THE CASE OF
D.B. COOPER'S
PARACHUTE

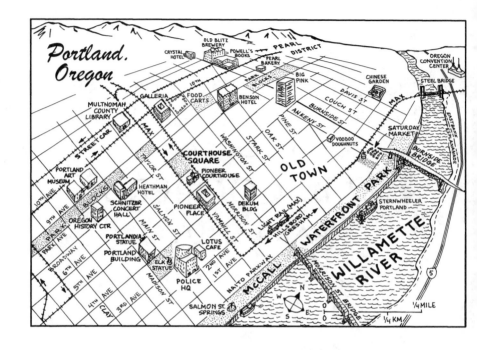

Also by William L. Sullivan

The Case of Einstein's Violin
The Ship in the Hill
A Deeper Wild
Listening for Coyote
Cabin Fever

Published by the Navillus Press
1958 Onyx Street
Eugene, Oregon 97403

www.oregonhiking.com

The Case of
D.B. Cooper's
Parachute

By
William L. Sullivan

Navillus Press
Eugene, Oregon

1

"You asked for cold cases, Neil," the captain said. He pressed the play button of the digital recorder and leaned back.

"Multnomah County 9-1-1," a woman's voice said. "What is your emergency?"

"My—my what?"

The male voice on the recording sounded frightened. Neil had heard the sound of fear often enough to know. But there was something else—an accent. Not Spanish. German? Neil glanced up to Captain Dickers. The young department chief simply sat there, poker faced.

"Your emergency. Do you need help?"

"Yes. Yes, I—" the man's voice faltered, as if searching for English words. "I know a crime."

"A crime? What is your name, sir?"

"Cooper."

"And where do you live, Mr. Cooper?"

"Not me! The man you want is Cooper. D.B. Cooper."

Lieutenant Neil Ferguson ran a hand over his face. Ever since Neil's promotion the captain had found little ways of letting him know where he really stood. If you become a detective in the Portland, Oregon police department at the advanced age of fifty-nine, you might as well ask for retirement. Subjecting him to a crank 9-1-1 call like this fit the mold.

"And what kind of crime do you think this Mr. Cooper might have committed?" The woman at the call center sounded even younger than Neil's daughter. Apparently she had never heard of D.B. Cooper, the airplane hijacker who vanished after parachuting into the forests of southwest Washington decades ago. Every year people called the police, claiming to know Cooper's true identity, and every single tip had led nowhere.

"Much crime. People work for him."

"Do you know of a specific crime, sir? I'm not sure how to help you if you don't have an example."

"They steal painting from church. Orthodox church in Woodburn."

Neil looked up, surprised. This wasn't what he had expected to hear from a prank caller.

"All right, sir. And why exactly do you suspect—"

"Because I work for him too," the caller interrupted. "I have a plan to stop. Are you listening?"

"Yes."

"Good. I tell Cooper to meet buyer for art at eleven o'clock tonight. We meet at Midland Library on 122nd Street. But we send police instead. Understand?"

"I'm not sure," the young woman replied. "Wouldn't the library be closed then?"

The caller sighed. "Of course. Tell police to meet in parking lot. Only one car, unmarked, with motor running. And no uniforms!" The caller hesitated a moment. "They must get D.B. Cooper. Please!" Then he hung up.

The captain didn't quite smile. "The call came from a pay phone at Powell and 134th at 9:15 this morning."

Neil rubbed his wrist, thinking. The fact that the captain had played the recording at all suggested he was expected to follow up. And although the paintings had been stolen months ago in a city thirty miles to the south, Neil suspected the police there hadn't found any hotter tips.

"This isn't really in our jurisdiction," Neil said. "That Russian art was Marion County and the whole Cooper thing was—I forget what— FBI?"

"But ensuring the safety of the Midland branch of the Multnomah County Library has always been one of our top priorities."

Neil studied the captain evenly. "I'll want backup." He added this not so much because the neighborhood was rough as to call the captain's bluff: If I raise the stakes are you still in?

"Take Sergeant Wu then." Finally the captain gave him a big smile.

"Are you sure you don't want me to drive?" Connie Wu asked as they got into the unmarked black Buick in the downtown precinct's underground garage.

She might as well have opened a valve to deflate him. Neil lowered his head onto the steering wheel. "Connie, I haven't been drinking. I swear, not a drop for six months."

"You asshole. I only meant—"

"Don't apologize." Neil started the engine.

Connie rolled her eyes. "I was thinking of your trauma."

Neil glanced at her from the side. Here he was, supposed to be a detective, and still he was surprised to realize she was completely sincere, without the bitterness you might expect from someone who had told you, just last week, to stop asking her out. She wore a touch of eye shadow to widen her eyes. The black pageboy haircut framed her features as smoothly as an oval cameo. Blue jeans and a ribbed black turtleneck stretched in the right places. No hidden weapons on Sergeant Wu tonight.

Neil put the car in reverse and backed out of the parking stall, talking over his shoulder as if to the backseat. "They say my trauma is only a problem if I try to sleep at night. Or if I'm in any more high speed chases. We should be OK at a library."

The darkness drizzled as they drove out Burnside. A cold, half-hearted February storm had been dragging through the city for days. Traffic signs and taillights reflected off the wet pavement, alternately blurred to nonsense and cleared by the wipers.

Neither of them spoke, but their thoughts filled the sedan. Neil was angry that he'd made an idiot of himself by getting involved with someone from the department. He should have known that he would have to admit why he had been promoted ahead of her. If anyone in the department could have filled the shoes of Lieutenant Credence Lavelle, the detective who had solved Portland's infamous Underground murders, it might have been Connie.

Connie was looking out the side window with a lump in her throat. She was sorry she had hurt Neil. He was basically a good man, someone who had already suffered more than most people knew. Maybe he would earn his promotion after all. And he was attractive—tall, blue-eyed, with the slender, athletic body of a much younger man. He rode his bicycle every morning, miles and miles, as if to outdistance the demons behind him.

They didn't talk again until they were parked in the empty lot beside the library, the motor running, the wipers on intermittent, the low beams reflecting off the few cars still sloshing past on 122nd.

"Waiting for a ghost," Neil said, checking his watch. Ten to eleven.

"How old would D.B. Cooper be?" Connie asked.

"He disappeared in 1971. The police sketch didn't look like much. Just a white man with dark glasses and a high forehead. He might have been thirty at the time."

"So our ghost would be in his seventies by now." She shook her head, and the pageboy cameo swept provocatively past her lips.

Neil closed his eyes and turned away. This too, he thought, was part of his private purgatory.

When he opened his eyes a burgundy SUV was slowing in the far lane across the street, as if to read the hours on the closed Bikini Babes Espresso booth. Connie was leaning forward, watching it too. A Honda. The driver wore a tipped-down baseball cap. When he drove on, Neil rechecked his watch. Two to eleven.

And then nothing. The traffic died. A shaggy old man in a clear plastic poncho pushed a shopping cart along the sidewalk, stopped to stare at them a moment, and then trudged on. A kid in a big-tired pickup squealed out of the Hawthorne light at 11:12 and roared down the empty street—just the kind of cry for attention that you strain to ignore.

Neil was about to pack it in, figuring he'd suffered about as much as Captain Dickers had planned, when the burgundy SUV slowly swung off the street and rolled up to the book drop, less than a hundred feet away.

"I got the license plate," Connie whispered. "Want me to run a check?"

Neil nodded. "But keep it quiet."

The SUV's window rolled down. When the driver leaned out to put something into the book chute, a streetlight strafed the side of his head. Beneath the baseball cap he was wearing a camouflage ski mask with holes for the eyes and mouth.

Neil pursed his lips in a silent whistle. "This guy must have checked out one hell of a hot book."

"It wasn't stolen," Connie whispered back.

"What?"

"The Honda. And it doesn't belong to anyone named Cooper. It's half a year old, totaled in a wreck two months ago."

"Doesn't seem damaged to me." In fact, the shiny SUV looked for all the world like a display model straight off a showroom floor. It growled quietly, idling.

"Now it's registered to Yosef Duvshenko, 13380 Southwest Division," Connie added.

"I guess he prefers the name Cooper when he's trying to fence stolen Russian paintings." It sounded stupid, but most thieves were even less creative than this. Neil reached for the door handle. "Guess it's our move."

Connie caught his arm. "No, let me do this."

"Why?"

"I don't want to alarm him."

Neil frowned. "You think I'm that alarming?"

Connie shook her head, bobbing that damned sweep of hair past her lips again. "You just don't look like an art collector."

Neil didn't have an answer for this. Maybe she was right.

"Cover me, OK?" Connie opened her door.

Neil rolled down his window and slid his service semi-automatic out of his jacket. Meanwhile Connie walked halfway across the parking lot, stepped over a divider full of bark dust, and held up her palms.

"Mr. Cooper?" she asked.

The masked face pulled back from the SUV's open window.

"Can we talk?" Connie took another step into the headlights' glare, her palms still up, showing she was unarmed. "I think you have something we want."

We! Just as Neil was thinking that "we" was the wrong word — that something seemed wrong about this stakeout — that he should never have let Connie walk out there alone — the police scanner below his dashboard suddenly squawked to life.

"Sergeant Wu?" The dispatcher's grating voice practically leapt out Neil's open window. "We've traced more information on that Honda."

A second later the SUV roared like a cornered lion and lunged forward. Connie started to turn, but the car had already swerved toward her. Rather than fall under the wheels, she jumped. The grille caught her in the stomach, banging her head on the hood. Somehow her fingers caught on the hood vents and held.

Neil had his semi-automatic out the window, but the SUV was careening so madly he'd be as likely to hit Connie as the driver. How on earth was she managing to hold on? The car spun around the lot one more time, bounced over the sidewalk, fishtailed into the street, and accelerated down 122nd with Connie still spread-eagled on the grille.

"Sergeant?" the scanner asked.

Neil squealed the Buick out into the street and flipped on the siren. Then he yanked the mike off its hook. "Sergeant Wu is on hood of that Honda, heading south on 122nd at sixty miles an hour."

"Copy that." The voice had turned grim. "On the hood."

"Yeah. So send an ambulance and every patrol car you've got."

"There's a squad on I-205 that's five minutes away."

"Five minutes? Then fuck it." Neil dropped the mike and gripped the wheel. It was his worst nightmare, all over again. The flashing lights, a carnival gone mad. The side streets, full of innocents. He could almost feel Layton beside him, cheering him on as if it were all a video game: "Cut left around the bus! Everyone's pulling over for the siren. We'll trap him at the railroad." But Layton was dead and Connie was clinging for her life.

Twenty blocks of hell, and then the SUV banked hard to the left through a red light onto Powell Boulevard. A rag doll slid sideways off the hood and rolled into the entrance of a beauty salon's parking lot.

Neil was trembling with cold sweat when he slewed up sideways in the street. He banged the door open and bolted through a haze strobed blue and red by the spastic lights in the Buick's back window. The cyber wolf howl of the siren might have been the keening within his own head: *Connie Connie don't die Connie it's my fault Connie it's always my fault —*

Her hair had been scraped off above the left ear, leaving a bleeding patch of meat the size of his palm. Her eyes were closed but he thought he felt a puff of life at her lips. Quickly he checked for a pulse at her wrist, and just as quickly his stomach turned at the sight of her hands. Ribbons of red flesh hung from her fingers. Somehow he managed to check her wrists anyway. The pulse was there.

"Stay with me, Connie." He clutched her bloody head between his hands, trying to slow the bleeding. "You're going to be all right, Connie. You've got to be all right. We're going to nail the guy who did this. I swear it, Connie."

Neil was crying by now, but even his tears couldn't drown out the voice inside him—the ugly voice that kept saying the guy who did this was Lieutenant Neil Ferguson.

The masked man who called himself D.B. Cooper circled a few blocks, watching out the rearview mirror of the Honda SUV. He hoped the undercover policewoman was dead. She hadn't been very alert after hitting her head on the hood, but you never knew how much someone at that close range could see. As for the bozo in the black Buick, he'd hardly been able to drive, much less offer any real pursuit. Cooper actually had to slow down, so as not to lose the police car too soon. Timing was everything.

Then Cooper took 136th north a few blocks to Division, rolling along at a lazy thirty-five miles per hour. Beside a shabby sheet metal sign for Foreign Motors Sales & Service he pulled down an alley and turned off his headlights. The parking lot in front of the shop was a glaring desert of mercury vapor and blacktop. Behind the hangar-like garage stretched a dark yard of sleeping wrecks. A shiny coil of razor wire topped a seven-foot chain-link fence around the perimeter.

Cooper took a remote control from the passenger seat and pressed a button. With a clank and a whir, a ten-foot section of the fence began rolling aside on little wheels in a buried metal track. He drove thirty feet into the yard, pressed a second button, and the gate began sliding back.

Suddenly a bare bulb blinked on above a shed door marked "Office" at the back of the building. A man stepped out and shaded his eyes against the bulb. He squinted into the darkness, looking puzzled. He was about thirty, with short, wavy black hair and a black Blazers sweatshirt.

Cooper stepped out of the car. He wore a long black raincoat, black gloves, and white hospital slip-ons over his shoes. He took a few steps toward the porch, smiling through the hole in his ski hat. "Yosef, you're working late tonight."

"Cooper? I thought—"

Cooper dismissed his anxiety with a wave. "That buyer of yours never showed up. Don't worry. It happens." Then he switched to Russian. "Is everything all right here?"

Yosef stammered back in halting, Ukrainian-accented Russian, although this should have been much easier for him than English. "No, I—the silent alarm went off, maybe an hour ago. There's been a break-in."

"Anything missing?"

"My gun. It was just a derringer revolver. And the Honda I've been working on for the past month. They started messing with my computer, too, but then they must have gotten scared and left."

Cooper nodded. "Your buyer double-crossed you. Come here, look what I found."

Yosef stepped down into the yard. When he got a closer look at the SUV, his mouth opened. "I spent the past two weeks repairing that car. Where—?"

"In the library parking lot. I brought it back to save you the trouble. But there's a ping in the motor, like they drove it too fast." He held his gloved hand toward the driver's door. "Try it. See what I mean."

Yosef looked worried now, and more confused than ever. The only person he had told about the library rendezvous had been the 9-1-1 operator, and that was just to alert the police. Could the police have broken into his office and taken his Honda? But then why would they leave it at the library? He got into the driver's seat, found the key in the ignition, and started the motor. It sounded fine. Out of sheer distraction he turned on the headlights and checked the wipers. Then he looked up uncertainly at the masked man beside the driver's window.

Cooper recognized Yosef's look—the ears-back pose of a disobedient puppy. The gesture touched him, despite everything. It was almost enough to change his plans. There was still time, just barely.

"You know, Yosef, I've had the feeling you're unhappy. You want out. Am I right?"

Yosef didn't dare speak.

"It's all right. I understand." Cooper took off his baseball cap and glanced at the sky. The drizzle had not quite stopped. That was good.

Yosef managed to clear his throat, but his voice still came out low and broken. "I owe you everything, Cooper. All of the cousins do. You brought Nadia. You got me the garage. It's just—" He ran aground.

"I said I understand. The rules are different in America, aren't they? I don't like playing the old small games any more than you do. This may startle you, Yosef, but I want out too."

"You do?"

"Yes. I think we're all ready for something better. Something bigger. Much bigger. And you're going to help take us there."

Yosef opened his mouth again, but could find no words.

"Watch closely." Cooper gripped the collar of his knitted ski mask and pulled it up over his head.

Yosef stared at the exposed face. "You—You're—"

"What did you think? And now it's your turn for a while." He held out the mask. "Put it on."

Yosef held the mask in his hands. His heart was beating so hard he could hardly think.

"Go ahead." Already the first mosquito whine of a siren was on the edge of hearing. "Put it on!"

Mechanically, Yosef pulled the mask over his head. Then he looked up with the same baleful, lost expression, as if for approval.

"Good. And now the cap too." Cooper reached in the window and helped him put the baseball cap on over the mask. "Look at you. You're the new Cooper! Look ahead. What do you see?"

The siren was unmistakable now, perhaps six or eight blocks away.

"Come on, Yosef. Tell me what you see ahead." He reached into the pocket of his raincoat and took out the derringer.

"Nothing?" Yosef gaped hopelessly out the windshield. "It's just black."

"Perfectly right," Cooper said, suddenly calm. "I'm sorry." Then he held the gun to the side of the ski mask and pulled the trigger.

The blast splattered blood across the dashboard and jerked Yosef's head onto his right shoulder. Cooper calmly reached in the window and fished up Yosef's limp hand. He wrapped Yosef's fingers around the handle of the derringer, held it out the window, and pushed the trigger finger. A shot fired harmlessly into the night sky. Then he moved the hand back inside and let it drop. The gun hit the steering wheel and clattered to the floor at Yosef's feet. The elbow caught on the windowsill and hung there.

Yes. It would be fine.

Cooper took off his gloves and stuffed them into a pocket of his raincoat. Then he unzipped the coat, took it off, and turned it inside out. He rolled it into a bundle and tucked it under his arm.

The siren was out in front now—just one car, but he knew there would be two policemen. They would take most of a minute thinking about the front door.

Cooper walked deliberately across the yard to a big Dodge pickup, stepped on the front bumper, and climbed onto the hood. He checked the pattern of raindrops on the hood where he had stepped. Then he climbed onto the cab roof, braced himself, and jumped over the razor wire of the fence.

He landed so hard on the alley gravel that he almost cried out. He really was getting too old for this, he thought. Gasping, he managed to crawl behind a hedge. There he took the hospital slippers off his shoes and stuffed them into the raincoat bundle.

A voice and a flashlight were starting to come down the alley, but Cooper knew how easy it was to disappear if you were merely walking. He ambled across a yard to the next street, heading toward his Prius a mile away. He had parked the car beside an apartment's recycling center. He would toss the raincoat in the garbage before going home to a lovely big snifter of cognac.

People were always looking in the wrong place, he thought. Portland cops were as blind as everyone else. He had counted on the stupidity of people for years, and they had never let him down.

That was why he was the only one who had ever discovered the true identity of D.B. Cooper.

2

The sky was still crying the next day, and Neil was bicycling through the tears.

He banked around the zigzag curves of the wet forest road to-ward the Washington Park zoo, pumping hard. Drips from the trees smacked against his teardrop helmet. The taut black-and-yellow Lycra of his racing shirt steamed. He sucked water through a plastic tube from a bottle on his bike's frame.

Water—endless water—was the only safe way to drown tears. He felt as if he had been holding his breath underwater all day. If he let go, if he took a breath, if he let himself coast downhill, he knew how easy it would be to spiral back into the depths.

Last night a patrol squad had found Neil shivering on the street, clutching Connie's bloodied head. Of course they had called Captain Dickers. Within an hour the captain had taken charge, tracked down the suicide driver, and solved the case.

Neil had ridden in the ambulance with Connie. At the hospital he had been dumped in a waiting room. They called it a lounge, but it seemed like an anti-lounge, an unfriendly barrens with the cold stench of pure alcohol. After eight hours in that brightly lit hell, a nurse told him to go home. Sergeant Wu's condition was serious but stable. She had abrasions, a concussion, and a cracked hip. A better time to visit would be between four and six that afternoon. Go home.

Neil had called headquarters and found he had the day off. Administrative leave. Captain's orders.

He had gone to bed and struggled with the fitful sleep of the damned. At noon he had awoken to a horrible hollow feeling that he knew was not just hunger. He had wanted a drink so badly it hurt.

Now he had been bicycling for three hours, and it was nearly time to face the hospital lounge again.

Neil pedaled past the zoo, looped over the freeway, and shot down the hellacious shoulder of Canyon Boulevard toward his apartment, dodging broken beer bottles. The traffic beside him roared, spraying water from the surf of an angry sea.

Just before the freeway tunnel he peeled off onto slightly saner city streets. Then he rode down his apartment building's basement ramp, slid his card through a slot to open the garage door, and parked his bicycle in the middle of the first open parking spot. The other tenants kept telling him to park his bike behind the recycling bins, but he didn't care. His rent included a parking spot, and his titanium-framed racing bicycle was worth more than most of their beaters.

Still dripping, he took the elevator up to the eleventh floor, left wet footprints across the hall carpet, and opened his door with his card.

A rhythmic creaking and the faint smell of garbage told him his daughter was there.

"Susan?" He took off his helmet and ventured into the living room.

She was sitting in the cane chair by the picture window, her eyes closed, gently rocking her upper body forward to a music only she could hear. At the sound of her name her dark eyes opened—so beautiful and so elusive.

"Hello, Papa."

Susan Ferguson had grown up with autism, and although her inability to make eye contact was the first thing most people noticed about her, Neil had long since learned to see the strengths of her character and the advantages of her exceptional mind. Yes, she abhorred touch and hated crowds. But in her thirty-two years, Susan had never succumbed to despondency, never doubted the worth of the universe. Why hadn't he learned these life arts from her? She had ignored taunts and overcome challenges all her life. For the past six years she had worked at a recycling station in Old Town, keeping her own apartment and managing her own boyfriends. She wore no make-up. She had straight hair and boyish features. But her haunting eyes gave her a compelling beauty that made everyone look twice.

When Neil looked at Susan, he saw the reflection of Rebecca. Bone cancer had forced his wife to give up her landscaping business in

Eugene four years ago. Just before Rebecca passed away she had told him, "Look for me in Susan. I am there."

When Rebecca finally died, Neil had been a wreck. But Susan had not cried. "Come with me, Papa," she had said. "Get a job in Portland like me."

And so Neil had sold the three-acre farm north of Eugene, with the fiberglass greenhouse and the old Ford pickup and the one-eyed nanny goat. He had quit his position with the Eugene police and had taken a job in Portland instead. He had moved to a place with no memories—an eleventh-floor apartment on the Park Blocks, overlooking a streetcar line, a yuppified Safeway, a lost wooden church steeple, and the thousand jumbled buildings of downtown's west side.

He had even given up running, a passion since his college days at the University of Oregon. There was nowhere he wanted to run here, not in downtown Portland. He had bought a bicycle instead.

He had also started drinking more that first year. A lot more. Susan had found it puzzling, watching with concern as he stumbled and stuttered through the evenings.

And then Layton had died.

"It's not just because of the plastic bags," Susan said.

Neil wiped the rain off his face, trying to bring himself back to the present. His beautiful daughter was sitting in front of him in the blue overalls of her recycling center, talking about plastic bags.

"This is about the new recycling machine, isn't it?" Portlanders had stopped trying to sort their recycling at home when the new machine had been introduced. Although the machine had eliminated many minimum wage sorting jobs, Susan had been lucky enough to transfer to a new position, cleaning out the plastic bags that gummed up the machinery. But she had never liked change. For weeks Neil had been telling her she would get used to her new tasks.

Susan's gaze shifted lower and to one side. "Something about it doesn't feel right."

"A new job is always hard at first."

Susan bit her lip. "I want you to come see."

"Again?"

Susan nodded.

Neil blew out a breath. "All right. When?"

"Now."

Neil held out his arms, as if his wet, skin-tight bicycling outfit were an explanation.

"Why not?" she asked.

Neil sighed. "Do you remember Connie Wu? The policewoman I introduced you to? She's been hurt. I have to go see her at the hospital. They said I should visit before six."

Susan wrinkled her brow. "Connie. I liked her. How badly is she hurt?"

"It didn't look good."

"Will she get better?"

"They won't tell me over the phone."

Susan thought for a moment. "I'm not sure she liked you enough."

"What?"

"She liked you, but I'm not sure it's enough."

Neil dropped his arms in exasperation. Now his daughter was jealous. Or worse, this really might be Rebecca talking. More maddening still, he found he cared about her opinion. Parents should not have to ask permission from their grown children—or their dead spouses—before going on a date. Besides, he wasn't going on a date! He was going to the hospital to visit a colleague who had told him never to date her again.

The whole thing made him so angry that he ran his hand through his hair, trying to think of what to say.

"Papa?" Susan said, standing up. "Let's go see the recycling station later."

"Right. Maybe Saturday."

"Don't forget, will you?"

"Sure, Susan. Remind me, OK?" Outside a streetcar rumbled by.

He followed her to the door, saying the usual good-byes and thank-you-for-comings. Then he hurried to the shower. The streetcar ran every thirteen minutes. With luck he could catch the next one to the hospital.

After the shower he paused, naked, in front of his closet. Not a tie—he was being paid not to go to work. Not jeans, either. Finally he pulled on what seemed like standard Portland garb: khaki Dockers, a Pendleton plaid shirt, and running shoes. As he waited for the elevator the hall mirror reflected a homeless man who had apparently stolen mismatched clothes from Nordstrom's after hours in the dark. But it was too late to change now.

He ran half a block to catch the streetcar, swung into a seat, and then fumed at how long the car took to get moving. The trolley trundled through the Portland State University campus at a jogging pace, stopping for every red light and clueless jaywalking student. When they had finally rolled under the concrete spaghetti of the Marquam Bridge he got out at the south waterfront and hurried across a plaza to the hospital gondola. The hospital had been built atop a Gibraltar-like knoll, as if to rise above the city's unhealthful vapors, so the only practical way to reach it was by ambulance or aerial tram. For three minutes a shiny aluminum egg carried Neil and a somber crowd of hospital staffers up through the drizzle to a misty cloud city.

The labyrinth of corridors finally led Neil back to the anti-lounge, where he asked a man in a brightly colored smock about Connie Wu's room.

"Mrs. Wu should only have one visitor at a time. Right now she's with Mr. Wu. Would you like to wait?"

Neil blinked. "Mr. Wu?" Connie had said she was divorced. She had said her ex-husband owned a scuba diving company in Kauai and didn't care about her in the least. "I thought Mr. Wu was in Hawaii."

"He flew in this morning. If you'll have a seat I'll tell him there's another visitor."

Neil sank into a green plastic sofa opposite a television. He should have been glad to know that Connie's ex was rallying to her side. But he couldn't help feeling that he'd missed a clue.

Meanwhile the TV had launched into the five-thirty news, with a report on the global energy summit coming up in March. Oregon was hosting the conference at Mt. Hood's Timberline Lodge. Top leaders from Russia, China, and the Middle East had already committed to attend. The newscaster tapped his papers together on the desk and glanced to his colleague. "How are they going to convince anybody about global warming when it won't stop snowing at Timberline, Angela?"

"I hope they're bringing skis, Marcus," the woman at the news desk smiled back. Then her voice dropped to an earnest tone. "A high-speed police chase through East Portland late last night ended with the suspect's apparent suicide—and with a big break for criminal investi-gators, according to Portland police. Karla Myers has the story."

Neil leaned forward, suddenly alert. Despite what people seemed to think, his work rarely showed up on television. Domestic violence, bar fights, and delinquent kids just didn't fascinate reporters. The few times the media had gotten excited about check scams, marijuana busts, or shootings, the stories had been spun from such an odd angle that he had hardly recognized his own case.

A blonde in a double-breasted trench coat was standing in the rainy parking lot of a car repair shop, holding a microphone. "I'm here at Foreign Motors, the repair shop at 112th and East Division where Yosef Duvshenko was found dead around midnight last night, ap-parently from a self-inflicted gunshot wound. Police are now saying stolen artwork and cars found at the site indicate this may have served as the headquarters for the Russian mafia in the Portland area."

The screen switched to a grainy passport photo of a thirtyish, dark-haired man with sad eyes. The reporter's voice continued, "Duvshenko immigrated to Oregon from Ukraine six years ago, claiming religious persecution in his home country. But those who know him say he didn't seem to lead a particularly religious life."

The blonde was back on screen. "Neighbors of Duvshenko's shop say he worked all day and most nights, never took vacations, and didn't attend a church. His wife Nadia and their four-year-old daugh-ter Sonya rarely left their apartment just four blocks away. But police are discovering that Yosef Duvshenko was not just another workahol-ic. This afternoon we spoke with Portland police captain John Dickers."

Neil tightened his lips at the name of his boss. Wearing a dress uni-form, the captain stood at a podium with half a dozen microphones. Apparently he had called a press conference at police headquarters to brag about what he had accomplished while Neil was on administra-tive leave.

"Acting on an anonymous tip," the captain said, "I sent an under-cover team to attempt to recover a stolen Russian painting in East Portland last night. Unfortunately the officers' identities were com-promised and the contact person fled."

Neil opened his mouth to object. The radio dispatcher at headquar-ters had blown their cover by calling back in the middle of a stakeout! But the captain was already moving on.

"By tracing the suspect's car we were able to track him to the car repair shop he owned about a mile away. By the time we reached the shop Yosef Duvshenko had already locked himself in the compound. Evidence suggests that he killed himself with a single gunshot to the head."

The captain stopped to wipe his nose with a handkerchief. Neil knew the captain's habit of fussing with his nose was merely a nervous tic, but on television it lent an air of pathos.

"Evidence retrieved at the scene includes a painting that had been missing from a Russian Orthodox church in Woodburn since December. We also recovered cars and documents indicating that the shop served as a center for modifying stolen or damaged cars and re-selling them as new at locations around the metropolitan area."

The screen switched back to the reporter in the trench coat. "Today it seems police are about to close the books on a long string of theft and fraud cases that may have originated at this unassuming car repair shop, a base some are saying was a foothold for organized crime from the former Soviet bloc. Reporting from East Portland, I'm Karla Myers."

The reporter shrank to a box in the corner of the screen. The anchorman at the main news desk looked up and asked, "Is there such a thing as a Ukrainian mafia, Karla?"

The miniaturized reporter nodded. "Actually, many of the contacts they're finding in the shop's computer system appear to be from Russia and Latvia as well as Ukraine."

"So this may be a more complicated network than we thought."

"Yes, and here's the strangest part. The code name for the network appears to have been D.B. Cooper."

"As in the name of the old missing skyjacker?" The anchorman shook his head. "That really is bizarre. Thank you, Karla."

The reporter in the corner box whirled off the screen, immediately replaced by a photograph of a baby elephant. The newscasters at the desk smiled and began talking about the zoo.

"You're here to see my mother?" A voice asked.

Neil turned around. A pudgy, tanned young man with shoulder-length black hair was standing behind him in a short-sleeved shirt.

"I'm sorry?" Neil asked.

"The nurse said a guy was out here waiting."

"You're Mr. Wu?"

"Yeah. Leighton Wu."

Neil stood up and shook the young man's hand. "I'm Neil Ferguson. I guess I thought your father was here."

Leighton frowned. "Dad doesn't leave the islands much anymore. So, uh, how do you know my mother?"

"I was her partner."

From the look on the young man's face, Neil realized how misleading his words must sound. He quickly added, "On the police force. I'm the lieutenant who was assigned with Sergeant Wu last night. How is she?"

Leighton still looked skeptical. "She's in a lot of pain. Her hip isn't broken, but it's got a hairline crack. They shaved most of her head and decided she doesn't need skin grafts. With luck I should be able to take her home in a couple days."

"Home? To Hawaii?"

"No, I'll be staying at her house here in Portland for as long as it takes. Why?"

"Nothing. I'm glad you're here. She never really talked much about her children." Neil regretted this as soon as he had said it.

"She never talked much about her partner either." Leighton gave a sharp edge to the word "partner." Neil knew that blade. Here was a son defending his mother. The young man had meant to cut him, and he had.

"Look, the captain sent the two of us out there last night. I'm sorry your mother got hurt. Believe me, I'd trade places with her if I could."

Leighton lowered his head. Suddenly he looked tired. His eyes were hollow from lack of sleep.

"Room 388," he said, brushing past Neil on his way to a chair.

Neil walked down the hall, counting room numbers. Now he realized he'd forgotten to bring anything. No flowers. No card. The doorways he was passing were wide enough for gurneys. Most doors stood open. Bottles hung in the rooms, connected by tubes to people in hospital gowns on beds. Clusters of Mylar balloons also hung in the rooms, silvery hearts and smiling suns tethered to the bed frames, as if love and hope might similarly be dosed out in slow drips.

The door marked "Wu, Connie," was nearly closed. Why did it frighten him so much to push it open?

"Hello?" he said, peering inside.

Connie looked at him and groaned. "You asshole."

A white football helmet of bandages covered her head, but her black eyes blazed. Lumps beneath the bed blanket suggested casts or braces or tubing.

Neil didn't know where to begin. "Connie, I stayed here last night until they threw me out, and they wouldn't let me come back until—"

"Come here," Connie croaked.

"What?"

"Shut up and come here." She raised a bandaged hand. "And turn off that damned TV. They give me drugs, but not enough to like television."

Neil switched off the newscast. Then he stood beside her bed. The bandages on her head covered everything but her eyes, nose, mouth, and chin. The features he could see were drawn and white, as if they belonged to a much older version of the woman he knew. Every few moments she closed her eyes, breathed through her mouth, and closed her lips tightly.

"I feel like this is all my fault," Neil said.

"But it isn't. You know that." She closed her eyes again and winced. "Shit happens when you're a cop."

"I can't imagine how much it must hurt."

Her black eyes looked at him sharply. "I saw you last night. Chasing after me with the lights flashing. Seventy miles an hour on a city street. That was the one thing they said you didn't have the nerves left to do." She took a breath and closed her eyes. "I can't imagine how that must have hurt."

Now it was Neil who found himself taking a long, steadying breath. Connie might be the only one who understood how much he had suffered that night. Out loud he said, "At least the guy we went after is dead."

"No." Connie twisted to face him and was kicked back by a wave of pain. Blackness swirled up into the room around her. She felt needles darting in and out, jabbing her on all sides. When the light began to sparkle back her head was full of clouds. Someone was in front of her, opening his mouth as if he were talking. Ferguson—it was Ferguson. He was worried, but worried about the wrong thing, and not nearly worried enough. When sound began to return she dimly heard him saying, ". . . call someone. I'm going to go get the nurse."

"No." This time she held still, trying to keep the blackness from rising up again.

"Connie? Are you all right?"

"Don't go." She had to take three breaths before she could speak again. "I saw him. Last night. He's not dead."

Neil looked at her, concerned. "It was on the news, Connie. Dickers said the driver of the Honda committed suicide."

"The picture on the news." Her voice came out as a whisper. "That wasn't the man I saw."

"How can you be sure? The man you saw last night was wearing a ski mask."

"His eyes. They looked older. And they had no fear, no anger. They were the coldest eyes I've ever seen."

"Perhaps it was the look of a man who realized his only way out was to commit suicide. After we spooked him he left a trail so wide even Dickers could follow it."

Connie managed to shake her head slowly. "The man I saw could kill anybody but himself."

Neil pondered this for a moment. "Connie, you're one of the sharpest people on the force. But you're also hurt. You're in pain."

"You asshole. You don't believe me."

"You know how trauma works. We both faced a lot of fear last night. Emotions like that don't just evaporate. You're going to feel shaky for a long time."

Connie coughed and closed her eyes. "If D.B. Cooper is still alive, and if he thinks we know, he'll kill us both."

"But he's dead, Connie. Welcome to the world of trauma. It's an uneasy feeling that doesn't go away."

Connie said nothing.

3

The man who called himself D.B. Cooper had an uneasy feeling. As soon as he saw the News at Noon and realized the policewoman had survived, he knew he would have to kill her, and possibly also the cop in the unmarked police car. A few quick calls identified the policewoman as Sergeant Wu, in Room 388 of the Oregon Health Sciences University. Cooper took a hiking guidebook from his bookshelf and flipped to the Portland entries. He could stroll to the hospital on a four-mile loop and get his daily exercise at the same time. Cars may be easy for police to trace, but an old man hiking the Marquam Trail would be invisible.

Cooper stowed the essentials for his outing in a fanny pack. Then he drove his silver Prius to the zoo and parked it amidst a sea of cars. He stepped out and squinted at the clouds. Although it had rained earlier that afternoon, the gray skies now looked brighter in the west. He decided to take along a folding umbrella just in case. Then he pressed his key to lock the car and set out on a trail behind the World Forestry Center.

By the time the Marquam Trail began climbing up into the woods on the far side of Canyon Boulevard, Cooper was wishing he hadn't worn his favorite walking shoes. February rains had left the path muddy, with puddles that were hard to avoid. Muddy soles are awkward at murder scenes. He would have to destroy the shoes afterwards and buy new ones. He hated shoe shopping.

Cooper noticed that the trilliums were not yet blooming. In fact, none of his favorite flowers were out yet. As he puffed up the bloomless slope toward Council Crest he had time to run through his possible murder options. Of course, hospitals are full of weapons. It helped that his target was already injured. People die in hospitals all the time. He narrowed his choices to three, and then argued with himself, ranking them.

It was six o'clock when he finally reached the sidewalk on Gibbs Street, a few blocks from the hospital. He stopped at a puddle in a driveway to clean the worst of the mud from his walking shoes with a stick—just as any retiree might do after walking in the woods. Then he stomped the water from his soles, stuffed his folding umbrella into his fanny pack so that he would have his hands free, and strolled to the hospital.

Cooper climbed the entrance steps unnoticed, walked past the reception desk without warranting a second glance, rode the elevator up three stories by himself, and followed the hospital's perfectly clear directional signs to Room 388 without meeting anyone in the hall.

Despite the bandages on Sergeant Wu's head, Cooper recognized at once the round face of the woman he had driven down 122nd Avenue the night before. To his delight, everything he needed for his preferred option was at hand. Someone had thoughtfully left an extra pillow beside the sergeant's head. Even a child could flip the pillow onto her bandaged mouth and hold it there until she breathed no more. The sergeant's hands had been conveniently wrapped in gauze to limit her struggle. If foul play were suspected—which seemed unlikely—forensics would find no troubling DNA beneath her fingernails.

Cooper paused in the doorway, admiring the perfection of this simple tragedy—a woman who had to die because she had dared to glimpse the impossible. She had looked into the eyes of the invisible man, D.B. Cooper.

4

Neil dreaded going back to work. He had fouled up a stakeout and had nearly gotten yet another partner killed. But because he had been given only one day's administrative leave—and because he hadn't heard otherwise—he got up the next morning at 5:30 and went through his usual routine. After bicycling ten miles to the Pittock Mansion and back he showered, dressed in a suit and tie, grabbed a yogurt at Safeway, and walked seven blocks through town to the central precinct office.

The Portland Police Bureau occupies about a third of the justice skyscraper on Chapman Square, between Madison and Main Streets. To find the police entrance you have to walk around to the back on Second Avenue, past the forbidding tunnel of the cops' parking basement. The art deco lobby has curving aluminum balustrades, granite walls, and a stylized eagle statue over the door.

Neil pushed through the glass doors at the back of the lobby and took the elevator up. He wasn't particularly surprised to find a note at his cubicle telling him to report to Captain Dickers ASAP. Might as well find out right away how bad things were.

The captain's door was ajar, so Neil tapped on the glass and leaned his head in. "You asked to see me, sir?"

Dickers looked up, his brow knit. "How's Sergeant Wu this morning?"

"This morning?" Neil faltered. Apparently the captain wasn't even going to let him sit down before unloading a double-barreled blast of guilt. "I saw her last night. Doesn't the hospital give you reports?"

Dickers shook his head. "We're just her employer, not her next of

27

kin. Or her partner." He paused a moment to let that barb sting.

"I've got the number of the phone in her hospital room," Neil said. "Would you like to give her a call?"

"No, no." Dickers waved him to a chair. "How was she last night?"

"Not good. I mean, she's stable. They say she doesn't need skin grafts. But I'm guessing she'll have to be at the hospital a couple more days. It'll be weeks before she can think about going back to work, and even then it would have to be a desk job for a while."

"How's her mood?"

"She's in a lot of pain." Neil sighed. "Her son flew in from Hawaii yesterday to stay with her. I thought I'd drop in each day after work."

"Do that."

"Yes sir. Oh, and one more thing. She was worried about the case."

"How so?"

"She had a feeling the guy who ran her down might still be alive."

Dickers blinked. "Well, she needn't worry about that. Right now he's in the Clackamas morgue. In fact—" he glanced at the wall clock— "we should get over there. I've got his wife coming in at 9:30 to identify the body. Let's go."

Neil hesitated. If there was anything in the world more horrible than what he had witnessed two nights ago on 122nd Avenue, it just might be Mrs. Duvshenko attempting to identify the bullet-shattered head of her husband Yosef.

"Don't worry, I'll drive," Dickers said. "You shouldn't be behind the wheel for a few days anyway."

"Are you sure you need me there, sir?"

"Of course." Dickers slipped on his suit jacket. "I'm handing this case back to you." He picked up a notebook-sized package wrapped in plastic bubble wrap. Then he led the way out of the office to the parking garage.

As they drove across town to the morgue, Captain Dickers explained that all of the significant work on the case had already been done. Neil would be left to clean up a few loose ends and complete the paperwork.

"You're sure about the identity of this Duvshenko?" Neil asked.

"Positively. Bringing in his wife is just a formality."

"I heard on the news report last night that it was most likely a suicide, but—"

Dickers cut him short. "They didn't tell the half of it. After Duvshenko got away from you, he drove straight back to his car repair lot. The yard is entirely surrounded by razor wire. The only way in is through an electric gate. He closed the gate behind him and left the remote control on the passenger seat. Then he took out a revolver — a derringer that had been registered to him for a year — and blew out his brains. His finger prints are all over the car, the gun, everything. Nobody else's prints — just his. And there's powder burns on his hand from the blast. It's an open and shut case."

Neil thought a moment as they waited for traffic to get around a stalled car on I-205. "What about the anonymous tip? Who made the phone call to 911?"

"A guy named Andrei Andropov," Dickers replied. "He owns a different car repair shop in Troutdale. He called yesterday to explain why he turned Duvshenko in."

"The voice on the 911 recording was pretty frightened," Neil recalled.

They drove past the stalled car and Dickers hit the gas, accelerating to sixty-five.

"Are we in a hurry?" Neil asked, his throat suddenly tight.

"Sorry, I forgot." Dickers eased back to sixty. "Anyway, about Andropov. Of course he was afraid. Apparently there are a dozen car repair shops around here that belong to East Europeans. Duvshenko had been blackmailing them all, using the code name D.B. Cooper. He picked up totaled, late model cars at insurance auctions, had the shops fix them up, forged new registration papers, and sold them as new. The whole story was in Duvshenko's computer, hidden behind a firewall and a password."

"The car shops must have been getting a cut," Neil observed. "If they were, why would they blow the whistle on the boss?"

"Duvshenko was cheating them. He wasn't even giving them enough for parts and labor. But what really scared them, according to this Andrei, was that Duvshenko had started stealing Russian paintings."

"Why is that more frightening than car fraud?"

"The paintings are religious icons." Dickers pulled off at the Clackamas exit and steered down a street lined with office buildings. "I guess icons like that are worth a lot if you resell them in Europe, but these car repair guys are superstitious. The wrath of D.B. Cooper they could face, maybe, but not the wrath of God."

Neil was more worried about the wrath of Duvshenko's widow. When they pushed through the doors to the waiting room of the coroner's office, he was a little surprised that they were not met by a hysterical, teary-eyed wife. Instead a middle-aged, red-haired woman with black-framed glasses and a blue business suit was speaking quietly to a nervous young platinum blonde. The girl wore far too much make-up, a dizzying dose of perfume, high heels, and a shimmery, low-necked party dress. If they hadn't been in a morgue, Neil might have guessed that this was a mother giving her high school daughter last minute instructions before the prom.

"Marial, good of you to help out once again," Captain Dickers greeted the red-headed woman. "I'd like you to meet Lieutenant Ferguson. He'll be finishing up the case for me. Neil, this is Marial Gresham — am I pronouncing that right?"

"Close enough." She smiled, revealing a charming little dimple that suddenly made her look five years younger.

"Marial's our Russian translator. I've asked her to bring a car you can use."

"Lieutenant," she said, extending her hand.

Neil shook her hand. "I thought Duvshenko was Ukranian."

"His wife is Russian," she said. "I speak both languages."

Dickers added, "I signed Marial up for the next week, if there's any driving or translation work you need done. I thought maybe you could take that painting back to Woodburn this afternoon." Then he turned to the girl. "And you must be Mrs. Duvshenko?"

The girl's bright eyes, swimming in pools of shiny purple shadow, darted from the captain to Neil.

"I'm very sorry for your loss," Dickers said. "Can you understand me?"

"No," the girl said, looking down.

Marial stepped in. "Nadia has been in America only six months. Most of that time she's been in an apartment with her daughter."

"Where is her daughter today?" Neil asked.

The two women exchanged a few low words in a language of harsh consonants and odd glides.

"The daughter is with cousins," Marial announced.

Neil asked, "Does Nadia know she is here to identify a body?"

Marial nodded.

Dickers held open the glass doors. "Then let's go." He glanced to the receptionist. She merely pointed down the hall.

No one spoke as they filed through the corridor to the morgue. Neil used the time to speculate about Yosef Duvshenko's marriage. His widow could hardly be older than twenty-two. If he had immigrated to America six years ago, as the newscaster last night had said, then Nadia would have been just sixteen when he left. Perhaps in Ukraine it was ordinary for a man in his twenties to marry a girl that age. Could she have been a mail-order bride? It seemed more likely that they had merely dated when she was sixteen, with Yosef promising to come back to marry her when she was older. Yes—that would account for the four-year-old daughter. And it might well have taken Yosef several years to wangle an American visa for his wife so he could bring her to Oregon.

The timeline seemed plausible. Everything about the case was straightforward. As far as Neil was concerned, only one troubling question remained: Where were the young widow's tears?

He had his answer at the morgue. Nadia began to tremble as soon as they entered the cold, brightly lit, tiled room. Her perfume vanished beneath the stench of chemicals and the scent of death. She clapped her hand to her mouth, watching with wide eyes as a somber woman in a white doctor's jacket walked to a wall of large drawers.

When the covered corpse slid out—a shape beneath a sheet—the last of Nadia's self-control gave way. She fell to her knees, wailing. She threw back her head, crying her husband's name. Great streaks of purple makeup ran down her face.

The translator knelt beside her with her arm about Nadia's shoulder, offering foreign words of solace. Neil looked at the floor, ashamed that he had doubted the young woman's love. Captain Dickers stood with arms crossed, waiting.

After a minute, when Nadia's wails had subsided to sobs, Dickers asked, "Can we get on with the identification?"

Marial looked up with an unhappy shrug.

"All right." Dickers nodded to the coroner.

The woman in the white jacket hesitated. "Just to warn you, we've done the best we could. Still, I can only show you the right-hand side of the face."

"Go ahead."

The coroner lifted a corner of the sheet, carefully exposing a white jaw, a Roman nose, and an open eye that seemed glazed by sadness and surprise.

Nadia's anguished cry left no doubt that this had been the man she loved.

Dickers waved for the coroner to close the drawer. As far as Neil was concerned, they were also closing the last doubts on the case.

But then the coroner paused. "There's still the matter of the ring."

"Oh, right." Dickers explained to Marial, "It's a department tradition. We leave the wedding ring on because some people want it to be interred with their loved one."

The coroner turned to Nadia. "Of course if you'd like to keep the ring as a memento, you may."

After Marial had translated this, the girl nodded and turned away.

The coroner folded back the sheet just far enough from the left side of the body that she could lift the left hand. She worked the ring loose from the fourth finger and was about to replace the sheet when Neil stopped her.

"Wait a moment."

Dickers glanced to Neil. "It's an ordinary gold band. No inscription. We checked."

Neil pointed just below the wrist bone. "There. The skin is slightly whiter where a watchband used to be."

"Yes, he wore a watch." Dickers said impatiently. "Of course we took the watch off."

"But he wore it on his left wrist, sir."

"So what?"

"Normally, only right-handed people wear watches on their left wrist." He turned to the girl. "Nadia, was your husband right handed?"

After Marial had translated this the girl gave a small puzzled nod.

Neil turned to the captain. "You see the problem? Duvshenko was shot in the left side of his head."

"Oh, honestly." Dickers shook his head. "The powder burns prove he fired the shot. And there's any number of reasons he could have held the gun in his left hand."

"Really, sir? I can't think of one. Was the window open?"

"What?"

"The car window," Neil repeated. "When you found the body was the driver's side window open?"

"Well yes, but—"

Neil cut him short. "Excuse me, sir. I need to use my cell phone. I'll be in the hall."

The captain stared after him. "Who are you calling?"

"Sergeant Wu, sir," Neil said from the door. "Suddenly I'm a little worried about her."

5

"Who?" A quavering, elderly voice answered the call to Room 388 at the hospital.

"Not who. Wu!" Neil said, exasperated.

The voice suddenly became distant and muffled, as if a hand were over the mouthpiece. "Nurse? I think I may have some kind of crank caller."

A moment later a young man announced, "This is the floor supervisor. May I help you?"

"This is Lieutenant Neil Ferguson of the Portland police. Is this Room 388?"

"Yes."

"I'm trying to reach Sergeant Wu."

"I see." There was a coldness to the nurse's tone that gave Neil a chill.

"Is she all right?"

"Mrs. Wu is in recovery. I'm afraid I can't tell you where."

"Why not?"

"Last night Mrs. Wu insisted that we move her to a shared room. She asked that we not give the number out by phone."

"Did she say why?" Neil asked.

"Yes. She has lodged a formal complaint with the hospital management."

"What kind of complaint?"

"Too many visitors," the nurse said, and hung up.

Neil folded away his cell phone, frowning. How many visitors could Connie have had? Did she have other relatives? And if she wanted to be alone, why had she demanded to be moved to a shared room? Neil wanted to go check on her himself, but without a car of his own, he'd have to wait until he was off duty that evening, and then take the streetcar again.

Suddenly the door opened and Dickers came out of the morgue, chatting with the coroner about pension plans. After they had commiserated about the state of the stock market, the captain gave her a small farewell salute. "Thanks for your help, doctor." Then he turned to Neil. "Was there anything else you wanted here? And how is Sergeant Wu?"

"She's in recovery, sir. But I have to tell you that Sergeant Wu and I feel this case might not be as simple as it looks. Maybe it wasn't just a suicide."

Dickers glanced back at the translator, who was still comforting Mrs. Duvshenko. Then he pulled Neil aside and spoke in a low voice, "Damn it Neil, I've done all the hard work on this one. Don't screw it up by pretending you're Credence Lavelle."

"I'm just—"

"Well don't." Dickers held out his hands, as if to diagram the explanation. "Look, we've got the Russian energy minister coming for a summit next month, so everyone's watching. There's a hundred thousand Russian immigrants in the Portland area. They've got a few bad apples like everybody else, and we treat them like everybody else. If you turn this into a witch hunt, the feds are going bust us for racial profiling and the press will go ballistic. Understand?"

"Yes sir."

"Good. Then finish it up, and get back to—" Dickers waved his hand uncertainly, "catching D.B. Cooper."

They walked out to the parking lot in silence. Dickers took the bubble-wrapped package out of his trunk and handed it to Neil. "Here's the painting Duvshenko stole. Return it and take care of the paperwork." Then the captain got into his car and drove off.

Neil blew out a breath. The captain was right that the case had to be handled delicately. But he wasn't about to drop it until he understood Yosef Duvshenko's death. And he knew exactly where to begin.

"Let's take Mrs. Duvshenko home," Neil told the interpreter. "I've got a few questions I'd like to ask her along the way."

"Of course, Lieutenant."

"Call me Neil, would you? I'm thinking we may be in this together for a while."

"All right. I'm Marial—just Marial. No one can pronounce my last name." The interpreter smiled, bringing out her girlish dimple. Her black-framed glasses gave her a professional, studious air. The thick lenses made her wide brown eyes seem even wider. Neil hadn't really looked at her before. Now it almost seemed as if she wanted him to look. He had to admit she was a handsome woman. Working with her would be no punishment.

"You don't mind driving?" Neil asked.

"Your captain says I have to." Her dimple deepened. "Are you that dangerous?"

"Probably. In fact, I think I should sit in back."

She looked at him skeptically. "Really?"

"Sure. Then it will be easier for everyone to talk. If you don't mind translating while you drive."

As Marial led the way to a boxy Ford from the city carpool, Neil noticed that the young Mrs. Duvshenko had regained her composure. She strutted in her high heels. The shoes had straps at the ankles and little bows at the toes, reminding him once again of a high school prom. When he opened the passenger door for her, he felt like a clumsy chaperone. She slid in, neatly tucking the shiny dress about her knees. While Marial got into the driver's seat Neil climbed in back, laid the painting carefully on the seat beside him, and clicked his seat belt in place.

Marial glanced at Neil in the rearview mirror as she drove toward the freeway. "You wanted to ask Nadia something?"

"Yes." Neil leaned toward the gap between the two front seats. "Nadia? Your husband had been in Portland only six years. That's a short time to become the owner of such a large car repair shop. I think he must have worked hard?"

The girl looked straight ahead as she spoke. Marial translated, "He worked very hard. He was a good mechanic."

"Did he have help, buying the shop and getting started?"

"Yes, of course. Everyone helps each other."

Neil wondered about the word everyone. He asked, "Did he ever mention a Mr. Cooper?"

She shook her head decisively. "No. Yosef never talked about business at home. I've never heard the name Cooper. I told this to the other policemen many times."

"Then you don't think your husband could have been Mr. Cooper, the one who organized the car fraud scheme?"

Neil expected the girl to agree, defending her husband's honor. To his surprise, she merely tipped her head slightly and looked out the side window. "I don't know. My husband was good at everything he tried. He always wanted the best for Sonya and me. He never did anything wrong, I'm sure of that. But yes, I think maybe he was this man they call Cooper."

Neil leaned back, stunned. The young woman had said she knew nothing about her husband's business. She had wailed genuine tears over his body. She believed he had never done anything wrong. But somehow she thought it possible he was a mafia ringleader. It didn't make sense — unless Slavic wives were very different from the wife he had known.

He decided to try a different approach. "What will you do, now that you are alone?"

Nadia lifted her chin. "I am not alone. I have my daughter Sonya."

"Of course. What will you and Sonya do?"

"We will do whatever we like."

This answer also struck Neil as peculiar. "But how will you support yourselves?"

"Everyone helps each other. The cousins will run the shop and support us until Sonya is grown."

"Cousins?" Neil asked. "Are these the same cousins that Sonya is staying with right now?"

For the first time Nadia's confident tone wavered. "We have many cousins."

Neil looked to Marial for help. "Is she talking about people that are still in Europe?"

Marial took the Division Street exit and headed east. "I don't think so. She seems to be using the word 'cousin' in a broader sense."

"But she does have relatives here in American that she can rely on, doesn't she?"

Marial turned past a gas station onto a potholed side street as she spoke with Nadia. "No, Nadia's parents are still in Europe. But she says her cousins are here. I think the questions are starting to disturb her."

"Yes, I can see that." The answers were starting to disturb Neil too. As they neared 112th Avenue, he made a sudden decision. "Turn left here, Marial."

"Here? But Nadia lives—"

"I want you to drive slowly around Foreign Motors."

"I don't know, boss." Marial turned left.

Nadia stiffened as they drove past the shabby car shop, its glass door draped with yellow crime scene tape.

"Turn down the alley," Neil said. The tires ground on gravel and bumped in potholes. When they reached the sliding gate of the back lot's fence, he said, "OK, stop here."

Nadia turned away, her hand over her mouth.

"Is this where they found the Honda? Inside the fence?" Neil asked.

Marial translated, and Nadia nodded.

"Did her husband have the only device for opening the gate?"

After a moment Marial translated, "She thinks so, but she's not sure."

Neil studied the fence, thinking. Then he said, "All right, let's take her home."

They drove in silence another four blocks and parked in front of a two-story turquoise apartment building. Laundry was drying on the balcony. Old tires and cable spools littered a vacant lot next door.

When they got out of the car, Neil asked, "What time will Sonya come home from playing with her cousins?"

Nadia's reply came back, "After you leave." She looked about nervously.

Neil followed her glance. Three teenage boys were in the vacant lot, trying to do wheelies with a broken bicycle. A dog was sniffing the recycling bin in the gravel alley. A block down the street an old man was out for a walk. Nothing seemed to explain her uneasiness.

Neil handed Nadia his business card. Then he looked to Marial. "Tell Mrs. Duvshenko to let me know if she plans to move. I might have more questions later. Oh, and see if she has any questions for me."

Marial translated. Then she told Neil, "Nadia would like to see the painting her husband had in the car when he died."

Neil opened the car door, took out the package, and unwrapped the plastic from a gilt frame. The notebook-sized painting inside—on a board, not a canvas — showed a trim-bearded man in a flowing white robe holding a haloed boy up to a sky of shiny gold. The two faces were strangely tilted and flattened. The copper-colored rocks beneath the man's sandals curved in a peculiar way, as if a jumble of ship planks had turned to stone. Red Cyrillic letters hung in the sky beside each head, evidently labeling the two people.

"Yosef!" Nadia gasped, clapping her hand over her mouth.

Neil glanced to Marial. She said, "It's an icon of St Joseph and the Christ child. Very beautifully done." She leaned closer and shook her head. "This is first-rate work."

Neil tilted the painting toward Nadia. "I'm guessing Joseph would have been your husband's patron saint. Do you really believe he stole this from a church, tried to sell it, and then attempted to kill a policewoman?"

Nadia's makeup-smeared eyes had gone wide with fear. With her hand still over her mouth — and before Marial could translate Neil's question — she whispered a single fierce "No!"

Then she fled up a metal staircase, unlocked an apartment door, and closed it behind her.

6

If Nadia had been Neil's focus for the first half of the morning, Marial managed to make herself a center of interest for the rest. Marial, it turned out, had translated so often for the Russian Old Believers in Woodburn that she knew the direct number of their church leader. She placed a call in Russian, arranging to return the painting and discuss the case that afternoon at one thirty.

This was the sort of competence that won Neil's respect, but there was something else about Marial that kept attracting his attention too, and he wasn't sure exactly what. She shouldn't really have been his type — he had never liked thick, dark-rimmed glasses, red hair, or blue business suits — but her every movement seemed to be sending out subtle, alluring signals. She twisted to buckle her seatbelt, pulling her woolen jacket taut between her breasts. She turned her head as she backed up the car, placing the tip of her tongue in the corner of her mouth to concentrate. She flashed small, surprising smiles.

Or was Neil imagining it all? He had to admit that the passenger seat had mysteriously enveloped him with the lingering scent of Nadia's perfume, a sweet musk that seemed far more effective in minimal doses. Even the freeway scenery had a soft, erotic glow. Neil found himself asking questions out loud about Marial.

"So what do you do when you're not translating for the police?"

"I'm a librarian."

Neil couldn't help but laugh.

"Is that so funny?"

"I'm sorry. It's just — " Neil faltered. "Well, you look like a librarian."

"I'm only a librarian part time." A shiny strand of red hair had fallen across her glasses to her cheek. With a curved finger she slowly slipped the strand behind her ear. "I also volunteer as a docent at the Portland Art Museum."

"I imagine there's a lot of demand for someone with your language skills."

"Especially at the library. That's why they hired me for the Midland branch."

This news stopped Neil for a moment. "You work at the library on 122nd Avenue?"

"Of course. That's where the immigrant population is. We have another part-timer who does Chinese and Vietnamese."

Neil's tone became earnest. "Two nights ago a man put something in your library's book drop. Can you find out what it was?"

She shrugged with one shoulder. "A book, I assume."

"Yes, but what was the title? And who checked it out?"

"Sorry. Customer records are confidential."

"But—"

"Strictly confidential." She shook her head. "Librarians won't tell you anything about their customer records, even if you have a warrant from the FBI. Besides, we get hundreds of books in that box each night. Still, I bet I know something about the case that you don't."

"What?"

She touched her index finger briefly to her lips. "Buy me lunch in Woodburn and I'll tell."

Her little gestures, her teasing tone—Neil had never known a woman who could play on emotions so skillfully. Or was she just being herself, and had he perfumed himself into a trance?

"Lunch it is," he heard himself say.

She smiled as she signaled for the Woodburn exit.

Neil had only seen Woodburn from the freeway. Stuck out in the flats of the Willamette Valley, split by the interstate's roaring concrete river of long-haul truckers and Salem commuters, the town had never tempted him. On one side, an asphalt parking lot faced a mall of factory outlet stores—a jumble of stucco California glitz dumped like unrecyclable garbage into the valley's farmfields. On the other side, overgrown signs hawked retirement condos along an empty golf course. But as Marial followed "city center" pointers east from the freeway, Neil began seeing sidewalks lined with 1970s ranch houses and 1920s bungalows—homes that reminded him of his old neighborhood in North Eugene.

Downtown turned out to be yet another surprise. Century-old brick storefronts—half of them abandoned, the rest with signs in Spanish—mustered up like war veterans along the railroad tracks. Rusty boxcars sat on a siding by a gigantic water tower. An Amtrak train rattled through town without stopping.

"This doesn't look very Russian," Neil observed.

"You'll see Russian soon enough," Marial replied. "Lunch first."

"OK. Where?"

Marial pointed to a taqueria wedged between a thrift shop and a store selling zapatos. "I like this El Salvadoran place. They do deep-fried cactus and bananas."

"Lead on."

They settled at a window table beneath garlands of colored paper flags, ordered the burrito special, and were brought iced tea.

Clinking his glass to Marial's Neil asked, "Your secret?"

"It's not much. Nadia Duvshenko sometimes visits our branch."

"Really? I suppose you won't tell me what she reads."

"No, I won't." Marial lowered her head and gave him a stern librarian's glance above her glasses. "But I can tell you why she's there."

"Why?"

"She brings her daughter Sonya for my bilingual storytime."

"And?"

"And nothing. Nadia dresses nicely, as you've seen, but she's actually quite shy. She's trying to fit into her new country. She's just not sure how."

"What about her daughter?"

"Sonya? She already speaks English better than her mother. By the time that girl starts kindergarten, no one will know she wasn't born here."

The burritos arrived with a side of lumpy fries that didn't look like potatoes. Marial held one up as if it were exhibit A. "You see, the immigrants in Portland are not like the ones in Woodburn."

"I don't follow you."

She dunked the French fry in salsa, took a bite, and puckered thoughtfully. "Prickly pear cactus. Mostly without the prickles."

"I'm still not following."

"Simple. The immigrants in Woodburn try to keep their culture. Immigrants in Portland try to lose it. The fries you get in Portland might as well be Burger King."

"And that's true of the Russians as well?"

"Especially the Russians. The Old Believers in Woodburn wear peasant clothes with a belt and a cross. They never eat meat on Wednesdays or Fridays. They have no restaurants because they refuse to use the same plates as non-believers. They drive cars and some have televisions, but many don't speak English."

"They sound almost like the Amish in Pennsylvania."

"Old Believers aren't as afraid of technology, but it's the same idea. They've been traveling the world for 300 years, trying to keep their culture intact. In the 1960s, ten thousand of them moved to Woodburn. They paid cash for the best farmland in the state."

"And the Russians in Portland?"

"They're modern Protestants. Baptists, mostly. When the Soviet Union broke up in the late 1980s they poured into Portland. They said they were escaping religious persecution back home, and I suppose they were. Of course they were really here to become Americans and get jobs. They came from places with no money—Russia, Ukraine, Belarus, Moldavia."

"Why did they pick Portland?"

Marial shrugged. "Who knows? Somehow we have the second largest Russian community in the country."

"What about you?" Neil looked into Marial's eyes. "You came here too."

"But not from Russia!"

"No?"

She leaned back, obviously offended. "Can't you tell?"

Neil shrugged.

Marial held out her hands, as if to offer herself as proof. "I'm from Latvia."

Neil knit his brow. "Latvia?"

"One of the Baltic republics."

"Oh."

"I grew up in the capital, Riga. Our national language is an old branch of the Indo-European group."

"And you speak Russian because—?" Neil left the sentence for her to finish.

"The Soviets occupied our county for fifty years. They made us speak Russian in the schools." She cast her eyes down. Her glasses magnified long, curving lashes. "Many people are misled because my last name is Russian."

Neil reached back in his memory to the captain's introduction that morning. "Gresham is a Russian name?"

Her eyes blinked back up, smiling. "Captain Dickers is a funny man. My name is Greschyednyev."

"I see." Neil made a mental note not to attempt this name without training. "Then your husband is Russian?"

"He was, yes. I married young, before Latvia was independent. Oleg was a vodka importer. Twenty years older than me. I loved him greatly. I miss him, every day."

"I understand." Neil looked down, thinking of Rebecca. Then he noticed his watch. "We should get going to the Russian church. Is it far?"

"A mile. After fried cactus, we'd better drive."

Neil paid the bill. Then they drove south along the railroad tracks out of town. Marial turned left, crossed Highway 99, and zigzagged on county roads through fields of raspberries and winter wheat. She passed Frolov Drive, where Neil could see a building with silver onion domes among the fields. Finally they turned right on Bethlehem Drive.

With no sidewalks or curbs, this street of cheap ranch houses might have been any sad rural subdivision from the 1970s, with flower planters in spare tires and kids playing basketball at a portable hoop. An estate sale in a garage offered old skis and a Toyota pickup. But the names on the mailboxes were Allagoz and Karpov. A white-bearded man sat on a porch, listening to minor music with a Slavic wail.

Neil pointed to a church on the left with a gold onion dome. Unintelligible lettering decorated the gate of a wrought-iron fence in front.

"That's the Turkey church," Marial said.

"What does that mean?"

"Turkey threw out its Old Believers in the 1920s." She drove on, past another church with onion domes. The street ended at a parking lot in a bean field with yet another onion-domed church. This one was white, with silver domes and garlands of plastic flowers over the entry. "Here's the church that lost the icons."

Beyond the church the bean fields stretched to a grove of old oak trees beneath a gigantic sky of puffy white clouds.

Neil took the painting out of the car. As he walked toward the church the front door opened to reveal a white-bearded monk in a black robe.

"You brought back Joseph! Excellent!" the monk exclaimed, surprising Neil with a broad accent that seemed to hail from somewhere east of Texas. The monk held out his hand to Neil. "Hey, Lieutenant Ferguson, you're the man."

"I'm sorry," Neil replied, flustered. "Are you the abbot?"

The monk pointed at him. "Good one. I'm Brother Larry. We don't have abbots. Why don't you come on back to the refectory. I'll get the samovar fired up for some tea, and we can talk."

Brother Larry led them around the sanctuary hall to a big white room with a vinyl floor and half a dozen folding dining tables lit by fluorescent ceiling panels. Icons and color snapshots decorated the walls. Large Cyrillic letters cut from red construction paper had been stapled to the walls to serve as labels.

Larry began filling Styrofoam cups from a brass pot on a table. "You folks like sugar?"

"Sure," Marial said.

Neil nodded, but then asked, "You're American, aren't you, Brother Larry?" It didn't seem quite possible that the conservative Old Believers would have accepted this mod squad hillbilly as one of their own.

"We all are." The monk dropped a cube of sugar in a cup and handed it to Neil. "All the Old Believers are Oregon citizens."

"Well yes, but—"

"I know." The monk set a third cup of tea on the table and sat down, settling his robes over a folding metal chair. "Our faith has always been a haven for refugees and outcasts. It started back in 1666, when the head of the Russian Orthodox church decided to change the whole religion to match some Greek texts he'd found. The Old Believers weren't buying the new rituals, so they were driven out of the church. Three million of them are still in the backwoods of Siberia. Our group went to Brazil, and then Oregon."

Brother Larry stroked his white beard. "You're old enough,

Lieutenant. Do you remember the protest days of the 60s and 70s? The student demonstrations?"

Neil nodded. "Sure. I was at the U of O."

"There you go. Everybody was trying out drugs, transcendental meditation, Hare Krishna, looking for answers?" Brother Larry turned up his palms. "Turns out the real answers were right here with the Old Believers. And you know what? They let us stay without question. People like me and Brother Daniel."

"Brother Daniel?"

The monk leaned forward and tapped the painting's frame "He's our rock star. Learned to paint right here at the monastery. Became one of the best icon writers in the world."

Marial pointed at him with sudden inspiration. "I've heard of him. Brother Daniel's supposed to be in that new exhibition at the Portland Art Museum."

"You got it. The man's a genius. But kind of reclusive. And maybe a little too angry."

"Angry?" Neil asked. "Because someone stole his painting?"

"Partly, I guess." Brother Larry frowned, awakening a wreath of wrinkles that pushed Neil's age estimate back to seventy or even seventy-five. "You see, all these evangelicals started coming here from Russia and Ukraine. Holy Rollers. They're not like us. Seems like the only thing sacred to them is money. Our icons started disappearing and Brother Daniel flipped out. Got a studio somewhere in Portland. He wouldn't say where. Said he wanted to proselytize among the damned."

"When did you notice the icons were missing?" Neil asked.

"That's tricky. We take them all down for Christmas. I know, everybody else decorates churches and houses for Christmas, but with Old Believers, it's just the opposite. We strip everything bare, and then we fast. And our Georgian calendar is two weeks later than yours, so it's January before Christmas comes and we can put all the decorations back up. Except this year we went to bring out our icons and a dozen of the best ones were gone. Some of them were from the Old Country, centuries old. A gray madonna and child that work miracles. All gone."

Neil nodded. "And then Brother Daniel's painting of Joseph turned up in the back seat of a dead Ukrainian car repairman named Yosef."

"Draw your own conclusions," Brother Larry said, shrugging.

"You're the detective."

Neil was starting to draw some unpleasant conclusions, although he suspected they might be different from the monk's. "You say no one asked questions when Brother Daniel joined the church. Do you remember when that was?"

"Well, it was just after Christmas."

"Of what year?"

Brother Larry wrinkled his brow, thinking. Then he brightened. "Come on outside. I can show you."

They pushed open a double door beneath a green EXIT sign and followed a walkway around to the front of the church. The monk pointed to a date chiseled in a cornerstone. "There, it was 1972. When Brother Daniel joined he turned over his worldly goods to the congregation. The money helped pay for the new church."

Neil exchanged a glance with Marial. Then he asked. "Is Daniel his real name?"

The monk cocked his head. "You mean his original birth name? I doubt it. We're all given new names from the Bible when we take our orders."

"Names like Larry?"

The monk shrugged. "It's short for Lazarus."

In the car on the way back to Portland Neil mused aloud, "What if Brother Daniel is actually Daniel B. Cooper?"

"You mean the hijacker or the mafia boss?" Marial asked.

"Maybe both. D.B. Cooper disappeared on Thanksgiving eve of 1971 with $200,000 in cash. A month later a penitent refugee turns up in Woodburn. He doesn't say a word about his past. But he donates enough money to build a church."

"And becomes a world-class painter of religious art," Marial added.

"I know. He doesn't sound like a killer. Still, I wonder if he and Larry are really Old Believer monks."

"They don't fit the usual pattern," Marial admitted.

"They seem to hate the new evangelical immigrants. Daniel would have been especially angry if he thought they were stealing icons."

"It doesn't look good that his painting turned up in a dead man's car."

"Exactly." Neil sighed. "I'd like to talk to this Brother Daniel. The problem is that he seems to have gone underground."

"Well he'll be above ground Saturday night," Marial said.

"He will?"

"I'll bet a dollar to a doughnut."

"A doughnut costs about a dollar these days."

Marial touched a fingertip to her dimple. "It's hard to keep up with American expressions. But I'm pretty sure Brother Daniel wouldn't miss the gala reception for the new exhibition."

"They're having a reception at the art museum?"

"Actually it's at the home of the museum's new director, Gerald Chandler."

"Gerry!" Neil laughed. "We were on the track team together at the university. I haven't seen him for years. I'll plan to go. I've got some questions for Brother Daniel."

"You would need a ticket," Marial cautioned.

"Fine."

"And a tuxedo. It's a formal event with a limited invitation list."

Neil frowned. He didn't like dressing up. And he couldn't exactly barge into a gala reception, even if it was at the house of a college chum.

Marial paused a moment before speaking again. "As a volunteer at the museum, I have an invitation. I might be able to get a second ticket if you want to come as my guest."

Neil shifted uneasily. He had not envisioned the evening as a date. "Is there someone who would object?" Marial asked.

Her tone was innocent, but Neil knew what she meant. His wife Rebecca had been dead for three years. His daughter Susan had no business telling him what to do. And Connie—well, she had told him to stop asking her out. There was no reason he couldn't go out with a librarian. It would be an evening of police business.

Finally he asked, "Would I really have to wear a tuxedo?"

Marial's dimple puckered back to life. "It all depends."

"On what?"

"On how good you look in a suit."

7

Dan Cooper's Last Will and Testament, Part 1

My time may be short. My "cousin" has become increasingly threatening. I cannot write for very long each day. I will start with the facts.

First, I have never called myself D.B. Cooper. That name was applied to me by a confused reporter who had talked with confused police. I bought my ticket under the name of Dan Cooper, and although I have not used that particular nom de guerre before or since, it can serve to establish my identity here.

I have not selected an heir, nor am I certain of my legacy, nor am I likely to secure the signature of a witness. In short, this document is less of a will and more of a testament. I have no time for apology, excuses, confession, or even exoneration. Only explanation—and even then I must cut to the chase. So let me start with the morning I chose to get out, and realized I needed out fast.

The day before Thanksgiving is traditionally a time for Americans to come home, and so it was with me on that rainy November morning in 1971. For me, however, there was no family waiting for me, roasting a turkey. Coming home had a different meaning, and it required two things: $200,000 in cash and a way to disappear completely. If you are being followed as closely as I was, by people as dangerous as they were, vanishing without a trace is the most difficult and important thing in the world.

That morning I filled a briefcase with a replica of a bomb—candles wrapped in red construction paper as dynamite, a searchlight battery as a detonator, and a spaghetti array of colorful telephone wires.

Enough to convince the uninitiated. I shaved, realized I looked too young, and spent a few minutes adding years. Then I put on a clean white shirt, a black clip-on tie that would be easy to remove, and the nondescript black business suit of Portland's Everyman.

When I left the building that morning I had a copy of the *Oregonian* tucked under my arm and a pair of sunglasses in the pocket of my black overcoat. I knew I would be invisible to most people, simply another business commuter. Most people weren't the problem. I knew I was being watched. Eyes had already noticed which bus I took. If those eyes had not actually followed me onto the bus to the airport, I knew they would be close behind.

8

"You haven't forgotten, have you, Papa?"

It was Saturday morning. Neil had just come back from his usual bike ride to find the telephone ringing. He stood there in his apartment, steaming in his yellow Lycra outfit. "Of course not, Susan. You wanted me to look at your recycling center again."

"Yes."

"And this time, it's not about unclogging plastic bags. There's something else. You're worried." He took a breath. "What is it, honey?"

"I have to show you. I'll meet you there, OK?"

"Could we meet at Powell's Books first? In forty minutes?" Neil had already been to see her recycling center a dozen times. Asking her to meet at a crowded bookstore was a test. He knew her autism made her shy from public places—even ones she liked.

"OK, Papa. I'll be at the new books section in Powell's in forty minutes."

When she agreed without hesitation, Neil knew she must be serious.

They met by the shelves of new books, prowled a few floors of Powell's together, bought a couple of titles apiece, and walked three blocks to the Pearl Bakery to compare their finds over lattes and a giant brioche. Susan had picked out books on vampires and string theory. She seemed puzzled that Neil had chosen books about Russian icons and Latvia.

"It's background for the art theft case I'm working on," Neil explained.

Susan glanced furtively from the Latvian book to him. "Why is

51

your face turning red, Papa?"

"It is not."

Susan always glanced furtively, even when she wasn't trying to be mysterious. She flipped open the book on iconography and asked, "Have you visited that sergeant who doesn't like you enough?"

"I try to get to the hospital every day."

"Is she better yet?"

"A little. She had a scare that set her back."

"Oh?"

Neil frowned. "She thought she saw D.B. Cooper again."

"The man who tried to kill her?"

"Yes."

"I thought he was dead."

"That's what my captain thinks too." Neil was still frowning.

Neil told his daughter what he had learned from Connie. Yesterday, after Connie had fallen asleep, a nurse had come down the hall rattling a dinner cart. The noise had woken Connie up. For an instant, with her eyes out of focus from the sleep and the drugs, Connie had seen the shape of an old man in her doorway. No one else had seen him, but Connie had been so upset that she had insisted on moving to a shared room.

Neil did not tell Susan what Connie had said next: *We've got to find him, Neil. We've got to find him before he kills us both.*

Susan listened intently. She was silent for a long time, slowly rocking. Then she said, "I think you need to find him, Papa."

"Who?"

"D.B. Cooper."

Neil sighed. "D.B. Cooper is a phantom. A ghost. People have been looking for him for forty years."

Susan collected the books and stood up. "Let's go now. Maybe I know someone who can help."

"You do?" He looked at her skeptically.

"Maybe." She closed her eyes a moment—something she did when the world around her began to overload. "Although I would rather take you to meet a ghost."

Susan hung her head, staring at sidewalks as they walked the half dozen blocks to Old Town. Her mood tore at Neil's heart. He loved to walk with his daughter—he was proud of her beauty—but her hunched gait tarnished her charm.

The day itself was one of those glorious, spring-like February miracles that only Oregon seems able to conjure out of gray winter. Parents had emerged with a flock of children, bringing the Park Blocks' playground to life. The tusks of the bronze elephant statue gleamed where they had been polished by the shoes of climbing kids. Big Pink, the trapezoidal office tower on Burnside, split the blue sky like the prow of a tropical liner. Tourists milled outside the Chinese Garden, talking dreamily of cherry blossoms (one month away!) and the prospect of dim sum.

The final two blocks to Susan's work place were a descent into the netherworld of Old Town's bowery—the same district that had shocked the world the previous year with the Underground murders. His predecessor Credence Lavelle had found the serial killer, but the bowery remained largely unchanged. Unshaven men in old clothes slept off Friday night's jag in abandoned entryways. Others staggered like zombies with their hands outstretched, begging change to start the new day's buzz. Every time Neil walked here he worried about his beautiful daughter—and about a shadow inside himself.

The One More Time Women's Cooperative where Susan worked was a public-private partnership that had renovated an abandoned brick warehouse and a weedy vacant lot. Once the site had been the heart of Portland's drug scene. Now the building's heart was the Recyclotron, a machine that did away with the need to sort recyclables. In the past, households and businesses had been expected to struggle with an array of bins and buckets, separating metal from glass, plastic from paper, and compost from the unredeemable refuse that remained—the incorrigible trash that had to be incarcerated in landfills without parole. One More Time, a cooperative that had spun off from the nearby Saturday Market, had raised money and won grants to install a patented sorting machine as a demonstration project.

And the women's co-op had hired Susan Ferguson. In the repetitive, technical business of recycling, her autism was more of a gift than a disability.

Susan took a chained key ring from the pocket of her overalls and unlocked the heavy metal door. Without turning on the lights they crossed the thrift shop showroom, with its displays of salvaged lamps, shoes, and bicycles. Only when they had gone through a second door marked "Employees Only" did Susan reach for a light switch. Great banks of fluorescent lights illuminated a vast workroom with Dumpsters and machinery. Despite the hum of ventilators, the air was thick with the same sour perfume that clung so often to Susan's hair and clothes.

Neil had been here far more often than he liked, reassuring Susan that her world would not end now that her duties had changed. One More Time had won awards for innovation and efficiency. Portland loved the Recyclotron project. People no longer had to sort their garbage, except for obvious things like batteries, paint, and electronics — and even when these were put in the trash they were caught by an intake team. The same team salvaged reusable items to sell in the thrift store for a profit. The Recyclotron did the rest, rumbling away as it generated tidy truckloads of raw material: glass, metal, paper, plastic, and compost. Toxic chemicals extracted from the garbage were mixed into harmless clay bricks. The amount of waste bound for the landfill had finally shrunk to zero.

"So what's the matter?" Neil asked.

His daughter walked to a small side door. "This."

"What? A closet?"

"It's locked. No one in the cooperative has the key."

"But they just renovated the entire building. Someone must have the key."

"Yes. The backers. The investors who put up money for the Recyclotron."

"Fine," Neil said. "You have a locker. Everyone who works here has their own private locker. The investors can have a closet if they want."

Susan tightened her lips in frustration. She did not argue well. She had trouble explaining things, even when it was all clear in her own mind.

Neil said, "The door disturbs you. But there's more to it than just a locked door, isn't there?"

She nodded silently.

"What is it?"

"I don't know."

He knew this was exactly the kind of frustration that could occupy Susan for months, if not years. He wanted to help. But what could he do? Harassing her employer about a locked door might get her fired.

Instead Neil tried shifting topics, although he knew this was diffi-cult for Susan. "You said you knew someone who could help with the Cooper case."

To his surprise Susan nodded. But her lips were still tight. A tear started to form in the corner of her eye.

Neil felt as if his heart were twisting. He wanted so much to hold his daughter, to comfort her at times like these. But touch was the one thing she could not bear to share. "Susan, I love you, but I don't always understand."

She turned away, walked across the workroom, took out her key ring, and opened her private locker. When Neil joined her, she handed him a bottle of what looked like a very nice California red wine. A tear ran down her cheek.

Neil's hands were suddenly so damp that he nearly dropped the bottle. "Why are you doing this, Susan? You know I can't drink."

"It's bait," she said, her voice thick.

"Bait?"

"Not for you, Papa. For the one who may know about Cooper."

"And who is that?"

"Dregs," she said. Her dark eyes were looking anywhere but at her father, blinking away tears.

"Dregs?" he repeated.

She nodded. "The key to unlocking his secrets is screw-top zinfan-del."

9

Susan led him down the MAX tracks toward the city's ancient waterfront.

"Every Monday and Wednesday at one o'clock," she said, as if to herself, "We let people take away the returnable bottles and cans from our intake line. The deposit is only a nickel, so it's not worth hiring someone to take them to a supermarket. We let others do it for us."

"Like this man Dregs," Neil suggested.

She nodded unhappily. "No one can take more than seven dollars' worth. That's the most the stores will let one person redeem in a day."

Neil considered. "Not a bad piece of charity. It's not enough to buy a bum a bed, but it could keep him fed."

"Or drunk."

"Yes. I bet you get a rough crowd." Neil worried again about his daughter's safety. He had known she worked near skid road. Elsewhere in the country, people called such districts "skid row", but in the Northwest, where the term originated, it referred to the gritty harbor fronts where logs from the backwoods had once been skidded down dirt roads to freighters. As a cop, he knew the dangers of Portland's waterfront. He hadn't realized her recycling center was a magnet for the homeless.

"How much trouble have you had?"

She didn't answer. Instead she simply walked onward, beneath the maze of the Steel Bridge's on-ramps. It was a shadowy place, echoing with the rumble of trains, the roar of traffic, and the cry of gulls. Where the sidewalk ended a chain-link fence had been peeled aside. To Neil's amazement, his daughter didn't even pause. She stepped through the gap into the darkness beyond.

"Suzie!" a man's voice cried from the murk.

The familiarity of the man's tone made Neil's blood run cold. He quickly stepped in after his daughter, his eyes straining in the gloom. The shapes beneath the bridge gradually resolved into a ragtag camp littered with cardboard, bottles, and sleeping bags. Neil guessed that half a dozen men might live here, but he could only make out three for certain — one huddled under a coat, one asleep on a plastic tarp, and one walking toward them with a yellow-toothed smile. Neil shifted the wine bottle, holding it by the neck like a club.

"And look, you've brought a guest," the man said, stopping two paces short of Susan. A bar of light from the bridge caught him diagonally. Neil judged him to be in his thirties, although life on the streets had added a few years. Sandy blond hair curled from the rim of a knit watch cap. His beard was blond and short. A face that might once have been handsome was disfigured by a scar that sagged his right cheek, leaving one eye slightly larger and redder than the other.

"Are you Dregs?" Neil asked.

The man smiled again, revealing that his teeth, though yellow, were apparently intact. "That's Dr. Egstrom to you, Lieutenant."

Neil scoffed, "You're a doctor?"

"Not a physician, perhaps, but I have a Ph.D. from Reed. Don't I, Suzie?"

This was too much. Neil demanded, "Just how well do you know my daughter?"

Dregs shrugged. "Well enough."

Neil turned to Susan, flush with anger and the growing fear this homeless man might in fact have become a part of her life. "Is this true?"

"No." She hugged herself, rocking slightly with her eyes closed. "I mean, I don't know. Dregs comes by the center twice a week and we talk. Just give him the bottle, Papa."

Neil lifted the heavy bottle, still holding it like a club. But he did not resist when Dregs took it from his hand.

"Ah! My favorite breakfast. Chateau Mondavi Reserve. From the Napa Valley. Not the industrial fields of Fresno." He opened the cap with a practiced flourish. "Care to join me?"

"No," Neil said.

"All right. Then we can use simpler stemware." He tilted back the bottle and drank three large swallows. Then he lowered the bottle and let out a long, slow breath of satisfaction.

"I've heard a lot about you, Lieutenant. You don't disappoint. I have to say, it's a pleasure to finally meet a member of the Portland police department in a social setting. Make yourself at home."

"This is not a social call."

Dregs looked to Susan. "Then why'd you bring your Daddy?"

Susan's eyes were still closed. "Tell him about the Recyclotron."

"So this is an investigation." Dregs took another drink from his bottle. Then he waved his hand theatrically as he savored the wine. "Your daughter, Lieutenant, doesn't believe it is possible for the Recyclotron to function as claimed. Seriously, how could you extract the toxic waste from an entire city's garbage every day and bind it into a few harmless bricks?"

"Doesn't the EPA check things like that?" Neil asked.

"Mindless bureaucrats, filling out forms."

"Are you suggesting the building is polluted with poisons?" Suddenly Neil worried that his daughter might be jeopardizing her health.

Dregs waved away the comment. "Oh, the workplace is clean. They make sure of that. But what makes the Recyclotron profitable is that so much nasty stuff disappears. The toxics haven't evaporated, and D.B. Cooper knows it."

Even for a conspiracy theory, Neil found this over the top. He turned to Susan. "Is this what you believe?"

"I don't know. I don't know anything about Cooper," she said.

"But I do," Dregs put in.

"Oh?" Neil asked. "So he's still alive?"

"Certainly." Dregs shrugged. "His real name is Curt Lammergeier. He was my old professor at Reed College. You know how Reed is the only college in the country with a nuclear reactor? Lammergeier wangled the grant to build it. He's always been a con man. Always needed money. When he retired he designed the Recyclotron. The money to actually build the thing came from Saudi Arabia. You want to know who has the key to the closet where the machine dumps its toxic waste?"

"Sure."

"Genghis Khan." Dregs laughed so hard he sputtered red wine

down his coat.

Neil eyed him steadily. "I suppose you heard all this from your professor at Reed?"

"Lammergeier? He's a back stabber. Because of him, I couldn't even get a post doc."

"So now, in revenge, you've decided he's D.B. Cooper. It's amazing how zinfandel makes everything clear."

Dregs took the bottle down from his lips. "If you don't believe me, ask The Keeper."

"The Keeper?"

"An old Dutch guy who hops freights south for the winter. He met Lammergeier in a freight yard in Kelso on Thanksgiving of 1971. The Keeper still knows where to find D.B. Cooper's parachute."

This was specific enough that it caught Neil's attention. Thanksgiving of 1971 would have been the day after Cooper went missing. "And where is this Keeper now?"

Dregs drank a few more swallows. The bottle was nearly empty. "He goes south each Thanksgiving and comes back on Washington's Birthday, just like a red-breasted robin. Should be here soon. Tell you what, you bring me another bottle then, we'll throw a party and figure it all out."

Neil shook his head. "Sorry, Dregs."

"Why not?"

"Oh, I'll try to track down The Keeper, but I'm not bringing you more booze."

"Really?"

"I don't trust drunk charlatans."

Dregs leaned back, roaring with laughter. "You've got me down perfect." He finished the bottle and tossed it aside. "But you know what? You and I aren't all that different. I'm the perfect completion of your daughter."

Neil stared at the homeless man. "What?"

"I'm the fucking yang to Suzie's yin. When she can't talk, I do. When I can't think, she does. We're meant for each other, man. It's a match made in Portland." He took Susan by the hand. Although she leaned away with a frightened look, she did not yank her hand free.

Neil balled his fists, suddenly wild with anger. "You are not the completion of anything. Stay away from my daughter!"

"Whoa!" The two other homeless men in the camp awoke from their torpor. They shambled up—big men with scraggly hair and missing teeth. "Is this dude bothering you, Dregs?"

"Careful," Dregs said. "He's police."

"Don't look like a cop to me." One of the men flicked the sleeve of Neil's jacket with a finger, as if to test the fabric. They loomed on either side of him like disgruntled bears.

Neil stood his ground, although his police training was shouting at him to disengage. He shouldn't allow himself to be within arm's reach of potential attackers. He was unarmed. He had no backup. But he was also the father of a young woman whose disability had made her a target for bullies all her life.

"Susan, listen to me. I know you're worried about the Recyclotron. I'll check the ownership and see what I can find out about the locked door. But don't get taken in by this man."

"Oh, so you think I'm lying?" Dregs pulled Susan closer.

Susan was shaking her head, crying quietly with closed eyes. "No. No. No."

"I happen to know a bit about Reed College, Doctor Egstrom," Neil said, his teeth clenched. "It's an undergraduate school. They don't give out doctoral degrees. And it's not the only university with a nuclear reactor. Even OSU has one. I bet you weren't at Reed at all, or if you were, your professor was right to flunk you out. He's a fraud, Susan."

Dregs' face flushed as red as the zinfandel he'd drunk. "Come here, Lieutenant. Right here. Can you tell me the name of your daughter's favorite band? That's right, what's her music?"

Neil felt the veins pounding in his head. He was so close to Dregs that the cloying stench of alcohol hit him with every breath. "Let go of my daughter."

"What's her online avatar?" Dregs demanded.

Susan intoned, "No. No. No."

"Let her go!"

Dregs smiled and pointed to the scar beneath his sagging red eye. "Here's the magic button, Daddy. I dare you to punch it."

Something inside Neil snapped. His right fist lashed out, and Dregs' head jerked back.

At the same time the two big men launched into Neil. He dodged a blow to his ear and deflected a fist to his stomach. Dregs had retreated to the shadows and Susan was still just out of Neil's reach.

Neil managed to parry a few more blows, fighting for his daughter, before one of the big goons spun him sideways with a powerhouse hook to his temple.

Then Neil was on the ground, and everything hurt, and Susan was holding her hands over her face, and he knew he would regret it all.

10

By the time Marial called to say she was on her way to pick him up for the gala, Neil had taken a long bath and had pieced himself back together as best he could. Still, there was no disguising the shiny blue half moon around his left eye. It was a mark of shame — the stigma of a naive middle schooler, lured with simple taunts into a fistfight behind the bleachers.

What hurt most was that he had let Susan down. It had not been easy for her to introduce him to the contacts she had made among the homeless. She had wanted to help him with his case. And even if it turned out the locked door and The Keeper were dead ends, it was true that he needed to learn more. He had lost his temper because he wanted to protect his daughter. Because of who she was, she had trouble recognizing when she was being victimized. Neil was certain that Dregs' motives were not pure. His conspiracy theory was an inebriated rant. But for Christ's sake, he could at least have let his daughter down gently.

Neil put on the black suit and the French cufflinks he had worn to Rebecca's funeral. Then he rode the elevator down, wishing that he had not promised to spend this particular evening in search of yet another unlikely D.B. Cooper.

When he walked down the brick steps to the sidewalk, his Latvian librarian was nowhere in sight. With offices and shops closed, the only people out at this hour were a bored Radio cab driver, a clueless couple trying to make a credit card work in a parking machine after hours, and a young woman beside a BMW waving her hand at something.

"Neil!" The woman called.

Neil looked more closely. Could this really be his dowdy translator, Marial? Coppery hair spilled in a shiny cascade across a chic green velvet dress of the sort you might expect to see in magazines or movies. One side of the outfit left her arm entirely bare, while the other had a full-length sleeve and a slit to her thigh. A choker with an emerald circled her neck.

"Neil, are you all right?" Marial asked. "What happened to your eye?"

"Oh, I—" he found himself searching for words. "I ran into some trouble researching the case. Nothing serious."

"Are you sure?"

"Yeah." He couldn't help but stare at her. "What about you? Where are your glasses?"

Marial smiled, and the dimple proved this was really her. "Contact lenses. Easy magic. Come on, let's go."

Her BMW was midnight blue, with tan suede upholstery. The interior smelled of leather and freshly ground coffee. After she started the motor—an almost inaudible purr—she paused with her hand on the shifter.

"There's something else wrong, isn't there?" She looked at him. "You're upset. I can tell."

Neil blew out a breath. "Oh, it's just my daughter. Her new boyfriend is a bum."

Marial laughed. "That's what every father thinks."

Neil was about to protest that no, in this case the boyfriend in question was in fact a homeless wino. But the lightness of her laughter, and the unexpected elegance of her company, convinced him to set the subject aside.

Marial slid the shifter to Drive and switched topics just as smoothly. "Did you really know our new art museum director when he was in college?"

"Chandler? Yeah, those were heady days down in Eugene," Neil reminisced. "Bill Bowerman was at the peak of his fame as track coach and Steve Prefontaine was this phenomenon, breaking all kinds of records in the longer distances. Prefontaine overshadowed the rest of us. I was just an also-ran in the mile, and Gerry was off doing his thing in the long jump."

"Did you keep in touch with him?"

"Not much. My brother knew him better. I know he got a job with Nike for a while. A lot of guys from the team got jobs at Nike back then. Why?"

"He's very popular at the museum. Everyone's talking about him. Apparently his apartment is a huge studio on the top floor of an old brewery in the Pearl District. That's why invitations for this reception are so hard to get."

"You'd think a reception for a new exhibit would be at the museum. How are we supposed to see the paintings?"

"The exhibit doesn't go up for a few weeks. Tonight's reception is kind of a sneak preview for donors and volunteers."

"And the whole exhibit's about Brother Daniel?"

"No, he's just part of it. It's called Icons of Oregon. Half of it will be about the local icon painters and the other half is about Mark Rothko."

"Who?"

Marial rolled her eyes. "Rothko is the most important abstract artist in American history. He grew up in Portland in the 1920s. One of his paintings recently sold for $87 million."

"Wow," Neil said. "Never heard of him."

She looked at him from the side. "Are you going to be on good behavior tonight? With that eye of yours, you look like you're going to start a fight."

"No ma'am. I mean, yes ma'am." Neil grinned.

It was only a mile to the address in the Pearl District—a cluster of brick factory buildings linked by skywalks to a modern, glass-and-steel highrise. A sandwich board on the sidewalk read, "Art Gala—Valet Parking." Half a dozen young men in white tuxedoes milled about like ushers before a wedding. Marial parked at the curb, got out, and handed her keys to a handsome young man.

"Where do we go?" Marial asked.

The young man pointed to a walkway between buildings. "Just follow the flashing lights."

Battery-powered blinkers marked the route. Marial slipped her arm in Neil's, following the winking white lights to a courtyard with a fountain. Water cascaded down a crooked metal mountain welded together from dozens of shiny aluminum beer kegs. To one side of the courtyard, condominium balconies towered into the night sky. To the other side, a jumble of water tanks, smokestacks, and pipes topped the old brewery.

"How would you like living in a place like this?" Marial asked.

Neil shook his head. "I don't think I'll get here on a detective's salary." He wondered how Marial, working as a part-time librarian and translator, had been able to afford her luxury car and clothes. Obviously she had other resources.

The blinking lights led them to an old loading dock. There a uniformed attendant in a red cap invited them to join two other couples in evening dress, waiting for a freight elevator. Giant chains rattled through pulleys as the metal cage slowly lowered. The attendant pulled aside a clattering metal screen to let them on board. Then the screen clattered back, a bell rang, and the metal platform lurched upward.

An elderly woman beside Neil gasped and caught his arm. "This isn't quite like the elevators in Macy's," she said. Cage lights cut shadows among the massive wooden beams supporting the floors. A sweet hint of malty brewer's yeast hung in the air.

At the top floor—the fourth—another attendant opened the elevator's metal gate, revealing a high-ceilinged hallway with the entry doors of half a dozen apartments. The little white lights blinked along the wall toward the final door and the muffled clamor of party voices.

The door opened ahead of them, increasing the clamor to a roar. The two other couples walked on in. Marial, however, hesitated. She clutched Neil's hand. "I have a confession to make."

"What?"

"I'm not really a party person." She gave Neil a shy smile. "I wanted to come here tonight because of the artists. But I wouldn't have had the nerve to do it alone."

"I'm not much for parties either," Neil admitted. He gave her hand a squeeze. "Let's see if we can corner Brother Daniel in his den."

Persian carpets and gilt-framed mirrors decorated the foyer of Mr. Chandler's loft apartment. A volunteer greeted Marial and Neil, checking their names off a list. Then they ventured out into the main room, a noisy, hangar-like hall filled with easels, spotlighted posters, and people in evening attire. Waiters in tails carried silver trays of appetizers. A string quartet on a platform struggled to make Mozart audible above the din. A glass skylight spanned most of the ceiling, while an entire wall of wavy glass windows rippled the lights of the city into rivers of diamonds.

"Look," Marial said, leaning to Neil to make herself heard. "There are hundreds of shoes hanging around the edges of the ceiling."

"Gerry worked at Nike for years," Neil replied.

"Ferguson!" A voice boomed out of the crowd with a familiar authority that made Neil stiffen.

Captain John Dickers, in a tuxedo with shiny black lapels and a red cummerbund, was waving for them to join him. Flanked by a young woman and an older man with sunglasses, he held a champagne flute in his hand.

Neil approached reluctantly. "I didn't know you were a fan of art, Captain."

"Me?" Dickers feigned surprise. "I'm the guest of honor. After all, I'm the one who recovered the stolen painting. Hey, Marial, you look good enough to eat."

Marial blushed—or was it a flush of anger? She exchanged a glance with Neil that let him know he wasn't the only one who was uncomfortable meeting their boss at a party.

"Let me introduce you all," Dickers said, waving his glass. "These are two of my staffers, Neil Ferguson and Marial Gresham. I'm sure you know our county commissioner, Ivan Combaugh."

The silver-haired man with sunglasses tipped his head. "A pleasure." Neil did recognize the commissioner, largely because of the mirror-lensed glasses. The man wasn't actually blind, if Neil remembered correctly, but had some sort of eye sensitivity. He also owned Ivan's Oyster Bar, a popular restaurant in Old Town.

Then Dickers lifted his champagne glass toward a young woman wearing black leather and white lace. "And this is Nancy Willis, the CEO of NovoCity Finance."

The young CEO might have been attractive, Neil thought, except that she had streaked her hair with the bright colors of a fright wig and had repeatedly punctured her face with silver jewelry. Neil found it irksome whenever presidents or CEOs were substantially younger than himself. Somehow it made him feel that he should have achieved more with his life, and a lot quicker.

Nancy Willis ignored Neil and smiled instead to Marial. "It's good to see you again, Mrs. Greschyednev."

"You know each other?" Dickers asked.

"When my husband passed away," Marial explained, "I sold his vodka importing business to NovoCity."

"The Otlichna brand still sells well in the Northwest," Nancy said. "But what really makes it work is that we've bought vineyards here and are exporting wine back. Our new Oregon Noir, a champagne-process pinot, is proving very popular in Europe."

"Isn't Nancy something?" the county commissioner said, shaking his head so their reflections swiveled in his mirrored glasses. "I've spent years struggling to get the county to create jobs, and NovoCity simply pulls them out of a hat. Now they've bought a cruise liner to base in Portland. Without NovoCity, we never would have landed the global energy summit, either."

Neil had been keeping his head turned slightly to one side, but finally Dickers caught sight of his black eye. "Say, Lieutenant, have you been letting Marial beat you up?"

"No, I—"

"And you'd think with your promotion you'd be able to afford an actual tuxedo." The captain was on a roll, inspired perhaps by the champagne. "Where are my manners? Waiter, bring a tray of drinks over for our new guests. There's vodka and that fizzy new red champagne. Or are you a designated driver tonight, Lieutenant?"

Neil's features hardened and his face went red. The captain knew Neil could neither drink nor drive. Already once today Neil had been taunted to violence. Now he covered his anger with a small laugh. But he knew the captain wasn't merely joking. Dickers was playing a dangerous game of power, obviously enjoying the risk of putting Neil down in public. And what could Neil say in response? He should be grateful to the captain for granting him the promotion at all. By all rights, Neil should still be a sergeant—no, he thought, by all rights he should be unemployed. Certainly he felt he didn't belong here, at a fancy reception with important people and a beautiful woman on his arm. He wished he could disappear, or that some magic wand would tap him on the head and make everything right.

"Neil?" There was a man's voice, and a tap on his shoulder. "Neil Ferguson?"

Neil looked up to discover that the crowd had made way for a mustachioed man in a rakish fedora, a white silk scarf, and a wide-shouldered, narrow-waisted gray suit. Had this man been watching all the time?

"Don't you remember me?" the man with a mustache asked.

Neil searched his brown eyes. "Gerry?"

"Hey, Neil, you're looking good. Still running marathons, I bet." Gerry Chandler turned to a group of perhaps a dozen people who had been following him. "Everyone, I'd like you to meet one of the most honest men I've ever met, Neil Ferguson. We were on Bowerman's legendary track team together back at the University of Oregon. Neil's the guy who paced the mile so his teammates could win. He ran in relays but gave others the glory. And when idiots like me were marching to burn down the ROTC buildings, Neil stood up and turned back the mob."

Gerry put his arm around Neil's shoulder. "How did an honest guy like you manage to sneak into a bash like this?"

The crowd laughed.

Marial said, "I invited him, Mr. Chandler."

Gerry widened his eyes theatrically. "You're Marial's guest? Now I'm really envious. Enjoy the evening, you two." Then he clapped Neil on the shoulder again and lowered his voice a notch. "It's been a long time, Neil. I hear you're a detective?"

"I'm a lieutenant with the Portland police."

Gerry looked him in the eyes. "We need to talk. Catch me before you leave tonight."

Then he was off, swirling with his white scarf toward the platform at the front of the room. The string quartet cut Mozart short and played a flourish. Gerry stepped up into a spotlight against the backdrop of windows overlooking the city. He took a microphone from a stand and announced, "Your attention, please. Welcome, and thank you all for coming. I'm Gerry Chandler, and tonight we're celebrating Icons of Oregon, the first major local exhibit I've had the honor to organize as museum director. The show opens March 14, celebrating not only the Russian art icons created here in Oregon, but also the work of Mark Rothko, who is himself an icon of Oregon. Of course, world-class displays like these are made possible by the generous gifts of our donors and volunteers. And can you believe it? I'm not going to hit you up with a pitch for money tonight. That's because the people in this room have already given so much. You know who you are, so please, give yourselves a big hand."

Applause rippled through the room.

Gerry continued, "In particular I'd like to thank our two corporate sponsors for the exhibit, Nike and NovoCity Finance. The folks at Nike put up with me as an art designer for nineteen years before I actually went out and got a degree in art. It's nice to see they've followed me here to become a major supporter of the museum. NovoCity is a new corporate sponsor for the museum. Their chief executive officer Nancy Willis is here somewhere tonight." Gerry shaded his eyes with his hand to search the crowd. "If you see Nancy, thank her for tonight's beverages. She might even be able to connect you with a case of that wonderful red champagne at wholesale. So raise your glasses, please, in a toast to Nike and NovoCity."

The room was a sea of raised glasses. Captain Dickers clinked champagne flutes with Nancy Willis and the county commissioner. It seemed Neil and Marial were the only ones without a glass. He made do by taking her hand and raising it, as if in victory.

"For security reasons, we haven't been able to bring paintings from the exhibit here to show you tonight," Gerry told the crowd, "but instead we have a special treat befitting an art loft.

"In the far corner," Gerry held out his hand toward the back of the room, "we've set up a reproduction of the New York studio where Mark Rothko produced so many of his important works. As you perhaps know, the Rothko family not only donated dozens of the artist's paintings—which now constitute the museum's most valuable collection—but they also gave us the materials that were in his studio when he passed away. Tonight, Mr. Rothko's grandniece is on hand to show you the brushes, paints, and easels he used, and to share her memories of Rothko's creative process.

"In the corner of the room to my left," Gerry said, holding out a hand to one side, "We are honored to have with us three leading lights in the Mount Angel school of religious iconography, Brother Gabriel, Brother Daniel, and Brother Marcus. They've brought a number of works in progress, so you can see how these icons are written. Notice that we say the icons are written, and not merely painted, because of the complicated stylistic conventions and symbology involved in the process.

"And if all that isn't entertaining enough," Gerry added with a big smile, "Captain John Dickers of the Portland police department is here tonight as well. As you've probably seen in the news, the captain was responsible for recovering one of Brother Daniel's most famous icons, stolen from a church in Woodburn in January. All you amateur sleuths, here's your chance to get the inside scoop on one of the state's most sensational art thefts."

Gerry pressed a switch on the wall, starting a motor to hum somewhere overhead. "And now to launch our upcoming exhibit, we're giving away a hundred free museum passes. But there's a catch—literally. I think everyone in this room already has free passes, so we've attached the passes to helium balloons, hoping to entice the outside world to visit the museum."

Volunteers at the back of the hall began bringing out nets filled with silver balloons. Meanwhile, the humming motor had opened the loft's enormous skylight, tilting back frosted glass panels to reveal a starry sky. At a wave of Gerry's hand, the volunteers opened the nets, releasing a cloud of silver spheres up into the night sky—a spectacle so magical that the crowd of partygoers gasped.

"Enjoy the evening, everyone," Gerry said, flipping the switch to close the skylight. "And thank you all for supporting the Icons of Oregon."

The applause that followed soon dissolved into voices and laughter as people began making their way to see the displays.

"Isn't he something?" Marial marveled.

Neil stood on tiptoes, scoping out the room. "There's a big crowd around the monks. We won't be able to talk to Brother Daniel for a while. In the meantime, I'd like to investigate something by that wall."

"What?" Marial asked.

"The appetizer table." Neil smiled. "I didn't really have dinner."

"Me either. I'm starving."

They edged toward the table and were soon exclaiming over delicacies. Mushrooms stuffed with smoked salmon. Prawns barbecued with pear tomatoes. Chevre cheese and capers on pumpernickel fingers. Huge strawberries, ready for dipping in a seven-tiered fountain of molten dark chocolate.

Mounted on the wall behind the table were color photographs of Mark Rothko and his paintings. The balding artist glowered behind wire-rimmed spectacles. His paintings consisted of large, fuzzy squares and stripes in various colors. To Neil, it looked as if workmen had been using the canvases to clean paint rollers.

"How could something like that be worth $70 million?" Neil asked.

"It looks simple, but Rothko's style was revolutionary at the time," Marial explained. "During World War II the center of the art world moved from Europe to America. But the leaders then were mostly surrealists like Miro and Dali. Rothko left them all behind with these abstract works of pure color, pure emotion."

"What kind of name is Rothko, anyway?"

"He changed it from Rothkowitz. His parents were Ashkenazi, Russian Jews. They moved to Portland when he was ten."

"Rothko came from Russia too?" Neil asked, surprised.

"From Daugavpils, actually. It was part of the Russian Empire in those days, but now it belongs to Latvia."

"Latvia. I see."

Marial nodded toward the far end of the table. An elderly bald man in a black robe was loading a plate with stuffed mushrooms. She whispered, "This may be our chance to corner the iconographer."

Neil stepped up to the monk. "Excuse me, are you Brother Daniel?"

"Marcus, actually." The monk waved his plate toward an easel. "Daniel is the one with the gilt demo."

Neil walked to the far side of the easel, where an elderly monk with wispy white hair was carefully burnishing a tiny leaf of gold foil onto a saint's halo.

"Brother Daniel?" Neil asked.

The monk made a vaguely affirmative noise without looking up.

"I'm Lieutenant Neil Ferguson of the Portland police."

Brother Daniel continued stroking the foil with a tiny metal tool. Neil couldn't help noticing how strongly the monk's stature and tall, white forehead matched the old police sketches of D.B. Cooper.

"I know this is a little awkward at an event like this," Neil began, "but I'm the one who delivered your icon of St. Joseph to the monastery in Woodburn yesterday. I talked with Brother Lazarus, and he said you can be hard to get a hold of. Would you mind answering a few questions?"

"First," the monk said, still concentrating on his work. "Brother Larry is an idiot. Second, there is no monastery in Woodburn."

"I don't understand."

"How could you fail to understand, Lieutenant? Larry is a certifiably brain-dead hippie, the detritus of a dissolute age."

Neil blinked. "I meant the monastery. It's right there behind the Old Believer church on Bethlehem Lane. Brother Larry took us to the refectory."

"What you saw was the social hall of a church. Churches are for everyone. Monasteries are for monks. The Old Believers have no monasteries in America. Those of us who want to study their ways have to enroll in the Benedictine monastery three miles away in Mount Angel."

Neil turned to Marial. "Is that the monastery you called to set up our visit?"

She shook her head. "I telephoned the patriarch of the Old Believers. He said he'd have an English speaker meet us at the Woodburn church."

Neil had been misled by his own assumptions, and he didn't like it. He asked Brother Daniel, "Isn't the Mount Angel monastery for Catholics?"

"At this distance from Constantinople," Daniel replied, "Romans and Russians have a lot in common. Art iconography, for example."

Neil decided to steer his questions closer to the Cooper case. "Brother Larry said the Old Believers accept refugees without asking about their past."

Daniel finally set down his burnishing tool to look at Neil. "Ignoring people is not the same as accepting them."

Neil sidestepped this with a question of his own. "Would you be willing to tell me what you did before you arrived in Woodburn?"

"My former life is irrelevant."

"Is it? You donated enough money to build a church in Woodburn. I can't help but be curious about that."

Daniel picked up an Xacto knife and weighed it in his hand. "If you sell your past, it is because you don't want it anymore. My job is to praise God with paint."

"And my job is to understand people's motives. It would help me if you could paint just a little window into your past."

Brother Daniel flexed the knife's blade sideways, as if testing it. "My mother was a schizophrenic middle school art teacher in Washougal. My father ran a Texaco gas station by day and beat my mother by night. I never found out which one of them shot the other first. I inherited the gas station and sold everything. Is that sufficient, Lieutenant?"

Neil lowered his eyes. "Yes." In truth, the monk's bitter childhood did not rule him out altogether as a candidate for a hijacker. Neil paused a moment before venturing, "What puzzles me is that a young car mechanic like Yosef Duvshenko would hit on the idea of stealing your paintings at all."

Brother Daniel bit out several angry sentences in Russian. Then he turned his back on Neil and began trimming the gilt halo of his icon with the razor-edged knife.

Neil was left to retreat with Marial. As they headed back toward the strawberries, Neil asked, "What did he say?"

"It wasn't pretty," Marial replied.

"How so?"

"He has a lousy accent. And too colorful a vocabulary for a monk."

"But what did he say?"

"He said the new immigrants are dogs. And the police are fools. But not in those words."

"He might be right about the police. I don't suppose he had any specific examples?"

"He said his stolen art is worthless compared to the Gray Madonna."

Neil thought a moment. "Quite a few icons are still missing. Brother Larry also thought they were valuable. Where are they? Already sold? And who would buy religious art like that? Someone from a competing church?"

"Or a museum," Marial suggested.

"I need to know more about the missing paintings," Neil admitted. "A lot of the research will be in Russian. Could you help?"

"I'd love to. Do I get a raise, stepping up from translator to research assistant?"

"I can ask."

All the strawberries were gone at the appetizer table. Only a few celery sticks remained on silver trays.

Marial looked about at the crowd of people. "Is it too early to go home?"

"I'm ready. Let's go thank our host."

They found Gerry near the door, saying goodbye to other guests.

"Neil!" Gerry motioned him aside and lowered his voice. "Could you come by my office someday soon? We have a problem at the museum that needs to be handled delicately."

"A problem?"

The director frowned. "Yes, I invited Captain Dickers so I could bring this up with him, but I think I'd be more comfortable talking with someone I know."

"It's been a long time, Gerry."

"Too long. Are you doing anything Monday morning?"

"I think I'm meeting an old classmate at the art museum."

"Good. Let's say ten." He handed Neil a business card.

"OK, but Gerry —"

"What?"

"You've got to give me a hint."

The museum director ran his hand over his brow. "That church in Woodburn isn't the only place with a problem."

"You mean —?"

Gerry nodded. "We may be missing some art as well."

11

Dan Cooper's Last Will and Testament, Part 2

"Sir?" The attendant at the Northwest Orient counter flashed me a smile that reflected careful training. Northwest really did want you to fly with these girls.

I should have been frightened to death. On the bus ride to the airport the blood had been pounding in my ears so hard I couldn't hear the driver call out stops. So many things could go wrong. Already they must be wondering why I changed the plan. Traitors are dead men walking. And double traitors? Two wrongs never add up to a right, but what if the sum were zero? What if I could vanish?

The trick was to use their knowledge against them. I began right there on the bus with the first rule I'd learned. To assume a different identity you must erase the old one. I closed my eyes and let out a long, deep breath, exhaling the spirit of a frightened runaway. When I breathed in, the air itself seemed braced with confidence. By the time I left the bus and put on my sunglasses, I had slipped into my new persona as if it were an old coat.

"How much room do you have on the next flight to Seattle?" I asked, glancing at my wristwatch with just the right casual concern.

"Flight 305?" She glanced at a clipboard. "Forty seats. Need that many?"

I smiled. "Must be a big plane. A Boeing 727?"

"Yes, sir."

This was the model we had trained for—the most common jet for domestic flights, with an aft staircase that could be lowered from the tail. "Give me a window seat. One way."

"First class?" she asked brightly.

"Coach will do."

Already she was taking a four-part ticket from beneath the counter. "That will be $18.52. Name?"

"Cooper," I said, taking a twenty out of my billfold. There would be no need to show my fake ID on a domestic flight like this. "Dan Cooper."

She took the money and gave me change. Then she tore out a carbon and slid the rest of the ticket into a folder with rental car ads. "There you go. Would you like to check your luggage, Mr. Cooper?"

But Mr. Cooper didn't hear her question because he had already evaporated. The moment I recognized the gravelly voice of Division Chief Swarovsky from the revolving glass door by the taxi stand, Cooper's suave business persona was gone. Instead I stood there naked, a terrified fugitive, watching from behind the insufficient protection of sunglasses as the big, barrel-chested man in a pin-striped blue suit scanned the crowds of holiday travelers.

"I'm sorry, would you like to check your briefcase?" A girl's voice was politely trying to pull me back to the fantasy world of Dan Cooper.

I stared at her. She was so beautiful. Nearly my own age. Incredibly, she would live out this day and I would not.

"Why don't you just take it as carry-on," she said gently, motioning me aside so she could help the next customer. "Take the first corridor to Gate B11. They're already boarding."

I took the ticket and fled, pursued by the rapid footsteps of Swarovsky's hard leather Wingtip shoes.

12

Marial limped as she and Neil descended the steps from the old loading dock to the courtyard fountain.

"Are you all right?" Neil asked.

"New shoes. They pinch. Sorry." She winced and clutched his arm.

"You've been on your feet all night." He slowed, noticing a bench beside the fountain.

"If we could just rest a minute." She sat on the bench, shook back her hair, crossed her knees, and slipped off a pointy green shoe.

She was so beautiful, poised there in the sparkling lights of the fountain, that Neil was suddenly speechless. He sat beside her, drawn as if by a spell. Her bare foot touched his knee as if by accident.

"My toes hurt. Could you—?"

His hand closed cautiously over her slender foot. When he touched her, a warm charge surged through him. He managed to massage her toes for a moment before he stopped and swallowed. He had never imagined that stroking a woman's foot could be such a sensuous experience.

She put on her shoe and smiled at him—the dimple again!

Although it was not a cold night for February, a chill had raised goosebumps the entire length of her sleeveless arm. Neil put his arm around her shoulder for warmth, and she simply folded up against his chest.

He held her there for a long moment, torn by a mixture of happiness and guilt. If she looked up at him—and he suspected she might—he knew he would want desperately to kiss her.

Marial lifted her head and looked at him questioningly through a strand of hair that shone like red gold.

"I—" Neil was fighting in internal battle. "I have to tell you something about myself. Before we go any farther."

She cocked her head. "What?"

"I'm an alcoholic. Or I was. I—"

She touched a finger to his lips to silence him. "Do you think I didn't know? My husband was a vodka salesman. I understand."

"You do?"

She nodded. "Now kiss me."

He leaned over and sank into a long and passionate kiss. The guilt was still there, but for a time he was happy to let it be drowned beneath the splashing patter of the fountain.

Later, when she parked her BMW in front of his apartment building, he said, "I'd invite you up for a cocktail but, well, you know. That cupboard's bare."

"I could make Brazilian lattes," she said.

"What are they?"

"A coffee thing. I just picked up some fresh Sumatran. Do you have milk?"

He nodded.

"A blender?"

He nodded again.

"OK then." She put the car in park and took out her key.

Neil's heart was beating far too fast as they rode the elevator up together. It wasn't just the anticipation of inviting a beautiful woman into his apartment. There was also the fear of what he would have to say.

When he opened the apartment door and turned on the lights Marial walked in slowly, examining the tidy kitchen alcove, the sparse living room, the shelves of books, the display of track jerseys, and the swing-out TV screen.

"You live very nicely here," she said.

"When I moved from Eugene I wanted something small," Neil said.

"I like it." She held her handbag in front of her. "Would you mind if I took out my contacts? I can only bear them for a few hours. Then they start killing me."

"Sure. The bathroom's off the hall."

She flashed a big smile and left with her handbag. Over her shoulder she called, "Start some hot water, will you?"

A minute later she was back, biting her lip as she ventured into the kitchen. "My glasses ruin the effect, don't they?"

Neil smiled. The thick black frames did in fact make her look like a librarian dressed up for the ball. But with her hair down, and with the emerald choker, she was a very attractive librarian indeed. He said, "Your glasses are fine."

"All right then, let's get to work. Do you mind if I boss you around a little?"

"You mean, about the lattes?"

"How much bossing can you handle?"

Neil hesitated. "I'd like to learn how to make lattes."

"Good. We'll need a pan for the milk. I hope you have cinnamon."

"Ground cinnamon, but it's kind of old."

"Then we'll make old Brazilian lattes."

For the next ten minutes they were working side by side in the kitchen. Neil took off his jacket and loosened his tie. He had never realized lattes were quite this complicated, or that it was possible to make them at all without an espresso machine. Finally she decorated the top of each cup with a coffee bean in the middle of a heart of foam. Then she clinked her mug against his. "Cheers!"

The lattes were unlike anything he'd tasted at Starbucks, full of jungly spice. The hot milky Sumatra was just far enough beneath the sweet froth that they both had to lick off foamy mustaches.

But then Neil's smile faded and he set down his cup. "This is lovely, Marial, but there's something else I feel I have to tell you."

She raised an eyebrow. "More? And this time I can't guess."

"It's something that happened you should know about. Before— well, I think you should know the worst about me."

"Mr. Chandler said you might be the most honest man in the world."

"Maybe that's part of the problem." Neil tightened his lips and stared down at his coffee drink.

"Maybe we should sit down in the other room," Marial suggested.

Neil nodded and followed her out to the sofa. He took a drink of his latte, sighed, and set it on the coffee table. "I started drinking too much three years ago, after my wife Rebecca died. It made the evenings less lonely. Because I was living alone, I figured I wasn't really hurting anyone."

"Perhaps not even yourself."

Neil shot her a questioning glance, but she seemed to be serious.

"You are a man with a strong physical constitution," she explained.

"That's true. I ran track for years, and I still bicycle ten miles every morning. For a while I simply burned off the alcohol. But then I started having a drink or two in the morning. Just for the headaches. To make it easier to go to work."

Marial said nothing.

"Six months ago I was out on patrol with my partner Jeremy Layton. We responded to a robbery in progress at a Vietnamese grocery on Sandy Boulevard. It's pretty unusual to get daytime robberies. Only the most dangerous, desperate types attempt it. We got there just as a car was squealing out of the parking lot. The store owner was outside, pointing for us to follow the guy. I was at the wheel. Jeremy hit the siren. I hit the gas, faster and faster."

Neil's hands were shaking, and his forehead was damp. He could feel the old carnival ride cranking up inside his skull, with the flashing lights, spinning and screaming. He still heard himself talking, as if he were somewhere outside his body, listening. Perhaps by telling this story he could drain it out of his life and be done with it.

"We chased him halfway to the freeway. At 85th a school bus suddenly pulled out in front of us. The sidewalk was full of children. The opposite lanes were full of cars. We shouldn't have been there, not at that speed, not in the middle of the day. We should have called in backup to seal off the street."

"What did you do?" Marial asked quietly.

"I hit the brakes, of course. But I also steered straight into a telephone pole. It was the only way to avoid hitting kids or cars. The airbags deployed. The wires came down. Sparks were everywhere. No one could get near us for minutes. Finally the medics pried open the car and got us out. We were lying there on two gurneys when Captain Dickers showed up. He leaned over, close to my face, and said, 'Your breath stinks. Damn it Neil, you've been drinking again.'

"I just looked at him, but I could see he knew. He'd known all along. He said, 'I can't have a DUI on the department's record. If you're in the passenger seat we don't have to check. So Layton was driving. Understand?'"

"Did that work?" Marial's voice was hardly a whisper.

"Yeah. We looked a lot the same, Layton and me. Except he was dead."

She caught her breath.

Neil closed his eyes. "So Layton's family thinks he drove into a telephone pole to save the lives of the kids. He's a hero. And to make the story work, the department had to turn me into a hero too. That was hard, because I had to take over the position of Credence Lavelle, the detective who retired with a million-dollar book deal."

"Dickers saved your career."

"I wish he'd fired me. The next day I asked to resign, but he wouldn't accept that either. The whole story would have come out, and all hell would have broken loose. Even Dickers might have lost his job. So instead he promoted me and ordered me to keep quiet. That was the worst punishment of all."

"And now you're a detective."

Neil nodded. "I couldn't tell the truth about myself, so I decided to try to find out the truth about all the other unsolved cases out there."

Marial stood up, walked to the sliding glass balcony door, and looked out across the lights of the city.

Neil couldn't guess her thoughts, but he was pretty certain that he had spoiled the evening, and perhaps their entire relationship. "I'm sorry, Marial. I shouldn't have dumped all this on you. Not tonight at least."

"No, honesty is important. Chandler was right. It's strange that a man who loves truth so much has been forced to lie."

Neil swallowed. She was so beautiful, standing there against the dark window, her light red hair spilling down her green velvet dress. "I was afraid when I told you, you'd leave."

"I'm going to."

"Seriously?" He was on his feet.

"Look, Neil, you've been hurt. But you're not the only person who has suffered. Others have been condemned to live lies as well."

"Who?" Neil asked. "You?"

"Perhaps. How would you know? You're so wrapped up in your own recovery that you haven't been able to investigate anyone but yourself."

"That's not true."

"Oh? What about Nadia Duvshenko? Even I could tell she was being pressured by somebody. How are you going to find out who it is?"

"I don't know."

"There's a memorial service for her husband tomorrow at noon. Maybe her 'cousins' will show up."

"If you'll drive, I'll go. Where are they holding the service?"

"At The Grotto."

"The Grotto?" Neil tilted his head.

"You know, the religious park full of Catholic statuary. At 85th and Sandy."

"But that's —" Neil stopped short.

"Right. Where they take busloads of Catholic schoolkids. Where your partner died. Still want to go?"

Neil's shoulders sagged, as if the weight of the day had finally pulled him down. "Pick me up at the downtown office at eleven."

Marial slipped her hands around his waist and hugged him, pressing her head against his chest.

Then she stepped back, kissed her fingertip, touched his lips, and walked out the door into the night.

Much later that night she magically returned, drifting into the apartment like a ghost, despite the locked door. This time Marial gave a light, musical laugh at Neil's fears, told him she had just the thing to set him right, and asked, "Mind if I change? This gown feels like Saran Wrap." She disappeared briefly into his bedroom. When she returned she was wearing one of his white dress shirts. The tails swooped around her bare thighs as she walked. The stiff collar points highlighted the deep V of pink skin at her throat. Because half the buttons were undone, Neil could glimpse astonishing pink curves. The familiar shirt pockets bulged and wiggled intoxicatingly as she walked toward the sofa. With a weightless pirouette, she sat on his lap and threw her arms about his neck. "There!" she exclaimed, dimpling her cheek as she tapped his nose with her forefinger.

He should have left her there, just like that. But he reached up, touched her shoulder, and the dream was gone.

All that remained were twisted sheets, the nightlight's glow, the bedside table photo of Rebecca, and of course, guilt.

13

A hangover would have felt better.

When Neil finally woke up Sunday morning his black eye throbbed as if some idiot were trying to inflate it with a bicycle pump. He ached all over. He had overslept his usual bike ride, but he felt as if he had already fallen in traffic.

Nothing hurt so much as the penance he knew he would have to pay for his Saturday full of mistakes.

Susan! Tomorrow he was supposed to cook her favorite dinner, spaghetti with eggplant. How could he face her after slugging her friends on skid row?

Marial! He'd repaid all her tenderness and charm with a self-centered horror story. Today she was driving him to a funeral on Sandy Boulevard, the scene of his crime. How was he going to keep from falling apart?

And then there was Connie. Yesterday, for the first time, he had failed to visit her in the hospital. Another broken promise.

Neil rolled over, flipped open his cell phone, and punched the hospital number. To his surprise he was told that Sergeant Wu had checked out.

"What do you mean, 'checked out'?" Neil sat up quickly on an elbow. "Is she all right?"

"I really can't tell you more than that," the voice said. "But we don't release patients unless they're stabilized."

"Who picked her up? Where did she go?"

"I'm sorry, sir."

Neil jabbed the "End" button and slapped the phone shut. He sat there fuming for a minute, rubbing his temples with his thumbs. Then he did the obvious, reopened the phone, and pressed the button for Connie's home phone. The number was still on speed dial, although she had told him never to call her there.

"Boop—beep—BEEP," a machine interrupted. "We're sorry. The number you are trying to call has been disconnected or is no longer in service."

Neil lumbered into the bathroom, groaned at the cadaver in the mirror, and began brushing his teeth to settle his thoughts. If Connie had been abducted from the hospital by D.B. Cooper—a phantom only she seemed able to see—the staff would not be calmly describing her as stabilized. They'd be grilling anyone who asked about her. But if Connie really had checked out on her own, why hadn't she told him?

Neil stepped into the shower stall, cranked the water back and forth from hot to cold until his skin woke up, and then soaped as much as he could away with a mean bar of Ivory. He found himself remembering Leighton, Connie's pudgy son from Hawaii. Probably he had done just what he'd said they would do. He had taken Connie to her house in the Hawthorne district to recover. Disconnecting the land line would have been Connie's idea. Captain Dickers had assigned Neil to check up on their damaged sergeant. He would simply have to go out there and see who was home on a Sunday morning.

Neil started to dress in the stonewashed jeans that Connie said suited him best. But then he thought—no, he would be going to a funeral later. So he pulled on the same damned slacks he had worn to the gala last night. The jacket collar even still smelled faintly of perfume.

He found a cold pancake and half a banana in the fridge, washed it down with guava juice, and took the elevator down to face the city.

The air outside was cool and clear, the same as it had been the night before, except that the sun now bounced off windows, flashing at odd angles through the urban canyons. Bus service is lousy on Sunday, and Neil felt weird waiting at a bus stop in a suit anyway, so he walked over to the Schnitz, a concert hall where cabbies seem to hang out, even if the Portland Baroque Orchestra went home long ago.

"Thirty-seventh and Hawthorne," he told the young man as he slid into the back seat.

"You got it." The cabbie had a little blond beard. He kept smiling at Neil in the rearview mirror when they stopped at red lights, as if he was hoping Neil would start a conversation. Neil figured the kid was probably a creative writing dropout from PSU, driving a Radio Cab to collect material for the Great American Novel. Neil had too much on his mind to deal with it now. Still, he gave the cabbie a five-buck tip when he got out in front of the Baghdad Theater.

Neil stood on the sidewalk, working up his nerve. He used to love Connie's neighborhood. He had taken her out several times here, first to an upscale Italian restaurant, then to a funky coffee shop with framed blueprints of Portland's bridges, and finally to a retro Coney Island hot dog shop where tie-dyed buskers played banjos by the door. As a former alcoholic he'd avoided the district's landmark center, the Baghdad. Connie told him that as a girl she had lined up around the block to see flicks like *Flubber* and *The Parent Trap* there. Since then a brew pub chain had restored the old theater as a beer hall with grunge bands. As a cop, Neil recognized the result: a neighborhood that's alive but nervous, with broken bottles in the gutter and iron bars in the windows.

Connie's own house, a block up a side street, had gradually become a fortress. A palisade of decorative but extremely sharp steel spikes topped a brick wall along the sidewalk. Neil pressed a buzzer on the gate's speaker box and waited.

"What do you want?" The voice of a world-weary surfer crackled from the box. Leighton. Neil could even see his shaggy black-haired head peering at him from a window up on the porch.

"A twenty-ounce latte to go. What do you think? I want to check on your mother."

"Name?"

"Oh come on."

"Name?" he repeated.

"Lieutenant Neil Ferguson."

"Password?"

"Jesus Christ!"

A moment later a buzzer and a click let Neil know the gate was un-latched. He pushed through and climbed the porch steps.

Leighton looked puzzled as he opened the front door for Neil. "Mom said you'd know the password, and you did."

"Cops think alike. Where is she?"

"On the Internet." Leighton waved a Smith & Wesson

semi-automatic vaguely toward the living room. "That's all she's done since we got home. That, and put me on guard duty."

"Whoa there, Leighton." Neil held his palms out toward the pistol as if it were an angry Rottweiler. He knew this model well, and it was lethal. "Are you aware that this weapon's safety is off?"

"It has a safety?" Leighton examined the gun front and back, wobbling the muzzle from his own forehead to Neil's left shoulder.

Gently Neil lowered his palms to pet the nice doggy. He managed to click the safety in place. Then he strode through the living room—past the white piano, the white sofa, and her roaming house turtle—expecting to find Connie in the den she used as her home command center.

The person who swiveled away from the computer monitor to confront him left him at a loss for words. The half-bald head looked as if it had been stitched together by a mortician, with red patches, bruised eyes, and a swollen jowl.

"In case you're wondering," she said, slurring her words, "I look better than I feel."

"You—" It took Neil a moment to find a way to finish the sentence. "You took off your bandages."

"Yeah, I'm supposed to give the wounds air." She winced as she tried to stand up.

"Careful! Don't you have a broken hip?"

"A hairline fracture." She straightened unsteadily. Despite her baggy housedress, it was obvious that she had lost weight. "They made me start walking as soon as I was consistently conscious. Without morphine, the whole world's on fire."

"Connie, you should still be in the hospital."

She shook her head. "Haven't you figured it out yet? We're playing this game for keeps."

"OK, so tell me," Neil said, trying to calm her down. "Do you remember anything else about the man you saw in your hospital room?"

She shook her head. "I just heard a noise and woke up. My eyes weren't focused. He turned and ran out. But I tell you, it's the same guy who tried to kill me with the car. He wasn't in the hospital to bring me flowers."

Neil pressed his lips together.

"I know what you're thinking," Connie said, sinking back into her office chair. "This lady's a lousy witness. No one else at the hospital saw the mystery man. And anyway, the department's written off the whole Duvshenko case as suicide. In short, I'm wacko."

"I think you're right."

"That I'm bonkers?"

"No, that the case stinks."

"Yeah?"

"Let me count the ways." Neil leaned against a table and began ticking off points on his fingers. "First, we know Duvshenko was right handed, but he shot himself with his left. Second, his widow's so frightened she contradicts herself every other sentence. Third, the most valuable artwork is still missing. And the only witness who saw the Russian crime boss up close thinks he's still alive."

"So what are you doing to clear things up?"

"Dickers ordered me off the case."

"He did?"

"He told me to find the real D.B. Cooper instead."

Connie laughed painfully. "Dickers wants you working on a forty-year-old skyjacking case? The statute of limitations must have expired long ago."

"It's no joke." Neil tapped the purple mark beside his own right eye. "Yesterday I followed a tip from my daughter and got caught up in an interview with some thugs. They seemed to think Cooper is a Reed College professor."

Connie considered this. "Reedies can be strange."

"Not that strange. And the Russian icon painter? Turns out he's just a sullen hermit from a bad home in Washougal. He might stab an art critic in the eye with a paintbrush, but he lacks that certain skyjacking flair."

"So you've run out of leads?"

Neil shrugged. "I'm thinking Cooper might be tied in with a smelly current case after all."

She looked at him skeptically.

"OK, so we both know it's an excuse," Neil admitted. "But I'm still going to Duvshenko's funeral today at noon."

Connie raised an eyebrow. "That could be dangerous. You should take backup. Someone who knows how to handle a gun."

"Definitely not your son, then. That reminds me, Leighton says you've been on the Internet. What's up?"

"I've just been sniffing around."

"I thought so. Look, Connie, I can work on the outside while you work on the inside. But we've got to keep quiet about this case, and we've got to share."

She studied him for a moment and then nodded. "All right. You want to see what I've got?"

Neil nodded.

Connie clicked one of the buttons at the bottom of her computer screen. "Here, I convinced the evidence tech guys to email me the list of car shops from Duvshenko's computer. Strange thing about these files. When you click on "Properties" you can see they were all last modified Wednesday evening around nine o'clock."

"Two hours before we met the guy in the red SUV at the Midland library. Maybe Duvshenko was working late? He could have driven straight from his shop to the rendezvous."

"Maybe. The previous time the computer was used to log out at 6:30."

"OK, so he went out for dinner and then came back. We could check with his wife."

"Good idea." Connie clicked a different button. A new screenful of figures popped open. "Here's a rundown of the guys in Duvshenko's computer file who own the other businesses. Counting transmission shops, boat dealers, and a couple of janitorial services, there's a total of nineteen. I had a hell of a time getting their immigrations records from Homeland Security, but it turns out they've been arriving in Portland at the rate of about one a year, almost every year since the Iron Curtain fell in 1989. All of them from Russia or Eastern Europe."

"That's a lot of cousins," Neil said.

"It's hard to tell who's related. Some of them really do have the same last names, but others are using patronymics."

"What's that?"

"Last names that are based on their father's first names. It's pretty confusing."

"How about Duvshenko?"

"The name Duvshenko is all by itself. But Nadia Duvshenko's maiden name was Andropov, the same as Andrei Andropov."

"Who's he?"

"The guy who called 9-1-1."

"Oh, right." Dickers had told him about the car shop owner who had ratted on Duvshenko. Neil had told Connie about it along with everything else. It bothered Neil that she had remembered the name and he had not.

"Of course the 9-1-1 caller didn't actually give his name at the time," Connie pointed out.

"So what are you saying? That Andrei and Nadia might be brother and sister? Why would they conspire to have Yosef killed?"

"Why indeed? Maybe the stool pigeon and the widow aren't related at all."

"Even if they are, it doesn't prove anything."

"But it makes you wonder." Connie tapped a finger on the table nervously. "There's something else that was odd about Yosef Duvshenko."

"What?"

"He was Catholic." She clicked a third button to reveal yet another screen, this time from the Immigration and Naturalization office. "All the other immigrants are Protestant. Roman Catholics are pretty uncommon in Ukraine. You're more likely to find Catholics in Poland or Lithuania. Nadia must have taken heat from her family for falling in love with the wrong sort."

Neil sighed. "That explains why the funeral's at The Grotto." He glanced at his watch. "I've got to head over there soon."

Connie stared at him. "To The Grotto? The place out Sandy Boulevard?"

Neil nodded.

"Dickers knows what caused your trauma. He can't make you drive out there again."

Neil held up his hands. "Dickers doesn't know about this. I'm not working on the Duvshenko case, remember? And besides, I've got a driver."

"Good. I was serious when I said you should have backup."

"Well, she's not armed." Neil immediately regretted using the word *she*. He quickly added, "The driver's a Russian translator."

Connie studied him silently.

Neil had the uncomfortable feeling that Sergeant Wu was starting to draw the wrong conclusion about his translator. Connie had an uncanny knack for picking up on clues. Of course there was nothing improper about his relationship with Marial. And Connie wouldn't have the right to be jealous anyway.

"Watch your back, Neil," Connie said.

14

Panic always made Neil thirsty. A frightened demon was hiding in his chest, shivering from the anxiety of loss. But hiding only made the loneliness worse. At times the craving was almost intolerable.

"Talk to me. Please." Neil closed his eyes tightly. Sandy Boulevard was cutting diagonally across Northeast Portland in his mind, a series of crazily angled intersections full of hazard. The Vietnamese grocery would be just ahead.

"All right." Marial's voice was low and steady. "I think I may have found the Gray Madonna."

"The what?" Engines were revving and horns were honking outside. Inside, Neil's blood was roaring in his head. If only he could have a drink!

"The seventeenth century icon stolen from the Old Believers' church in Woodburn."

"The icon, right. You actually found it? Where?"

"On the Internet. You told me to do some research, remember?"

"Right." Now he remembered. Last night was a long time ago.

"I'm a librarian, so I don't trust a lot of what you see online, but last week a St. Petersburg newspaper reported that an anonymous donor had returned a gray madonna painting to a monastery on the Solevetsky Islands. The monks there claimed the icon had been stolen in 1689."

"Did they have a picture of it?"

"No. I couldn't find a photograph of the one from Woodburn either. I suppose madonna icons are pretty stylized anyway. It's just I've never heard of another gray one."

"We need to know where they got it."

"Provenance," Marial said.

"Where's that?"

Marial laughed, and Neil opened his eyes to look at her. To his surprise, the frightened beast inside him did not howl in pain. Perhaps the demon was waiting because Neil had backup. He had told Marial about his fear. She was here with him. He decided to focus on her and what she was saying. "Provenance isn't a town in France, is it?"

"It's the history of an artwork. If you don't know the provenance, anything could be a fake."

"I take it the monks in Russia don't think their madonna is fake."

"No. The original was said to work miracles. Apparently the new one already has."

"What kind of miracles?"

"The monks wouldn't say."

Neil humphed. "It must have taken a miracle to smuggle it from Woodburn to Russia. Customs is pretty tight about art."

"I think it's tighter if you bring art into the United States. It's less common to smuggle Russian art into Russia."

"Probably true." Neil thought a moment. "What about the anonymous donor?"

"It might be possible to track him down. He bought the painting at an auction in Novgorod a month ago for twelve million rubles."

"Wow."

"That's only about half a million dollars."

"Still a lot," Neil mused. "You wouldn't pay that unless the auction house had pretty solid evidence the thing was authentic. But why would he turn around and donate it?"

"To atone for sins? That's the usual reason churches get gifts."

"The bigger the sin, the bigger the donation." Neil looked out the windshield. They were coming up on 85th Avenue. Already he could see the sidewalk and the telephone pole of his nightmares. His stomach twisted so hard he had to clench his teeth to keep from throwing up. But he kept his eyes open, hoping he could face down the fear.

Marial's voice seemed to come from another world. "The auction house says its records are confidential, but I bet things would be different if you actually went there. Someone in Novgorod knows who bought that icon and where it came from. In Russia, every secret has its price."

Blood was gushing across the street as Marial set the right-hand blinker to turn into the entrance of The Grotto's parking lot. In the rearview mirror, Neil saw their tire tracks run red for a dozen hectic heartbeats. Then the tracks began to fade to ordinary asphalt, strewn only with brown fir needles.

Ahead the gigantic Douglas fir trees of the sanctuary's grove towered on either side of a long parking lot. No spaces were free. For a moment Neil was afraid they would have to turn back to confront the street yet again.

But then a hulking black Titan with tinted windows pulled out, leaving the perfect parking space. Right at the front, next to a little silver Prius.

15

Dan Cooper's Last Will & Testament, Part 3

My heart hammered.

When you've been trained as a spy, you know that everyone looks like a spy, because spies are trained to look like everyone.

Swarovsky had been stopped at the gate, ticketless, while I hurried ahead to board Northwest Orient flight 305 for Seattle. Of course he could have taken a shot at me then. It would have been messy, but I don't think that stopped him. He knew I was trapped. Either he had an agent already aboard the plane, or he'd have an undercover team waiting for me at the Sea-Tac airport.

I craned my neck, watching the stewardess smile her way down the aisle, serving drinks from her cart. Perhaps because I was the last to board, I'd ended up in 18E, a window seat in an otherwise empty row near the tail. One by one the heads of potential assassins bobbed up and spoke. Seven-Up for the ponytail with big round glasses. V-8 juice for the crewcut with double chins.

I took a long breath, trying to slow my heart. Then I took a piece of paper out of my suit pocket, unfolded it, and re-read what I'd written that morning: "I have a bomb in my briefcase. I will use it if necessary. I want you to sit next to me. You are being hijacked."

Finally the smile landed on me. "Would you like coffee or Coke or something?"

Her shiny blond hair had been hair-sprayed into a flip, curling up at the shoulders of her tight blue uniform. Shiny frosted lipstick made her mouth lighter than her tanned face. A bronze nameplate identified her left breast as Lisa.

"Bourbon, sweetheart. Straight." This was not my style, but then this was not me. It was Dan Cooper.

She blinked slowly, her lashes weighted with mascara. "All right." She poured the drink and handed me a plastic cup with a little cocktail napkin and a packet of peanuts. "Here you go, sir."

In return I held out the folded note. "Lisa, this is for you."

With the same bright smile she took the note, tucked it unread in the tiny pocket at the waist of her uniform, and rolled her cart to the next aisle. Behind me I heard the recording replay, "Would you like coffee or Coke or something?"

Minutes passed while I waited, nervously sipping my bourbon. Out the window the clouds were so deep that even Mt. Rainier couldn't poke through. Finally I took my briefcase and made my way to the bathroom in back. Lisa was rearranging her cart at a closet by the door. When I came out of the lavatory, still clutching my briefcase, I whispered, "Miss you'd really better read that note."

This time I didn't have to wait long. I was hardly in my seat before Lisa scooted in beside me, her glossy lips quivering. "I—I thought you were just trying to give me your phone number."

"Shh." I took the note and tucked it into my jacket pocket. "I don't want to have to hurt anyone."

"My God," she whispered. "What do you want?"

I took out a second note and handed it to her. She unfolded it and read through the demands: When we landed in Seattle, they were to bring me a briefcase with $200,000 in unmarked $20 bills. They were also to bring me a total of four parachutes—a main backpack chute and a reserve front-pack chute in each of two styles, military and civilian. In exchange I would spare the plane's passengers.

When she had read the note she looked up at me, more puzzled than frightened. "You want parachutes? Why?"

"Just walk calmly to the cockpit and repeat my demands to the pilot. Tell him I'll blow up the plane unless he does exactly what I ask. Do you understand?"

She nodded.

"Good. Off you go."

She stood and walked up the aisle. I had time to finish my bourbon before she came back. I knew what she was going to ask, so when she sat down beside me again I set the briefcase on my lap, flipped the latches, and lifted the lid for two seconds—just long enough for her eyes to widen at the display I had prepared that morning. Seven sheets of red construction paper, rolled into tubes and bundled with white masking tape to resemble dynamite. A large nine-volt battery of the type used in searchlights. A confusion of brightly colored wires stripped from a telephone cord.

I closed the lid, snapped the latches, and let my thumb hover nervously over a red plastic button I had glued near the handle.

"Don't make me push this button, Lisa."

She held up a trembling hand. "Please. The captain said if you really have a bomb, he'll get everything you want."

"Good girl. Tell him not to land until the parachutes and the cash are ready." I gave her a Cooper smile. "And while you're up, why don't you bring me another bourbon?"

16

Neil's heart was still hammering, but his head was clearing, as if the demons were scurrying back into the shadows. He had driven through his nightmare. Marial had piloted him through that vortex of blood. They had come out the other side in The Grotto. A sign on a post read, "A Sanctuary of Solitude, Peace, and Prayer."

Marial was watching him from the side. "Are you going to be all right?"

"Maybe, yeah." He felt as if he were clearing the cobwebs away. Last night Marial had been right — he had been too entangled in his own issues to focus properly on the case. He wasn't here to treat his own trauma. He was here for a memorial service. Yosef Duvshenko was dead. Suicide was a simple but improbable explanation. Murder, on the other hand, opened a door into labyrinths.

"We're late for the memorial, aren't we?" he asked.

"A little." For the first time that day she smiled, and it brought back the dimple that lent Marial's ordinary features a touch of extraordinary beauty. Neil looked down and swallowed, suddenly remembering his dream from the night before. "Let's go."

They got out of the car and walked a gravel path alongside the glass wall of a gift shop. Statues grimaced in rows behind the store window — weeping disciples, tortured Christs, sorrowing Marys with their hands raised in despair.

Suddenly there was a click-clunk behind them. Neil spun about, half expecting to face the muzzle of a pump-action shotgun. No one was there. What he had heard were the doors of Marial's unmarked police car, automatically locking. Still, the sound gave him pause.

Connie had told him to watch his back.

"Wait a moment." He walked back to the car, picked up two tiny pieces of gravel, balanced one on the driver door handle, and set the other on the middle of the hood.

Marial rolled her eyes. "Detectives! Come on, Neil."

Beyond the gift shop the path curved through a mossy rainforest of big Douglas fir trees, some of them three feet in diameter. Plaques on the trunks had Roman numerals identifying stations of the cross — where Jesus fell, or was crowned with thorns, or was given a drink of water.

After a hundred yards the walkway opened onto a broad plaza backed by a 150-foot rock cliff. Inside a cavernous overhang at the base of the cliff a gigantic white statue of Mary wailed silently over the limp body of her crucified son. Banks of candles flickered on either hand. Semicircles of green benches spread out across the plaza from the altar like ripples in a baptismal lake. Although there was room to seat a multitude, only a few dozen people remained after the Sunday morning services, meditating, lighting candles, or greeting friends.

"Marial!" A young woman was pushing an old man in a wheelchair their way.

"Nancy Willis," Marial smiled in reply.

Neil was grateful that Marial had greeted the woman by name. He otherwise would have had difficulty placing the young CEO they had met at the art gala the night before, especially now that she was wearing black jeans and a black T-shirt. The jeans had dangerous-looking silver studs and an actual chain as a belt. The shirt was sequined with a skull and unreadable graffiti. It seemed to Neil that a slightly different arrangement of piercings now disfigured Nancy's otherwise pretty features, although the black lipstick and multi-colored hair streaks looked the same.

"You guys left early last night. Missed the dance. Lieutenant Ferguson, isn't it? This is my father." Nancy leaned over and shouted, "Dad! These are my friends!"

The old man's head hung slightly to the left, as if pulled aside by his few wisps of white hair. Was he trying to smile? His mouth quivered open. A string of drool dripped to the plaid scarf about his shoulders.

"Damn." Nancy took a tissue from a bag on the back of the wheelchair and cleaned his mouth. "Sometimes I wonder why I keep taking him here."

Neil was ready to move on, but Marial asked politely, "Do you come for the services?"

"Hell no. We're not even Catholic." Nancy stopped short. She gave Neil a flustered look. "God, now I've done it. With an Irish name like Ferguson you probably come here all the time."

"Actually it's my first visit. I'm not very religious."

"Well, this place grows on you. Dad used to love it." Nancy pointed to the shrine in the cliff. "It's an old gravel pit. The Union Pacific railroad originally quarried it to build their line through the Columbia Gorge. A monk bought it for a song in the 1920s, set a few last charges of dynamite to make a grotto, and started collecting statues. Now it's like some spiritual healing center. Crazy what you can market, huh?"

"Selling a religious hideaway to Americans?" Marial mused. "I think that would be as easy as selling vodka to Russians."

Neil let that disturbing comment hang for a moment. Then he said, "We're actually trying to find a memorial service."

Nancy's black-shadowed eyes widened. "The Ukrainian mafia guy? You know, I saw a black canopy on the upper level in the Joseph Grove, but I just assumed it was for a goth wedding. You have to take an elevator to get there. Tickets are in the visitor center by the restrooms."

"Thanks."

"Sure. See you, Marial. Take care, Lieutenant." She pushed the wheelchair down the gravel path toward the stations of the cross.

While they were waiting for the elevator to descend beside the cliff, Neil had time to consider what he was going to do at the service. This was no place for an interrogation. But if Duvshenko really had been murdered, there was a fair chance the perpetrator would be there. Murderers really were fascinated by the funerals of their victims, just as arsonists can't help but watch their own fires. The description he had from Connie—a person with ruthless eyes—could apply to almost anyone in the right circumstances, even a woman. The one person Neil felt confident could be ruled out as the killer was the person who had called 9-1-1. No crime boss would call the police to set up a trap for himself.

The elevator door opened and they stepped inside. When the door closed again, Neil took a small digital music player and a pair of ear buds out of his suit pocket. "Marial, I'd like you to listen to something before the service."

"Funeral music?"

"Sadder than that, I'm afraid. It's a recording of the 9-1-1 call that started us looking for D.B. Cooper a week ago. You know Slavic accents. I want you to tell me if you hear this same man at the service."

She put on the earphones and pressed "play".

Outside the glass windows of the elevator shaft, the plaza sanctuary below began shrinking. They rose past the treetops into a bright sky — as if they really were transcending a vale of tears to heaven. Except that this heaven included a jumbo jet slowly descending toward the airport along the Columbia River. In the distance, cars waited on a stretch of freeway, backed up before the long white arc of a river bridge.

Neil knew what Marial was hearing, and it was not tidings of the Almighty's eternal joy. *"They must get D.B. Cooper. This is important. Please!"* Heaven was not supposed to echo with the voices of the damned.

The door opened, revealing a short bridge from the elevator tower to the sanctuary's clifftop gardens — lawns and shrubbery amidst the skeletons of leafless February trees. Marial took off the earphones and handed the player back.

"What kind of accent was it?" Neil asked.

"Terrified."

"But what nationality?"

Marial shook her head. "If he'd been speaking Russian, I'd know. In English, it's harder to tell."

"It's supposed to be the voice of Andrei Andropov, one of the other repair shop owners. He called the downtown police station later to confess that he was the informant."

They walked to a small circular patio. Marial asked, "You're not convinced?"

Neil shrugged. "Like everything about this case, it's too easy. Besides, Andropov was Nadia Duvshenko's maiden name."

"Andropov is a common name. Still, I suppose they could be related. She kept talking about her cousins."

"Exactly. If this Andrei is here, I'd like to meet him."

A directory at the far side of the patio had an arrow pointing left to St. Joseph's Grove. A smaller gravel path meandered along the edge of a lawn toward a black canopy with a cluster of about forty people. Empty folding chairs before a statue of Joseph suggested that the service itself was already over. The crowd had moved on to the reception. Women in white aprons were serving food on paper plates.

"Mama! It's the lady from the library!" A dark-haired little girl in a pretty pink dress rushed out to meet Marial, but then stopped halfway, suddenly uncertain and shy.

Marial held out her hand, as if to a fawn. "It's all right, Sonya. You always come to my storytimes. I wanted to come to your father's service. Is it OK if I bring friend?"

The little girl ran back to the canopy and hid in the black skirts of her mother Nadia. Mrs. Duvshenko still looked far too young to be a widow, but now she carried herself with the matronly manner of a woman in charge. She waved Marial and Neil closer and gave orders in Russian to the servers. Within moments Neil found himself swept up in a crowd of Slavic conversations, holding a paper plate of strange food.

"These are *shashlik*," Marial explained, pointing to skewers of meat that looked like shishkabob. "I assume you know *pirogi*, the cabbage pockets."

"No, actually I —" but Neil's words were lost in the general babble, and Marial had already turned to talk to someone else. As he sampled the food he watched the crowd. These were young families, with parents in their thirties and children that ranged from suckling babies to surly teenagers. Although they wore black, their mood was anything but somber. Neil wondered if most of them had not mourned the loss of Yosef Duvshenko, or if this were like an Irish wake, where you celebrate death with a party. No one looked like a criminal, much less a murderer.

A priest with a black shirt and white collar made his way to Neil. "I understand that you are Lieutenant Ferguson?"

Neil swallowed his mouthful of *pirogi*. "Yes. I'm investigating the death of Yosef Duvshenko. Did you know him?"

"Not well. He rarely attended services, and only came in for confession once."

Neil raised an eyebrow. "He confessed?"

The priest smiled. "Confessions are confidential. But I can tell you that Yosef was a troubled man. A man who had difficulty fitting in."

"Because he was Catholic? I understand most of the Ukrainians are Orthodox."

"That may have been part of it. Certainly that's why the family asked me to give the eulogy, even though my own background isn't Slavic. But there were other differences as well. The rest of the extended family are Baptists, from Russian villages between Pskov and Novgorod. Even their language was substantially different from Yosef's."

"If they were so different, how did Yosef meet his wife Nadia?"

"I asked that too. They both attended a conference in Riga for victims of religious persecution. They fell in love. It happens."

"In Riga." Latvia again. "I suppose a troubled man who doesn't fit in might decide to take his own life."

The priest tightened his lips.

Neil added, "But is it possible that an outsider like Yosef could become the ringleader of a Russian crime syndicate?"

"I can't say."

"Does that mean you don't know, father?"

In reply the priest gave him only a slight bow.

Suddenly a hand grabbed Neil's shoulder and spun him about. An angry man demanded, "What are you doing here?"

Neil had automatically caught the man's wrist, a move that would allow him to twist or break the arm. Now he let it go. The man was in his forties, with short black hair and dark eyes that really might be described as ruthless. He wore the kind of dark suit you would expect at a memorial service, but his thin black tie had been loosened crookedly. His breath smelled of cabbage and vodka.

"My name is Lieutenant Ferguson," Neil said.

"We know who the hell you are. Why can't you leave us alone?"

To one side Marial was holding up her hands in a gesture of apology. "You asked me to find Andrei Andropov."

"You're the one who called 9-1-1," Neil said.

Even before Neil recognized the flash of confusion in Andrei's eyes, he knew this couldn't really be the informant. The frightened voice on his iPod had a stronger accent. Andrei didn't have to search for English words.

"Yes, I did call." Andrei puffed himself up for this assertion.

"All right then, what time did you tell me to be at the library that night, 10:30 or 10:45?" The actual rendezvous had been at 11 p.m. If

Andrei was the informant, he would know.

"It doesn't matter."

"Maybe it does. Is Nadia Duvshenko your sister?"

When Andrei had no answer, Neil knew his guess had hit home. Despite himself, he pulled the trigger on the second barrel. "If Nadia is your sister, how could you turn your own brother-in-law over to the police?"

All the other voices at the reception had fallen silent. Everyone's eyes were on Neil and Andrei.

Andrei held out his hand to the gathering. "Look at these people, Ferguson. We are the cousins, families from the old country trying to make a new life here. For years we have lived in fear of Cooper. Cooper forced us to commit crimes in our shops. Now he is dead, and we are free. Yosef is gone, and yes, we are mourning. But you—you would bring this evil back to life. No one wants you here, Ferguson."

The silence that followed seemed to signal the end of the reception. People began leaving their paper plates on the folding tables, saying their good-byes to Nadia, and walking back along the path to the elevator.

Neil looked at the plate of food in his hand. It was greasy, cold, and foreign. He had no appetite for it now—and not very much appetite for his job either. He had told himself that a memorial service was no place for an interrogation, but in the heat of the moment, confronted by an angry man, he had allowed himself to go too far. A detective should not have a temper.

The priest touched his sleeve. "The Lord works in mysterious ways, Lieutenant."

"So do people. My job is to figure it all out."

"One thing I can tell you is that Yosef found solace in the shrines of this grove." The priest pointed to a path that led deeper into the woods. "He asked his wife to hold a service here if something were to happen to him."

Neil nodded. "Thank you, father." Then he set down his plate, caught Marial's eye, and indicated with a tip of his head that they might as well take a stroll in St. Joseph's Grove.

When they had walked out of earshot of the reception, Marial ventured, "Well, that could have gone worse."

"Really?"

"I think we learned a lot about the case. For one thing, it looks like Andrei Andropov really is Nadia's brother."

"I'm also pretty sure he wasn't the one who called 9-1-1."

"Yes. His voice sounded different." Marial thought for a moment. "I wonder if there's a way to compare the recording electronically with different people's voices to find a match."

"No point. I'm convinced the person who left that message is dead. It had to be Yosef himself. But there's no way to prove it. We don't have other recordings of his voice, and everyone we ask would lie. Even his own wife."

"Sonya would tell the truth."

Neil looked up at her sharply. "A four-year-old girl? Yeah, we might be able to terrify her by playing the voice of her dead father, but nothing she said would stand up in court."

A chilly wind blew through the grove, clicking the bare branches of the seemingly dead trees. Neil wondered how Yosef could have found solace in such a setting.

Marial said, "If Yosef was murdered, the person with the strongest motive is probably Andrei. He must have been furious when his sister married a Ukrainian Catholic. I can tell you from experience, Russians can look down on people who are different from them. Especially Latvians, Ukrainians, and Catholics. You saw how strong Andrei's sense of family honor is."

"You know, I could imagine Andrei as a crime boss—maybe even a killer. He seems to have some sort of power over the rest of the extended family. But I have trouble believing he's D.B. Cooper."

"Because he's too young?"

"Not just that. Cooper seems to be a code name for a mafia don. But is it really a name Andrei would pick? He was in diapers in Russia when Cooper hijacked that plane out of Portland. I get the feeling there's something bigger we're missing."

They had reached a shrine in the woods. Red votive candles flickered before a large bronze bas-relief panel. On the left, a haloed figure labeled "Joseph" prayed on his knees in a barren, rocky landscape. The eye of God beamed from the storm clouds above, but the Lord's gaze was not turned toward the kneeling man. Instead the rays of enlightenment and glory shone to the right, illuminating a rapturous pregnant woman.

"Joseph had a hard time of it, didn't he?" Neil said.

"What do you mean?"

"I dropped out of Sunday school in the seventh grade, but I remember thinking even then that Joseph got a raw deal. Here's a guy cuckolded by God, but he's not supposed to complain because his wife's still technically a virgin. She's been impregnated by some sort of angelic artificial insemination, without her permission. Then Joseph has to raise the boy as his own, with no child support from the actual father. He goes to the trouble of training Jesus as a carpenter, but does the boy help by taking over the business? No, he wanders off as a holy man."

Marial clicked her tongue. "You really aren't a believer, are you?"

"I don't think Joseph gets to speak a single line in the whole Bible. The man was used, humiliated, and then forgotten."

"Like our Yosef?" Marial asked.

"Exactly. The priest said Yosef used to come here for solace. I think Yosef knew he was being set up as a scapegoat."

"If that was Yosef's voice on the 9-1-1 recording, then you're right, he was scared to death. But there's a lot of evidence saying he committed suicide."

"I'm working on that." Neil took a last look at Joseph. Yosef wouldn't have asked his wife to hold a service for him in this grove because of its sense of solace. There was no solace here. Yosef had wanted to make a statement about his intolerant "cousins". He had wanted to leave a clue for someone like Neil.

"Let's get back to the car," Neil said.

The black canopy had already been removed by the time they returned from the woods of St. Joseph's Grove. As they rode the elevator down, descending from the bright sky of the upper level to the murk of The Grotto's plaza, it struck Neil that he seemed to be dealing with two different kinds of D.B. Cooper—one hidden by the blinding light of a folk hero, and one obscured by the darkness of a criminal underlord. The original D.B. Cooper had invented skyjacking before that particular crime got a bad reputation. He had hurt no one, taken money from an unpopular airline company, and vanished.

The new D.B. Cooper, by contrast, was a force of terror. Yosef Duvshenko had been afraid of him. Andrei Andropov had described him as evil. Even Connie had barricaded herself in her house for protection.

If both Coopers were the same man, then he would have to be a bipolar Jekyll and Hyde.

"Where do we go from here, Neil?" Marial asked. They were walking back through the stations of the cross.

"Two ways," Neil said. "I'm going to handle this as two completely different D.B. Cooper investigations. One's the Russian boss. To track him down I'll need to examine the forensics report from the shooting scene. I'd also like to find out more about if and how his stolen icons wound up in Russia. And I've got a meeting tomorrow morning with my friend Gerry at the art museum that might prove important. For the other Cooper, the old skyjacker, all I've got are some thin leads from my daughter Susan."

"Oh?" Marial looked surprised. "Actually I was asking where you want me to drive you next, but what's this about your daughter? Or am I being too nosy?"

"No, we're in this deep enough together, you might as well know. Remember how I said my daughter's new boyfriend is a bum?"

"Yes," she said slowly.

"Well, he really does live under a bridge. But he claims to have connections with people who know about the actual skyjacking case. Apparently there's a transient named The Keeper who may know the location of the original parachute. There's also a Reed College professor who's supposed to have led a secret life. He had an odd name—Lammergeier."

Neil thought he heard Marial catch her breath, but when he looked, her expression revealed nothing. She stopped in front of the gift shop and took out her car keys. "Is that where I'm driving you now? To Reed?"

"No. I'm heading home. But I could drop you off on the way and take the car back to the station."

"I thought you weren't supposed to drive."

"I think I can do this now. To be honest, it's because of you. For six months I haven't been able to drive past the scene of my accident. Today you took me through my fears. The world didn't end. I feel a lot more confident."

"Maybe so, but I'm still your designated driver." Her eyelashes fluttered with a half wink.

Neil's heart skipped in his chest. How was she able to pull his emotions about so easily? Half a wink and suddenly he was spinning back to his dream from the night before.

"All right," he managed to say. "But I owe you, Marial. I really do."

"Good. Then maybe you could buy me that icon."

"What?"

She nodded to the window of the gift shop. "The madonna in the window display. I noticed it on the way in. I don't know what the gray madonna looks like, but this one seems strange for a Catholic shop. What do you think?"

A bit bewildered, Neil followed her into the gift shop. There were three versions of the madonna icon for sale, in different sizes. The one she had pointed out was only thirty dollars, so he bought it.

He was waiting for the clerk to wrap it in tissue and put it in a bag when he noticed Marial was gone. The glass door was slowly closing. She was already halfway to the car.

An indefinable panic gripped him. He dashed across the shop and burst out just as Marial was sliding into the driver's seat.

"Wait, Marial! Stop!"

She rolled her eyes. "Honestly, Neil. The gravel was still balanced on the door handle where you left it."

He looked at the hood. The piece of gravel was still there as well. He had been overreacting. It was part of the stress from the trauma.

Still, when she leaned forward to put the key in the ignition he heard himself say, "No. Pop the hood first." Something was wrong, and he couldn't even figure out what it was. The white cars on either side? The scuff marks in the gravel of the lot?

"Neil!"

"Just do it."

She sighed and pulled the hood release lever. The gravel chip hopped and rolled to one side. Neil walked to the front of the car, found the spring latch, and lifted the hood.

The bomb was sitting there atop the starter motor in plain sight. Seven red sticks of dynamite, a large nine-volt battery, and a confusion of colored wires. It was almost as if he had expected it to be there, just like that.

"Can I start it now?" Marial asked.

"No! Don't! Get out of the car. I want you to see this."

She got out, looking bored. But when she reached the front of the car her mouth opened in horror. "My God!"

"That was my first reaction."

"Neil! You just saved my life!"

"Not really, but you can count us even if you like."

"What do you mean?"

"Can't you see what's so impressive about this?"

"Whoever did this put the pieces of gravel back right where they'd been."

"No, I would have done that too. But look—it's not even really a bomb."

The sticks of dynamite were actually tubes of red construction paper. The wires were mostly unconnected. And the battery wouldn't have been necessary for a car ignition bomb anyway.

"But why?" Marial reached out her hand tentatively.

"Don't touch. Forensics will want to look at it for clues."

"It's a warning." Marial looked at Neil, her lips pale. "Any one of the people at that memorial service could have done this. They all wanted you to drop the case. They're afraid of what you might find."

"Most of those people wouldn't have replaced the gravel. At least one was a professional."

"How could they have known you'd come to the service?"

"They knew I'd come if I thought Duvshenko's death wasn't a suicide. I'd come to look for the murderer."

"And they didn't leave a real bomb because they wanted to give you a second chance?"

"Not likely. I think it's just that we parked at The Grotto."

"Why would that matter?"

"Because it's a sanctuary."

17

Neil awoke with the strange and delightful feeling that he did not have to ride his bicycle into the hills. It was 6:30 a.m. on a Monday, but the compulsion simply was not there. Every other morning in the three years since his wife Rebecca had died, he had opened his eyes to panic, and the overpowering need to escape. At first he had tried alcohol. That had led to disaster. Then he had tried bicycling. He had pedaled through thresholds of pain.

He stretched under the warmth of his comforter, folded his hands behind his head, stared at the pre-dawn shadows of his ceiling, and listened to the sleeping city begin to stir. Miraculously, nothing hurt. From his stomach to his limbs, there was only a faint, pleasant tingling.

To be sure, he could have died yesterday. The car bomb could just as easily have been real, and Marial could just as easily have turned the ignition key a moment before his warning. A professional killer was almost certainly following him.

This should have been disturbing. But to Neil, it was a relief.

Whoever Cooper might prove to be—and Neil had long since labeled the killer with the name Cooper—he was no phantom. Demons dwelling in the folds of your tortured brain, or in the cracks of your broken heart, do not plant car bombs.

Cooper was a flesh-and-blood person. A clever person, yes, but a human being with a mind that could be outwitted and a body that could be put behind bars.

The fake car bomb had not been just a warning. It had been a challenge. Maybe, Neil mused, it was just the sort of challenge he needed to give him traction in a life that had grown slippery.

The odd tingling lingered all morning as Neil showered, dressed in a slightly casual sport coat, drank a large glass of orange juice, checked the ammunition in his police semi-automatic, and put on his bright yellow rain outerwear. He rode the elevator down to his bicycle in the basement, but then he broke his routine. He carried his bicycle up a flight of fire stairs, wheeled it across the lobby (to the dismay of the frowning concierge), and rode down Salmon Street through the heart of the city to the riverbank. He had never before joined the crowds of bike commuters along the riverbank. Now he crossed the Steel Bridge, looped back along the Eastbank Esplanade—a bike path floating on pontoons—and recrossed the Willamette on the Hawthorne Bridge. Never before had he been to the Heathman Hotel. Now he locked his bike to a handrail, walked across the paneled lobby to the restaurant, and ordered breakfast. If he was forced to be unpredictable because he was being stalked by a killer, he might as well enjoy it.

Over eggs Benedict he took out his cell phone, started to call Connie, and then thought better of it. With the pain medication, Connie might still be asleep. Besides, he couldn't discuss anything important on a cell phone in a restaurant. He had already had a long talk with her yesterday afternoon, after Marial had dropped him off at his apartment. Connie had been both angered and intrigued by the fake car bomb. She had vowed to redouble her computer research efforts to find out more about Andrei Andropov. And then Neil had puzzled her by asking a favor. "I'd like you to dig up whatever you can find about the Recyclotron."

"The garbage sorter?" Connie had asked. "Doesn't your daughter work there?"

"Yes, and she's worried that something's not right. Something about the engineering or the building remodel. It bothers her that there's a locked door no one seems to have a key to."

Connie had paused before replying, "You know, Neil, that's just the sort of thing that would bother a person with autism."

"I know, but I promised her the department would look into it. Could you find out which architect oversaw the remodel?"

"Sure, sure." Then they had talked about other things—her son Leighton's terrible cooking and Captain Dickers' laughable golf obsession—before hanging up.

Now, sitting in the Heathman restaurant with the cell phone in his hand, Neil decided to call Luis in forensics. He punched in the number.

"Portland police forensics, Espada here."

"This is Ferguson in homicide. Don't you guys have caller ID yet?"

"Naw, the bureau doesn't want us to have too many clues."

"Listen, I've got a 10 o'clock meeting, but if I stopped by this morning, say in about twenty minutes, would you have any news for me?"

"We're all done with the shooting scene. I just started work on this other little bomb you dropped on us — scared the hell out of me when I found it on my desk this morning."

"Sorry. Your colleagues brought it in yesterday. They must have left it for you as a surprise. See you soon."

"OK."

Neil paid his tab, rode his bike to the station, and took the elevator down to forensics.

Luis Espada was a small, round man with an overgrown mustache and quick dark eyes that darted about as if trying to keep up with the connections lighting up his neural synapses. He was madly mousing through computer screens of information when Neil walked in, and didn't even turn around. "That you, Lieutenant?"

"Yes. What's up?"

"Let's start with the suicide car, since that case is supposed to be closed. Ooh!" Luis raised his eyebrows at something on the computer screen, typed a few words, and then moused on. "Don't know how you guessed, but you were right about the fingerprints. Duvshenko left beautiful prints on the door handle, ignition key, gun, and steering wheel — but everything else is a mess."

"What do you mean, a mess?"

"Just smudges. On the shifter, the window button, the hand brake — all the same kind of smudges."

"Could someone leave smudges like that if they were nervous?"

"Then they'd leave oil from their fingers. No, these smudges were from gloves. Probably latex, like the ones we wear."

"Are you saying someone from our own forensics team contaminated the scene?"

Luis let go of the mouse and swiveled in his chair to confront Neil. "We don't do that, Lieutenant. It's far more likely that Mr. Duvshenko shifted the car into park, took off his gloves, and ate them."

Neil laughed. "I think the coroner might have noticed that earlier."

"That's not my department."

"What about the footprints?" Neil asked. "Did you find anything on the car hoods near the fence?"

"Yes, sir. On a big old Dodge Ram. Two on the hood and three on the roof. Men's size 8 or women's size 11, take your pick."

"What brand shoe?"

"Uh uh." Luis wagged his finger. "All smudged by little folds of fabric."

"Meaning?"

"My best guess? Disposable hospital overshoes."

"Jesus Christ." Neil ran his hand over his face. The killer had not merely been a professional—he had been an expert. "All we've got are smudges. I can't get a conviction out of that."

"You can't get a conviction until you've got somebody to convict," Luis pointed out. "And that got me thinking. The smudges don't prove a thing. The case could still be a weird suicide. But if somebody did manage to switch places with Duvshenko and jump over the fence, what about the ski hat?"

"That's right." Neil wondered how he could have overlooked the hat. "Duvshenko was wearing the same kind of balaclava as the guy who ran down Sergeant Wu. Either they had two of them, or they switched hats.

"So I took the liberty of checking the hat. A few of the hairs inside matched Duvshenko's DNA. But a lot them didn't." Luis held up a test tube.

Neil turned the tube in his hands. White hairs. Most of Portland's Slavic immigrants had dark hair. Duvshenko's parents were still in Eastern Europe. If the hairs really were Cooper's, it suggested he was old, and possibly not Slavic at all. Neil looked to Luis. "Can you tell from the DNA who it is?"

Luis shook his head. "I couldn't find any matches in our databases. But if you give me a suspect, I can tell you whether he's been wearing the ski hat of a dead man."

"Good work." Neil handed back the test tube. "I suppose it's too early for you to tell me much about the fake car bomb."

"It's a fascinating artifact, Lieutenant." Luis stood up and crossed the room to an examination table where lights and microscope surrounded the imitation bomb. Luis took a small metal rod and turned the red paper tubes to one side. "I've only had an hour to work on this, but two things struck me about it right away. First, it looks a lot like the bomb D.B. Cooper had in his attache case in 1971."

"You're kidding. It can't be the same bomb."

"No, but it's a remarkable replica. Only one person saw D.B. Cooper's bomb—a flight attendant named Lisa Brockman. She told the FBI there was a bundle of seven red sticks of dynamite wrapped with white masking tape. She also saw what looked like a nine-volt search-light battery and a bunch of colored wires. After Cooper showed her the bomb he closed the case and took it with him when he jumped. It's never been found."

"How many people know about this?"

"That's what I was checking when you came in. The FBI restricted the description to law enforcement agencies. It's still classified. I only knew about it because it's become a kind of cult classic in the forensic biz."

"So where's this flight attendant now?"

"Mrs. Brockman is a 63-year-old grandmother living near Seattle on Bainbridge Island. She's the only one in the general public who's supposed to know."

"Except for D.B. Cooper himself," Neil said slowly.

Luis gave a small nod. For once his eyes had stopped darting.

Neil looked back at the bomb. "You said there was one other thing that struck you right away."

"Yes. The shiny metal case of the nine-volt battery is a perfect surface for collecting fingerprints. All of them are smudged except for this one very obvious and very beautiful thumbprint." Luis pointed his metal rod to the side of the battery. An oval of light gray powder clung to the patterns of swirls and whorls.

"You've already dusted it." Neil's heart was starting to beat faster. Could it be that they were really this close to identifying the original Cooper—and connecting him to Duvshenko's murder?

Luis nodded. "I've already identified it. It was easy to scan, and came up with a positive match within seconds."

"Within seconds? That was easy. Who's the match?"

Luis sighed. "You're not going to like it, sir."

"Just tell me. Who?"

"This is the thumbprint of Lieutenant Credence Lavelle."

For a moment Neil merely stared at the forensics technician. This was not a good joke. "Lieutenant Lavelle is in the Caribbean. She retired there six months ago to write a book about solving the Underground murders."

"I know. I just checked her blog. She left this morning in a 32-foot sailboat with her dog Bingo on the crossing from Barbados to Grenada. She'll be out of cell phone range for three days. Yesterday afternoon she uploaded a picture of herself that's time dated in Port-au-Prince. As far as I can tell, she really is in the Caribbean."

"Then how the hell did her thumbprint get on a battery under my car's hood?"

"That's what I'm trying to tell you. The print is too perfect. It's got to be fabricated."

"Fabricated? Is that possible?"

"It's a complicated, delicate process, but yes. If someone has access to a really clear fingerprint, it's possible to make a gel cast, load it with some plausible oil, and leave a print. I'll run some tests, but it's hard to prove. It's just my first reaction—one perfect thumbprint from an impossible person? That's got to be a fake."

"Just like the bomb."

Luis nodded. "Just like the bomb."

Neil reeled at the scale of Cooper's chutzpah. The man was thumbing his nose at them. And he was using the department's own thumb to do it.

Neil walked to the Portland Art Museum by a circuitous route that took him through stores with multiple entrances. Along the way he had time to think about the challenge Cooper had left him. The man's arrogance was his weakness. That flaw had not been a factor in the murder of Yosef Duvshenko. Cooper had nearly succeeded in arranging that crime so carefully that no one wanted it solved. The Russian community—even Duvshenko's own wife—had somehow been bribed or threatened into silence. The police department wanted the case filed away as a suicide. Cooper's one mistake had been that Connie had survived. Her suspicions had kept the case alive.

The fake car bomb at The Grotto, however, was different. It was a statement of disdain. This time Cooper was toying with them, laughing at the incompetence of the police. But in so doing, Cooper had left several valuable clues. Neil considered them one by one. First, the code name "Cooper" was not a fluke. The similarity of the bomb to D.B. Cooper's original bomb proved that. Either Duvshenko's killer was in fact D.B. Cooper, or he knew the flight attendant, or he had access to police files. Neil suspected the latter was true, especially because of the second clue Cooper had left: the thumbprint. That proved he had more than a passing familiarity with the Portland police. How else would he have the print of a retired homicide detective? Either Cooper had been saving the print for at least six months or else he had pulled it from police files in the past week. In short, Cooper had revealed the troubling possibility that he was in fact one of Neil's own colleagues—or at least that he had power over someone in the department.

Neil remembered Connie saying, "Watch your back."

With all his detours, Neil arrived at the art museum five minutes late. The front door was locked and the windows were dark. A sign said the museum was closed on Mondays. So he walked around the building. Beside a loading dock he found an unobtrusive metal door and a buzzer. He rang.

A woman in a guard uniform opened the door halfway.

"I'm Lieutenant Ferguson, Portland police. I have an appointment with Gerry Chandler."

She led him inside to a concrete corridor with a security office window. Half a dozen black-and-white video monitors flickered behind the glass, channeling every few seconds through pictures of hallways, sculptures, rooms, and paintings.

"Fill this out and wait here while I call." She handed Neil a clipboard and went into the office. He filled in his name, the time, and the purpose of his visit. Then she opened the window and slid him a necklace with a plastic visitor tag.

A minute later Gerry strode down the corridor, his arm outstretched. His mustache framed a big smile. "Neil! Good to see you again. Come on down to my office and we'll catch up on old times."

Gerry led him past a row of lockers, a large loading bay, and a staff lunchroom before showing him into his office. Neil was surprised that the room was small, especially after seeing Gerry's lavish penthouse studio. Bare fluorescent bulbs lit the windowless room. Prints and posters cluttered the walls. Neil was drawn immediately to a small gold trophy on Gerry's desk — a marble-based statue of a running man holding up a laurel wreath.

"I have one of these," Neil marveled.

"From the NCAA track championship in Eugene, in the spring of 1971." Gerry nodded. "I remember. You placed in the 400 meters."

"Actually I placed in the relay, and only because the fourth man on our team was Steve Prefontaine." Neil read the trophy's inscription. "Gerald Chandler, Third Place, Long Jump."

"Those were the days, huh?" Gerry sat in a black vinyl chair behind the desk. He motioned for Neil to take a seat opposite him.

"You've weathered the decades well," Neil said. Without the fedora from the gala, Gerry was actually a balding man with only a tonsure-like ring of white hair above his ears. The boyishly smooth face that Neil remembered from college had become wrinkled, especially around his eyes. But he still had the musculature of an athlete.

"How do you keep in shape?" Neil asked.

"In winter? I go cross-country skiing. Do a little ski jumping. I was up at Mt. Hood yesterday — beautiful powder. I don't race anymore but I can still lay down 20K. He nodded to Neil. "How about you?"

"I bicycle in the hills."

Gerry nodded. "We should have kept in touch. I'm a lousy correspondent. But I did get a Facebook page a few years ago and ran across your brother Mark."

"Really?" Now Neil remembered why he and Gerry had drifted apart. When he was a sophomore at the U of O, his older brother Mark and Gerry had been seniors. Mark had been kicked off the track team for smoking pot. Gerry and Mark had hung out together anyway, growing their hair long, joining radical student groups, and organizing sit-ins to protest the Vietnam War. Everybody had been doing that kind of thing back then, but Neil had disapproved.

"I guess Mark's still in Eugene," Gerry said.

"And he's still a hippie. He lives on a commune in the hills, making wooden toys."

Gerry shook his head. "What about you? I guess you went straight into police work?"

"Pretty much."

"But you're not married?"

Neil tightened his lips. "My wife passed away three years ago."

"I'm sorry. How are you doing?"

"I'm recovering. And you? How'd you get into art?"

Gerry shrugged. "Actually it was my major at the U of O. Turns out there wasn't much of a market for installation pieces of Army boots splattered with pig's blood. I finally got a job at Nike. Designed shoes for nineteen years. Then I went back to school for a master's in art administration. I landed a job at the Getty in LA for a few years, and now here I am."

"Marial says the volunteers at the museum consider you the most eligible bachelor in Portland."

Gerry laughed. "Life's complicated enough already. Tell Marial I'm yielding that title to you."

They both grinned. It was Neil who finally brought them back to the business at hand. "So, other than taking all these women off your hands, how can I help you?"

Gerry touched his fingertips together in a tent shape. "It's a delicate matter. I haven't even brought it up with the museum board yet. I need you to keep this strictly confidential."

"Fair enough. But if there's an actual crime involved, we may have to play by different rules."

"That's just it. I'm not yet absolutely certain there has been a crime. But I suspect that six of our most valuable Rothko paintings have been replaced by fakes."

Neil whistled. "Aren't these Rothko things worth millions?"

"Yes."

"I'm not an art specialist, Gerry. I'm a homicide detective."

"I know. But I need someone I can trust. And I'm starting to think this might be connected to that other case you're working on. The business with the stolen Russian icons."

"Tell me what you know."

"First of all, it's not easy to fake a Rothko painting."

Neil stared at him. "Come on. From what I've seen they're just big blocks of color. Even I could copy that."

"No, you couldn't. Rothko knew his new style looked simple—that was the whole point, to express basic, universal truths. So to stop copycats he developed his own secret paint medium. He mixed oil paints with a blend of egg whites, powdered metal, and who knows what else. Even his own staff wasn't allowed to learn the recipe."

Neil considered this. "So even today you could test a sample of the paint and tell if it's an original Rothko."

"That's right. Usually you take a chip from the edge or the back of the canvas. Rothko didn't frame most of his works, you know. He'd just extend the painting around the edges. It's pretty easy to take a sample from the side where it's not very visible."

"I assume you've already done this with the six paintings in question?"

Gerry frowned. "Yes. The sample I took didn't match the Rothko formula."

"What made you suspicious about these paintings in the first place? Did they look — well, sloppier than usual?"

"No, they look fine. If they're fakes, they've been done by a master. It's just that a colleague of mine from the Getty museum sent me an email last week asking what I knew about an online Rothko auction. The Getty is always looking for top quality art, but they've been burned before. While I was there we repatriated some Greek vases that had been bought under suspicious circumstances in the 50s. Just between you and me, there are dozens of works in the Getty right now that are almost certainly counterfeits."

Neil stopped him. "Wait. You were talking about an auction of Rothko works. What exactly is for sale?"

"The same six paintings we've got in storage. Except that the auction house had experts take paint samples, and theirs have the authentic Rothko oils. Of course it's quite possible that their paintings are fakes and they've been lying about the test results."

"Where is the auction house?"

"In Novgorod, Russia."

Neil blew out a breath. The Gray Madonna had been auctioned in Novgorod as well. Most of the Russian car repair shop owners in Portland came from that area. There had to be a connection — even though the car repairmen hardly seemed to be art experts.

"How much do you think these paintings are worth?" Neil asked.

"The starting bid is $100,000 apiece, but if they're authentic, the set of six would probably go for at least $30 million."

"Jesus." Neil thought a moment. "From what I've seen, the security here at the museum looks tight. Who could have switched the paintings, and how?"

"I've wondered about this too. There may have been a lapse in security the day I took over." He stood up and motioned toward the door. "It would be easiest to show you in person."

Gerry led Neil down the corridor to the loading dock. At the back of the bay he inserted an ID card into a slot. There was a click and a whir. A large metal garage door began to open, revealing a cavernous storeroom—a hall so large that Neil could hardly believe it fit inside the building. They stepped inside, Gerry touched a button, and the metal door slowly rattled back to the floor.

Neil marveled at the rows of twenty-foot-tall shelves, stacked with statues and furniture and paintings and boxes. "Wow. Looks like the biggest, most expensive antique mall in the state."

Gerry laughed. "That's what I always think, too. We have ten times more artifacts than the museum can display. So we rotate exhibits all the time. That's the whole trick to getting repeat visitors."

"Where do you keep the Rothko paintings?"

"Over here." Gerry opened a drawer by the wall. Gently he lifted out a two-foot-wide canvas painted yellow and red. To Neil, it looked as if an angry cafe customer had smeared his placemat with mustard and ketchup.

"The paint on this doesn't match Rothko's formula?"

Gerry shrugged. "Sometimes Rothko ran out of his formula and used regular paint. I don't know. The provenance for these six works is otherwise incontestable."

Provenance. Neil remembered the word from Marial's discussion of the icons. "So if the paintings here are supposed to be from Rothko's studio, what happened? When could the originals have been switched with fakes?"

"The only real opportunity would have been the day I became director, a year ago. The previous director was fired because he was lousy at drumming up big donations. The board called the museum's old Asian art specialist out of retirement as a temporary director while they held a search. It took three months before they decided to hire me. In the meantime the temporary director had this brilliant idea. She threw a big party in the loading bay for my inauguration."

"In a loading bay? That doesn't sound very fancy."

"She wanted to invite all the major donors and volunteers, give them tours of the collections in the storeroom, and have them brainstorm ideas for new exhibits I could put on in the coming year."

"So everyone had access to the Rothko paintings."

"It was insane. I objected, but she overruled me. She wanted to show off our hidden treasures. Her idea of security was to never let both of the garage doors open at once. Sort of like an air lock. At first only the loading bay's outside door would be open and people would have drinks and appetizers out there. Then they'd close the outer door and open this inner one. Even with guards and volunteers posted around the room, there was no way you could watch everything, especially after people had a few drinks. It was a nightmare, and I was supposed to smile and chat up all these people I'd never met before. The very next day I rewrote our security procedures and ordered a complete inventory."

"Still, it would have been pretty obvious if someone had carried in six paintings, switched them, and carried the originals out."

"Not necessarily. The loading bay was full of caterers. They had boxes stacked all over for food, wine, paper plates, chairs, tablecloths, and sound system equipment. The paintings are small enough they would have fit into any of those boxes."

"But how could anyone have made convincing copies in advance? The originals were hidden here in the storeroom."

Gerry shook his head. "They'd been on display for years. You can even buy postcards of them in the gift shop. The temporary director had just taken the originals down because she had this idea for organizing an even bigger Rothko exhibition."

"An idea you actually used."

"I expanded the exhibit to include other icons of Northwest art, but yes. That idea was sound."

Neil glanced at his watch and rubbed his eyes. How was he going to handle this investigation on top of everything else? He'd promised Gerry to keep things confidential, but if there really was a multi-million-dollar counterfeiting operation, and if it really was connected to the stolen Russian icons, it would be a huge expansion of his current case. A $30 million art theft would make headlines across the country. Meanwhile, Captain Dickers had warned him not to let the Russian angle blow up into a scandal. And the whole story about the fake Rothkos might turn out to be a misunderstanding. Gerry's request for help was genuine dynamite.

"I'll need a guest list," Neil said. "Get me the names, addresses, and phone numbers of all the caterers, guards, donors, and volunteers."

"That's easy. We used the same list for the gala at my studio Saturday night. I suppose we had a few new faces—you, Captain Dickers, and the Mozart trio—but otherwise, not many."

"Brother Daniel?"

"Yes, he was there. The idea was to invite people with ideas for future exhibits."

"Marial?"

Gerry frowned. "Well yes, but surely you don't suspect —"

"Everyone, Gerry. Until I know more, everyone is a suspect."

18

Connie pulled her living room curtain aside. "Who's in your car?"

Neil sighed. "My chauffeur, Marial Gresham. Dickers doesn't want me to drive for a while."

"Gresham?"

"It's hard to pronounce her real name. She also does Russian translation. She found the website where they auctioned the Gray Madonna."

"Huh." Connie's expression didn't change—Neil suspected the bruises made it painful for her to stretch her face—but he heard a frown in her voice. Could she be jealous?

"Backup is good," Connie said, "but you need armed cover. Civilians aren't much use. How much longer before you can drive again?"

"I don't know. Yesterday was tough, going out past the scene of my accident. Now I feel like I'm getting back on my feet." He switched the subject. "How about you? How's your walking?"

"Not bad. I've dumped the painkillers, and plan to lose the cane soon." She walked stiffly across the living room toward the den. "Let's look at that list from the art museum."

Neil followed her to her computer desk. Among the papers stood an empty Soy Queen milkshake cup, a box of Wheat Thins, and a jar of green olives. Leighton's cooking really must be impossible.

Connie eased herself into a swivel chair padded with tasseled sofa pillows. Then she moused the computer awake and maximized an Excel file to fill the screen. "So it looks like we've got sixty-seven suspects for the role of D.B. Cooper."

"That's jumping to a lot of conclusions," Neil cautioned. "Just because someone was at Chandler's inauguration at the art museum doesn't mean they're Cooper. We're not even absolutely sure the Rothko paintings in the museum are fakes."

"When six identical Rothkos are being auctioned in Russia? It's even the same auction site where the Gray Madonna was sold. That can hardly be a coincidence."

Neil had to admit this was true. If Cooper had stolen the madonna, he would certainly be tempted by a set of paintings worth $30 million.

Connie tapped her fingers. "On the phone you said Chandler thinks the Rothkos would be hard to counterfeit. Do you agree with him?"

"Honestly? No. They're big abstract blotches. As long as alarm bells aren't ringing here in Portland, no one's going to look too close at the paintings in the museum. The only people who would bother to have the paint chemically analyzed are the buyers in Russia."

"So let's assume Cooper switched the originals for copies. From what you've told me, the best opportunity was at the party six months ago. In short, we have sixty-seven suspects."

"If, if, if," Neil countered. "But go ahead."

"All right. And we think Cooper may have white hair, because of the ski cap. How many suspects does that leave?"

"Pretty much all of them. Most of the people I saw at the gala on Saturday were silverbacks. Oh, there's Nancy Willis, the young NovoCity CEO. She had multi-colored hair. Other than that, the only non-white-haired people I remember were waiters. The caterers hired college-age kids. They're too young to be Cooper, but he might have hired one of them."

"I'll check them out." Connie scrolled down the list. "Outside of the waiters, this isn't a very promising list. Here's a couple of multi-millionaire bigwigs from Nike. They don't need money. We've got a dozen or so wealthy philanthropists. They're more likely to give paintings than steal them. There's a county commissioner."

"I met him," Neil said. "Ivan Crombaugh. He's a friend of Captain Dickers."

"That's not necessarily proof he's evil. What else do you know about him?"

"He's about seventy, wears mirrored sunglasses, and owns Ivan's Oyster Bar. I suppose he could have been the original D.B. Cooper in a previous life, but it would be hard for a politician to cover up that kind of past."

Connie nodded. "And then there's Brother Daniel."

"Yes, I keep thinking about him. An angry artist. He's got exactly the right profile to be Cooper—age, height, facial features. He has a tense relationship with the local Russians. And he's got the skills to copy a painting."

"Except if he's Cooper, that means he also stole his own painting from that church in Woodburn," Connie pointed out.

"The Joseph icon? Why not? The guy we're looking for is clever enough to try to throw us off the track."

A cat rubbed against Connie's chair. The smell of bandages and disinfectant leaked from the edges of the room. This wasn't the romantic setting Neil remembered from his earlier dates at Connie's house.

Connie's attention had shifted to a name on the list. "Hello? Who's this Marial Greschyednev? Don't tell me she's your translator lady?"

"She volunteers at the museum," Neil said, as casually as he could.

Connie swiveled her chair and studied him a moment. "You went with her to the gala on Saturday, didn't you?'

This time he did blush, and it made him angry. "Dickers assigned her as my driver."

"She was also at the party six months ago. Gresham is a suspect."

Neil doubted that Connie envisioned Marial as a probable Cooper. Realistically, the librarian waiting for him in the police car was not the ruthless-eyed monster who had driven Connie down, cracked her hip, skinned the hair off her head, and left her for dead. If Connie imagined Marial was damaging her in other ways, whose fault was that? Connie had dropped her claims on Neil's spare time. She wasn't in a position to accuse anyone of an emotional hit-and-run.

"Everyone on the list is a suspect," Neil said, his voice even. "Find out what you can about them. Arrest records, odd finances, underworld connections. Even where they were on November 21, 1971."

"That may be hard."

"Try. Meanwhile, have you got anything for me about the Recyclotron building?"

Connie blinked at this sudden change of subject. "The owner of that building is a blind trust for the One More Time Women's Cooperative. In other words, no one knows who really owns it. But the remodel was handled by the firm of Stafford, Kahle, and Meredith. Here's the contact info for Jim Stafford, the chief architect."

"Thanks." Neil took the slip of paper. He knew he had treated her with a colder tone than she deserved, and he was about to say he was sorry. They had never quite been lovers, but she was still the best friend he had on the force. She had every right to be bitter that he had been promoted ahead of her, but she mostly wasn't. Now more than ever, recovering from her wounds, she needed him.

"You shouldn't keep your driver waiting," Connie said, stressing the word driver.

Neil's apology died on his lips.

At the gate by the sidewalk Neil used his cell phone to call the architect. A secretary put him through to James Stafford. The man didn't seem surprised to be talking with a detective. They could meet in half an hour if Neil wanted.

When Neil got into the car Marial was reading a Kate Wilhelm mystery on the steering wheel. The glassine sheath on its dust jacket, and the sticker on the spine with the word "Mystery" in spookily rippled letters, announced that it was a library book.

Marial had gone in heavily for the librarian look today, wearing her hair in a bun and a pair of reading glasses on a chain. Neil couldn't explain why this suffused Marial with an erotic glow. He couldn't look at her without imagining her unpinning that bun, allowing red hair to cascade over her white silk blouse. The reading glasses had thick, black-and-red-striped earpieces and narrow lenses she could peer over. The thought of her slowly taking off those glasses made his pants tight.

"So where are we going?" Marial asked.

Neil handed her the slip of paper. "To see an architect in Old Town."

She tipped her head up to read the address, pursing her lips. A loose strand of red hair dangled by the pearl in her ear lobe. Neil looked away and closed his eyes.

"Do I get to come with you this time? I've almost finished my book."

He nodded, still looking away.

She drove them to a Smart Park garage on Third. As they walked the block and a half to the address, Marial asked, "Why are we visiting an architect?"

"It's about my daughter."

"Susan? The one with a boyfriend you don't like?'

Neil cut her with a glare. "I don't think they're actually dating. God, I hope not. Susan's always been a little fragile. She's autistic."

"Oh." The word rose and fell, a tone that bespoke neither surprise nor disapproval, but interest. "That term covers a pretty broad spectrum. Does she have a job?"

"Yeah, at the garbage recycling plant. She's a great worker. Absolutely reliable."

"I can imagine. Autism tends to make people fastidious."

"That's the problem. She notices anything out of the ordinary. Now she's worried about the Recyclotron building."

Marial responded with a small shrug that cocked her left shoulder.

The office was a walk-up in an ancient brick building with an Irish pub downstairs. The bricks had been sandblasted until they were as pink and fresh-looking as a stack of new erasers. The glass door at the top of the stairs opened into a lobby with antique oak furniture and tall, wavy-glassed windows. A fan turned lazily below the exposed joists of a fifteen-foot ceiling.

Neil told a receptionist his name, and was pointed back to an office door. He tapped twice, lightly, and opened the door a crack. "Mr. Stafford?"

"Come in, come in. You must be the police lieutenant." A tall, thin man stood to meet them. His brown eyebrows were so bushy they appeared to be sprouting wings.

"I'm Neil Ferguson, and this is my assistant Marial Gresham." He gulped her last name, embarrassed that he still hadn't mastered it.

"Your office is in a wonderful old building," Marial said.

"Just don't shake anything too hard." The architect's eyebrows flexed as if they were warming up for flight. "The brick dates to 1886. When the next big earthquake hits, this will all be rubble. Only historic preservation architects and Irish drunks would be maudlin enough to set up shop in a building that can't feasibly be retrofitted."

"I should tell you why we've come," Neil began.

"Oh, I've been expecting your visit. Frankly, I'm surprised you waited this long to get in touch. Won't you have a seat?" He motioned them to wicker chairs. He sat in his leather chair and put his elbows on the desk, perfectly at ease.

Neil was taken aback. "Mr. Stafford, I'm a homicide detective."

"I know," the architect replied. "I worked closely with your predecessor, Lieutenant Lavelle. When she retired some months ago she suggested that you might be contacting me."

Now Neil was completely adrift. "She said I might contact you? About what?"

"Why, about the Underground murders, I assume." It was the architect's turn to express surprise, turning his eyebrows up sharply. "I mapped the Underground system for the historic landmark review process. When she suspected the missing people might be linked to the Underground tours, she came to me."

Neil still wasn't clear why Lieutenant Lavelle would have mentioned him. That case had been solved and closed. Five people had gone missing in as many months, with no apparent connection to each other. Finally Lavelle had discovered that they had all ridden on public transportation—buses and MAX trains—where an entrepreneur had passed out scratch-it coupons to win free visits to the Portland Underground tour. It had been a struggling new tourist trap trying to mimic the success of similar tours in Seattle and Pendleton by leading people through spooky passageways beneath the streets. Shanghai men, prostitutes, and opium dealers had once hung out in that underworld. It turned out that the tour promoter, a Los Angeles mortician with a checkered past, had actually been killing the people who won the "grand prize" coupon. The fact that he had then embalmed them and included them among the mannequins of the Underground displays had been so sensationally gruesome that a book publisher now wanted Lavelle to write up the story.

The architect leaned back in his chair, looking out the window at the gray sky. "That was my fifteen minutes of fame, I suppose. The historic landmark status thing turned out to be a dead end. The national review board wanted an identifiable landmark, not a collection of disused basements, sewers, and tunnels. Altogether eighty-three different landowners were involved, and a lot of them didn't want their rotting foundations on the historic register. So it all fell through."

"Mr. Stafford," Neil said, "I'm not here about the Underground murders. The case I'm working on isn't really a criminal investigation at all. It's just a routine background check."

"I see." The architect looked disappointed.

"I understand you helped with the renovation of a historic building at 228 North First Street."

"The Recyclotron project."

"Exactly. There's a locked door to a closet or room of some sort near the back of that building, and none of the people who work there has a key. This seems unusual for a recent remodel. I'm wondering if you can tell me about the owners, the contractor, the engineer — anything that might have struck you as odd."

The architect stared at him, his eyebrows suddenly still. "You're not serious, are you?"

"Why shouldn't I be?"

"Lieutenant, that building is the northern end of the Underground system. The door you describe seals the entrance that Lieutenant Lavelle used when she discovered the tour operator's suicide. How could you not know this?"

"I —" Neil groped for words. "I didn't read her reports because I was a sergeant at the time."

The architect considered this. "Actually, she might not have put it in the reports. The building on First Street had been a drug house. After the murders the owner was afraid of liability. He sold to a consortium. They're the ones who hired me to do the remodel, although I never met them. I only dealt with a lawyer, so I don't really know who owns the building. Still, I insisted the Underground access be preserved. It's an historic part of the site."

"Then who has the key?"

"I thought you did," the architect said.

"Me?" Neil asked.

"Yes, you and the engineer."

"I'm sorry." Neil rubbed his eyes with his thumb and forefinger. "I'm not aware that I have any such key."

"Peculiar." The architect sat back again, his brows drawn into a pensive V. "Lieutenant Lavelle told me she left the key in the drawer of her desk for her successor. She also said you'd come to see me." He toyed with a pen. "Did she expect that I would tell you about the key? Why would she think you would come at all? It doesn't make sense."

Neil was also baffled. But he realized he should at least sound confident. "I'll look for a key in my desk. If it's not there, perhaps you could tell me the name of the engineer with the other copy."

"Todd? He's the Recyclotron guy. It was a rush job, renovating the building and installing the machinery in three months, so we worked together closely. Todd can be—how do I say this?—difficult. Opinionated."

"Todd who? How can I get in touch with him?"

"I always had trouble with his last name. I actually alphabetized him under T." He turned to a small cylindrical box on his desk, opened the lid, and shot Neil a smirk. "My Rolodex. I know, you don't see them anymore. They're from the century before computers. I love this old stuff."

He flipped through the wheel of index cards. "Here you are. See? It's faster than a computer." He turned the Rolodex toward Neil.

Neil read Todd's last name.

Lammergeier.

19

Dan Cooper's Last Will and Testament, Part 4

Lammergeier.

I knew his name and number. The man would only trust an American contact with his information. And he had to have $200,000 in cash. Making the trade would have been difficult enough with the approved plan. But now that I knew the nature of the information Lammergeier actually had for sale, I'd changed my mind. My new plan was far more complicated. I'd gotten a good start by shaking Swarovsky at the Portland airport. Now I had to shake the rest of his agents in Seattle, get the money, double back, lose everyone else, and still make the contact with Lammergeier. There were so many ways things could go wrong.

"Mr. Cooper?" Lisa was back, whispering with a concerned look that I imagined she saved for difficult passengers. Could she really be this calm, even when I had threatened to blow up her plane?

"The pilot says everything you wanted is ready at Sea-Tac. Can we land now?"

"Sure, sweetheart. Tell him to park out on the tarmac, away from the buildings. Have a truck come out to refuel the plane. And I want one person—just one—to bring the parachutes and cash to you on the back stairs."

"Then you'll let us go?"

"Not you, hon." I was trying my best to out-cool her, but there was sweat on my brow. "I'll need the pilot, co-pilot, and flight engineer to stay too. Once I've checked the chutes and the cash you can let everyone else out the back stairs. Think of it as a trade. By the way, do you have any dinners on board?"

She blinked her black lashes. "Dinners? This is a beverage flight."

"Then have them bring half a dozen dinners too. I don't want my flight crew to go hungry."

"Thanks. That's thoughtful of you."

I marveled that she was serious. "Oh, and one more thing. As soon as we land, dim the cabin lights."

"Dim the lights? Why?"

To frustrate police snipers, of course, but I wouldn't tell her that. "Just do it, Lisa."

"OK." She walked back up the aisle. A minute later a man's voice came over the cabin speakers, talking over the rush of the engines like a tour guide behind a waterfall. "This is your pilot. Sorry for the delay, folks. We finally have clearance to land in Seattle."

One of the passengers responded with an unenthusiastic cheer.

"Make sure your seatbelts are fastened, your seats are in the full upright position, and you've extinguished any cigarettes or other smokes. We should be on the ground in about ten minutes."

I didn't know it at the time, but the authorities had made quite an effort to comply with my demands. As soon as the pilot told Sea-Tac air traffic control about his situation, they'd contacted the Seattle police and the FBI. Then the FBI had called Northwest Orient's president. He didn't want to risk blowing up a planeload of customers, so he authorized the payout.

I'd counted on the FBI. I wasn't surprised when I found out later they'd taken the two hundred grand to a microfilm machine that could flip through all ten thousand bills and photograph their serial numbers. It was OK with me if the cash was hot. I only needed to make one purchase from Lammergeier.

Rain streaked the windows as we slid down through the clouds. The wet runway emerged from the white just seconds before the wheels hit. The engines roared backwards. We rolled a minute, turned onto a side lane, and then stopped.

The ponytail who had ordered Seven-Up stood up and started to get a backpack out of the overhead bin. Suddenly the lights dimmed.

"I'm afraid we've got another delay here," the pilot announced.

Several passengers groaned.

"If you could stay in your seats for a few more minutes, we're going to bring out a maintenance truck to run a little check and bring some supplies. It looks like we'll be here ten to fifteen minutes. Then we'll be asking you to deplane by the aft stairs."

"Oh, for crying out loud." It was the double-chinned man who ordered V-8 juice. "Now they can't even get the front door to work?"

After a few minutes a tanker truck pulled up below the starboard wing. Two men in yellow slickers climbed out and began connecting hoses for the refueling.

Lisa sat down beside me again and whispered, "Northwest Orient has a manager ready to drive out with the things you wanted."

"Good. Tell him to park beside the plane where I can see him."

"OK." Lisa bit her glossy lip. "There's also a man from the airport who'd like to talk to you."

"A man? Where?"

"He just wants to talk. He's driving out with the manager. We thought after you'd let the passengers go you could meet on the stairs and talk about any problems you might have."

"No. There's nothing to talk about. Tell them to stop the car. Only one person is allowed to drive out here with the stuff. No officials from the airport. Do you understand?" I lifted the attache case to show her my thumb was still on the red button.

She nodded nervously. Then she stood up, walked to the cabinets by the bathroom at the back of the plane, picked up the intercom handset, and spoke quietly. A minute later a pickup parked outside my window. I could see the man inside scanning the plane for faces. I leaned back. Meanwhile Lisa unlatched a lever on the back door. With a clunk and a whine, hydraulic pistons began opening the door and lowering a metal staircase from the tail. A cold gust blew in.

A moment later the driver's door of the pickup door opened. A man in a clear plastic poncho walked around to the passenger side. He took out a green canvas duffel bag and four gray parachute packs. He carried them across the tarmac, out of sight behind the plane. I tensed, watching the back door, half expecting a commando with a machine gun to come charging in. But that's why I'd left the plane full of civilians.

Lisa's heels dinged musically on the metal stairs—notes on a scale. Then she was there in the aisle beside me, setting everything on the empty seat.

"Is this going to be OK?"

The parachutes looked standard — I could check them more carefully later. When I opened the canvas duffel, I was surprised to see a stack of six plastic trays. Then I remembered that I'd ordered dinners. I took them out and handed them to Lisa. Underneath was the money. Thirty bundles of $20 bills, each with a pair of blue rubber bands that read "$6000". That only came to $180,000, but at the bottom I found two larger bundles of $10,000. I flipped through a couple of the bundles and checked a few random bills. Then I closed the bag and nodded.

"Very good, Lisa. You can let the passengers out now. Then we'll be ready to take off."

She swallowed. Now she was obviously frightened. "Where are we going?"

I winked. "I'll let you know when we're back in the air, sweetheart."

20

Back at headquarters Neil went straight to his desk and pulled out the front drawer. Marial stood by as he rummaged around among the bank pens, rubber bands, and paper clips. Finally he jerked the whole drawer loose and set it on the desktop. Taped to the back was a large silver key with a paper label. Written on the paper was "228W1".

Marial sat on the edge of the desk for a closer look. The maroon leatherette fabric of her just-above-the-knee skirt stretched taut and shiny across her thigh.

"Is it in code?" she asked.

"An easy code. The address of the Recyclotron building is 228 West First."

"Then it really is the key your daughter wanted."

"Yes, but now what? I can't barge into a private building and unlock a door without a search warrant. And no judge is going to give me a warrant without a good reason. Which I don't have. It's just a door that bothers my daughter."

"It also bothered Lieutenant Lavelle. Call her up and ask why."

Neil shook his head. "She's sailing in the Caribbean, on a three-day crossing between islands."

"Poor thing." Marial gave her lips just a hint of a pout.

Neil pocketed the key and tried to shove the drawer back into his desk. It wasn't as easy as taking it out. "Why would a person hide a key at the back of a drawer and then tell an architect about it? It's like she was worried about something, but was even more worried about telling anyone."

"Just like your daughter Susan."

Neil sighed. "Like Susan. That girl lives on intuition."

When Neil looked up, Marial was watching him over the rims of her glasses. "At least your daughter isn't sailing in the Caribbean. She's probably near a phone."

"I need to call her anyway," Neil admitted. "Monday nights I cook her favorite dinner, spaghetti and eggplant."

Marial swung her legs down from the desk and smoothed her skirt. "Well then. What can I do for you while you call? I'm yours for another hour."

"Get me copies of Lavelle's reports. Everything from her last two months of work. If Archives gives you any trouble, call."

"Yes, sir." She gave him a salute and turned to go. Her shiny skirt creased left, right, and left again all the way to the door.

Neil opened his cell phone and poised his thumb over Susan's speed dial button. He held that pose a long time, thinking of what he would say. Susan got off work early on Tuesdays, so she was probably already at her apartment. First he would have to apologize for losing his temper. Then he would have to apologize for not apologizing sooner. He'd been more than a little distracted with Cooper's threats since Saturday, but how could he explain that to Susan? It wasn't part of her life. Dads have no excuses.

Finally he pushed the button. He could hear the phone ringing—double buzzes, three times. Then her voice, quiet and cautious as always, "Papa?"

"Hi, honey. I have some news about that locked door, but first I wanted to say how stupid I feel about the way I behaved toward your friend on Saturday."

There. He'd got it out. Now he held his breath as he waited. Susan processed things in a flash, but long and circuitous channels separated her thoughts from speech.

"That's OK," the answer came at last. "I knew you'd be mad."

"I—well, I was just surprised." This was dangerous terrain. He didn't want to sound judgmental. "I plan to follow up on Dr. Egstrom's tips about the D.B. Cooper case. Did he say his old professor's name was Todd Lammergeier?"

"No, it was Curt."

"Curt, right." He had known that. Still, the name was rare enough that the two people may be related.

For a moment Neil was unsure what to say next. He glanced up at his wall clock. A fly was walking erratically around the rim of the dial, as if chased by the second hand.

"Washington's birthday is Tuesday," Susan said.

"I'm sorry, honey. What?"

"Washington's birthday. The real one. It's tomorrow."

Finally he made the connection. "Right. That's when the D.B. Cooper witness usually shows up."

"The Keeper. We can meet him when I get off work."

Neil hesitated. If he had to make another trip to the homeless camps beneath the river bridges, he'd rather not take Susan. But once she had decided to do something he could spend hours trying to change her mind and still fail.

"OK," he said. "I think I have the key to your locked door."

"Good. Bring it tomorrow."

Once again Neil was left to unravel the subtext. Obviously the date tomorrow was now set in stone. Susan also imagined they could simply unlock the door and walk in—a misperception he would have to deal with later. But there was a third, more disturbing message here as well.

"Susan, aren't you coming to my apartment for spaghetti tonight?"

"No."

"Why?" He knew she couldn't have forgotten.

"I sent for fish and chips. From the cafe on Broadway."

"Do they deliver?"

"It should be here soon."

"You could have told me."

Silence.

"Then I guess I'll see you tomorrow?"

"OK." Her tone was flat. It was always flat. Still, Neil knew he had opened a rift. He wished he could just sit down and talk it out, as he had always done with Rebecca.

"Susan, I love you," he said.

"I know, Papa."

Another silence. The fly buzzed away from the clock and bumped repeatedly on the window.

"Bye, Papa," she said.

"Bye."

Neil covered his eyes with his hand, as if to hide his hurt even from himself. It was true that Susan had inherited much from her mother. But somehow he was the one who had inherited Rebecca's emotional doubt.

When the door opened, Neil quickly wiped the dampness from his eyes.

Marial was carrying a sheaf of papers against her breast. When she saw him she tucked her lower lip against her teeth. "Your daughter?" Neil nodded.

"If there's anything I can do —." She lowered the papers to his desk. He smiled with one side of his mouth. "Can you eat spaghetti with eggplant?"

It had been three days since Marial had made Brazilian lattes in Neil's apartment, but she swept in with the ease of a familiar spirit. She hung her tailored tan raincoat on the hood behind the door, took a glass from a cupboard, filled it from the tap on the refrigerator door, took a sip, and excused herself to go freshen up.

Neil put away his bicycling raingear and started boiling water for the spaghetti. He had mixed feelings about inviting Marial to dinner. She was attractive, and yes, there was a hole in his life he wanted to fill, but he had started to wonder if there was more behind her seductive glances than merely a widow seeking companionship. She kept managing to involve herself more deeply in the Cooper case, both as an investigator and as a suspect—as Connie had pointedly reminded him.

He took out the eggplant and hacked it into cubes. Connie had her own motives. Maybe she was miffed that the man she had just dumped wasn't spending his time alone. And Susan? Marial was stepping in to take her place for an evening, eating her favorite dinner. Susan hadn't forgotten. She had just said no. Neil slid the eggplant into a frying pan and turned up the gas. By the time he heard the bathroom door open, he had made up his mind.

To Neil's disappointment, Marial came back into the kitchen with her red hair still pinned up in a professional bun. Perhaps this would be a business dinner after all.

"Let's see," she said, surveying things. "You've started the spaghetti.

Maybe I could work on a salad."

"Have at it."

She folded back the cuffs of her white silk blouse. When she reached for a cutting board beside the microwave Neil found himself speculating that she didn't appear to be wearing a bra. Hadn't she worn one at work that day? With a silk blouse, one would have thought it essential. A detective ought to remember such details. Certainly there were no strap creases on her shoulder blades now. When she peeled bright green strips the length of a cucumber, the swells beneath her blouse swung with each stroke. The silk definitely puckered against nipples. She must have taken off her bra and put it—where? In her purse?

"Do you have cream?" she asked.

"Cream?" Neil asked, wrenching his thoughts back to food. "There's a carton in the door of the fridge, but I'm not sure how old it is."

"Let's check. I'd like to make a cream dressing with black pepper." She opened the refrigerator, took out the carton, and sniffed. "Smells fine, but it's really best if the cream is sweet."

Marial dipped in her index finger, white to the first knuckle. She let her fingertip drip twice into the open spout. Then she parted her lips in an O, arched a curve of pink tongue toward her finger, and stopped.

When she looked up at Neil over her glasses, his heart was beating in his throat. He felt himself stiffening and rising toward everything she was doing. How the hell did she know such simple things could be so arousing?

Marial set the carton of cream aside. Slowly, she took off her glasses. She held up her white fingertip and painted his lips with the cream. Then she leaned forward on tiptoes and licked it off.

"Sweet enough?" she asked.

Susan lay on her bed, covered only by a sheet, as the fifth Brandenburg concerto thundered from speakers on either side. It was starting to get dark by five at this time of year, but she had pulled the blinds and closed her eyes to make the blackness absolute. A Baroque cello the size of a bus picked up the theme and sawed down to an open string. shivering the apartment walls. She lived on the top floor of a rundown Queen Anne, where no one complained when she blasted out Bach.

The music was far too loud for her to hear the steps on the stair, or even the click of the front door latch. She knew he was there, however, from the oily smell of fish and chips. With her eyes closed she could see the theme passing from violin to harpsichord to cello and back, as if Bach were weaving a basket, or a rug, made of vibrations in her head. When everything crashed to a halt for the harpsichord solo, she could hear the shower running. Yes.

The harpsichord riffs jangled with incredible speed, not a circle of broken chords but a spiral — subtly twisting closer and closer. Faster. Closer. Turning. Until. Almost.

When all the instruments roared back in with the theme, she knew he was in her bedroom. Still dark. A drip of water on her forehead as he pulled the sheet aside. The sweet, damp scent of vanilla soap. The warmth of his breath on her bare shoulder. No kiss. No talk. He knew the rules.

The mattress shifted as he positioned himself above her, dripping, supporting himself only by his hands and feet. How long could she make him stay that way — an athlete ordered to hold a push-up half-way to the ground? The concerto slowed, the big notes of the cello booming back toward the tonic. Five. Four. Three. Two.

She nodded, her eyes still closed.

"Now, Dregs."

21

When Neil arrived half an hour late for work the next morning, he guiltily asked Marial to drop him off a block away from the station. He told her to circle the block before taking the car down to the basement garage. As he was trying to slip through the lobby however, the receptionist called out, "Lieutenant Ferguson?"

Ranah was an India Indian, with a head shawl and a crimson dot on her forehead. She spent most of the day smiling prettily as she told people how they could retrieve their towed cars. Neil knew her name only from the sign on the counter. He was surprised she knew his.

"You're late this morning. Captain Dickers asked to see you as soon as you came in." Ranah gave him a pretty smile.

By the time Neil made it to Dickers' office the captain was livid.

"Damn you, Ferguson! Didn't I tell you to stop harassing the Russian community?"

"Yes sir."

"Then what the hell are you doing making an ass of yourself at a private funeral?" He waved to the papers on his desk. "I've got three complaints here so far. You barge into a reception, eat their food, make a scene, and accuse people of who knows what. Why am I the one always cleaning up your messes?"

Neil stood his ground. "When I got back to the parking lot after that reception there was a fake car bomb on the engine of my car."

"And you know what? That's not illegal. You've made a lot of people angry. What do you expect?"

"Sir, a bomb threat is in fact illegal."

Dickers picked up a photograph from his desk. "Construction

paper and masking tape. If we were going to deal with every prank-ster we'd have to lock up half the ten-year-old boys in Portland. No, something's gotten into you. I want a straight answer: Why aren't you closing the Duvshenko suicide?"

"Forensics has turned up some new evidence at the crime scene."

"Smudges." Dickers shook his head. "The man was running a chop shop. Half the cars on his lot were hot. When you're in that line of work, you wear gloves a lot."

"There were also white hairs in the ski mask that don't match the victim's DNA."

"For crying out loud, Ferguson, when you're disguising yourself to sell stolen art, do you just take your old familiar ski mask off the closet shelf? No, you go to a goddam Goodwill store and get one that lots of people have tried on. Why do I have to explain this? It's like you're stuck in Detection 101."

What stung most about the criticism was that the captain really might be right. Everything could be explained just as he described. An impartial observer might say that Neil had let himself be infected by Connie's hysteria. Except for one thing.

Neil laid his hands on the captain's desk. "Then explain why Lieutenant Lavelle's thumbprint was found on the car bomb."

Dickers sat back in his swivel chair and crossed his foot on his knee. "That detail is disturbing. Most disturbing."

"Sergeant Espada believes the print was fabricated from records and planted on the bomb."

"Yes. That suggests it was put there by someone in our own depart-ment. The forensics team worked in pairs, so it had to be someone else who was there that day."

Dickers looked directly at him.

Neil felt the blood drain from his face. "What? You don't seriously think that I—?"

Dickers spread his hands. "I'm keeping an open mind. I just want you to know, I'm watching you, Ferguson."

"Watching me do what? Try to track down the original D.B. Cooper?"

"Fine, you can keep working on that too. It's better than stirring up panic about Russians. In a few weeks we'll have to provide security for the Russian energy minister. But right now I need you to focus on something new. There's a fish kill at Crystal Springs. Some kind of pollution at the rhododendron garden out on SE McLoughlin."

"A fish kill?" Neil puzzled over this sudden assignment. "Wouldn't that be the Parks Department, or maybe the DEQ?"

"They've both been there since 7:30 this morning. Half an hour ago the caretaker called us. Apparently fish aren't the only thing dead in that lake."

"I see."

"You still got your driver on call? The Gresham woman?"

Neil nodded. "I think she's in the garage."

"Crystal Springs, is it?" Marial took them across the river on the high, narrow arch of the Ross Island Bridge. The strap creases were once again beneath the silk of her blouse, but she'd left the top button undone, revealing a pink cleft as a reminder of the night before. "A lot of people get married in the Crystal Springs Rhododendron Garden. Nice lakes, flower gardens, cute little footbridges."

"Somehow I've never made it there."

"Well, it's almost part of the campus, you know. Right across the street from Reed College."

Reed. For the rest of the drive Neil felt a vague foreboding. Dregs had once warned him that D.B. Cooper might be his old Reed College professor, Curt Lammergeier.

When they arrived the parking lot was already full of flashing blue lights, including an ambulance and the forensics van. Neil headed for the park entrance, a breezeway in a shake-roofed building that resembled a Japanese pagoda. A nervous older man with a mustache, a beret, and green suspenders stood by the glass ticket window, wringing his hands.

Neil showed his badge. "Lieutenant Ferguson, homicide."

"Oh, my."

"Are you the caretaker who called?"

The man nodded unhappily.

"Did you know the victim?"

"I'm not sure. The body was face down. They told me not to touch anything."

"Well, let's take a look. Can you tell me what happened?"

The caretaker walked with a slight stoop as he led Neil down a paved path to a footbridge. Marial followed a few steps behind.

"We're all volunteers here," the man began, "so we're not really trained for something like this. In winter we don't even charge admission. Mostly we just sweep paths. I got here at seven—I have trouble sleeping in the mornings, an age thing I guess—anyway, I went down to get a broom from our maintenance shed by the lake. And there they were, all dead."

"They?"

The man stopped in the middle of the bridge to look at Neil. "The trout. The water from the springs is so pure, and we don't allow fishing, so they get quite large. They're like pets. I don't understand why anyone —"

Neil cut him short. "Did you notice anything else?"

"Not then. I went back to the office and made some calls about the fish. What kind of person would poison our fish?"

"When did you find the victim?"

"Only later, after I'd taken the parks people down to see the lake." He walked on, lost in thought. "Whoever it was must have fallen in and been poisoned too. How gruesome."

The path descended a slope of unblooming bushes, crossed a shallow lake on a 100-foot bridge, and curved left to a waterfall where a crowd of dark figures stood along the shore. Silver fish bellies glinted on the water. As Neil neared the waterfall he could see why the victim had been overlooked, hidden among the reeds of the shore. Garbage bobbed in the water nearby, evidently left by people who couldn't be troubled to carry their litter home.

Luis Espada caught sight of Neil. "Lieutenant, I'm glad you're here. We've got our initial samples. We'll collect the trash in the lake later, just in case. Now we'd like to turn the body over."

Neil surveyed the surroundings, imprinting the scene in his memory. Then he nodded. "Go ahead."

A parks worker with rubber boots stepped down into the reeds. Half a dozen hands with latex gloves helped pull the stiff body to the shore. When they hefted it onto the gravel path the corpse teetered briefly on one shoulder. Then it flopped onto its back.

The caretaker gasped at the bald head and white eyes.

"You know him?" Neil asked.

The caretaker nodded. "He was supposed to close up last night. Volunteers shouldn't stay after hours, you know, but I think sometimes he did. He loved the garden so much."

"Who?"

"Why, the professor, of course."

"Which professor?"

"Professor Curt Lammergeier."

22

The dead man in the lake, Curt Lammergeier, had a wife. Neil dreaded having to tell Rachel Lammergeier what had happened. He didn't have many answers. The doctor at the scene had estimated that Lammergeier had been dead twelve to fifteen hours. That put the time of death between six and nine o'clock the previous night. There were no obvious signs of trauma. He wouldn't know until after the autopsy whether Lammergeier had drowned or died from the same poison that killed the fish. Even the kind of poison would remain a mystery until forensics ran tests.

Meanwhile, the death scene had left Marial shaky. She leaned against the police car, her face as white as the floating corpse's. She took long, tremulous breaths. Her silk blouse hung like a shroud on a zombie.

Neil put his arm on her shoulder. "I can drive, Marial. Let me take you home."

Marial nodded weakly.

Neil helped her into the passenger side of the car. "Where to?"

"Not far. Bybee and 13th, in Westmoreland."

It really wasn't far—just a mile to the west. Still, when Neil slowed at the corner where Bybee turned to become 13th Avenue, he wondered if she had led him astray. The only building here was an abandoned five-story concrete mortuary, clinging to a clifftop above the Willamette River at Oaks Pioneer Park.

Marial took a key chain out of her purse and pressed a button. A corrugated steel garage door, defaced by the florid graffiti of vandals, slowly rose to reveal a loading bay with tiled walls, a beveled glass portico, and a familiar midnight blue BMW.

"You live in a remodeled mausoleum?" Neil asked.

She nodded. "My husband got it cheap at auction twenty years ago. I think it reminded him of the USSR. I'd invite you in, but—"

"No, I have to work."

"Yes, of course." She leaned over and kissed him on the cheek. "I'm sorry I get weak-kneed at the sight of a body. You'd think, living in a place like this, I wouldn't care.

What else could he say but "I understand"?

She got out, holding onto the car door. "Neil? I want you to know that I care about you a lot. Last night was perfect, and I'm not one to talk lightly about such things."

Neil cleared his throat. "I care about you too, Marial."

"Promise me you'll call tomorrow."

"Tomorrow. I promise."

"Good. I want to help. We've got to find D.B. Cooper."

He gave her a flustered smile. "Who can say if there really is such a thing?"

"There is," she said, and closed the car door.

On the way to Lammergeier's house, Neil had time to worry about Marial's motives. Even before the Cooper case had been reopened, Marial had signed up as a volunteer at the art museum. She had landed a job doing Russian storytimes in a library near Duvshenko's car repair shop. She had become a translator for the police bureau. Any one of these things might have been a coincidence, but together, they suggested she knew more about Cooper than she was letting on. What was her angle?

Neil was already investigating more than he could handle, but he resolved to run a background check on Marial's late husband. The Soviet vodka importer had left her enough money that she could live as she chose. Neil wasn't yet sure if he was going to wind up in bed with Marial again, but he wanted to know more about the guy who had been there before.

Neil drove slowly down Carlton Street, looking for house numbers. This close to Reed College, most of the homes were large and old, built by professors in the boom years of the early 1920s. Lammergeier's address was a brick Tudor house with half-timbered gables and leaded glass windows.

He parked, walked up a curving brick path, and pressed the doorbell.

Nothing happened.

Then a woman who had been working in the side yard raised her head. "Hello?"

Neil turned. "Mrs. Lammergeier?"

"Yes." She was kneeling by a freshly spaded bed, holding a trowel in her gloved hand. She wore jeans and a sweatshirt. Seed packets and stakes lay nearby. Some Oregon gardeners dare to plant peas in late February, trying to be the first on their block with homegrown produce. Mrs. Lammergeier had chosen a bed by a sunny south wall.

He cleared his throat. "I'm Neil Ferguson, a lieutenant with the Portland police bureau."

"Really?"

He showed his badge. "I'm afraid I have bad news. It's about your husband."

The woman stood up. She was tall, with short dark hair and quick gray eyes. "What about my husband?"

Neil hesitated. This was even harder than he had imagined. "Could we go inside? Maybe sit down?"

"No. Just tell me, now. What's happened?"

"Professor Lammergeier was found this morning at the Crystal Springs rhododendron garden. In the lake."

"Oh!" She caught her breath. "Are you telling me he's dead?"

"I—I'm afraid so."

For a moment it looked as if her tears were starting to form in her eyes. Then she tightened her lips and threw her trowel into the bed. "Thank God."

Neil wrinkled his brow, taken aback. "Mrs. Lammergeier?"

"I've been waiting fifteen years for this." She gave a nervous laugh. "Don't tell me he drowned by accident."

"We don't know. But I am with the homicide department."

"Then we'll want to go inside after all. Do you drink rooibos ?"

"I don't really drink."

She took off her gloves and opened the front door. "Rooibos is a South African tea, made from red desert bushes. It doesn't even contain caffeine."

Neil followed her inside, troubled that such a recently widowed woman was able to lecture him about tea. He couldn't help but contrast her with Nadia Duvshenko, the widow who had wailed in anguish when she saw her husband in the morgue.

"If you could wait here in the library," Mrs. Lammergeier said, indicating a wood-paneled room with glass bookcases and maroon wingchairs. "I'll just wash up and get our tea."

For a minute he heard the sounds of water running and dishes clinking from a room beyond an arched doorway. Then she leaned in the opening, wiping her hands on a dishtowel. "You do know that Curt and I are separated?"

Neil started to say that death was a permanent form of separation, but then he thought better of it, and switched instead to a noncommittal "Ah."

She went back to prepare the tea, shouting so that he could hear. "For me, our marriage was a biological time clock thing. I'd spent so long working on my career—I earned tenure in medieval studies, you know—anyway, when I turned forty, I panicked. He was twenty years older, with a nasty teenage son I never liked, but at least Curt was single and male. God, I'm glad he couldn't get me pregnant."

Mrs. Lammergeier backed through the door, a bamboo tray in her hands. "Curt turned out to be the greediest, least pleasant person I've ever met. Fortunately we'd signed a pre-nuptial agreement that split everything fifty-fifty." She set the tray on a round table and pulled up a wingback chair for herself. "By denying me an actual divorce, Curt came out slightly ahead. Sort of forty-sixty."

Neil tried to stop her with an even gaze. "Because you were still married at the time of his death, I assume you'll inherit everything."

She lifted a teapot from the tray and poured two cups. "Most of Curt's assets go to his son Todd. But I will finally have sole ownership of this house. Would you like a biscuit?"

Neil accepted a cracker. Although she had a motive, she didn't seem like a murderer. "Your husband was supposed to close up the park yesterday, but it seems he stayed there after hours. He died sometime between six and nine last night. This morning the fish in the lake were dead."

"All the fish were dead?"

"Yes, I think so. If your husband liked the park as much as they say, it's unlikely he poisoned them. That means someone else was there."

"No doubt. Dozens of people wanted Curt dead."

Neil looked at her.

"Don't look at me, Lieutenant." Mrs. Lammergeier blew steam off her cup of tea. "It's true I disliked Curt, and I don't have an alibi. I was here alone last night. But I abhor cruelty, and I respect life. I take houseflies outside in paper cups to release them. With Curt, all I had to do was wait. Someone was sure to kill him eventually."

Neil took a notepad out of his suit pocket. "Then maybe you could tell me about other possible suspects."

"Where should I start?" She waved her hand as if at a multitude.

"Was Professor Lammergeier originally from Portland?"

"Good heavens, no. He was born in Vienna, just before World War II." She took a sip of tea. "His parents were Jewish. After the Anschluss they couldn't get visas to leave Austria, so they sent him on one those save-the-children flights to New York. They later died in the Holocaust."

"Both his parents died?" Neil sat back, unsure how to respond to this horror.

"Curt never really knew them," she continued calmly. "He was three years old when a childless couple in New Hampshire adopted him. They were carpet factory workers."

"Were they Jewish?"

"Atheist. He grew up as one of those adamantly scientific non-believers. Neither of his adoptive parents had been to college, but Curt was bright, so he won a scholarship to a state school. He went on to get a doctorate at MIT. Impressive, really, for a war orphan."

Neil looked up from his notepad. "Did he make enemies at college?"

"Probably. I think he didn't start collecting them in earnest until he got a job at NASA. He worked seven years on the Apollo project. He left suddenly because of some big scandal he wouldn't talk about. He said he switched to private enterprise because it pays better."

"I'm told your husband had a strong interest in money." Neil fell back on what he'd heard from Dregs.

"That's certainly true." She leaned back and crossed her legs. The knees of her jeans showed grass stains. "After NASA he spent a year working for nuclear power companies. I think he switched from Westinghouse to General Electric as soon as he collected enough industrial secrets to demand a higher salary. Then he came to Reed College."

"Why Reed? Teaching at a college doesn't pay that well."

She shook her head. "In engineering, the big money is all about grants. Then you can pay yourself an extra salary. Curt got the grant that built Reed's nuclear plant. It's still the only one of its kind in the country."

Neil paused, remembering that Dregs had made a similar claim. "Other universities have nuclear plants, don't they?"

"Graduate schools do, yes. But Reed is the only undergraduate program with one."

"I see." It troubled Neil that he had contradicted Dregs so forcefully on this point. Without looking up he asked, "I don't suppose Reed ever offered a graduate engineering degree?"

"No, Reed's strictly for undergraduates."

"I thought so."

But then Mrs. Lammergeir gave a slight shrug. "Well, there was one brief experiment. It was Curt's idea, a collaboration with Caltech. I think they approved only one doctoral candidate before the program collapsed."

Neil was holding his pencil so tightly that he nearly snapped the lead. "Was this student named Egstrom?"

She brightened. "Yes, Dirk Egstrom. Do you know him?"

Neil nodded, ashamed at how deeply he had wronged Susan's friend. "I think Dr. Egstrom may qualify as one of your late husband's enemies."

Mrs. Lammergeier laughed. "Absolutely. Those two were impossible. They used to joke about which one would strangle the other first." She stopped, flustered.

"Go on."

She poured herself another cup of tea. "Of course Curt had many other enemies. I just don't know their names. You see, he gambled."

"He gambled? Did he have debts?"

"Lots, but he always paid them off. Strange people would show up night and day, threatening him. He kept wangling grants and coming up with inventions to get cash. Like that Recyclotron thing."

Neil picked up this new subject. "Did your husband hold the patent on the recycling machine?"

"Yes." She said the word slowly, as if she were thinking. "I suppose it's the most valuable thing he owned. Todd will get the patent now, but that's only right. They'd worked together on the Recyclotron for years."

This confirmed what Neil had already suspected— that Curt Lammergeier's son was the engineer who had installed the Recyclotron. Neil had one key to the Underground, and Todd had the other.

"I'll need to talk to your stepson next," Neil said. "He hasn't yet been told about his father's death."

She frowned. "Todd can be difficult. He idolized his father. His reaction to this news could be—well, it could be violent. Do you know where he lives?"

Neil nodded. Yesterday he had copied Todd Lammergeier's contact information from the architect's Rolodex.

"Let me call him first," she said. "Todd knows me."

"I thought you said you didn't like your stepson."

"I don't. He's an animal. But even animals deserve sympathy, don't they?"

Neil nodded. It would make his job easier if she paved the way. Then he stood up and put his notepad away. "Well, I don't want to take up more of your time. Thank you for the tea. What did you call it?"

"Rooibos."

"Yes." He handed her his business card. "I'll let you know if we find out more about what happened to your husband."

She accompanied him to the door. "Don't you consider me a suspect?" She sounded a little disappointed.

"Poison is traditionally a woman's weapon," Neil replied. "Still, I wonder if you would be able to kill that many fish."

This time her eyes really did grow damp. She shook her head.

"I'd like you to stay in the area. Give me a call if you plan to leave Portland for any reason."

"Certainly."

He turned to leave, but then paused in the doorway, thinking. "You know, this is going to sound strange. But did anything about your husband make you think that he might once have had another identity?"

"Another identity? What do you mean?"

Neil took the plunge. "Could Curt Lammergeier have been D.B. Cooper?"

She did not burst out laughing, as he had anticipated. Instead she slowly touched her fingertips to her mouth and stared past him into space.

"There was a rumor among his students," she said, her voice distant. "I think he encouraged it, as part of his aura."

"So it's possible?"

"I'm not sure. The night I seduced him—oh, I wanted a baby so badly back then—he told me he'd known who D.B. Cooper was. He said he'd confronted Cooper, the night after the skyjacking, on a bridge over the Willamette River. Curt said he tried to arrest him, but he just dived in."

"Cooper dived into the river?"

"Yes. Just dived in and vanished." Mrs. Lammergeier's eyes refocused. She looked at Neil, her brow knit. "Curt never talked about it again. But he loved money. He was a gambler. Do you think—?"

23

Dan Cooper's Last Will and Testament, Part 5

"Don't you think they could refuel a little faster?" I had already let the passengers go free. Now we were waiting for two bumbling technicians by the jet's port wing. The storm's twilight had given way to the dark of night. White reflective stripes on the workers' slickers glowed through the drizzle.

"They're having some trouble with the tanker truck." The stewardess set another plastic cup and a paper cocktail napkin on the seatback tray beside me. "Here's your bourbon, Mr. Cooper."

I took my wallet from my pocket, but she shook her head, "There's no charge." I could see her makeup was shiny with tiny beads of nervous sweat.

"You're a gem, Lisa." I put my wallet back with my right hand, always keeping my left on my briefcase. "Just two more little things. Could you send the flight engineer back so he and I can have a chat? And tell the pilot to make those clowns outside hurry up. If they take much longer refueling I'll have to press this little red button. I don't think they should be fooling around with jet fuel when that happens."

"Oh!" Lisa said. "Yes sir, Mr. Cooper." She hurried toward the cockpit, her heels clicking.

I had some time to sip my bourbon and consider the rest of my plan. If I didn't make the trade with Lammergeier within twenty-four hours, he'd get scared and back out altogether. So far I'd succeeded in getting the $200,000, and I seemed to have ditched my KGB tail. Now everything depended on timing—and one gigantic leap of faith.

Outside I could see one of the lazy maintenance workers answering a pager. A moment later he was shouting to his colleague and frantically connecting hoses. Good boy.

"Mr. Cooper?"

I jerked back from the window. How could I have let down my guard? Blame the bourbon. In the dim light of the cabin I could see Lisa had returned, but she'd brought a man in a blue uniform. For a second I thought he was a cop.

"You wanted to talk to First Officer Matacek?"

"You bet, Lisa. You take a seat right here, hon. Officer, I'd rather you didn't come any closer. I have my thumb on the bomb's detonator."

The flight engineer stopped, watching me. "You won't get away with this."

"If I don't make it, neither do you."

"What do you want us to do?"

"Fly this plane as slow as possible. Keep her just under ten thousand feet, with the flaps and landing gear down."

Even in the dim light I could see him raise his eyebrows. "Why would you want us to do that?"

"Not your problem, Officer."

He thought a moment before asking, "Where are we going?"

"Mexico City."

Lisa gave a little gasp.

The flight engineer, however, was shaking his head. "Can't do it. Flying that slow would triple our fuel usage. The 727 is a mid-range plane, and Mexico City is two thousand miles away. We'd have to refuel."

I hadn't considered this. He was probably right. "Where could we stop along the way?"

"We might make it to Phoenix, but even that would be tight. Reno would be safer."

"Fine, we'll refuel in Reno. What route will you take?"

He frowned. "Victor Twenty-Three, I suppose. It's a low altitude federal airway west of the Cascade crest."

This fit my plan. "Good. Fly over Portland, Medford, and Red Bluff before heading to Reno. Then on to Mexico City."

The flight engineer hesitated. "Mexico City would still be a long ways. We'd need to refuel once more after Reno."

I suspected he was inventing obstacles, but I couldn't be sure. "What's the last place we can refuel in the U.S.?"

"Yuma, I think."

"OK, that's the plan. How slow can you go?"

"In this weather? Maybe a hundred and seventy knots, unless you want to risk stalling."

"How much is that in miles per hour?"

"About two hundred."

"Do it. But don't pressurize the cabin."

"What!"

"You heard me. If you don't go over ten thousand feet we won't need cabin pressure."

The man stared at me. He looked completely baffled.

I pointed to the cockpit. "You've got your orders. Let's go."

24

Neil was so preoccupied with Curt Lammergeier's death that it took him a while to realize he was being tailed. A black Lexus with tinted windows had changed lanes to follow him over the Marquam Bridge to the Fourth Avenue exit.

Fine, Neil thought. He was six blocks from headquarters. Why should he care if someone tracked him to his office? He memorized the license plate anyway.

He pulled into the basement garage, took the elevator up, and wrote a report about the body in the lake. After he'd given Mrs. Lammergeier plenty of time to tell Todd about his father's death, Neil picked up a phone and punched in the number.

Before it even rang he heard a click.

Neil hesitated . "Hello?"

There was a scraping sound on the line, and then a voice — male, but nervous and high-pitched. "Rachel said the police would call."

"Is this Todd Lammergeier?"

"Yeah."

"I'm sorry to have to call you at a time like this. Can we meet somewhere to talk?"

"Sure. You're in the downtown police station, right? I can be at the Lotus Cafe in twenty minutes."

Neil avoided the Lotus. It was an old brick dive across the street from headquarters, with ceiling fans and barstools. Neil had spent many an evening there, downing three-dollar pints, in the months he'd tried to drink Rebecca back to life. But the cafe also served a good lunch.

"All right," Neil said. "How will I recognize you?"

"I'll find you." Todd gave a small laugh.

Half an hour later Neil had already started work on a plate of fish tacos when an overweight young man swiveled off a barstool and walked toward Neil's table with a tall beer glass.

"Mr. Lammergeier?" Neil asked.

The man's pasty skin and puffy cheeks made him look younger than he probably was. He wore a short-sleeved houndstooth shirt. He sat down heavily.

"I'm sorry about your father," Neil said. "I understand you were very close."

"My father—" Todd began, and closed his eyes. "My father was a freedom fighter."

"A freedom fighter?"

Todd opened his eyes. "That's what you call a man who's trying to save the world."

"You're talking about his invention of the Recyclotron."

"That was part of it."

Neil pushed his fish tacos aside. "I want to find out why your father died. If he was involved in something dangerous, I need to know."

"He was."

This was slow going. Neil took a little risk. "Your stepmother said he had gambling debts."

But Todd just shrugged. "Trivial." Then he leaned forward again. "My father dedicated his life to the struggle against socialism."

Neil blinked. "So he had political enemies?"

The puffy face nodded.

"Do you know who these enemies are?"

Todd swirled the beer in his glass, as if to clean the foam from the sides. "Not exactly. Not yet. They're part of a secret movement. Highly trained people. For forty years they've been infiltrating everything—universities, businesses, governments. "

Neil nodded. He'd heard conspiracy theories like this before. But the people who believed such things were seldom found floating in fish ponds. "Look, I'm a detective. To investigate this case, I need names."

Todd smiled with just the left half of his mouth. Either he was smirking, or he had once suffered a stroke. "If I give you a name, you'll laugh."

"Try me."

"How about D.B. Cooper?"

Neil didn't laugh. "Your stepmother thinks Cooper may have met your father the night after the skyjacking."

"Yeah." Todd pushed back in his chair. His weight made the metal legs screech like nails on slate. "Cooper was the one who started the trouble. My father spent his life trying to stop him. When we find Cooper, we'll know who got my father."

Todd stood up, as if to leave.

"Wait," Neil said. The young engineer didn't seem violent, as Mrs. Lammergeier had warned, but he obviously knew a lot more than he was willing to share. To buy a little more time, Neil reached into his pocket and held up a key. "I found this in my desk."

"So?"

"It's a key to a door in the Recyclotron building. I think you have one too."

"Maybe. I have a lot of keys."

"Then you don't mind if I use it?"

Todd's doughy face flushed pink. "People stick their noses into places like that at their own risk. Portland's Underground is dangerous as hell."

Alone with his cold fish tacos, Neil took out his cell phone and called Susan. He wasn't going to let her go with him to investigate the Underground, but he had promised to meet her today. On the third ring the muted clatter of machinery began echoing from his palm. He could almost smell the sour crush of the Recyclotron.

"One More Time Women's Co-op," his daughter's voice intoned.

"Hi, Susan. How are you doing?" It was a pointless question, because he knew how she would answer.

"Fine."

"We'd talked about getting together today to meet The Keeper. You know, the transient who might have seen D.B. Cooper. Is he in town yet?"

"Yes."

"Good. Should I meet you after work?"

"No." One of Susan's long silences followed. Then she said, "Now is better. At Voodoo Donuts."

Neil repositioned the phone against his ear. "I'm sorry, did you say Voodoo Donuts?"

"Yes."

"The one off Burnside?"

"Can you come now?"

"Uh, well, give me half an hour."

"OK. Bye."

"Love you, Susan," he said, but of course she had already hung up. The conversation with his autistic daughter left Neil so frustrated that he took a jalapeno pepper from his fish tacos and bit it in half. The burn spread through his mouth as he chewed. Then he paid his bill and crossed the street to headquarters. In his office he strapped on an under-the-shoulder holster for his Glock semi-automatic. His last visit to the homeless camps under the river bridges had ended badly. This time he was definitely not making a social call.

Further armed with an overcoat and a folding umbrella, he walked the ten blocks up Third Street, keeping a close eye on the traffic and the passersby.

A line of young, tattooed customers snaked out the door of the donut shop. Neil had heard that people sometimes booked the shop for weddings. This puzzled him, because the donuts themselves contained odd mixtures of bacon, pretzels, and Fruit Loops.

Susan was already waiting on the sidewalk with six large boxes.

"We're taking weird donuts to transients?" Neil asked. Last time they had taken screw-top zinfandel, so anything seemed possible.

"No, Papa." She handed him three of the boxes, but her wide, dark eyes looked aside. "It's for the dragon boaters."

Had she told him about this before? Neil dimly recalled that Susan's group was sponsoring an entry in Portland's dragon boat competition. Each fall, teams of paddlers raced giant Chinese canoes down the Willamette River. As Neil and Susan carried the donut boxes to Waterfront Park, he learned that this year's event had been shifted to March to capitalize on the media attention surrounding the global energy summit. The Recyclotron's twenty-four-member team was not widely viewed as a serious contender because it consisted of hobos and garbage handlers. Donuts, apparently, were their reward.

Susan led him across Waterfront Park to the river promenade.

There she unlocked the gate of the gangplank to the *Portland*, a stern-wheel riverboat.

"I thought this was a floating museum," Neil said. The old steam-powered ship creaked and sloshed in the muddy river. Four white decks, each smaller than the next, swayed like a teetering stack of children's blocks. The air smelled of fish, oil, and garbage.

"The museum is closed on Tuesdays," Susan said. As she walked down the narrow gangplank, half a dozen people stood up from folding chairs on the ship's rear deck.

"Voodoo! Voodoo!" a large woman in blue overalls said, pumping her fist.

An elderly bald man with a shabby backpack and a huge white beard eyed the donut boxes. "Did you get the kind with Cap'n Crunch?"

Susan set her boxes on a life raft case. Then she stepped back to the railing and lowered her eyes, leaving Neil to fend for himself. He set down his boxes and smiled awkwardly. Among these people he was obviously a policeman in a suit. The bulge of the gun under his coat felt like a deformity.

The large woman brushed back her wavy gray hair and put her hands on her substantial hips. "So, you're with Susan?"

"I'm her father, Neil Ferguson."

"Well, I'm Martha, captain of the Riff-Rafters." She began flipping back the lids of donut boxes. "We always get some plain ones, just in case. Now don't anybody take more than one until the rest of the crew gets back with the boat." Then she looked sideways at Neil. "You ever been in a race before?"

He wanted to say yes, he had run track for years, but he shook his head. "Actually, Susan asked me here to meet a man called The Keeper."

"Now there's a role model for you. He's seventy-five and paddles like a banshee. Joined the Riff-Rafters this morning." She turned to the bald man and raised her voice. "Keeper! This here's Neil, Susan's dad!"

The man had just bitten into a donut. He chewed for a while, picking crumbs of colored cereal from his beard. Then he held up two gnarled fingers in greeting. "The pleasure is mine."

"My name's Ferguson." Then Neil added quietly, "I'm a lieutenant with the Portland police."

"What?" The Keeper cupped his ear.

Neil motioned him to a railing amidships, where they could shout without alarming the others. "I'm Lieutenant Neil Ferguson! With the Portland police!"

"No!" The old man's eyes widened.

"It's all right, you're not in trouble. I just want to ask you about D.B. Cooper."

"Cooper?" The Keeper stroked his beard. "All these years I've been trying to tell people, and they wouldn't listen. No one would listen."

"I'm listening." Neil noticed that Susan had edged up along the rail. She stared into the choppy river, but he knew she was listening too. He turned to The Keeper. "I'm told you met D.B. Cooper in Kelso, Washington in 1971. Is that true?"

"No! I never said that. Cooper died when he jumped out of that plane. He wasn't trained to use a parachute like I was."

This speech raised a number of questions, but Neil decided to follow Cooper. "Why do you think Cooper died? Tell me what you know."

"Well, I was riding the rails south, like I've done every Thanksgiving since, and I got stuck in a freight yard outside of Kelso. It was about noon when this guy comes out from underneath the Coweeman River bridge. At first I thought he'd been sleeping there. He had a duffel bag and a civilian parachute case. He looked like he'd been in the rain, but he was wearing a suit. Guys like that don't usually sleep under bridges."

"You didn't think it was Cooper himself?"

"No! His name was McGill. He told me about the whole skyjacking thing. If he'd been Cooper, he would have made up a different story, wouldn't he?

"Maybe. What did he look like?"

The Keeper squinted at Neil. "Like you. Tallish, fit, clean-shaven. Younger, I suppose."

The description sounded a lot like the FBI description of Cooper. "Did this McGill tell you he'd found Cooper?"

"Yes. He said he'd wanted to help with the manhunt, so he'd gone out looking. He figured if Cooper was an amateur, the parachute might never have opened. In that case, people would be looking too far south. So McGill drove up the Coweeman River. He stopped when he heard a pack of coyotes howling in a field. They were fighting over a body. The chute really hadn't opened. McGill dragged what was left of Cooper to a ditch and covered him with branches to keep the coyotes away. But by the time he got back to his car, it wouldn't start. So he walked down to the train yard, looking for a telephone."

Neil found the story improbable. "Pardon me," he said, taking out his cell phone as if it had been vibrating. It hadn't been, but he wanted an excuse to photograph The Keeper. He flipped the phone open, pretended he was reading a message, and snapped a picture.

Neil folded the phone away. "You were saying McGill wanted to find a telephone. Then what happened?"

"Well, there weren't any phones near the train yard. I was going south, and McGill said he lived that way, so I convinced him to come along. By then a slow train of scrap metal was rolling through. I knew it must be headed for the docks at Vancouver. We hopped on and hid between junk car bales. Sure enough, it switched into a siding and stopped across from the Vancouver Amtrak station."

"I thought he wanted to find a telephone," Neil objected.

"He did. McGill used the pay phone outside the station to see about getting his car fixed. He said the Triple A was sending a tow truck to get the car. Because it was Thanksgiving, it was going to take a while. He said they'd pick him up at eleven o'clock that night."

"What did you do until then?"

"We'd gotten chummy, so I unpacked a bottle of brandy and we sat under the railroad bridge by the Willamette. I've always liked it down there. Quiet, but close to everything you need. Good place to sleep. It's easy to catch a train south in the morning too."

"Did he leave that night at ten o'clock?"

The Keeper wrinkled his brow. "Yes, but here's the strange thing. He didn't go back to the Amtrak station. Instead he walked out onto the bridge. He just walked out and never came back."

"Did you think his duffel bag might be full of money?"

The old man pursed his lips. "Not until later."

The most convincing part of the story, for Neil, was the railroad bridge. Just that morning Rachel Lammergeier had said Cooper might have been on a bridge over the Willamette River the night after the skyjacking. But neither story had any solid evidence.

"I was told," Neil said, "that you know where to find D.B. Cooper's parachute."

"No! How could I know that? McGill left the chute with the body."
The old man looked out across the river. A big canoe with a dragon
head was paddling their way. "But McGill did take Cooper's parachute case. I noticed it right away, because it reminded me of my time
smokejumping in Alaska."

"You parachuted in Alaska?"

"I had a summer job with the Forest Service. We were the best hot-
shot crew in the Tongass, trained to drop into hell and build a line.
When it got to be November and the fire season was over, they let us
all go. I thought we'd stay together, the hotshots. But everyone just
drifted away. There's nothing to do in Alaska in winter. I was running
out of money fast. So I took the ferry to Bellingham and started riding the rails south, looking for warmer weather. When I saw McGill's
parachute case, I got all misty eyed. I even asked him if I could swap
my knapsack for it."

Neil raised an eyebrow. "He didn't trade, did he?"

"He did. In fact, he seemed glad to get rid of it."

"Where is this case now?"

The old man hesitated a moment. Then he slipped the backpack
straps off his shoulders and held out a bedraggled gray bag.

"This is it?" Neil asked, taken aback by the smelly, ancient artifact.
"This is the case of D.B. Cooper's parachute?"

The Keeper nodded.

"Ahoy, Lieutenant!" A shout from the river interrupted them. A
thirty-foot boat with a snarling dragon at its prow was pulling up
alongside the railing. Nine pairs of rowers fumbled with their oars. At
the back, holding the tiller in one hand and a megaphone in the other,
was a scar-faced man Neil remembered all too well.

"Hey, Daddy!" Dregs shouted through the megaphone. "Looking
good today!"

The dragon boat bumped along the side of the *Portland*. Before they
reached the giant wooden blades of the stern paddlewheel, the crew
tied ropes to cleats and climbed aboard the ship. About half of the
rowers wore the blue overalls of Recyclotron workers. The rest wore
sweatshirts and ripped coats. All of them headed straight for the donut boxes.

Dregs swaggered toward Neil with a chocolate donut in the shape
of a gingerbread man. A voodoo pretzel stuck out from the donut's

heart. Dregs bit off the head and talked with his mouth full. "I see you met our friend The Keeper." He put his arm around Susan's shoulder. She flinched and looked down.

Neil took a deep breath. This time he was not going to lose his temper, no matter how Dregs provoked him. Neil held up the parachute case. "Is this why you call him The Keeper? Because he keeps a memento of the skyjacking?"

"No!" The bald man stepped between them, waving his hand in protest. "That's not why at all."

"Then why?" Neil asked.

"I grew up in Holland. My name there was DeKuyper. Gregor DeKuyper. When I went to Alaska the firefighters couldn't pronounce it. They're the ones who started calling me The Keeper."

The old man reached for the parachute case, but Neil didn't let go. "I'm afraid I need this as evidence."

"What?" Dregs rolled his eyes. "Give him back his bag, man."

"I want it checked by forensics," Neil said. "If it's not Cooper's, I promise I'll bring it back. But if it was used in the skyjacking, it's important to our investigation."

"Get a grip, Dad," Dregs said. "Your investigation should be over. I already told you about D.B. Cooper. His real name is Curt Lammergeier."

Neil turned to Dregs. "I owe you an apology, Dr. Egstrom. It seems Reed College may in fact have awarded you a Ph.D. I was wrong to doubt your credentials."

"Glad to hear it."

"But there's a bigger problem." Neil kept his voice steady. "When was the last time you saw Professor Lammergeier?"

"I don't know. A year ago?" Dregs lifted his head — with innocence, disdain, or guilt?

"Professor Lammergeier was found this morning in a lake near Reed College. He's dead."

Dregs' cocky attitude evaporated. He took his arm from Susan's shoulder. "So this really isn't a social call."

"I asked the professor's widow for a list of his enemies. She was able to give me only one name. Yours."

Dregs frowned.

"I have to ask you, Dr. Egstrom. Where were you last night between the hours of six and nine?"

"Papa!" Susan's face flushed. She was actually looking Neil in the eye. "Dregs is not like that! He could never hurt anyone."

"I'm sorry, Susan, but I need facts. I need to know where he was last night."

"No." Dregs shook his head. "I can't tell you."

Neil studied him. The scar across the man's cheek flamed red. His sagging eye stared straight ahead. "Do you understand what you're saying? Without an alibi, you become the department's top suspect in what is almost certainly a case of murder."

"I understand." Dregs stood as rigid as a soldier at a court martial. "I still won't tell you."

Everyone on the Portland had fallen silent. If a distant siren had not wailed from the far shore, and if the river had not continued to slosh against the hull, time could have been standing still.

"He was with me," Susan said, looking at the scar-faced man beside her. "Dregs was in my bed."

25

That evening Sergeant Connie Wu was talking to her turtle Luigi, always a sign of trouble.

"Do you want out?"

Connie wanted out. Her house was starting to feel like a prison. She lifted the hubcap-sized tortoise down from his terrarium and set him on the white living room carpet. Then she put a dish of romaine lettuce in front of him. At first Luigi kept his head under his brown-and-yellow shell. But then he slowly extended his neck and pumped with his front legs, sniffing the air.

"Are you hungry, Luigi? God, I am."

Luigi blinked his small black eyes. He lifted a scaly claw and dragged himself forward.

'Mmm, lettuce." Connie kneeled on the carpet and winced. The hairline fracture in her hip flashed out electrifying but useless distress calls whenever she bent. By the time the pain had cleared, the turtle had snatched a stalk. Each time he opened his beak to lunge for a bite, she could see his pointy pink tongue.

"You know what I'm hungry for?" Connie asked. "Meat. Food with protein. Anything but milkshakes."

Her son Leighton had left her alone again. He was out of the house longer each day. Connie knew what it meant. She was recovering and her son was getting bored.

Leighton had always had a short attention span. At the age of twelve he had bought Luigi, promising to take care of him forever. But turtles can live for a century. Within a year Leighton had followed his father to Hawaii, leaving the turtle with Connie. She didn't mind keeping Luigi—turtles demand so little, and reptiles really aren't allowed in Hawaii—but her son's lack of commitment rankled. Even now, faced with the threat of an armed maniacal assassin, he had lost interest after a week.

"Should I call Leighton?" Connie asked. Luigi lunged for another bite of lettuce.

"I'll take that as a no. All right, should I call Ferguson?"

The turtle lifted his head, paused, and blinked.

"Luigi! How can you say that?" Connie sat back and winced again. "Ferguson is the guy I told never to call me. Just because you've got a shell, it doesn't mean everyone is bulletproof. You know what he did?"

The turtle pumped his legs, sniffing.

"He stole my promotion. I should have been lieutenant. Then he would have been the sergeant walking out there to get run over by D.B. Cooper. The man has a drinking problem—and here's the crazy thing—he got promoted because he was driving drunk! How am I supposed to deal with a guy like that?"

The turtle had stopped eating. He had a glazed expression that Connie knew all too well. But it was too late. Luigi was already peeing into the carpet.

She cleaned up the wet spot with paper towels. Turtle pee was a lot like water, so it wouldn't stain the carpet or smell. Still, it was a statement.

She took our her cell phone. When she realized she still had a speed-dial button for Neil, she hesitated, embarrassed. Why had she kept it? But then she punched it anyway.

After four rings his voice answered. "Connie?" He had a lost, distant tone.

She cleared her throat. "Yeah. I've got some new data on the Cooper case. Just checking in."

"I was going to call you." He sighed. "I've been busy, but that's no excuse. I'm sorry. How are you feeling?"

"Better. I'm walking fine. I could probably return for duty, it's just that everything hurts."

"You should rest."

"No! That's just it. I'm so cooped up here, I could scream."

There was silence on the line. Was he hiding a laugh or not

paying attention?

Then he said, "You know what, Connie? You sound just like yourself."

"Well I am." She walked into her den and sat in her swivel chair.

"No, I mean it. It's good to hear you again."

She scoffed, spinning slowly in the chair. "OK, Mr. Busy. Tell me what you've been doing."

"Well, this morning Dickers sent me to check out a fish kill at the Crystal Springs Rhododendron Garden."

"A fish kill?" Connie gave a satiric whistle. "Hot stuff for a homicide lieutenant."

"It turns out there was a body in the lake too."

"Oh. Whose?"

"Curt Lammergeier's. He's the professor my daughter's homeless friend thinks might be D.B. Cooper."

Connie considered this. Twice in one week, people linked to Cooper had died. She asked, "Could this professor have been murdered by the same person who killed Duvshenko?"

"Somehow I doubt it. The scene wasn't rigged to look like suicide. Lammergeier was either poisoned or drowned. I won't know which until I hear from forensics tomorrow."

"Any obvious suspects?"

"When I told his wife he was dead, she was delighted. She said she'd been waiting for this news for years."

Connie thought of her ex-husband, and understood why a widow might say such a thing. "Does she have an alibi?"

"No. But she claims she isn't even able to kill houseflies."

"Women can surprise you." Connie rolled her chair to the door, swiveled to look at herself in the hall mirror, and frowned at what she saw. "What other suspects have we got? How about the homeless man? What's-his-name. Dregs."

Another long silence. Finally Neil said, "Susan says she can vouch for him."

"Your daughter was with him the whole time?"

"Yeah." Neil sounded tired. "That whole night."

Connie heard the pain in his voice. There was obviously a lot more going on than he was saying. Connie's injury had left her isolated. She was healing quickly. Neil, on the other hand, had been smashing into crises with his daughter, Captain Dickers, and, a dead professor. His librarian translator had been spending a disturbing amount of time with him as well. Connie was worried about him.

"Neil? We need to talk, and not just on the phone. What are you doing tomorrow?"

The voice on the telephone sighed. "Looking for ghosts again. This time in the Portland Underground, beneath the Recyclotron."

"Not without armed backup, you're not."

"Look who's giving orders."

She ignored the comment. "Are you able to drive by yourself again?"

"Yes."

"Pick me up at my house tomorrow. I'll go with you."

"Connie, are you sure you're up to this?"

While they were talking the turtle had walked through doorway into the den. Luigi lifted his head, pumped his legs, and sniffed at her.

Connie held the phone aside and mouthed the words, "Luigi! What I do is none of your damned business."

Then she put the phone back to her ear and said, "I'm sure. What time will you be here?"

"As soon as I'm done with forensics. About ten."

"Good. And Neil?"

"What?"

"Can you take me out to lunch?"

Yet another long silence. "I thought you didn't want me to — "

"It's not a date, Neil. Just take me out to lunch. I'm starving."

There was a short laugh — a good kind of laugh, the kind that made her think things were going to be OK after all.

"See you tomorrow, Connie."

26

The next morning Neil skipped his usual bike ride. He felt like he was racing all the time now. Instead he went straight to his office. While he waited for forensics to open he wrote a report about The Keeper, complete with the photograph from his cell phone. Captain Dickers had told him to keep out of trouble by working on the ancient D.B. Cooper case. Here was proof he was making progress.

Neil did not report his proudest achievement: He had not slugged Dregs. Neil still didn't like the homeless Ph.D. The man was a rude wino. But Neil was beginning to respect him. Dregs had not lied about his doctorate. He had not betrayed Susan, even when threatened with a capital crime. And Susan seemed to actually like the guy.

The phone rang. "Espada here, returning your message. Just letting you know I'm in, we're open, and I've got results."

Neil grabbed his parachute case and made tracks for forensics.

Sergeant Luis Espada welcomed him with a salute. "I'm glad you're the detective in this case, and not me."

"Why?"

"Because Crystal Springs was not crystal pure yesterday."

"What kind of poison did you find?"

"You name it, we've got it." The sergeant held up a long printed list. "Arsenic, mercury, dioxins, lead, PCBs. Extremely low levels, but that lake had some nasty stuff."

"What could cause that?"

The sergeant's dark eyes darted about the room. "Apocalypse? Insanity? I don't know."

"So whatever killed the fish also killed Professor Lammergeier."

"No." Espada placed his hands on his desk. "That part you've got backwards, Lieutenant."

"Backwards? How?"

"The fish had minor levels of the toxins. I'm surprised they died at all. But Mr. Lammergeier's toxicity is off the charts." Espada turned his hands on edge. "The lake didn't poison him. He poisoned the lake."

"What! How could that be?"

Espada lifted his shoulders.

"Well, at least we know he didn't drown," Neil mused.

Espada gave a short laugh. "Actually, he did. I checked with the coroner. Lammergeier fell in the lake and drowned. That's what killed him. But with toxins like these in his stomach, he wouldn't have lived another ten minutes on land."

"Jesus."

"Please, Lieutenant. No profanity in forensics."

"Sorry. It's just—how could you get that much poison in your body?"

"Not by accident. You'd have to drink an ugly cocktail. A blend like that would be hard to find."

Neil thought at once of his daughter's suspicions about the Recyclotron. "I think I know where to look."

"Really?" Espada shook his head. "I'm so glad I'm not a detective." He pushed the list of poisons across his desk. "Have fun."

"Wait. There's one more thing." Neil held out the bedraggled backpack he had taken from The Keeper. "I want you to tell me if this is authentic."

"What's it supposed to be?"

"The case of D.B. Cooper's parachute."

Espada raised an eyebrow. He took a metal rod from his desk and lifted the rumpled gray bag from Neil's hand. "Did you find this in your car, like the fake bomb?"

"No, this one I got from a homeless man on the waterfront."

"You know what, Lieutenant? We get stuff like this all time. It's been forty years since Cooper disappeared, but people keep bringing us shoes, parachutes, belts, money bags—all kinds of garbage. Nothing has ever been definitively linked to him."

"I thought some of his stolen money turned up in a riverbank."

"All right, except for $5880 in twenty-dollar bills. Everything else has been a waste of time."

"Then you're sure this couldn't be the backpack used in the sky-jacking?"

"I didn't say that." Espada laid the dirty bag on his desk. He lifted its top flap with his metal rod. "At least this nylon is from the right era. Most of the parachute materials we get for Cooper are either canvas, obviously from World War II, or lightweight synthetics that are too modern."

He turned the case over on his desk and shook his head. "The label is too worn to read. The straps have been repaired or replaced. This artifact has seen years of heavy use."

"Are there tests you can run on it?" Neil asked.

"I can try."

"Do what you can. This is my best chance to verify a Cooper witness."

Espada looked up. "You're kidding."

"No. I've found someone who might have seen Cooper after he jumped."

"Sure," Espada said. "You and everybody else, Lieutenant."

Back in his office, Neil slipped his Glock pistol into the holster under his suit jacket. He was worried about visiting the Portland Underground—and not just because it might be a repository for poison. Last night he had stayed up late, reading Lieutenant Credence Lavelle's reports on the Underground murders. Had there been a touch of doubt in her conclusion about the serial killer's motive? The Underground tour promoter, Tony Daugherty, had strangled five very different people, embalmed them, and used them in his displays. The connection Credence had found among his victims was that they had each won a "grand prize" ticket to his tour. But could there have been another link? Daugherty had hanged himself before she could ask.

Neil went to his desktop computer and checked Lavelle's home page. She had posted pictures of her dog and her sailboat in a sunny green sea. But her last entry was now four days old. It still said she was setting out from Barbados for Grenada, and would be out of cell phone range for three days.

He called her cell phone. After it had rung a while he Googled the Grenada police. A page for the Royal Police Department popped up with a picture of black men parading in white pith helmets. The "Contact Us" link led to a fill-in-the-blanks form. Neil filled in the blanks, asking them to be on the lookout for a thirty-two-foot sailboat arriving from Barbados. He gave his name, rank, and telephone number. He told them he wished to speak with retired Lieutenant Credence Lavelle as soon as it was convenient.

Neil looked at his watch. It was time to pick up Connie. He grabbed his coat and headed for the parking garage.

On the way, struck by a sudden touch of vanity, he stopped at a bathroom to comb his hair. Looking in the mirror, he worried that his hair was even thinner and grayer than he remembered. Wrinkles surrounded his blue eyes. The Keeper had said Neil looked just like the man he'd met on Thanksgiving Day in 1971, only older. If D.B. Cooper really was still alive, he might look like the man in the mirror. An old man, afraid of losing his way.

For some reason this thought reminded him that he had promised to call Marial today. He really did feel that he was racing all the time now. But where was he going?

He took one of the department's unmarked Buicks from the basement garage, headed out Hawthorne, and parked in front of Connie's fortified house. By the time he had walked up to the wrought-iron gate, the security latch was already buzzing. He pushed through the gate, continued up the stairs, and tapped on the door. It opened on the second knock.

Connie had dressed in civilian clothes, and looked surprisingly good. She wore a black felt fedora, canted to one side to cover the part of her scalp that had been scraped raw. Makeup masked the bruises. A black jumper and tights revealed that she had indeed lost weight, but mostly not in high profile areas. Black gloves covered the damage to her hands.

Neil lowered his eyes. "I don't know, Connie. Maybe you should sit this one out. It could be dangerous out there today."

"What? It's that risky eating lunch with you?"

"I meant going into the Underground."

She laughed. "Sorry. I'm totally focused on lunch."

"All right, let's focus on lunch first." Neil said. "What are you hungry for?"

"Oysters."

"Seriously?"

"I know where we can get them this early in the day."

"Where?"

"Ivan's Oyster Bar."

Neil nodded slowly. "Owned by Ivan Crombaugh, one of your six-ty-seven Cooper suspects."

"Even lunch can be research."

"Agreed."

She stepped down from the porch and gave a small gasp of pain. Her expression hardened. "I'm afraid I need an additional weapon for this mission."

She went back to the house, fetched a black metal cane, and closed the door behind her. "Let's go."

While they were driving to the restaurant in Old Town, Neil told her what he had learned that morning—that Curt Lammergeier's body had contained a mixture of poisons.

"Sounds like toxic waste," Connie said. "You'd think the inventor of the Recyclotron would know better than to take his work home."

Neil glanced at her cautiously. It felt good to be sharing a police car with the sardonic Sergeant Wu again. A week ago he had been afraid of losing her altogether. But it still seemed there was an invisible ribbon between them that read, *Police Line Do Not Cross*.

He fell back on business. "Last night you said you'd found some new information about the Cooper case."

Connie faltered. "Nothing important. I was just checking alibis for the people at the art museum parties. I thought I should tell you about Marial Greschyednev."

Neil gripped the wheel a little tighter. "I'm impressed you can pronounce her name. What did you find out?"

Connie looked away. "She's clean. She was living in Latvia in 1971, so she can't be connected to Cooper. She came to Portland with her husband the next year. After he died in 1993, she got a job as a librarian. She's been volunteering at the art museum at least that long. She's never even gotten a parking ticket."

"Good, good," Neil said, and immediately regretted adding the second good. "I have to admit I did a little background checking too. On her husband."

"Her husband?" Connie turned. "She remarried?"

"There's no proof she was ever widowed. Her husband Anatoly went missing during an Oregon Chamber of Commerce retreat in Yachats. The official report says a sneaker wave washed him into the surf, but the witnesses weren't close by and his body was never found."

"Why would he fake his own death?"

"He had a business importing vodka. Last night I ran a search and turned up a rumor that he had been working with the KGB on the side. Not as an agent, just running errands in exchange for perks."

"If that's true," Connie mused, "he would have been on his own after the Soviet Union collapsed in 1989."

"Yes, and by then he might have made some enemies."

"How much of this does his wife know?"

"No idea." Neil sighed. He wasn't looking forward to talking to Marial about it. "Still, I wouldn't cross Mrs. Gresham off our list of suspects just yet."

"Yes, sir."

The on-street parking near Ivan's Oyster Bar was full, and the private lot nearby wanted ten bucks, but Neil simply paid it. Then he walked around the car to open the door for Connie.

"An officer and a gentleman." She stepped out onto the pavement with her cane, and winced.

Ivan's Oyster Bar was in an old brick building with cast iron curlicues beside the windows. The restaurant had just opened for lunch, and they were the first customers. A young man in an apron led them to a window seat where passersby would notice them.

Connie studied the menu as if for a final exam. "Look, they've got smoked salmon. Oh my God, fish and chips, but I don't need the grease, not really. Bouillabaisse is just soup. I want the bucket of oysters."

"Fine," Neil said."I'll have a bowl of clam chowder."

She looked at him askance. "Not at an oyster bar."

"What, then?"

"Oyster stew."

"All right." He waved the waiter over. "We'd like a bucket of oysters and a bowl of oyster stew."

"Very good. And to drink?" He picked a tri-fold brochure off the table. "Our special today is the Oregon Noir."

"I've heard the name Oregon Noir before," Connie said. "What is it?"

"Carbonated wine," Neil replied. He had already avoided the drink once this week at the art museum gala. "We just want two glasses of water."

"You got it." The waiter retreated.

While they waited for their food, Connie set off looking for the bathroom. On the way she noticed a chained stairway to a basement.

She didn't mention it until later, after they had eaten. When the waiter came with the bill she asked what was downstairs.

"You want to see the Underground?" The young man's hair had been cut short on the left side, but hung down on the right.

Neil looked up sharply. "You have access to the Underground?"

"Our restaurant was one of the stops on the old Portland Underground tours. We took down the signs last year. Even though the murders happened four blocks away, our owner was afraid it might scare away diners. I'm only allowed to show people if they ask."

"We're asking." Neil took out his wallet and paid the bill. It seemed unlikely that the basement here could be connected to the Recyclotron four blocks away, but he was curious.

"Let me ask the manager," the waiter said, retreating with the bill.

A minute later he was back. "Sure, come on." He led them to the head of the stairs, unclipped the chain, and launched into a spiel. "This building dates to 1882. Back then it was on the riverfront. Tides and floods changed the water level so often that most buildings had two levels. After the city decided to fill in the streets, the lower levels were left as a network of basements."

The young man led them down the stairs, opened a door, and turned on a switch. Bulbs in wire cages lit a brick passageway ahead. "Watch your heads on the doorway."

The hall smelled of mildew and mortar. There were cobwebs and rubble along the walls. The damp air was so cold that their breath puffed out as fog.

After a hundred feet they turned a corner to a vaulted brick room divided by a railing of two-by-fours. Beyond the railing, spotlights lit three mannequins dressed in nineteenth-century garb. A sailor and a

Chinese man with a long pigtail were struggling with a slumped man in work clothes. The wall behind the statues had been painted to depict a doorway overlooking a riverfront with tall-masted sailing ships.

"It's a shanghai parlor," Connie said.

"That's right," the waiter said. "In Portland, captains had trouble enlisting crew members to sail their ships to China, so they sometimes slipped the locals a few knockout drops. When the men woke up, they were already on their way to Shanghai."

In addition to the painted doorway, there was one real door with a large padlock. Neil asked, "Where does the door lead?"

The waiter widened his eyes and whispered, "To China!"

"I mean the real door."

The waiter shrugged. "We're supposed to say the door leads to China. Then everyone's supposed to laugh and we're done."

"I see." Neil nodded. "Well, thank you for the tour."

"Tips are OK."

Neil dug out a fiver.

The young man bowed and led them back the way they had come.

As they climbed the stairs Connie winced with each step. Still, when she reached the top she managed to ask the waiter, "Does the restaurant's owner come here often?"

"Mr. Crombaugh? Not really. He's a county commissioner. There's some pictures of him by the front door."

"Thanks."

Neil and Connie went to look at the framed photographs. They showed a bald man with mirrored sunglasses shaking hands with the governor, or putting his arm around a chef, or fishing from the deck of a houseboat.

"I know what you're thinking," Neil said. "D.B. Cooper wore sunglasses too. But Crombaugh's almost blind. I think his eyes are sensitive to light."

"If he's almost blind, wouldn't his eyes be less sensitive to light?"

Neil considered this. "Maybe they're disfigured, and he doesn't want to upset people.

Connie looked again at the photos. "I'd like to see Mr. Crombaugh's eyes. I'll never forget the eyes of the man who ran me down."

The man who called himself Cooper covered his eyes and ducked around a corner. The two cops were leaving Ivan's Oyster Bar. He had had so little time to prepare. But short notice made life interesting. He loved taking advantage of sudden opportunities. Quick thinking and creativity had always kept him ahead.

He pulled down the bill of his trucker cap and shuffled across the street, checking to see if the two cops were going back to their Buick. They were—but only to get a large flashlight.

The Asian woman was carrying a cane. How could she be walking so well after everything she'd been through? He had nearly killed her twice. The lieutenant with her actually turned around and looked right at him, just half a block away. But shuffling old men with trucker caps are invisible in Old Town.

When Cooper was certain they were going to the Recyclotron he ducked into an alley and unlocked a door. Then he took out a pocket flashlight and went down a metal staircase. The abandoned hardware store in this basement had once been a stop on the Underground tours. A narrow, winding passageway extended nearly a block to the Recyclotron's basement.

In the dark corridor, rats scurried away from his light. Water dripped from rusty pipes. Wooden beams sagged overhead. Debris cluttered the floor. Twice the narrow hall appeared to deadend at sharp corners.

When Cooper reached the room with the tour's saloon scene he hid behind the bar and set up a row of empty whiskey bottles as cover. He took out a Glock 26 semi-automatic. It looked exactly like the one Lieutenant Ferguson carried. Cooper smiled. It was easy to get pistols of the type used by Portland police. He checked that the ten-round magazine was full, clicked it back in place, and took off the two safeties. Then he switched off his flashlight and waited.

The darkness and silence seemed absolute. He slowed his breathing. He counted his heartbeats to gauge the time.

After four hundred and fifteen heartbeats—just under six minutes if he was as calm as he thought—he heard the distant rattle of a lock. A door creaked. There was a pause. Then the door closed with a faint clunk.

Cooper closed his eyes, trying to understand the echoed whispers. The two cops were alone. Good. They were arguing about the flashlight. Obviously they hadn't figured out how to turn on the lights. That would make his work even easier.

Footsteps rang on the metal steps of the stairway. Soon they would be in the bordello gift shop. The Underground tours had always ended in the gift shop. Victorian dolls in petticoats, history books with pictures, and barrels of old-fashioned candy had been an easy way to wring a few more dollars out of the crowd. The whorehouse theme had been Daugherty's idea, but Cooper had to admit it was genius. After the gruesomeness of the saloon, the tourists needed busty mannequins in black lace to lift their mood.

A flashlight beam strafed the wall outside the saloon, and the voices became clearer.

"—no storage tanks or pipelines." The lieutenant was no longer whispering. "We're getting farther away from the Recyclotron. Maybe there aren't any toxics down here after all."

"I can't believe they left half-naked statues at a crime scene," the woman's voice said.

"That was just a gift shop. I think the murders actually took place in the next room."

Cooper crouched lower behind the bar. He aimed his pistol between bottles.

"This is it," Neil said, swiveling the flashlight across the room's broken chairs and overturned tables. Cases of old Blitz Weinhard beer bottles, a brand discontinued for decades, stood stacked against a wall. Then his light flashed across a row of empty whiskey bottles on an ornate wooden bar.

"A speakeasy," Connie said.

"More of a Wild West saloon," Neil replied. "Daugherty had hoked it up to look like a bar brawl. Two of the bodies were supposed to be cutting each other with broken bottles. Two others were sprawled out with gunshot wounds. He even had one body on the floor with an ax in his back. The murders looked so real that some people felt queasy."

"They were real." Connie shivered. "Where did they find Daugherty?"

Neil scanned the ceiling with his flashlight. "Up there."

Cooper didn't have a clear shot at the policewoman yet. He wanted to kill her first. If he shot the lieutenant the flashlight would drop before he could take aim again.

Connie followed Neil into the center of the room for a better look. A broken chain hung from the ceiling. Neil explained, "When the police were closing in, Daugherty stood on a table, tied a rope to a light fixture, and kicked the table away."

"Really?" Connie said. "Doesn't that seem a little strange?"

Cooper was waiting for Connie to turn her head. He wanted the deaths to look like a murder-suicide. The public had seen this kind of story before. Rejected in love and frustrated at work, Lieutenant Ferguson had shot his former sweetheart and then turned the gun on himself. The bullets would match the type of weapon, and the lieutenant's pistol would have been fired twice. No one would think that a second, identical gun might have been used, and then switched.

"Strange?" Neil asked. "You don't think a serial murderer would commit suicide?"

Connie shook her head. "All of it seems strange. This whole Underground setup is just — I don't know — odd."

When she stopped shaking her head, Cooper sighted in on a patch of raw skin between her fedora and her ear.

Finally it was perfect.

He began to squeeze the trigger.

Dan Cooper's Last Will and Testament, Part 6

The Boeing took off from Seattle at 7:40 p.m. We were headed for Mexico City — although I didn't plan to go that far.

Lisa, my once cheerful stewardess, was silent now that she and I were the only two people left in the passenger cabin. When the plane started leveling out, still in the thick of a relatively low cloudbank, she pouted her glossy lips at me.

"What's wrong, sweetheart?" I asked.

"Am I the one who doesn't get a parachute?"

It took me a moment to understand. Counting the flight crew, there were five of us on board. But I had ordered only four parachutes.

"You think I'm going to make everyone bail out?"

"I don't know." She blinked her damp lashes. "No one knows what you're doing."

Bing! The "Fasten Seatbelts" signs blinked out above our heads. I had work to do.

"I really don't want anyone to get hurt, sweetheart. Now I need you to go join the others in the cockpit."

We stood up in the aisle, an arm's length apart.

"Are you sure, Mr. Cooper? You don't need anything else?"

For a moment I was afraid she was going to tackle me, right there in the aisle. What would I have done if she did? Push the little red button I had glued onto my briefcase?

"Just go to the cockpit," I told her. "Stay there, and don't open the door again until you get to Reno. No matter what happens."

She looked at me a second — a standoff that seemed to last an hour. "No matter what?"

"No matter what, Lisa."

She turned, straightened her cap, and walked up the aisle in her high heels.

Before she was even out of sight I was trying to figure out how to tie a duffel bag of money around my waist. The last thing I wanted was for the money to blow away when I jumped. I found a roll of webbing in an overhead bin and strapped the bag on over my suit. My necktie was in the way, and it was just a stupid clip-on anyway, so I tore it off. Of course by then I'd forgotten that I'd tacked it in place with a mother-of-pearl tie clasp, so I ripped my shirt in the process. No matter. The money bag would serve as body armor against the storm outside.

Next were the parachutes. The Army chutes didn't have ripcords, so I tossed them aside. Instead I strapped on the two civilian skydiving chutes — the main case on my back and the reserve on my chest. Months later I would read in a newspaper article that the airline had inadvertently supplied me with a dummy reserve chute, used only for packing demonstrations. It wasn't able to open. I'm glad I didn't know that at the time.

Then there was the briefcase. Call me vain, but I didn't want the FBI to find out how cheesy my fake bomb had been. I untied the webbing on my money duffel, positioned the briefcase over my crotch as an additional layer of armor, and bundled myself back up again.

Now I could hardly walk. I checked my watch. We'd been in the air half an hour. At two hundred miles per hour, we had already flown a hundred miles. I needed to leave soon, or I would miss Portland altogether.

I staggered back to the tail of the plane, grabbed the "AFT STAIR EXIT" lever, and yanked.

A freezing gust of sleet knocked me onto my back. The roar of wind and jet engines blasted from a door-shaped hole in the tail. My ears popped and my head swam.

"Mr. Cooper?" The pilot's voice came on over the cabin speakers. "We've got a door warning light here, and there's been a fluctuation in cabin pressure. Is there anything we can do for you?"

"No!" I shouted. My hands were already getting cold. The wind was whipping snow back through the open hatch. When I sat up I could see the aft stairway descending into a void. There was no turning back.

I gripped the railing, pulled myself to my feet, and faced the darkness. Then I ran two steps and jumped headfirst into hell.

28

Connie jerked her head back, startled that the lights had suddenly come on.

Neil pulled out his service pistol. "Who's there?" The words echoed. Fluorescent tubes, spaced out along the brick walls, had lit the basement so brightly that he had to squint.

Connie drew her pistol cautiously. She crouched and crept back toward the entrance stairs. "Hello?"

A shoe scraped faintly on the metal landing at the top of stairs.

Neil motioned for Connie to stay back. Then he ran across the abandoned gift shop and flattened himself against the wall by the stairs. He took a breath, held the gun in both hands, and jumped to face the stairway.

"Freeze!"

Susan threw her hands in front of her face. "Papa!"

Neil lowered his weapon. "What are you doing here?"

"I work here, Papa."

"I know, but—" He ran out of words. It was rare for Neil to run out of words, and rarer still for his daughter to answer so quickly.

"You left the door unlocked," Susan said. "When you couldn't turn on the lights, I asked Dregs to help. He knows about wiring."

A sandy-haired man leaned into the doorway. "Hey, Dad. The circuit had been tripped. Don't shoot us, OK?"

Neil put his gun back in his holster. "You just happened to be here today?"

"Yeah, well it's Wednesday. Mind if Suzie and I come down for a look?"

"Yes, I do."

"Then get over it. You're not supposed to be here either. At least Suzie's an employee." Dregs clomped down the stairs.

Neil pressed his lips together to silence his anger.

Susan kept her eyes on her feet as she followed Dregs down the stairway. "They come every Monday and Wednesday at one o'clock."

It took Neil a moment to figure out what she meant. Twice a week the Recyclotron staff let homeless people take away returnable cans and bottles for the five-cent deposit. Today was Wednesday, and it must be almost one o'clock. It disturbed Neil to think that his daughter's boyfriend would line up to get a bag of old cans.

"Whoa, these dolls are hot." Dregs laughed at the bordello mannequins. "See? I knew you'd find poison."

Susan looked about the room and shook her head.

Dregs took her hand and pulled her toward the second basement room.

When they entered the old saloon, Neil was surprised to see Connie coming out of a narrow passageway at the far end of the room. She looked tired.

Connie surveyed the group. "Hi, Susan. This must be your friend."

"The name's Dregs." He didn't hold out a hand. "Are you a cop too?"

Connie nodded.

Neil asked, "What were you doing?"

"Covering your back." Connie sighed. "I heard a noise. When I went to check it out I thought I saw the shadow of a person."

"A shadow?"

"I know, another shadow. Trauma victims have to learn to deal with this kind of thing."

Meanwhile Dregs had picked up an empty bottle from the bar. He read the raised lettering on the side, "'Federal law prohibits reuse or resale of this bottle.' Hey, this one dates to Prohibition."

Then he noticed the beer bottles. "And look! Four whole cases of Blitz. When I was an undergrad I lived on that stuff. We called it 'vitamin B'. Too bad beer doesn't age like whiskey."

Neil looked around the room, taking a mental picture of the scene. Then he waved everyone back toward the stairs. "All right, we've been here long enough."

When they had all climbed the stairs to the Recyclotron room, he locked the door and put the key in his pocket. Susan was standing beside him, looking down.

"I did what you wanted," Neil told her. "I found out what's hidden in your closet."

"No, Papa."

"No what?"

"You didn't find it. Connie was right. There still is a shadow down there."

As soon as Neil and Connie had walked back to the police car, she asked him to take her home. With some embarrassment, Connie admitted that the lunch, the walk, and the fruitless investigation of the Underground had left her exhausted. She just wanted to sleep.

At her house in the Hawthorne district, she let Neil walk her up the steps to the door. "Tell the captain I'm going to need a few more days before I can go back on duty full time."

"Thanks for coming with me, Connie. A week ago, I was afraid you might never go back on duty."

She smiled. "You need someone to watch out for you, Lieutenant." Up close, the makeup could not hide the bruises and swelling on her jaw.

Neil remembered kissing her while standing on this same porch. Now he said, "Keep researching those sixty-seven Cooper candidates. I'm not ready to cross Mr. Ivan Oyster Bar off our list."

She pulled down the brim of her fedora. "Yes, sir."

Back in the black Buick, Neil felt cheap when he took out his cell phone and called Marial.

"Neil?" the Latvian librarian's voice poured from the tiny speaker like sherry into a glass. "I have someone here I think you should meet."

"Where are you?"

"At work. Have you forgotten? I do have a real job."

"So you're at the Midland branch library?"

"Mmm." She hummed a lovely affirmative sound. "Are you free this afternoon? You need to see this yourself."

"I've got a car. I'll be there in a few minutes, OK?"

"Drive safe, love."

He closed the phone, already worrying about driving back to the library where Cooper had run Connie down. When he put the car in gear, he forced back the fear. Ten minutes later he was in the library parking lot. He had opened the car door and stepped out before he remembered the pistol under his suit coat. A Glock semi-automatic didn't seem right for a library. He leaned back into the driver's seat and slipped his gun into the glove box. Then he locked the car and walked in through the building's sliding front doors. He didn't visit libraries often, and was half expecting the security gates to sound an alarm for some reason—because his card had expired years ago, or because he hadn't read a book for a month, or maybe just because he was a cop.

The building resembled an aircraft hangar filled with bookshelves and giant artworks. He passed a rack of DVDs and stopped at a reference desk. "Excuse me. I'm looking for—" he paused to get the pronunciation right—"Marial Greschyednyev."

"Children's department."

Neil followed her finger to a stage where a dozen kids sat cross-legged on mats beneath a swarm of salmon sculptures. Marial, sitting in an ordinary library chair, was holding the children's attention by reading a large picture book in a language Neil could not even faintly comprehend.

Marial raised her voice as if to ask a question, and the kids shouted back an unintelligible reply. Marial lowered her voice, and the kids clapped their hands. When she turned the last page, parents emerged from the stacks to thank her and gather their children.

"Neil," Marial waved him closer. "I want you to meet my friend Sonya. Sonya, this is Mr. Ferguson. He came to your father's funeral."

A black-haired four-year-old girl in a lavender dress looked up at him shyly.

Neil cleared his throat. "Hello, Sonya. Where's your mother?"

Marial answered for her. "Nadia Duvshenko is out looking to buy a new house. She left Sonya here with me for the afternoon."

"A new house? How exciting." Neil lowered himself to one knee. Interrogating a four year old might get him in trouble, but surely there was no harm in a friendly little chat. "I thought you lived in an apartment."

Sonya lifted her head. "We did, but now we're going to live in a house."

"Oh. That will be quite a change. How did that happen?"

"Well." Sonya tossed her hair. "Mr. Cooper is buying us a house."

"Mr. Cooper?"

"Yes."

"Have you seen him?"

She frowned. "No one ever sees Mr. Cooper. Besides, there are two of them."

"Two?" Neil asked.

"Yes. A good one and a bad one." The little girl paused. "Although I'm not sure about the difference."

"What have you been told?"

Sonya wrinkled her brow. "One of them is very bad. He took away my father. Another one is buying us a house, so he must be good. But then there's a different one too."

"A third one?"

"No, just a different one." Sonya shook her head. "No one's supposed to know about him at all. I think he's the magic one."

"I see." Neil nodded. He looked to Marial. "I think we've taken up enough of Sonya's time for one day."

"Sonya," Marial said, "You like the Big Bird game. Why don't you play on the computer until your mother comes back?"

"OK." Sonya bounced off toward a computer station.

When they were alone, Neil asked Marial, "What do you think?"

"Four year olds never lie, even when they're lying."

"What does that mean?"

"It means they like to play make-believe, but there's always truth underneath. If Sonya says there are two Coopers, there are."

"A good one and a bad one." Neil said.

"For her, it's like the tooth fairy," Marial said. "Sometimes Cooper takes things away and sometimes he gives you money. But you never see him."

Neil rubbed his eyes, thinking. He wanted to examine Nadia Duvshenko's bank account to see if large sums of money were appearing, and if so, where they were coming from. But that would be a direct violation of his orders to leave the Russian community alone. And he already could guess that the money's source would be disguised.

"I'll be off work in half an hour," Marial said, picking up picture books for reshelving. "If you get some take-out food I could show you my mausoleum. I've straightened things up for company."

"Marial—" Neil began, but then he looked down.

"Is everything all right?"

"I've got some questions. We need to talk."

"Well, you're not supposed to talk in a library. Go get some take-out and meet me at my house in an hour."

He sighed. It was hard to say no to Marial, and the worst part was that he didn't want to say no. He wanted to eat dinner at her house.

By the time Neil was standing outside the mausoleum's garage door with a paper bag full of Thai food, he had steeled himself to resist whatever seductive loungewear Marial might have chosen for the evening. But when the spray-painted metal door clattered up, she was standing there in ordinary blue jeans and an unassuming pink fleece hoodie.

She took the bag and looked inside. "Do we need to microwave anything?"

"No, it should be hot enough." He was a little disappointed. He had been looking forward to testing his resistance.

Marial pressed a button to lower the garage door. Then she pushed open the glass front door. "Would you like the grand tour?"

"Five stories of mortuary vaults?"

She laughed, bringing her dimple to life. "Most of the building is still abandoned. I couldn't figure out how to remodel unheated concrete boxes into anything useful. On the other hand, the foyer didn't need any work at all."

Almost everything in the foyer was purple—the plush carpet, the velvet wall drapes tied with velvet ropes, and the somber sofas with buttoned plush upholstery. Six-foot Doric pillars supported Greek urns with large green ferns.

The word that sprang to mind was funereal, but instead Neil said, "It's quieting."

She opened a paneled mahogany door. "I still use the old office as an office. The bathroom is still a bathroom. The consultation room became my bedroom." She breezed him past an office, where there was a computer, an easel, and a sewing machine. The bedroom was much more elegant, with a coffered wooden ceiling and a large canopy bed.

"But I spend most of my time in the old chapel." She pushed between a pair of swinging mahogany doors.

The gigantic room might have been the great hall of a medieval castle. Wrought iron chandeliers hung from the timbered peak of a thirty-foot ceiling. A wall of glass overlooked the Willamette River and the distant skyline of downtown Portland. A dining table stood where the altar might once have been. The choir on one side had been converted to an open kitchen with a wooden counter. The opposite wall had couches and bookshelves.

A little disturbed by the kind of wealth this room suggested, Neil set his bag of take-out food on the table. It was only then, when he turned around, that he realized the entire far wall of the room was occupied by a pipe organ. Ranks of silver tubes arched toward the ceiling.

"The organ was already here," Marial said. "For funerals."

"Do you play?" Neil asked.

"Not very well. But the mausoleum was too cheap to hire an organist, so they installed a player piano mechanism. Do you want to hear?"

"Sure."

She walked to the console and flipped a switch. Lights blinked on. There was a slow, wheezing whoosh of air. She typed a number onto a keypad. After a moment the organ began softly tooting a classical piece Neil didn't recognize.

"Bach's Goldberg Variations. Would you rather listen to Brahms' Requiem? Most of the repertoire is dirges, I'm afraid."

"No, no. This is fine."

"Then we should eat while the food's still warm." Marial set out plates, chopsticks, and tumblers of water. She opened the take-out boxes, lit a candle, and said, *"Erst kommt das Fressen, dann die Moral."*

"I'm sorry?"

"In America you would say, 'Dig in.'"

They ate. The rice noodles stuck together and the pad Thai was runny with coconut milk, but it didn't matter. As evening fell the sky pinkened and Portland's skyscrapers morphed into light-spangled silhouettes. The stained glass panels on either side of the main windows dimmed to black. When the pipe organ stopped, the candle between them flickered.

Marial touched his hand. The candlelight reflected in her glasses and made her red hair glow. "You wanted to talk?"

Neil sat back. "Yes." He glanced around at the pipe organ, the chandeliers, and the stained glass windows. "This is not the home of a part-time librarian."

"You don't think I really live here?"

"You obviously do, Marial, but you haven't told me everything about yourself."

"What do you want to know? You haven't asked much about me."

This was true. Neil should have talked with her before running a background check at headquarters. Still, he plowed ahead. "Your husband must have been a wealthy man. How much did you know about his business?"

Marial leaned back and sighed. "Too much. And not enough."

"What does that mean?"

"Let's be honest with each other, Neil. You're a detective. By now you must have heard the stories that my husband was a spy. That's not true."

"No?"

"He was a vodka importer. For business reasons, he had to do some favors for the Soviet government. They did favors for him in return. That was life in the USSR."

"The favors paid well," Neil said. "Do you know what he was asked to do?"

"From time to time someone at the Riga warehouse would put a sealed envelope in one of the vodka cases. When the envelopes arrived in Portland, Anatoly was supposed to drop them off behind a certain bench in Washington Park."

"He was a courier."

"He didn't want me to know. I found out because he was spending so much time trying to learn what had happened to the courier before him."

"Who was the courier before him?"

Marial pushed up her glasses. "You know as much about him as I do. The previous courier went missing on the evening before

Thanksgiving in 1971."

Neil shook his head to clear his thoughts. "You're suggesting that D.B. Cooper may have been a courier for the KGB?"

"Anatoly believed he was. I don't think Anatoly had proof until after the Soviet Union fell."

"What did he find out?"

"By 1993 some of the people who had worked for the KGB were willing to talk. One day Anatoly came home very excited. He said D.B. Cooper was still alive. He said he would know more after a meeting that weekend on the Oregon Coast."

"A chamber of commerce meeting?" Neil suggested. He knew her husband had died—or at least had gone missing—during a convention at a coastal resort in Yachats.

"Yes. I should have been more worried." She stacked the empty take-out boxes onto the plates and carried them to the counter. "Anatoly and I were very much in love. It was hard for him to keep secrets from me. By then Cooper had become an obsession for him."

Neil hesitated. "I'm told your husband was swept out to sea."

She closed her eyes. "My Anatoly was murdered. Someone killed him because he was getting too near the truth."

"His body was never found."

She took off her glasses, covered her face, and turned away.

Neil could tell she was crying. He wanted to hold her, to comfort her. But she was weeping for her husband, and Neil didn't feel he had the right to put his arms around her just now.

Finally she daubed her face with a cloth napkin. "I'm sorry."

"It's all right," he said. Whatever else Marial might believe, it was clear that she did not think her former husband might still be alive.

Marial filled a coffeepot with water from a sink. Her voice was a little shaky. "Anatoly had provided for me, so I didn't have to work. Still I promised myself to find out why he had died."

"What did you do?"

She managed a wry smile. "Who do you ask when you need to do research? You ask a librarian. Or, in my case, you become one."

"That's also why you signed up as a police translator, isn't it?"

She nodded. "I wanted to find the truth. I still do. It's not a conflict of interest, Neil. I'm on your side."

Neil wondered if seducing him had also been part of her plan, but he couldn't bring himself to ask. Instead he said, "And your volunteer work at the art museum?"

"No." She shrugged her left shoulder. "I've always done that. I like art."

He hadn't told her about the museum's missing paintings. Still, he wondered if her interest in the museum could be entirely coincidental. Although he had never actually caught her in a lie, she had not been very open with him either.

As if she had read his thoughts, she walked back to the table and stood there, hanging her head. She hadn't put her glasses back on, and half of her tied-up hair had come undone. "You must think I'm horrible."

"No," he said. Once again he wanted to put his arms around her. This time he wondered whether it would be for her consolation or his own. "As you said, I didn't ask about your past."

"But I should have told you. Now you won't trust me."

He hesitated. Had he ever entirely trusted her?

"Neil." She took his hands and held them together. "I want the same thing you want—the truth. I have never lied to you. Ever." She was so close now that the pink polar fleece brushed his fingers. "Especially when I told you how much I care about you."

Then she put her hands on his thinning gray hair, gently holding his head. He did not resist when she pulled his head against her.

For a moment he just closed his eyes. Her heart beat with a reassuring rhythm. The curves under the polar fleece felt wonderful.

Then he slowly pulled away from her. "Marial, I care about you too. But I need to go home now."

"Wait." Marial reached toward him. "I want you to go with me. To Russia."

"Russia?"

"Yes. For an auction. It's less than two weeks away."

"What auction?"

"An auction of Rothko paintings."

Neil stood up and studied her. "What have you been doing?"

She lowered her eyes. "I've been doing what you asked me to do. I've been watching the website where they sold the Gray Madonna. I found out that the same auction house in Novgorod is selling six oil paintings by Mark Rothko. Those paintings are supposed to be here in

Portland. I've seen them in exhibits. I knew at once they must be stolen, even if the museum hasn't reported the loss yet."

"They have." Neil had been ready to suspect her of subterfuge, but her explanation made sense. And if he was going to make much progress solving the theft, he would need a Russian translator. "We're not supposed to let the public know about the Rothko auction until we're sure they're originals."

Marial looked up. "Do you think the paintings could have been stolen by Cooper?"

Neil shrugged. "Which Cooper? A little girl told me today there are two Coopers, one bad and one good. The bad one kills people, but the good one has money. Both of them sound like suspects."

"The place to track them is in Russia. Tell me you'll come."

"I don't think so," Neil said. "I already have too much work to do here. And the department would never pay for a trip like that anyway."

"I'll pay. I'll get the visas. Once those paintings are sold, they're gone. We'll never get this chance again."

Neil held up his hands. "I'll think about it."

"Then think about this." Marial leaned in and gave him a kiss so passionate his head spun.

29

The next morning Neil lay in his bed, watching the numbers on his clock. There were so many things he should be doing, so many unfinished investigations. Curt Lammergeier had died two days ago, and Yosef Duvshenko six days earlier. Paintings worth millions were missing. Neil didn't have a solid suspect for any of these cases. He felt like he'd been racing all this time on an exercise bicycle, going nowhere.

When the red numbers jumped from 6:59 to 7:00, he threw off the covers angrily, pulled on his Lycra bicycle clothes, took the elevator to the basement, and rode his bike half a dozen miles out Skyline Boulevard.

But there were no answers in the hills that morning either. When he finally showed up at his office in a suit and tie, he was an hour late.

The answering machine on his phone was blinking. Captain Dickers wanted him in forensics. The thought of meeting his boss again soured the yoghurt Neil had shoveled down for breakfast.

When Neil walked down to forensics and opened the door, Luis Espada and the captain were standing around a table with a muscular, crewcut black man Neil didn't recognize.

"There he is at last," Dickers said, smiling at Neil. "Our famous investigator, Lieutenant Ferguson."

Neil was used to Dickers' taunts, but this time the captain almost sounded sincere.

The black man held out his hand. "Steve Owen, FBI. Let me shake your hand, Lieutenant. What you've done here is simply incredible."

Puzzled, Neil shook the man's hand. Owen had a grip that could crack bones. Then Neil saw the gray bag on the table, and he began to understand. "The parachute case. It's genuine?"

Espada nodded. "The label was unreadable, but that size and style of tag was used only in one skydiving shop near the Seattle airport, and only in 1971. Every chute they owned that year is accounted for, except for the two used in the skyjacking. The reserve chute was a front pack. This one held Cooper's main chute."

The crewcut FBI agent wouldn't let go of Neil's hand. "We've been hoping for a break like this for years. Cooper is one of the biggest unsolved cases on the books. We've tracked down more than a thousand false leads. There was John List, the guy who killed his family in Jersey just before the skyjacking. Then Duane Weber confessed on his deathbed that he was really Cooper. For a while we thought Cooper might really be Kenneth Christiansen, a baggage handler for Northwest Airlines. And then a woman in Oklahoma announced her uncle Lynn Cooper was the real skyjacker. All of them turned out to be frauds or hoaxes."

"But now we've got the actual parachute case," Dickers said.

The FBI agent nodded. "When I saw your report, Ferguson, everything fell into place."

"Everything?" Neil asked.

"An unemployed smokejumper." The agent punched his big fist at Neil's shoulder with respect. "A parachute specialist who needs money. That's exactly the profile our agents proposed back in the day. They just didn't think to look in Alaska."

Neil realized what the man saying. "You suspect The Keeper?"

"Even the name fits. People call him The Keeper, but his real name is DeKuyper." The agent chuckled. "In English, I'd pronounce that D. Cooper."

This stopped Neil for a moment. Why hadn't he noticed this similarity himself?

Dickers laid a photograph of The Keeper on the table next to the FBI's composite sketch of Dan Cooper from 1971. "With age progression and a beard, and without the sunglasses, it could be the same person."

"Slow down," Neil cautioned. "The homeless man we're talking about has been trying to tell people for years about Cooper."

"Reverse psychology," the agent said.

"He's an old man." Neil said. "He may have mixed things up a little, but I don't think he's Cooper. Besides, I may have corroboration for part of his story."

Captain Dickers looked up sharply. "You didn't mention that in your report."

"It was in my other report, the one about Lammergeier." Neil turned to the agent to explain. "We found a professor poisoned in a lake near here two days ago. No arrests yet."

"Yes, I've heard of the case. Is it connected?"

"Maybe. When I talked with Lammergeier's widow, she said he might have met Cooper the night after the skyjacking. Somehow Lammergeier figured out Cooper's true identity and confronted him on a bridge over the Willamette. This is all third hand, but she said Cooper escaped by diving into the river."

"Interesting." The agent frowned. "That would explain why some of the money turned up on the riverbank later."

Dickers asked Neil, "Any leads yet on the Lammergeier poisoning?"

Neil shook his head. "Not many."

But the FBI agent had put his finger on The Keeper's photograph. "I've got a suspect for you right here."

Dickers latched onto this. "DeKuyper? Why?"

"Because I think he really is Dan Cooper. If the professor met him on a bridge in 1971, then the professor was a witness who could identify him. DeKuyper killed the professor to shut him up."

Neil wasn't so sure The Keeper was the kind of person who would track down and poison someone after forty years. But what did he really know? The only certainty seemed to be the identification of Cooper's parachute pack.

"This is a federal case now," the FBI man said. "I'm going to ask the U.S. marshal to let me take command. The statute of limitations may have run out on the skyjacking charge, but it never runs out on murder."

Captain Dickers nodded. "I want this solved. I can give you clearance to take charge immediately."

"Done." The agent picked up the photograph. "First priority: Bring DeKuyper in for questioning. Captain, can you get me some patrol cars?"

"Give me twenty minutes."

"Good." He turned to Neil. "Lieutenant, you've done excellent work so far. Do you know where to look for DeKuyper?"

Neil nodded uncertainly.

"Then let's go."

On the way to the basement garage Neil learned that Steve Owen had spent four years running intelligence operations during the war in Iraq. After mustering out of the Army, he had trained for the FBI. It seemed to Neil that Owen organized the search for The Keeper with as little subtlety as a counter-insurgency patrol in the Middle East. Blue lights flashed as their column of five police cars cruised along the Naito Parkway, slowing to check every shabbily dressed old man in Waterfront Park.

At the Burnside Bridge, Neil pointed to a cluster of men sharing a wine bottle. "There he is, on the fountain steps."

Owen unhooked a microphone from the dash. "This is the FBI." His voice boomed through the bridge's girders. "Stay where you are. Put your hands in the air."

"Take it easy, Owen," Neil objected. "They're just homeless men."

The FBI agent clacked the ammunition clip into his pistol. "One of those bums may be a skyjacker and a killer, Lieutenant. Let's bring him in."

Reluctantly, Neil followed the armed policemen toward the men at the fountain. To Neil's dismay, one of the men with the Keeper was Dregs.

The scar-faced Ph.D. shook his head at Neil. "*Et tu*, Brute?"

"Look, Dregs, this wasn't my idea."

"You're just going along for the ride, Dad?"

Neil couldn't countermand a special agent of the FBI. Instead he said, "We found out the parachute case is genuine. It really is the one used by D.B. Cooper."

The Keeper held up his hands. "That's what I've been telling everyone. Now you believe me?"

A television crew was hurrying along the sidewalk with a camera and a fuzzy boom microphone. Neil wondered how they could have known to be here at just this moment.

The FBI agent demanded, "Are you Gregor DuKuyper?"

The old man dropped the wine bottle. His mouth was a red O in the midst of a great white beard. "I didn't do anything. I've never stolen nothing, at least not anything important. I'm just—I'm just—don't take me away."

Special agent Steve Owen took out a pair of handcuffs, snapped them over the old man's wrists, and announced, "Mr. D. Cooper, in the name of the FBI, I hereby arrest you on charges of hijacking and murder."

That clip played on the evening news throughout the nation.

Neil walked away from the scene of the arrest, leaving others to book The Keeper and brag to the cameras. Owen had said they were only going to bring The Keeper in for questioning. It didn't seem to Neil that they had enough evidence for an arrest. Maybe the FBI agent knew more than he let on.

On the way back to his office Neil paused in the door of the Lotus Cafe, testing the pull of its alcoholic gravity. The TV screen over the bar repeated, "Mr. D. Cooper, in the name of the FBI, I hereby arrest you—."

Neil turned away, went back to his office, and clicked angrily on his computer's email button. He wanted to think about something else. But he hadn't really wanted to think about Grenada.

"Greetings, Honorable Lieutenant Ferguson," the email began. This part had sounded so much like a Nigerian lottery scam that Neil nearly clicked past it.

"Your request for information pertaining to a sailboat belonging to Lt. Credence Lavelle is duly recognized. This boat drifted ashore on Grand Anse Beach at approximately 7 a.m. today. No one was on board, but a large Irish setter dog has been recovered. The boat is damaged by surf. We are towing it to the St. George dock near the Royal Police Station. Please advise."

Neil held his hands over his face. How many blows could he take in one day?

He walked to Captain Dickers' office. Through the open door, he saw the young captain at his computer, watching news reports about the capture of D.B. Cooper. Neil knew at once who had alerted the camera crews about the arrest at the Burnside Bridge.

"Ferguson?" The captain grinned. "I'll admit, I doubted you, but you're golden. I gave you the old D.B. Cooper case as a joke, and you got us our first big break."

"The case isn't solved yet, sir," Neil said. "I've got bad news."

"What do you mean?"

"It's about Lieutenant Credence Lavelle."

"Our famous Credence." Then the captain's expression clouded. "Bad news, you say?"

"Yes, sir. I think she's dead."

Dickers studied Neil a moment, twisting a ballpoint pen in his fingers. "Lieutenant Lavelle is retired. She's sailing a boat in the Caribbean."

"Yes, sir. Her sailboat washed ashore this morning on a beach in Grenada. Her dog was still on board, but she wasn't."

"What are you saying?"

"It could be an accident. People can fall off of sailboats. But foul play might also be involved. I think she made some enemies while working on the Underground murders."

Captain Dickers set down his pen. "What do the authorities in the Caribbean say?"

"The Royal Police of Grenada sent an email asking our advice. They've towed the boat to their dock. I thought I should report to you before calling them back."

"This is not good. Lieutenant Lavelle was one of our own."

Neil could almost see the wheels turning in the captain's head: We need to find out what happened to "one of our own". The Cooper and Lammergeier cases seem to be solving themselves. And wouldn't it be lovely if the troublesome Lieutenant Ferguson went far away?

"Ferguson," the captain said, "I'd like you to go to the Caribbean."

"Sir?"

"I know it's a big trip, but Lavelle is important. I want you to find out what happened. Fortunately, we've got agent Owen here covering for you. We're getting close to locking up the Cooper thing. So what do you think?"

"You want me to fly to Grenada?"

"Tough assignment, huh?" Dickers winked. "Neil, you've done some good work after all. You deserve a few days away."

30

Three hours beyond Miami, Neil's flight tilted around a jungly, mountainous island in a blue-green sea. Pastel buildings with red roofs careened about a horseshoe-shaped harbor. Then the long asphalt runway of Maurice Bishop International Airport rose up to meet the wheels.

According to the in-flight magazine, this was the same airport where five hundred U.S. Army Rangers had parachuted in 1983. President Reagan had authorized the invasion of Grenada because the island nation's president, Maurice Bishop, had been killed in a coup by Communist hard-liners.

Neil worried that he might be dropping into trouble as well. The Grenada police had not wanted to discuss the case further by email or telephone.

Neil yanked his carry-on bag from the overhead bin, made his way to the front of the cabin, nodded good-bye to the smiling flight attendant, and stepped out into a bright wall of heat. He descended a metal stairway and joined a line of passengers crossing the shimmering asphalt. Beside the terminal door, a very black man in a blindingly white uniform was holding a piece of paper with the felt pen lettering, "Ferguson."

"I'm Lieutenant Ferguson," Neil said.

"Constable DePuis." The officer clicked his heels. "Do you have other baggage?"

"Just this."

"Then come with me." He led Neil around the terminal building to a white sedan. A coat of arms on the car's door depicted a red armadillo and a blue parrot holding up a shield.

Only after they were driving out of the airport—on the left-hand side of the road—did the constable speak again. "Forgive me for not telling you more before your arrival. Our government is very concerned about anything that could frighten tourists. Since the hurricanes destroyed our nutmeg plantations, tourism is pretty much our only industry."

"You still haven't found Lieutenant Lavelle?"

"No. It is unusual in these cases not to hear by now." The constable had a British accent with a Caribbean lilt.

"Hear what?"

"A ransom demand, of course." The officer glanced to Neil.

"Then you suspect she was taken hostage?"

"It is always our worst fear. Even a rumor of piracy would make yachters avoid our island." He adjusted his white officer's cap. "Now I will take you to your hotel."

"I'm not that tired yet. I was hoping we could go to your police station and look at the sailboat."

The constable shook his head. "Slow down, Lieutenant. In Grenada, no one hurries. I will pick you up tomorrow at ten o'clock. By then, we should have either a body or a ransom request. Either way, there is nothing you can do but wait."

There was no arguing with the constable. He dropped Neil off at a pink concrete hotel where cantilevered balconies overlooked a mile-long beach of orange sand.

Neil checked in, changed out of his sticky suit, showered, and came back down to the lobby in slacks and a white shirt with rolled-up sleeves. He found a local newspaper on a table beneath a potted palm. It had no mention of a stranded sailboat. Likewise, the desk clerk claimed not to have heard of a missing sailor.

"But you're not too late for the oil-down on the beach," the clerk told him. "Would you like some thongs?"

"I'm sorry?" Neil replied.

"Thongs for the oil-down. They're complimentary. We want our guests to be comfortable." The man held up a pair of sandals.

"You mean flip-flops?" Neil asked.

"We call them thongs."

Neil took the shoes. "And what's an oil-down?"

"A specialty of the island. It's traditional at beach gatherings. There is a charge of twenty East Caribbean dollars, but I can put it on your tab." He pointed to a crowd of sunburned tourists on a patio between a swimming pool and the beach.

Neil went outside to investigate. He was a little disappointed to discover that an oil-down is a picnic stew. A chef had filled a cauldron with coconut milk, pigs tails, salt beef, chicken, green bananas, yams, dumplings, and breadfruit. As the hotel guests stood around in the sand, watching and sipping fruit drinks, the stew boiled down until the coconut milk was absorbed by the other ingredients, leaving a puddle of coconut oil at the bottom.

After eating a bowl of the tropical goulash, Neil walked the length of the beach in his flip-flops and watched the sun set into the drooping green leaves of a banana tree. He was starting to think Grenada's unhurried lifestyle might be just what he needed to calm his nerves.

But then he went back to his room and turned on CNN. Like a bad memory, the video clip was back, showing the ring of policemen closing in on the homeless men beside a fountain. Yet again the special agent said, "Mr. D. Cooper, in the name of the FBI, I hereby arrest you on charges of hijacking and murder."

The television cut to an anchorman with a red tie. "After more than forty years, the FBI may be about to close the books on the nation's only unsolved skyjacking case. Yesterday law enforcement officers apprehended a suspect with the actual parachute pack used in the crime. For today's developments, we go now to our correspondent Angela Flint in Portland, Oregon. Angela?"

"Thank you, Marcus." A woman with a blonde bob and lots of makeup was standing in front of the post-modern Portland building by City Hall. Behind her, a two-story copper statue of Portlandia reached out toward the camera, trident in hand.

"At a press conference today, Portland police chief John Dickers explained why the hijacking suspect has been charged with murder. This was not clear yesterday, because murder was not part of the hijacking in 1971. None of the hostages were harmed when D.B. Cooper parachuted out of an airplane with $200,000. But earlier this week police found a body floating in a lake in a Portland park. They now believe the dead man, a retired college professor, may have been a witness to the 1971 crime."

The scene switched to Captain Dickers, wearing his dress uniform. Neil covered his eyes and sighed, but he kept listening.

"In a police lineup today, one of the volunteers at the Crystal Springs Rhododendron Garden identified our suspect, Gregor DeKuyper, as the man he had seen at the park on the day of Professor Lammergeier's death. If the professor was able to identify DeKuyper as the skyjacker from 1971, as we believe, then DeKuyper had both the motive and the opportunity for murder."

The reporter's voice added, "The statute of limitations has run out on the original hijacking, but this new charge could allow authorities to put DeKuyper behind bars. Back to you, Marcus."

The anchorman asked, "You mean it's possible to steal $200,000 and get off scot-free?"

"Apparently yes, if they don't catch you for twenty-five years. But it doesn't work once you start killing witnesses. There is no statute of limitations on murder."

Neil zapped the TV silent and went out to his balcony. Constellations he did not recognize shimmered in the warm sky. He closed his eyes. At least the roar of the ocean was a sound he understood.

When Constable DePuis drove up to the hotel the next morning, he seemed unaware that he was half an hour late. "Good morning. Did you sleep well?"

"Fine. Have you heard anything about Lieutenant Lavelle?"

"Slow down. I have good news. Get in."

Neil got in. "She's alive?"

"Probably not." DePuis rolled his hand in the air. "The good news is that I have decided pirates are not involved."

Neil sank back.

"Think about it," the constable continued. "They did not take the sailboat. There still is no ransom demand. I am beginning to feel confident that this is not about pirates."

"Then what happened to her?"

DePuis steered the car to the left around a traffic circle. "Probably suicide. You say she had just retired. She was alone. Was she depressed?"

"I don't think so. She'd just gotten a million-dollar contract to write a book."

"Then most likely she drank too much rum and fell off in rough seas. This happens when tourists underestimate our waves—and our rum."

"Wouldn't her body have washed ashore by now? The sailboat did."

"Sailboats drift with the wind. Bodies drift with the water. They're slower. And then of course there are the sharks."

"Oh." Neil didn't want to think about sharks.

"That doesn't mean we won't find her, Lieutenant. Sharks don't like human flesh, so they just take bites. We get a lot of feet washing ashore, usually still inside the shoes. A few heads."

The constable parked at a stone seawall beside a palm-lined harbor. Women with bandannas over their hair were selling fish from carts under brightly colored awnings. Across the street, a police station in a yellow French colonial building broke up a row of two-story warehouses.

"So Lieutenant, now you are here. What would you like to see first? My office or the sailboat?"

"The sailboat."

"Very well." The constable unlocked a chain-link gate and led Neil out a concrete dock past a police speedboat and a Coast Guard cutter. At first glance Lavelle's sailboat looked salvageable—other than the aluminum mast, which had been bent over the cabin. The white fiberglass hull was scuffed but intact. But then he saw the deck's floorboards were buckled, the windows broken, and the railings twisted.

"How long was it in the surf?" Neil asked.

"Less than an hour, but waves can wreck a light boat fast. It washed up on a popular beach yesterday at seven in the morning. We don't like to alarm our country's guests, so we removed it quickly."

"People saw the boat as it came ashore?"

The constable nodded. "Not many beachcombers were out that early. One went to call us. Several others stayed to watch. There was no looting, and no one came ashore from the boat. Other than the dog, of course."

"Bingo," Neil said.

"Pardon me, Lieutenant?"

"The dog's name is Bingo. Where is he now?"

The constable hesitated. "My wife took him home. He's a very friendly dog. We've gotten to like him. I suppose you'll want him back."

"Maybe." Neil thought Bingo was likely to stay in Grenada. He was glad the dog was in good hands for now. "Can I go on board the ship?"

"Of course. Be careful, there's still water in the cabin."

Neil stepped onto the deck, tilting the boat. Through a cracked window he could see debris floating in knee-deep water inside the cabin. If Lavelle had been the victim of foul play, there would be little hope of finding fingerprints or DNA evidence of an intruder. The entire boat had been washed by the surf. Neil walked around the edge of the boat, avoiding gaps in the mahogany floorboards. He knelt on the front deck to examine a cut rope.

"I'm not a sailor," Neil said. "Can you tell me what this rope was used for?"

"I wondered about that too," DePuis replied. "That's where you usually keep the anchor."

Neil looked at him steadily. "You didn't find an anchor on the boat?"

The constable thought about this for a moment. "So that's why we haven't found a body. It was tied to the anchor and thrown overboard." He frowned. "Bloody hell. That means it was pirates after all. They botched the attack and killed her by mistake."

"Would pirates bother to hide her body? Wouldn't they just leave her?"

The constable frowned. "True. Then who was it?"

"I think it was someone worse." Neil took off his shoes and rolled up his pants. "Did you find a computer on board? Maybe a laptop?"

DePuis shook his head. "No. Why?"

"Lieutenant Lavelle was writing a book. Could her computer have washed overboard in the surf?"

"I don't think so. The cabin door was closed. The windows are cracked, so water leaked in, but nothing could have washed away. "

Neil unlatched the cabin door, pushed it open, and sloshed down the steps. In Oregon he was used to cold seawater, but this felt like a bath. Plastic dishes, bags, and towels floated from side to side as the cabin rocked. He waded past a kitchen table, checking each of the cupboards. Beyond was a bench that doubled as a bed. He lifted it to look underneath. The bathroom was full of floating plastic bottles. Finally at the bow he found her office. The desk faced straight ahead to the broken windows of the prow. Pinned to corkboards on the tilted walls to either side were photos of Credence with talk show hosts, with Captain Dickers, with her dog, and with a million-dollar check.

The desktop was empty. The computer, notes, letters, and trash one might expect at a writer's desk were gone. There was no printer, although the cables remained. What had she been writing that was so dangerous it could provoke murder?

Then Neil remembered his own desk in Portland. Lieutenant Lavelle had left him a key to the Underground at the back of the top drawer. The memory gave him an idea. He yanked on the drawer beneath the desktop. It wouldn't budge. There was no keyhole. How was it locked? He rattled it harder.

Behind him the constable was clicking his tongue. "Easy, Lieutenant. No one wants drawers on sailboats to slide out fast. Things would fall out with every wave. You have to lift the drawer before pulling."

Neil lifted the drawer and pulled. It held the usual array of pens and rubber bands. He yanked the drawer loose and set it on the desktop. Taped to the back of the drawer was a small plastic device, the size of a pack of gum. A thumb drive.

He pulled it loose and held it up to the constable. "This is why they killed her."

"Who?"

"I don't know."

DePuis looked at the device in Neil's hand. "What do you think is on it?"

Neil examined the memory device. There was no label. "Do you have a computer that can read it?"

"Perhaps, in my office."

"Then let's go." Neil climbed up from the cabin. He wiped off his feet and put on his shoes.

As they walked back along the dock, the constable asked, "Was Lieutenant Lavelle in trouble?"

"She solved a series of murders in the United States. The killer committed suicide by hanging himself."

"Usually that would eliminate the trouble."

"Usually, yes. But I'm beginning to think she didn't really solve the crime. The real killer may still be loose."

"Ah." The constable nodded as they walked across the harbor road to the police station. "So often, the troubles we see here in Grenada come from somewhere else."

The lobby of the police station was a bare, high-ceilinged room with glazed tile floors and peeling tan paint. DePuis led Neil back to an office with fluorescent lights and desks. A small green lizard scurried across the wall.

"Let's see if we can salvage the data," DePuis said, inserting the memory stick into a slot on his desktop computer. He clicked his mouse a few times, waited a moment, and then said, "The Underground murders? That's rather different than murder on the high seas."

Neil pulled up a chair. "May I?" He took the mouse and scrolled through the manuscript. Of the thirteen chapters in the book, twelve appeared to be complete. A glance through them revealed that they chronicled Lavelle's investigation. She described how she had tracked the missing people to the bus and light rail lines where they had been given "grand prize" coupons for the Underground tour. The thirteenth chapter, "Tightening the Noose", was a fragment. It read:

"Before you read this final chapter, I should warn you that I am not entirely free of doubt. Thomas Daugherty was a mortician. He was an unlikable worm. He had surely lured these five people to their deaths in the Underground. Morticians know how to deal with death, after the fact. They are experts in the deceased. But rarely are they killers. Worms usually follow the true murderers. The day I retired, I left a key to the Underground where my successor could find it. Why? I'm not sure. Think of it as a safety valve. An escape, in case there are more bones to be unearthed than I have yet discovered. Success has made me lonely and suspicious. I am able to sail the warm seas of the Caribbean with my beloved Irish setter, Bingo. But I fear that no crime is ever fully solved. The culprit lies too deep within us. We are all D.B. Cooper, the mastermind who can never be caught."

31

Dan Cooper's Last Will and Testament, Part 7

Welcome to hell.

I had jumped into a sub-zero snowstorm on a November night at ten thousand feet without knowing where I was.

What I did know, with reasonable certainty, was that Air Force fighter jets would be trailing us. No one had ever commandeered a commercial airliner before. The U.S. military would be watching.

As long as my parachute remained unopened, they couldn't see me. A man falling through a blizzard is invisible in a storm cloud at night, even with radar. I aimed headfirst with my arms to my side, dropping like a meteor. The cold was astonishing. I could feel my skin freezing. I counted out loud, one-one-thousand, two-one-thousand, estimating that I had to wait through thirty seconds of agony before I could pull my ripcord. I needed to drop out of radar range. My whole plan hinged on disappearing completely.

It's strange, but in those moments I thought of Lisa, the glossy-lipped flight attendant. She was still in the cockpit with the pilots, unaware that I was no longer on board. She could open the door to check, but I knew she wouldn't. I had gotten to know Lisa, and I trusted her. When the plane finally taxied to a halt in Reno, she would be surprised that the aft staircase was scraping sparks across the runway. Federal marshals would surround the plane. Only then would she realize that I was gone, and that the first skyjacker in U.S. history had vanished into thin air.

When my count got to twenty, my fear swelled to outright panic.

Had I really jumped at ten thousand feet? I had told the flight engineer to stay *below* that elevation. And how high was the ground here? Mt. St. Helens was practically on our flight path, and it was over nine thousand feet tall. I was still in a cloud, but the freezing snow was turning into a warmer, low-elevation rain.

I grabbed frantically at the wire loop of the ripcord on my shoulder strap. The loop was covered with ice. My fingers were too cold to grip. Seconds ticked by as I struggled to bend my fingers around the ripcord. I was plummeting at terminal velocity, too scared to think.

Finally I managed to jam a thumb through the loop and pull.

Wham! The chute yanked me back with the force of a car wreck. I didn't have a helmet, so my head whiplashed onto the chest pack. The blow was so painful I was afraid I had broken my neck. But then the roar of the wind ebbed and I was rocking in the familiar cradle of parachute straps. I turned my head and looked down at a ghostly, polka-dot hillside. No trees. I just had time to crook my legs for the blow. I rolled as I hit, downhill through dirt and wet branches. Then all was quiet.

I lay there a moment, in the dark, in the cold drizzle, marveling that I was not yet dead. I had no idea where I was, but that was the best part. If I didn't know, then neither would the people pursuing me. Including my former best friend, and now worst enemy, Vasiliy Swarovsky.

I staggered to my feet and began unstrapping my backpacks, money bag, and briefcase. Even at night, the dim white circles on this hillside told me that I had landed in a clearcut where trees had recently been logged. Loose branches and duff had cushioned my fall. Fortunately I had not hit one of the stumps.

I gathered up the parachute, cut it loose from the backpack with my pocketknife, and stuffed it under a big pile of branches. In the spring, when the logging crews returned, they would burn the slash piles to clear the way for tree planters. After a moment's thought, I stuffed my reserve chute and the briefcase with the fake bomb under the branch pile as well. Let it all burn.

What remained was the main parachute backpack and the duffel full of money. I needed to travel light. I had to be back in Portland within twenty-four hours. But now I was shivering from the cold and the fear. My clothes were stiff with ice. Soon they would be soaked through. I could hardly feel my fingers. I was running on adrenaline. Where should I run?

The obvious choice was downhill. It was the easiest way, and would take me to a creek that must eventually lead to the Columbia River. But I decided it was the wrong choice. Clearcuts are not logged downhill. Cables pull the tree trunks up to a landing with road access. So I set out uphill, fighting my way through loose branches and ferns.

Half an hour later, exhausted, I stumbled out onto a gravel flat full of mud puddles. The loggers had left a caretaker's trailer here, with no caretaker. I jimmied the door with my pocketknife—a technique I had learned from Swarovsky. Then I lit the propane heater, took off my wet clothes, crawled into a sleeping bag, and flew from a world of nightmares to a land of dreams.

In the morning the storm had lifted. My clothes were nearly dry. My neck hurt and I was hungry, but I had $200,000 in cash and I wasn't dead yet.

I put on my damp suit and ate a box of cold Pop Tarts the caretaker had left. I tried to stuff the duffel of money into my backpack, but it wouldn't fit. So I put on the empty backpack, grabbed the duffel, and set out down the gravel logging road.

The logging roads of the Pacific Northwest are mostly unmarked, and dangerously confusing. By keeping downhill at every junction for six miles I managed to find a paved road along a river. The only sign pointed the way I had come. It read, "10-30.2", which didn't help. I turned left, following the paved road downriver. Gravel driveways on either side of the road led to rundown houses with junk cars. When a pickup truck whined toward me on the pavement I ducked off the road into the brush. After another mile I could hear the roar of a freeway. An on-ramp sign announced Interstate 5. If you're a fugitive, I-5 is both alluring and frightening. It's the magic carpet of the West, but it's also where police look first. By now the morning newspaper headlines would be screaming about my escape. I had to change personas, and I couldn't use I-5.

By crawling through the brush along the river I managed to make my way beneath the twin freeway bridges without being seen. Then I scrambled under a railroad bridge on the far side of I-5.

When I emerged at a railroad freight yard, however, I was suddenly confronted by a young man in a khaki uniform. He stood in front of a string of boxcars, glowering at me with his arms crossed.

I thought: This is it. After all I've been through, I am going to be arrested by a Forest Service ranger.

"Who are you?" he demanded.

It was time for a new identity, and quick. "McGill?" I suggested. "I've been looking for the skyjacker."

He cocked his head, looking at my backpack suspiciously. "What's a skyjacker?"

"You haven't heard?" I nearly laughed with relief. Then I held out my hand. "McGill's the name. What's yours?"

"It's hard to pronounce right." The young man seemed a little embarrassed, but he shook my hand. "People just call me The Keeper."

32

When Neil returned to PDX he expected to see someone from the Portland police waiting for him in the airport lobby. He was surprised that it was Sergeant Wu.

"Connie! Back on duty?" Less than two weeks after her run-in with Cooper, her bruises seemed to be gone. She wore gloves to hide the damage to her hands, and she had tipped her cap jauntily to one side to cover the damage to her scalp. Still, either her injuries had been less severe than Neil had thought, or she had willed herself well.

"Part-time. Sitting at home is just too boring when we've got a killer to catch. Did you bring me anything from the sunny Caribbean?"

"Actually, I did." Neil wheeled his carryon bag past the concourse shops. When they reached a quieter part of the terminal he spoke in a low voice. "You know what the native girls were wearing on the beach?'

She looked at him skeptically. "No."

"The women say it's a lot easier to go through airport security when you wear them, so I got you a couple." He unzipped his carryon bag and held out a pair of beach sandals from the hotel.

"Flip-flops?"

"What did you think I'd bring you? Thongs?"

"Neil, you really are an asshole."

"But in a good way, right?"

She sighed. "Let's get you back to headquarters. Everyone wants to know what's going on with Lieutenant Lavelle."

"They won't like what I'm bringing them either."

He followed Connie across the street to the parking garage. A cold drizzle sagged from a cold sky in shades of gray. Brightly colored "Synergy" banners on the light poles advertised the upcoming energy summit, but they hung limp and wet. Above logos of Portland and NovoCity, a picture of a blue-green Earth had been digitally altered to make the planet's clouds resemble a sassy smile with sunglasses. The image reminded Neil of a cross between the California Raisins and Joe Camel.

Once they were on the freeway Connie asked, "So is Lavelle really dead?"

Neil looked out the side window. "She wasn't on board when her boat drifted ashore. Her computer and all her notes were missing. And the anchor."

"The anchor was gone?"

He nodded. "Someone didn't want her to finish her book."

"What's so dangerous about a book?" Connie changed lanes, trying to escape the slowest traffic on the Banfield.

"I found a thumb drive taped to the back of Lavelle's desk drawer. It had the first twelve and a half chapters. She was starting to doubt that she'd found the real killer. We're going to have to reopen the case."

"The Underground murders? Well why not?" Connie threw up one gloved hand in mock celebration. "What's five more unexplained deaths? We're already investigating two murders, an art theft, and a forty-year-old skyjacking."

"I thought Special Agent Owen had taken that off our hands."

Connie pulled off the freeway and looped over the Morrison Street bridge to downtown. "I don't want to spoil Captain Dickers' surprise for you, but the FBI isn't having as much fun with the D.B. Cooper case as they'd hoped."

Neil thought a moment. "I'm glad."

Ranah, the receptionist, waved Neil over as soon as he and Connie walked in the door. "Lieutenant Ferguson?"

"Let me guess. Captain Dickers wants to see me."

Ranah smiled patiently. "Yes, but he's in a meeting until five. He apologizes, and asks if you could see him then."

"Sure." Neil looked at his watch. It was 3:30.

Connie suggested, "Time enough to write up your report?"

"We've got more important work." He pushed through the door to the hall. When they were riding the elevator up to his office, he explained. "We've got to find a crack in the Underground murder case."

"What, are you nuts?"

"I know Dickers. If we don't have more than Lavelle's vague suspicions, he's going to keep that case sealed. He won't let us touch it."

Connie nodded slowly. "He calls her Credence Clearthinker. Solving the Underground murders was big for Lavelle, but it was huge for Dickers too."

"Reopening the case wouldn't be just admitting a mistake. It would be a public relations nightmare. Can you imagine telling the press that the Underground serial killer may still be loose?"

Connie whistled.

"Officially, Lavelle's still a missing person, not a homicide victim," Neil said. "Dickers is going to want to keep it that way."

"Where do we start?"

The elevator door opened.

"With the other victims." Neil walked to his office, logged onto his desktop computer, and opened the archived file of Lavelle's old reports. "We know a lot about the people who were strangled in the Underground."

"Five very different people," Connie said.

"Six, counting Tony Daugherty."

"I thought he hanged himself. You showed me the lamp where the rope was tied."

"And you didn't like it. Neither did Lavelle. It's an awkward way to kill yourself. A mortician wouldn't do it."

"You're thinking he had help?"

Neil nodded. "Even the coroner wouldn't have noticed if Daugherty had been strangled before he was put in the noose. The rope marks would look the same."

"If someone else killed Daugherty, he didn't leave any clues."

"The victims are the clues." Neil scrolled down the computer screen. Lavelle's report had a chart with statistics about the five people who had been lured into the Underground with 'grand prize' coupons.

Mark Kellman, 25, single, Apple computer repair technician, Tigard

Louise Callahan, 42, divorced, Wellcare assisted living nurse,
Gresham
Dominic Murphy, 63, married, lawyer for Mason & Barney,
NW Portland
Fyodor Milovich, 32, single, Clark College flight technician
student, Vancouver
Martin Blodgett, 47, single, Erratic Vineyards manager,
McMinnville

"They're mostly men," Connie noted.

"Yes, and there's one with a Russian-sounding name. What does it mean that Fyodor Milovich was studying to be a flight technician?"

"I think it's an airplane maintenance program."

Neil nodded. "Sort of like the Ukrainian car repairmen. But Fyodor struck off on his own. That suggests a connection to the Duvshenko killing."

"Possibly."

For the next thirty minutes they checked. Milovich was indeed a Russian immigrant, but he came from a city near Moscow, claimed no religious affiliation, and apparently had nothing to do with the people in the Duvshenko case. His girlfriend said he was fascinated with ghosts and Halloween parties, so he had been excited to win a private Underground tour. She had found the whole idea creepy, and had stayed home.

"We only have an hour left," Neil said. "Let's go back and start at the top of the list."

Mark Kellman had a long record of traffic violations—speeding, parking tickets, running red lights. He had lost his license after causing an accident, and had ended up taking the bus to work. One morning he had been handed a grand prize ticket on the bus. That evening he took the Underground tour and never came back.

Louise Callahan had been through a messy divorce. Her ex got the car and was so distraught he wrecked it. Meanwhile she rode the MAX train to the assisted care facility where she worked in North Portland.

"Why would a woman like her want to go on an Underground tour?" Connie asked. "She sounds too busy for foolishness."

"The grand prize included a hundred bucks in cash. She probably needed the money."

"Still, she wouldn't go on a private tour with a man she doesn't know." Connie scrolled through pages of information about Louise Callahan, but could not find anything more to explain the woman's actions.

"If you think that's odd, take a look at Dominic Murphy," Neil said. "He's a 63-year-old lawyer with a BMW. While his Beemer's getting a ten-thousand-mile checkup he rides the streetcar to a Starbucks in the Pearl District. A stranger on board gives him a grand prize ticket. Murphy doesn't need the money, but for some reason he still walks over to take the Underground tour."

"Maybe he was interested in history?" Connie suggested.

"I'd like to know what legal cases he was working on."

Neil and Connie tried to find out more about Murphy's work as a lawyer, but they kept running up against confidentiality firewalls.

They gave up on the lawyer and turned to the fifth victim, Martin Blodgett. Time was short.

Blodgett had driven from McMinnville to the Sunset transfer center in Beaverton. He had left his car there and taken MAX downtown. In his pocket he had a thirty-percent-off coupon for a luggage sale at Pioneer Place. But when he was handed a grand prize ticket on the train along the way, he suddenly skipped his shopping and went straight to the Underground. He was never seen alive again.

"Wait a minute," Neil said. "If the operator of the Underground tour gave Blodgett a grand prize ticket on the train, and Blodgett went straight there, who led the tour?"

"Apparently they walked to the Underground together."

Neil shook his head. "None of the five victims had a compelling reason to drop what they were doing and go on a tour. Why'd they do it?"

"If they were targeted, they'd have something in common."

"But they don't. They're different ages. They had different professions. There doesn't seem to be a motive for killing any of them. We can't reopen the case unless we find a motive for at least one."

"Maybe Lavelle was right." Connie sighed. "What the victims have in common is that they all rode public transportation."

Neil frowned at the wall clock. Four thirty. Then he looked back at the list. "If someone killed Lavelle, you can be sure the Underground murders weren't random."

The word made him stop. Random. Erratic.

"What kind of a name is Erratic Vineyards?"

"The place where Blodgett worked?" Connie asked. "I think it's named for the erratic rock."

"What's an erratic rock?"

"It's a rock that's out of place. In Oregon, they're mostly Canadian rocks that floated south on icebergs in big floods during the Ice Age. There's a little state park with one on a hill outside of McMinnville."

Neil clicked the Google icon on his laptop and typed "Erratic Vineyards McMinnville."

When the page popped up, a young woman was sprawling seductively on a car-sized rock above a slope striated with grape trellises. A sidebar beside the image flashed an advertisement for a sparkling red wine. Oregon Noir.

"That's the same wine the waiters were pushing at Ivan Crombaugh's Oyster Bar," Connie said.

"And Oregon Noir was one of the concessions at the art museum when the Rothko paintings went missing."

Connie shook her head. "No, the wine was provided by NovoCity Finance. I know the guest list for that event inside out."

"NovoCity Finance owns the Oregon Noir brand."

Connie frowned. "Are you sure?"

"Yup. They bragged about it at the gala."

"Then who is this Martin Blodgett? If he was at the open house, he must have been using a different name."

Neil clicked through the Erratic Vineyards site. "Nothing here about Blodgett. But it looks like Erratic Vineyards ships Oregon Noir directly to Murmansk, Russia. In return they get Otlichna vodka."

"Your librarian's vodka company. I seem to recall they have a history of smuggling secrets."

"That was years ago. But it does make you wonder if they've been shipping stolen artworks in wine cases."

"The problem is, who do you ask?" Connie looked at her watch. "We've got twenty minutes."

Neil picked up the phone and punched the number Gerry Chandler had given him at the Portland Art Museum.

"Chandler here."

Neil cleared his throat. "Hi, Gerry. This is Neil, you know, with the

Portland police?"

"Hey, buddy. Long time no hear. Congratulations on catching D.B. Cooper."

"Or maybe not. Don't celebrate yet."

"Really?" Gerry sounded surprised. "Well, do you have any leads on our problem at the art museum?"

"Actually, I was wondering how much you knew about Erratic Vineyards."

"Not much. They donate wine for our events."

"Did you ever know an employee there named Martin Blodgett?"

"No. Why?"

"He was one of the people killed in the Underground murders a year ago."

After a moment's silence, Gerry said, "That's disturbing. What are you thinking?"

"I'm thinking Blodgett could have switched the Rothko paintings at your open house and smuggled the originals out in a wine case."

"And a few weeks later he's killed by a psychopath in a tourist trap? I don't get it."

"Neither do I. But I do know Erratic Vineyards exports cases of Oregon Noir wine to Russia."

Gerry caught his breath. "That's where they're holding the art auction. But then—" He paused. "God, this is getting messy. Are you keeping the investigation quiet?"

"I'm going to have to tell my captain something soon."

"Just don't let word leak out to the media. Please, Neil. My job is on the line."

Before Neil could answer there was a knock on the door and Captain Dickers walked into the office.

"Welcome back from the sunny Caribbean," Dickers said.

Neil spoke into the phone, "I'll call you tomorrow." He hung up, trying to organize his thoughts. It was still five minutes to five. He wished he'd had more time to sort things out before facing the captain.

Dickers settled into a padded chair and leaned forward with his elbows on his knees. "So what's the word on Lieutenant Lavelle?"

"Still missing, sir." Neil glanced to Connie. She had moused the computer screen to replace the Underground murder list with a website about Grenada.

The young captain frowned. "I need good news, Lieutenant. The FBI investigation about D.B. Cooper is going south on us. Finding the parachute case was a great start, but unless we get some more evidence against DeKuyper, we're going to have to release him. The whole country's watching."

"Well, the news from Grenada isn't good. People on the beach saw Lavelle's sailboat drift ashore with no one aboard. I checked out the boat in the police dock. It had been in the surf an hour, so any blood or fingerprints had been washed away."

"Fingerprints? Isn't it most likely she fell overboard in an accident?"

"Sir, the boat anchor was missing. The rope was cut. I think someone killed her, tied her to the anchor, and threw her overboard."

Dickers leaned back. "What do the local police think?"

"At first they thought pirates took her hostage. Apparently that sort of thing happens down there. But they never got a ransom demand, so now they're leaning toward robbery as a motive."

"How much was stolen?"

"That's the problem. I checked the cabin. The door was closed when the boat drifted ashore, so nothing could have fallen out in the surf. The only obvious things missing were her computer, her printer, and the notes she'd been using to write her book about the Underground murders." Neil hesitated a moment before taking the plunge. "Sir, I think someone involved in those murders killed her because they were afraid of what she might write."

To Neil's surprise, the young captain leaned forward and covered his face with his hands. "I was afraid of this."

"Sir?"

"There's another possibility, Ferguson." Dickers lowered his hands. He looked from Neil to Connie and back. "Lavelle was too clever for her own good. I never trusted her."

Neil waited, unable to guess where he was leading.

"Keep this under wraps for now, but I want you to investigate the possibility that Lieutenant Lavelle faked her own death."

Connie opened her mouth as if to speak, but then closed it again.

The captain said, "I know, it's not what you want to hear. But I've been thinking about it ever since she left a thumbprint on the fake car bomb in your car."

Neil ran through a mental calendar. The thumbprint had been left at Duvshenko's funeral eight days ago. Aloud he said, "She would have had to fly to Portland from the Caribbean and back."

"You've done that, Lieutenant." Dickers shook his head. "Lavelle kept secrets. Her reports didn't tell half of what she knew. I think she was bored with law enforcement. If she dabbled in crime on the side, it wasn't just for money, but for entertainment. Faking her death on a sailboat would be more of the same."

Neil and Connie exchanged a look that telegraphed questions. Could Lavelle be Cooper? While feigning retirement in the Caribbean, could a homicide detective have orchestrated art thefts and murders in Portland?

At that point Neil remembered the thumb drive. "I did find one other piece of evidence in Lieutenant Lavelle's boat. Taped to the back of her desk drawer was a memory stick with the first chapters of her book." He inserted the drive into his computer's USB port. When the file opened, he scrolled to the final chapter.

Dickers came over to the desk to read the screen. After a moment he pointed to the last line. "You see? She writes, 'We are all D.B. Cooper.' She thought she could toy with us."

"All right." Neil held up his hands. "You've given us another Cooper suspect. Now I need to tell you about another possible crime that may be tied to Cooper."

"I think we have enough."

"Remember the gala for the Portland Art Museum?"

"Sure."

"While we were there, the museum director, Gerry Chandler, told me they'd discovered what may be another art theft."

"You mean, like the Russian paintings from Woodburn? Why haven't you reported this?"

"Gerry asked us to keep it quiet. He still doesn't want us to go public. But he thinks the same people are involved as in Woodburn. This time they may have replaced six modern-art paintings by Mark Rothko with fakes. An auction house in Russia is offering six Rothko paintings for sale next week, and they look like the originals."

"How would these paintings have gotten to Russia?"

"Probably in wine cases. There's really only one time when the paintings could have been replaced, during a museum open house a year ago. Sergeant Wu and I have narrowed the suspects down to the employees of Erratic Vineyards. They ship Oregon Noir wine cases to Russia."

"Wait." Dickers held up a hand. "Oregon Noir is owned by NovoCity Finance. You've met Nancy Willis, the CEO. They're not smugglers."

"Sir, I'm afraid all these cases might be tied together. The art thefts, the murders, Lavelle, and even D.B. Cooper. The connection may be Oregon Noir. I need to interview the people there."

Dickers paced across the room. Then he pulled out a cell phone, punched a few buttons, and waited. "Hi, working late?" The rest of his conversation came in segments. "No, it's just one of my lieutenants. I think you met him, Ferguson. Yes, and he's worried that someone at Erratic Vineyards might be shipping more than Oregon Noir to Russia. Actually, paintings from the Portland Art Museum. I know, but still. OK. When? Thanks. Bye."

Dickers closed the phone and turned to Neil. "She'll meet you at the warehouse in McMinnville tomorrow morning at ten."

"Yes, sir."

"And Ferguson? NovoCity is a big player in Oregon. Don't screw up."

The next day Neil drove a Crown Victoria to McMinnville while Connie reclined in the passenger seat, waiting for her pain medication to kick in.

"Sometimes I think being bored might be better," she said.

"Isn't your son Leighton at home?"

"No! The kid went back to scuba diving in Hawaii. You'd think he had mothers to spare."

"Are you still worried that Cooper's after you?"

"Where can I hide? Now my own captain tells me Cooper might be a retired detective."

After an hour of stop lights and traffic on Highway 99W, Neil veered off past Dayton and pulled into the Erratic Vineyards parking lot. The cluster of green metal barns seemed unromantic for a winery. Visible just beyond was the Titan rocket of the Evergreen Air Museum, a white spire beside a gigantic glass-walled hangar.

They followed a "Tasting Room" sign to a dim lobby paneled with oak casks. Candle-shaped bulbs flickered in green wine bottles. A blond girl with blue eye shadow greeted them cheerily, "Welcome to the home of Oregon Noir! Are you ready to explore the dark side?" Neil flipped out his badge. "Lieutenant Ferguson, Portland police. We're here to meet Nancy Willis."

"Oh!" The girl faltered. "I think she's upstairs."

An elevator took them to an observation deck overlooking the farmland of the Willamette Valley to the south. The Titan rocket reared to the east. Irregular rocks had been bolted erratically to railings and eaves on all sides.

Nancy Willis was wearing black boots and chains. Her spiked hair was a bouquet of color. "Lieutenant Ferguson, how nice to see you again. And this must be Sergeant Wu."

Connie shook her hand. "I'm impressed to meet you in person. You're kind of a celebrity."

Nancy laughed. "Don't be modest. You're the ones who are always on TV, fighting the mafia, tracking down D.B. Cooper. Would you like a sample of Oregon Noir to kick off the morning?"

"No, thanks, I'm trying to cut back," Neil said.

"So how can I help you today? Your captain mentioned stolen paintings, but he didn't give me any specifics."

"We're curious about an employee named Martin Blodgett. He was one of the victims in the Underground murders."

"That's pretty old news. It was tragic, of course, but your colleagues were here a year ago, asking questions about Martin Blodgett." Nancy turned to a mustachioed man at a nearby counter. "Paolo? Do we know anything more?"

Paolo typed a moment on a laptop computer. "Not really. Blodgett worked in shipping for fifteen years. There's nothing new."

"Could he have been at the Portland Art Museum open house on February 23?" Connie asked. "Perhaps under the name of Michaels?"

Paolo typed again. "Actually, we do have Blodgett on the payroll for overtime then. I don't know anything about a Michaels."

"I do," Nancy said. "The usual booth tender called in sick that day, so Blodgett filled in."

"You say Blodgett had been with you for fifteen years. Was he one of the employees you acquired from Otlichna, the vodka importers?'

Paolo clicked a file on his computer. "It looks like he'd been with them, but I can't tell how long."

Neil nodded. "And have you sent any Oregon Noir to Russia since February 23?"

"We ship every few months." Paolo scrolled down a list. "Here. Containers went to St. Petersburg in March, May, July, and October."

Nancy looked skeptically at Neil. "You don't really think Blodgett shipped paintings from the Portland Art Museum in wine cases?"

"Six Rothko paintings are being auctioned in Russia next week. The originals are supposed to be in Portland. The best opportunity to switch the paintings with fakes would have been during the open house."

Nancy frowned. "And you suspect Blodgett because he happened to be killed by a serial murderer a few weeks later? That's a peculiar link."

"Look, you must have known when you bought Otlichna that they were passing messages to the KGB."

"Who told you a story like that?"

"Marial Greschyednyev. She says her husband was a courier for the Russian secret service."

Nancy paced to the railing and looked out across the checkerboard of Willamette Valley vineyards. "I should have known Greschyednyev was lying. She said the rumors weren't true. She wanted to sell, and I was young enough I wanted a bargain. I'd grown up thinking all that Cold War stuff was ancient history."

Ragged V-shaped flocks of Canada geese winged above distant fields, faintly honking. Neil waited.

At length the young CEO turned, her expression set in stone. "I've built NovoCity's reputation on honesty. I want this cleared up. What do you need from me?"

Connie said, "It would help if I could have access to your records."

"Done." Nancy nodded to Paolo. Then she looked to Neil. "And how about you, Lieutenant? I'm thinking you should go to that auction in Russia."

"I'm starting to think so too."

"If Captain Dickers gives you any trouble, tell him I'll pay your way."

"Thanks, but I've already got an offer."

Connie looked at him with surprise. "You do?"

Neil shrugged. "Marial wants to clear up suspicions too. She's offered to come along and pay both fares."

"How nice." Connie's voice was dangerously flat. "That way you'll have your translator with you."

Neil felt his face flush warm.

33

Some hungers fade, Neil had learned, and others slowly grow until they become tigers, pacing in cages.

When he returned the patrol car to the downtown headquarters that afternoon, a crowd of protesters had gathered on the front steps of the Justice Center. Protests like this happened so often in Portland that he paid little attention. He went up to his office and wrote up a report about his trip to Grenada, watering things down for Dickers' sake. He left at five, thinking he would stop at Safeway on the way home to buy spaghetti. It was Tuesday, after all, the night he cooked for Susan.

But when he made his way through the protesters outside — by then the circus had spilled across the street into Chapman Park — he found his daughter at the curb, holding a candle in a cup. Only then did he read the homemade signs of the protesters: "Free D.B. Cooper!"

"Susan?" he asked.

Her beautiful dark eyes stared at the flickering flame in her hand. "We're not with them, Papa."

"Who aren't you with?"

"The others. The dragon boat team decided to hold a vigil here every evening until you release The Keeper. He's a member of our team, Papa. We don't think he's Cooper."

"And the 'others'?"

"They do."

Only a dozen people held candles. Most of them wore the blue overalls of the One More Time women's collective. Dregs wasn't there, but the large woman who captained the team was eyeing Neil coldly.

The rest of the crowd, perhaps a hundred people, apparently had showed up because D.B. Cooper was their folk hero—a magnificent escape artist who had defied the establishment. The crowd reminded Neil of aging hippies at a rock concert. Some wore tie-dyed sweatshirts. One played a harmonica. Three long-haired men had climbed up on the elk statue and were hanging to the antlers, chanting, "Fly the Coop! Fly the Coop!"

"I missed you last week at dinner," Neil told his daughter, and immediately felt awkward, because it wasn't quite true. He had been intoxicated with Marial that evening. But it was true that he would want his daughter's reassuring company at dinner tonight, and he already knew from her silence that she wasn't coming.

"Susan, promise me you won't tell anyone," Neil said, leaning closer and lowering his voice, "But they don't have much evidence on The Keeper. They're likely to release him before long."

She looked at his shirt pocket—why there? Because she knew her gaze cut to his heart?—and said, "Call me then, Papa."

Neil walked past Safeway on the way home, thinking of hunger. Food was like sex. You could lose your appetite. You could skip a few meals and not care. But eventually it crept up on you, the body demanding its due. Alcohol was a different craving altogether. For the three years after Rebecca died, it had been his daily bread. Since he quit, those hunger pangs had mostly dimmed. When you sail away from that sunny shore, the memories live forever in a scrapbook you don't want to take down from the shelf. For Neil, the danger had always been loneliness. When he was alone too long, the scrapbook called. Then fear would begin to knot his stomach and make his upper lip sweat. That was when the memories of his old liquid friends returned.

Back in the apartment, he opened the fridge and stared past the empty shelves. Connie had hardly spoken during the drive back from McMinnville that afternoon. When he dropped her off at her house she had said it made sense for Neil to check out the art auction in Russia. She still tired easily, and didn't want to go. She could do research here in Portland, trying to excavate the Underground murders, while he flew to Murmansk. But she had called him Lieutenant, rather than Neil.

Neil slammed the fridge shut. Something obvious and evil was staring back at him from the flea market of facts they had gathered about the Underground murders. To see it, he needed to throw out all the junk. He needed to go for a bike ride. But he also needed to break his routine. He would go at night. And he wouldn't ride into the hills.

He changed into his bright yellow Lycra bicycling outfit. Then he replaced the batteries in his headlight, turned it on high, and strapped it to his forehead.

A dangerous hunger sent him down Salmon Street. The warm orange neon of the Lotus Cafe whispered to him from the familiar brick building. He lowered his helmet and sailed past, accelerating downhill to the river. Across the Morrison Bridge he turned right on the riverside path. After two miles he had left the roar of the city behind. An unlit bike path cut across Oaks Park, between a railroad track and a slough. Not even the homeless spent the night here. The dark wings of herons lifted from a tree beside the path and flew overhead toward the void of a lake.

Neil coasted to a stop, his heart beating in his throat. He didn't have a kickstand, so he laid the bike down gently in the grass beside the path. Then he climbed up the gravel of the railroad embankment. He had seen the tracks here, in the distance, last week. And now, when he stood between the steel rails and looked across the lake, he could just make out a distant light in a peaked window atop a dark cliff.

The hunger was strong here.

He took out his cell phone, lighting his face with a cold glow, and pressed a button.

"Hello, lover," Marial said. "Are you free tonight?"

He nodded. "I can be there in five minutes."

Marial met him at the door of the old mausoleum wearing her black-framed librarian glasses and a short terrycloth bathrobe. Two black pins held her copper-colored hair in a bun.

She laughed at Neil's skin-tight bicycle suit and commanded him to the bath. While she ran hot water in the tub, she peeled off his clothes, piece by piece, as if she were slowly preparing an exotic fruit.

"Into the tub" she said, pointing with the authoritative air of a reference librarian. He climbed in without a word, gasped at the heat, and gasped quietly again as she leaned over the tub in her insufficient bathrobe, to gently run a scented sponge back and forth the length of his body.

"Do you know what excites a woman most?" she asked.

He shook his head.

"It's not the bad boys, as everyone thinks. It's the bad boys who catch the bad boys." She kissed him on the lips and stood up. "Now, out of the tub."

He stood up, dripping, and shivered.

"Hold up your arms."

Uncertainly, he put his hands over his head.

She laughed. "Not that high. I'm not going to rob you." She took a large bath towel from a rack and dried him as carefully as she had washed him. Then she stood back and surveyed her work. "Now sit down."

The only place to sit in the bathroom was a small straightback chair.

"Well, go on."

He sat on the chair like a punished boy. He held his knees together, but his member insisted on jutting out like a gear shift. It nodded slightly with each throb of his heart.

"Perfect." She took off her glasses and set them on a shelf. She pulled the pins out of her reddish gold hair, letting it fall to her shoulders. Then she untied her bathrobe so that it gaped open in front. With an easy swing of one leg she stood above him, straddled. Then she put her hands on his shoulders, leaned back her head, and slowly lowered herself onto his lap until he was deep inside her.

The next morning Neil walked into the conference room still wearing bright yellow, skin-tight bicycling clothes. He hadn't slept much, and had woken up with a disturbing explanation for the Underground murders. If true, it would make a research trip to Russia all the more important.

Captain Dickers had called two dozen people together for an 8:30 a.m. briefing. He raised his eyebrows at Neil. "We don't do casual Wednesdays here, Lieutenant."

"No, sir. I'm bicycling to work in honor of the energy summit."

A young sergeant sniggered.

Dickers silenced him with a glance. "We've got a lot on the agenda. I'd like to start with an update on Lieutenant Credence Lavelle. The police in Grenada have changed her status from missing to presumed dead."

Everyone lowered their eyes—as if the captain were a pastor who had just said, "Let us pray." Neil looked at the faces, wondering what they were really thinking. Dickers himself had suggested she may have faked her death. How many of them believed that a homicide detective would die in an accident, falling overboard? Or was he the only doubter? In a room full of uniforms, his yellow bicycling pants stood out.

"All right, next up is the Lammergeier case," Dickers said, cutting the silence like a classroom buzzer. "We're under pressure to clear this up fast. The energy summit is just thirteen days away. VIPs from twelve countries are coming to town. The feds are sending diplomatic security agents to help organize security at the Benson Hotel and Timberline Lodge. We'll have to focus staffing on motorcades and crowd control. By then I want to prove that Portland is a safe city. Owen, you're on."

The FBI agent stood up and squared his shoulders, straightening his suit coat. "The bad news about the Lammergeier case is that we're getting nowhere with DeKuyper. We haven't been able to link him to the poison and now we've got a witness who says he was at a freight yard in Salem that night. In short, I no longer see DeKuyper as a viable murder suspect."

The young sergeant raised his hand. "What about as a suspect for D.B.Cooper?"

"That's tougher." Owen sighed. "He really did have Cooper's parachute pack, and he'd trained as a smokejumper. But the more we question him, the less likely he seems. Frankly, I don't think he's smart enough to pull off a hijacking plan that complicated. Besides, the crime's too old to be prosecuted. The statue of limitations cuts off robbery after twenty-five years. Without the murder charge, we can't hold him."

"What's the good news?" Neil asked.

The special agent held out his hand to Ray Masoli, a crewcut lieutenant with thick glasses. "Lieutenant Masoli has been doing background work on Lammergeier's widow."

Masoli pushed up his glasses. "For the past six months Rachel Lammergeier has been romantically involved with a chemistry professor at Reed. They haven't been able to marry because Curt Lammergeier wouldn't give her a divorce."

Dickers nodded. "That's a strong motive. She also inherited her husband's share of her house. And she admits she doesn't have an alibi. I want her and this chemistry professor in here for questioning. Espada, get a forensics team out to the chemistry lab at Reed. See if they have anything on hand that matches the poisons in the body. Owen, without the Cooper angle, does the FBI want to stay in charge of this?"

Owen eased himself back down into his chair. "For the time being, yes. My interest is in the hijacking, and there's evidence Lammergeier was involved. He might even have been Cooper."

"All right, we've got work to do. Anything else?"

Neil raised a finger. "What about releasing the old homeless guy?"

Dickers frowned. "That's delicate. It needs to be done quietly. DeKuyper doesn't have a residence. If we just dump him on the street, the media will tear into us."

Heads nodded. Dickers didn't need to remind them of the time they had released a drunken veteran without his wheelchair.

"Let me handle it," Neil said. "I know a place where he can stay out of sight."

"Fine." Dickers looked about the room. "That's it then. Let's get to work. Dismissed."

Neil lingered, waiting for the right moment to ask the captain for permission to take yet another trip abroad. Marial had spent a lot of the past night planning, even when she was lying in the canopy bed with her head on his chest. Tourist visas to Russia normally took three weeks to clear, but with police business, the process could be handled in hours. Marial had the names of contacts at the Otlichna vodka warehouse in Murmansk, the art auction house in Novgorod, and the Solovetsky Island monastery with the Gray Madonna icon. One thing she didn't have was a contact with the KGB, something they would need if it was true that Cooper had been a courier for the secret police.

Neil also needed permission from Dickers. Russia was a long ways from Portland. If the captain said no, Neil was prepared to ask for personal leave without pay.

"So, I hear you want to go to Russia?" the captain said as he gathered his papers from the conference table.

Neil groped for words. Could Marial have called to plead her case?

"Don't look so surprised. Nancy Willis checked in with me as soon as you left McMinnville."

"I see." Neil found it a little disturbing that the captain had such a close relationship with the young finance executive. "And what do you think?"

"I think the timing's terrible. We're shorthanded as it is, with the energy summit coming up. But NovoCity is important."

"If it weren't for them, the summit wouldn't even be in Oregon," Neil said, repeating a line he had heard the captain use.

"Exactly. Nancy wants this cleared up fast. Keep your work quiet. Be back before the summit. And change out of those stupid tights."

"Yes, sir." Neil walked quickly toward his own office, with no intention of changing his pants.

Then he called Connie at home. She answered sleepily, but switched to high alert when she heard his theory about the Underground murders. "Whoa! You know who this puts on the death list next?"

"You and me."

"Yes. And The Keeper."

That made Neil stop. "We're releasing DeKuyper today."

"Don't. Or at least hide him until I've done some checking. It's going to take me a while."

"Did you get access to the NovoCity files?"

"Yes, but it's oceans of information."

"You can wade in as deep as you like when I'm in Russia. Right now I need you to focus your research on the Underground murder victims."

"I'll try."

"Keep in touch, Connie."

"Stay safe, Neil."

Neil hung up and called his daughter Susan.

"Papa?" she said. "I told you to call when The Keeper was free. Is he?"

"Almost."

"Not good enough."

"Don't hang up!" Neil put his elbows on his desk and lowered his voice. "We need a place to hide him for a while. We can't just release a homeless man onto the streets. I'm thinking your dragon boat team might find a motel room for him somewhere quiet, and keep an eye on him."

"Hide him?" Susan asked. "From what?"

Neil sighed. "The media are going to be all over him. If he really was a witness in the Cooper case, there might be others after him too."

"Then the police should protect him."

"Susan, that's what we were doing. But you don't want him in jail, and neither do we. We need someplace else."

There was a long silence. Then she said, "Bring him here."

"What? To the Recyclotron?"

"I'm at my apartment, Papa. I've got an extra bed. I'll watch him."

"No, no." Neil rubbed his eyes. "I won't let you take that risk."

"Yes you will." Susan hung up.

"Damn it!" Neil flipped his cell phone closed. His daughter was maddeningly headstrong. Of course he couldn't hide The Keeper in her apartment. But if he refused her now, she wouldn't speak to him for months.

He fumed, pacing his office. It took a while, but gradually he realized that Susan was not just brave—she might even be right. People would expect to find The Keeper in a motel. They'd never guess the police would put him in a garbage recycler's apartment.

Neil still wasn't sure what he was going to do, but he had to do something. He rode the elevator down to the jail, filled out the paperwork for Gregor DeKuyper's release, took him down to the basement garage, and drove him in an unmarked car out Third Avenue.

"Where are you taking me?" The old man wrinkled his brow. "I just want to go back to the Burnside Bridge."

"Do you want to be on television again?" Neil asked.

"No!"

"Then you have to stay off the streets a few days. You've become something of a celebrity, showing up with D.B. Cooper's backpack. What do you say we put you up in a nice motel?"

"No! I don't want to be alone. I just got out of jail."

They stopped at a traffic light while the MAX light rail rumbled by. Neil looked at him. "You know the dragon boat team. If I took you to the apartment of one of the people on the team, would you promise to stay there for a week?"

The Keeper scratched his big white beard. Then he nodded.

"And you'll keep out of trouble?"

"Maybe. Who am I staying with?"

The light changed. Neil hit the gas. "With my daughter."

After Neil had smuggled The Keeper up the stairs to Susan's apartment, he checked the locks, pulled the curtains, and gave a lecture about keeping undercover. Then he handed them Connie's card and said if they noticed anything suspicious — anything at all — they should immediately call Sergeant Wu.

"Papa," Susan finally said. "Go home."

And so he did. He drove the unmarked car back to headquarters and rode his bike home. Worry clung to him even after he showered and changed clothes.

To take his mind off Susan, he took out a suitcase. It was high time to pack for the trip to Russia. Should he attempt to take a gun? He wouldn't get far. Realistically, he couldn't even take a pocket knife. Warm clothes would be a good idea. He would also want to bring the books he had bought about Latvia and icons.

As soon as he packed the books, he realized how inadequate they were. He ought to be doing a lot more research for this journey. And the most important things were not going to be in books.

With sudden resolve, he grabbed a notepad and a digital camera. He rode the elevator down to street level, walked a block to the Portland Art Museum, and asked for Gerry Chandler.

Neil's college friend looked worn, as if the missing paintings had been stealing his sleep. "Just passing by?"

"Yes, on my way to Russia."

Gerry held a finger to his lips. Then he led the way across the lobby and down a stairway to his office. Only after he had closed the door did he ask, "You're not really going to the art auction?"

"You asked me to."

"I've changed my mind." He ran his hand over the bald spot on the top of his head. "I mean, what's the point? Sure, we'd like to find out who's selling the Rothko paintings in Russia, but the sellers at these auctions are anonymous. You can't just ask for the names of art thieves and forgers."

"Maybe not." Neil recalled Marial suggesting that a well-placed bribe in Russia might in fact loosen tongues. "But wouldn't you like to know which one you're dealing with?"

"What do you mean?"

"Whether the seller is a forger or a thief. It has to be one of the two."

Gerry leaned back, thinking. "I suppose you're right."

"Is there some way I could tell if the paintings are originals, just by looking at them?"

Gerry pulled out a drawer and took out a manila folder. "I've thought about this." He spread six photographs on the table. "What do you see?"

Neil saw six white rectangles. "Not much. What am I looking at?"

"The backs of the original Rothkos. I remember you saying his paintings looked sloppy."

"Honestly, to me they look like they were done by a two year old."

"Mark Rothko was actually quite fastidious. Because he seldom framed his work, he painted the sides of the canvases carefully. As you can see, not one brush stroke slopped onto the back."

Neil considered this a moment. "A forger might not know that. Most people have seen the fronts of the paintings. But I thought the auction house did a chemical analysis of the paint and found it authentic. You know, it used Rothko's secret formula."

"Yes, but they said they took a sample from a place that wouldn't show. The only place that wouldn't show is on the back."

"So someone is lying."

Gerry pushed the photos across the desk. "Deceit and art are two names for the same thing."

Neil slipped the photos into his notepad. "What happens if I find out the paintings are authentic?"

"You're the cop. I suppose you'd blow a whistle or something. Presumably you'd also ask the Russian police to confiscate the paintings."

"And what if they're fakes?"

"Then you let the auction continue, but you explain why the paintings are worthless. Either way, you'll be a very unpopular man in Novgorod." He leaned forward. "I'm sorry I got you involved, Neil. Don't go."

That afternoon Neil skipped lunch to do a different kind of research. He walked two blocks from the art museum to the Multnomah

County Central Library, a massive stone and brick monument to the book. The city's ritziest thrift store stood right across the street, a Goodwill with Wedgwood and rhinestones. Unlike the buskers at Pioneer Courthouse Square, the young men here didn't bang pots and plastic tubs, pretending to be rock band drummers. The loiterers in front of the library had dogs and banjos and backpacks, but no bottles. A girl in fishnet stockings and a beret sat on a bench marked "Victor Hugo", tapping a touchscreen in her hand.

Neil was pushing through the library's massive oak doors when his cell phone rang. He made a U-turn and found a quiet stretch of the balustraded stone wall where he could sit under a big elm without being overheard. The phone's screen said the caller ID was blocked.

"Hello?"

"I knew you didn't get him," a man's voice smirked.

"Who is this?"

The voice laughed — a dry, grating sound that made the hairs on the back of Neil's neck stand on end.

"You gave me your fricking card, Lieutenant. You're the one who said to call if I thought of something more."

Neil thought back on all the people he'd given his card in the months since his promotion. It was a long and often ugly list, but this voice was recent, and seemed to match the puffy white face of an overweight young engineer in the Lotus Cafe.

"Todd Lammergeier?"

"You're not going to find D.B. Cooper in the gutter, Lieutenant. The man who poisoned my father was no bum. You have to look for bigger fish."

"You said you had something new to tell me, Todd. What is it?"

"You first, Lieutenant."

"What?"

"Go on. You've been tracking down leads while the rest of the cops sit on their thumbs. Tell me something I don't know."

Neil took a risk. "I think there may be two Coopers."

"Who told you that?"

"A little bird." When Neil thought of Sonya Duvshenko, the four-year-old girl in the Midland branch, he was reminded of a forest wren. "I'm told one of the Coopers is bad and one is good."

"I like that theory. You may be getting close."

"Now it's your turn, Todd. What have you got?"

"Synergy."

"You mean the energy summit?"

"I mean the invitees. Secret agents have been in town for weeks, preparing things."

"That's not what we've been told."

A man with a mustache thrust a community newspaper at Neil. "Buy a paper for a dollar, mister?"

Neil waved him on, trying to focus on the voice in the cell phone. "What?"

"They're called 'secret' for a reason. And they're not just from the U.S. The Russian energy minister will be here too. Some of these people have old scores to settle with Cooper."

"Which Cooper are we talking about?"

"Both. You already know Cooper was with the KGB, don't you?"

Neil didn't answer.

"Good. And do you know what was going on with the Cold War in November of 1971?"

Neil still didn't answer. This was precisely what he had planned to research in the library.

"Am I boring you, Lieutenant?"

"No, go on. The Cold War is a big subject. What should I be looking for?"

"You've heard that the U.S. energy secretary, Stanley Caulfield, grew up in Seattle?"

"Yes."

"And that the Russian energy minister agreed to the summit at Mt. Hood because he's a long-time chum of Caulfield's?"

This time Neil answered more cautiously. "Yes."

"In 1971 Stan Caulfield was playing bass guitar in a Troutdale garage band called the One World Express. I found out he missed a gig on Thanksgiving. He showed up in Seattle the next week with his hair cut short."

"And based on that, you think he's D.B. Cooper?"

"Look at what these politicians are doing. It's exactly the kind of world government my father was fighting. That's why they killed him."

Neil closed his eyes. He had forgotten that Todd was into

conspiracies. The Lammergeier murder wasn't really Neil's case anymore, but as long as Todd had called up, trying to rattle him, he couldn't resist rattling back.

"Do you think someone could have used the chemistry lab at Reed to put together a poison like the one we found in Crystal Springs?"

The breathing Neil heard could have come from an animal. "Maybe. If an agent told someone the right story, and paid the right price."

Neil knew the Central Library had back issues of the *Oregonian* in digital format, but the files were hard to search and awkward to scan. He preferred the old technology. He walked through the lobby, past a a row of giant green Synergy posters. In the Periodical Room on the second floor, twenty-foot-tall windows lit oak tables. But entering the news morgue—the archives at the back of the building—was like descending into catacombs. Dusty boxes with typewritten labels lined gray steel shelves. Microfilm reading machines hunkered against a dim wall, like automatons waiting through the decades to be brought to life.

Reduced to boxes of film, a century and a half of the *Oregonian* filled three banks of shelves. Neil found 1971, pulled out the two "November" boxes, and powered up one of the machines. Its glass eye lit up and its fan began to hum.

Each of the boxes held a spool the size of a doughnut. He threaded the first reel's microfilm into the machine and pressed a button marked "Forward." Pages whirred past in a blur on the milky glass screen. He stopped to focus, first on classified advertisements for furnished apartments, then on a Lil' Abner cartoon where hillbillies were attempting to capture the Vulgarilla from Slobbovia.

The forward button whirred again, landing on the front page for November 6. Citizens were being alerted to watch the night skies for the fiery reentry of Kosmos 347, a Soviet satellite of uncertain purpose.

Neil fast forwarded again, a leap of nearly a week. Playtex Living Gloves were eighty-three cents a pair. Communist Khmer Rouge forces in Cambodia had attacked the Phnom Penh airport. The Portland Zoo had just received a strange raccoon dog from Sapporo. And Led Zeppelin's fourth studio album was on its way becoming one of the biggest sellers of all time.

Neil rubbed his eyes. What was he looking for in this haystack? He rewound the spool until the film flapped angrily. Then he threaded in the other reel and whirred it a long ways forward, aiming for November 24. He landed on the 29th, the day NASA announced the names of the three-man crew that would pilot Apollo 16 to the moon.

A final rewind brought Neil to the inch-tall headlines of the Thanksgiving Day weekend. A mysterious bomber had hijacked a Northwest Airlines flight and vanished with $200,000.

For twenty cents, Neil could copy any page on the screen. He lined up the articles and started work.

Perhaps it was the repetition. Perhaps it was the copier's light, scanning in the darkness. Neil found himself transported back to the torrid night he had spent in Marial's home.

Suddenly a throbbing in his pocket jolted Neil back to the newspaper morgue. His phone. He had set his cell phone on vibrate when he went into the library. He fished it out of his pocket. Phone conversations weren't allowed in the library, but he flipped it open anyway. "Hello?"

""You were right, Neil."

"Connie?"

"If we disregard the Russian student and the wine shipping guy, all three of the other Underground murder victims had the same problem. They were riding public transportation because they'd lost their cars. And you know where the cars were being repaired?"

"In Yosef Duvshenko's shop?"

She clicked her tongue. "Only one of them was at Foreign Motors. The other two were at Andrei Andropov's place in Gresham."

Neil's throat was dry. "Then there really is an evil Cooper."

"Yes. A man with Russian connections who's willing to kill anyone who gets in his way, even if all they've done is see something at a car shop they shouldn't."

"You've gotten in his way too, Connie. He's tried to kill you, and he'll try again."

"I know. But I think the guy going to Russia is the one who needs to worry most."

34

"I have a confession," Marial said. The Aeroflot jet was descending over a mosaic of snowy tundra and gray lakes on the last leg of a long sleepless journey from Portland to Frankfurt to Saint Petersburg to beyond the Arctic Circle.

"Another?" Neil yawned.

"This is my first trip to Russia."

He rubbed his eyes. "I thought you grew up over here."

"Latvia is different. We'll fly out of Riga next week, after we find Cooper."

"You bought tickets back from Latvia?"

"It's not far from Novgorod." She shrugged. "Anyway, I'm paying. I haven't seen my homeland for thirty-nine years."

When they landed, Neil couldn't help but think how different Murmansk was from the tropical world he had seen in Grenada just a few days before. Flight attendants offered Aeroflot umbrellas to passengers at the cabin door. A cold gust cut into his thin business suit as he descended the metal stairs to the tarmac. It was raining sideways, a sleet that stung. The gray clouds and gray land merged at a dim gray horizon unbroken by trees or hills.

One thing was the same as in Grenada — a hand-lettered "Ferguson" sign by the terminal door. But this time the person holding it was a heavily made-up blond wearing a short fur parka, nylons, and pointy-toed, high-heeled shoes with glittery bows. She reminded Neil of Nadia Duvshenko.

Marial spoke with the girl in Russian for a minute. Then she introduced Neil to Ludmilla, a human resources manager at Otlichna's headquarters.

"Pleased to meet you, Ludmilla," Neil said, tipping his head.

Unsmiling, she offered a gloved hand for him to shake. "Pleased to meet you, Mr. Ferguson. I speak English, but not *otlichna*."

He shook her hand. "Does anyone speak Otlichna?"

"Oh yes. You do."

He glanced to Marial for a translation. "It's a joke," she explained. "Otlichna means excellent."

"Ah." Neil managed a small laugh.

The girl finally smiled. "I take you to hotel. On way we see city. Tomorrow, Otlichna. Yes?"

Neil did his best to remember something from the phrasebook Marial had made him read during the flight. Mostly he had concentrated on memorizing the Cyrillic alphabet, hoping to be able to read signs for place names.

"*Stross-vee-jee?*" he said.

From their laughter, he couldn't tell whether he had said "thank you," "hello," or "I'm sorry."

Ludmilla directed a uniformed worker to load their luggage into her car — a small, boxy Lada with rusty fenders and go-kart-sized tires. Neil hunkered in the passenger seat while Ludmilla drove, rattling away in Russian as the car rattled across potholes. Wipers smeared sleet across the windshield.

"She says Murmansk is the world's largest Arctic port," Marial translated from the back seat. "Because of the Gulf Stream, the sea here stays ice-free all year. In World War II the Americans shipped war materiel to Russia here. Forty-three convoys made it past the German blockade, bringing five thousand tanks and seven thousand planes."

Ludmilla pointed through the blur of the windshield to a gigantic dark shape — an ominous figure hundreds of feet tall on a bluff to the left.

"What is it?" Neil asked.

"A statue of Mother Russia, holding up her palm against the west," Marial said. "The Nazis attacked with ten thousand men from northern Norway in 1941. After all their victories in Europe, the Germans were amazed that they couldn't take Murmansk."

When the wipers swished again the dim gray clouds had decapitated the Russian statue of liberty, leaving a gigantic torso draped in a concrete sheet, her arm outstretched in what appeared to be terror.

"Is the weather always like this here?" Neil asked.

Marial translated the question while Ludmilla tailgated a bus, bucking slush-filled potholes and sooty fumes. The answer came back, "This is spring, the loveliest time, when the snow of winter is melting and the mosquitoes of summer have not arrived. Murmansk is farther north than most of Alaska. The sun never rises in December or January, and never sets in June or July."

So far Neil had seen little more than garbage-strewn fields and rusty metal sheds. Suddenly, as they rounded a corner, the city itself came into view — thousands of seemingly identical six-story concrete buildings. A gray river cut through a forest of cranes and smokestacks. There were no suburbs, no single-family houses, no wooden structures at all. They drove down a vast treeless boulevard flanked with long blocks of signless concrete buildings. Only a few dark figures in thick coats shuffled past the melting piles of plowed snow. An electric tram sparked overhead wires.

"What do people do for a living here?" Neil asked.

Ludmilla responded by raising her hand in a gesture of surprise.

"As she told you already," Marial translated, "Murmansk is a major port. It is home to Russia's fleet of nuclear submarines and icebreakers. The railroad provides a direct link south to Saint Petersburg. Otlichna is not the only company to recognize the many advantages of this location."

Ludmilla added in English, "You see? Luxury hotel Poliarny Zori? How you say?"

"The Arctic Circle," Marial said. She exchanged a skeptical glance with Neil. The hotel was the only freshly painted building they had seen, but the peach exterior did little to disguise what appeared to be a huge concrete prison cellblock.

Ludmilla helped them lift out their suitcases and roll them up the monumental, hundred-foot-wide concrete steps to the covered entrance. A sculpture of what appeared to be glass and stainless steel water heater parts dominated the cavernous lobby. Clusters of square plastic orange armchairs huddled on the bare terrazzo floor.

"You rest, yes?" Ludmilla said. "Tomorrow at nine I come with car, we tour Otlichna."

"Sure. Thanks," Neil said.

Ludmilla whispered, "The discotheque here, Club Ledokol, very happening spot. But the hotel restaurant, no. Go to Cucina Romana, five hundred meters." She pointed back toward the city center and winked. Then she turned on her spike heel and clopped across the lobby to the door.

Marial walked up to the reception desk, where she traded her passport for room keys. The ponytailed receptionist flipped through the passport and raised her eyebrows. "Portland?"

"Yes, we're from Portland. Do you know it?"

"Synergy!" the receptionist replied. Then she said, "Breakfast is included, seven to nine."

Marial asked, "Where is the nearest bank machine?"

The receptionist pointed to the far corner of the lobby.

A minute later the machine was spitting out brightly colored ruble notes in large denominations—one handful for Marial and another for Neil.

"The ruble is about twenty-four to the dollar," she told him. He nodded absently. The tension of the long flights had left him dazed. As if in a dream they rode a creaking elevator up several floors and walked a very long, echoing corridor past dozens of identical doors.

The room itself looked less like a prison cell than a college dormitory, with twin beds, a simple bathroom, and one large window. Neil was too tired to question why Marial had chosen twin beds. When he pulled the heavy drapes aside he saw more multi-story apartment blocks. A street lamp was already on, although it was only four o'clock. Construction rubble and garbage had begun to emerge from the snow in the wasteland between buildings. Half a dozen men in thick leather jackets were standing around a flaming barrel. He couldn't tell if they were burning trash, barbecuing something, or just keeping warm.

"You can have the first shower," Marial said.

"All by myself?"

"Yes, and don't fall asleep in there."

"Maybe just a nap. It's 5 a.m. in Portland."

"If you sleep now, you'll wake up at midnight. The only way to beat jet lag is to stay up until you're on the new schedule."

"Gah." He shambled into the bathroom to shower and shave.

It was dark by the time they left the hotel in search of dinner. The sleet had turned into tiny white flakes that sparkled beneath the streetlamps.

"Look, the snowflakes really have six points." Neil held out his overcoat's dark sleeve to watch the crystals crash.

"That means the clouds are cold. In Oregon, the flakes melt together before they land." She stopped beneath the streetlight and looked up, trying to catch one of the falling stars with the tip of her tongue.

As she paused there, with snowflakes on her eyelashes, Neil sensed that she wanted to be kissed, and he wanted to do it, so he did.

He came up from that long, warm embrace more confident about everything. Even tracking Cooper in Arctic Russia no longer seemed entirely insane.

"Now I'm hungry," Marial said, her voice husky.

"Dinner's on me tonight." Neil looked around. "We should be near the restaurant, but it's hard to tell when they don't use signs." The nearly identical buildings facing the street had small windows covered with roll-down metal blinds.

"I guess they don't have to advertise." Marial read a small notice posted beside an unlit door. "This place is a shoe shop and dentist office during the day."

Neil pointed to the snowy sidewalk. "When in doubt, detectives always follow the footprints."

The tracks ahead of them led around a corner to a side street, where a bare light bulb illuminated an unlikely-looking sheet metal door with the small label, *Cucina Romana.*

He pushed open the metal door. Inside was a dark, three-by-six-foot chamber lined with boots and umbrellas. The heavy wooden door beyond, however, opened onto the improbable warmth, light, and laughter of an Italian trattoria. Young couples with cappuccinos leaned across candlelit tablecloths. Framed movie posters from the 40s decorated the walls. A vitrine by the bar displayed layered torts, tiramisu, and cheesecake.

"Can I afford this on a lieutenant's salary?" Neil whispered.

Marial shrugged. She let a waiter in a white apron lead them to a table for two. He brought them menus and a basket of bread.

Before touching the bread Neil examined the menu. It was printed in English as well as Russian and Italian. He reminded himself that rubles were about twenty-four to the dollar. But he still couldn't figure things out because each entry was followed by several numbers:

Fettuccine (200) 75,-
Borscht with sour cream and meat (175/15/20) 48,-

"Why are there so many different prices?" He asked Marial.

"I don't know." She waved the waiter back and spoke with him in Russian.

"Well?" Neil asked.

"The number in parentheses is the weight in grams. If you ordered the beet soup, for example, you'd get 175 grams of borscht with 15 grams of sour cream and 20 grams of meat."

"That makes it sound like a formula for a physics experiment, not a soup."

"Apparently government inspectors require restaurants to be quite specific."

"Then the last number is the price in rubles?"

"Right. A four-course dinner here costs about ten dollars."

Neil held out his hand grandly. "Order whatever you like, my dear."

It had stopped snowing when they walked back to the hotel. Neil was thinking about the work waiting for them in the morning.

"You know, I don't think Ludmilla is going to be much help," he mused.

"Our chipper young tour guide?" Marial shook her head. "I agree. She's not the one to ask about the Russian mafia or the KGB. I have the name of a retired Otlichna employee who might know something."

"We need to talk to people outside the company too. I want the local gossip. I'm just not sure how to get it."

They had reached the corner of the hotel. At night the front entrance was a sleepy glass door with a dim "Poliarny Zori" sign, but the side entrance for the discotheque strobed hectic colored lights.

"Maybe in the icebreaker?" Marial suggested.

Now Neil noticed that the "Club Ledokol" sign had a logo of a ship cracking ice floes, and he could guess what a *ledokol* was.

"Alcohol is the universal truth serum," she said.

"Not for me."

"I know. Give me an hour to see what I can dig up."

He tightened his lips, but nodded. "An hour."

"Don't go to bed without me." They squeezed hands and walked away, each toward their own entrance.

Neil pushed wearily through the hotel door. If he went to his room he knew he'd fall asleep.

In one of the lobby's orange plastic armchairs a man with a laptop and a cigar was drinking a cup of coffee. Without thinking, Neil asked in English, "Where can I get one of those?"

The man looked up. He was balding and freckled. His off-white business suit was substantially better tailored than Neil's. He asked, "The Cuban cigar or the Arabian coffee?

"Either. Both."

"You are new here?""

"Just got in today. I'm sorry, can you really order coffee in the lobby?"

The man said a few Russian words over his shoulder to the receptionist. Then he motioned for Neil to join him at one of the chairs. "The Wifi is terrible in the rooms. You can only do business in the lobby. I think they arrange it on purpose, still thinking the old way."

"The old way?"

Instead of answering, the man studied Neil. "You're American. What brings you to Murmansk?"

Neil hesitated. The man spoke with a slight accent, but it didn't strike him as Russian. "I'm looking into an import/export deal. American wine for Russian art."

The man took a drag of his cigar and blew smoke up toward the glass and steel scraps of the lobby's sculpture. "Then we are not competing. I import shoes and export nickel. These things work, since the change."

A waiter brought a tray with a cup of coffee and a cigar. Neil started to reach for his wallet, but then decided to hold up his room key instead. The waiter read the number, nodded, and left.

"Where else in Europe can you smoke cigars in a hotel lobby?" The businessman leaned forward with a lighter.

Neil hadn't smoked a cigar for most of a year, since the last Ferguson family reunion. Stogies were the only vice of his brother Mark, the hippie who lived in a commune outside Eugene. Now Neil puffed quickly a few times to make sure it was lit. Then he filled his mouth with the sweet thick fog, rounded his lips, and puffed out a ring with his tongue. The smoky doughnut expanded upward, rolling itself inside out.

Neil held out his hand. "Neil Ferguson, Portland."

The businessman shook hands. "Wim Daalder, Antwerp."

"What was the old way of doing business in Murmansk?"

Daalder snorted smoke, an unpleasant sight. "For the Soviets, business was politics, and vice versa. Every conversation in this lobby was monitored."

"But not anymore?" Neil took a sip of coffee. It was strong and bitter, just what he needed.

"Who would listen to us now?" Daalder spread his hands and shrugged. "Since they closed the KGB training center here, the old spooks have found other work. You and I, they want us in Murmansk for business now. All they listen to is the sound of money."

"I don't know much about Europe," Neil admitted, "But there must be quicker ways to ship shoes to Russia than to send them halfway to the North Pole. Why Murmansk?"

"Why are you here?" His eyes smiled. "These days, a quiet Arctic port has certain advantages."

Neil rolled the cigar between his fingers, thinking. During the Cold War, the Soviet secret service had operated a training center in Murmansk. Couriers from America might have studied here. Vodka shipments could have carried concealed messages. But with the collapse of the Soviet Union, many of the KGB men had been out of work. The intelligence hierarchy and the shipping network were already in place. With enough bribes to keep the Russian government from looking too closely, Murmansk would be the perfect haven for a black market shipping operation. It was only a guess, but Neil was willing to bet that the Belgian businessman wasn't paying duty on his imported shoes, at least not to the proper authorities.

"I'm new to Russia, still searching for contacts." Neil aimed his cigar toward the faint thump of rock music down the hall. "My partner is in the discotheque, looking."

Daalder laughed. "Only the little people live in a frozen hole like Murmansk. The big ones own castles. And in the Icebreaker? All you find there are Navy officers on shore leave, hoping to get a foreign woman in bed."

Neil set down his cigar.

"They're good, though, these sailors," Daalder went on. "With the right vodka, I've seen them break down married women in less than an hour."

Neil glanced at his watch and stood up. "Excuse me, I think I have an appointment."

He reached the door of the discotheque just as Marial was coming out. The smoky room, with its flashing lights and thunderous noise, reminded him of the nighttime Mideast war zones he'd seen on television.

"I do not need to be rescued," Marial said archly, but her breath was sour and her ankle wobbled.

When Neil took her to the elevator she fell asleep on his shoulder, standing up.

35

Dan Cooper's Last Will & Testament, Part 8

I liked The Keeper. He was a simple, honest young man, an out-of-work Alaskan firefighter who believed my odd story without much curiosity. To this wonderfully credulous Dutch wanderer, it seemed perfectly understandable that I had volunteered to search for a parachuting hijacker, that I had found a body surrounded by coyotes, that my car refused to start, and that I now wanted to head toward Portland in order to find a telephone. He had no interest in involving the police. He himself was riding the rails south toward sunnier climes with just enough money to put bottles of brandy and cans of sardines in his knapsack. All he wanted from this world were things I was happy to provide him: companionship, a nice suit coat, and the nylon parachute case I was using as a backpack. When we were done exchanging coats and packs he didn't quite look like a skyjacker, but neither did I. I was now David McGill, another unemployed firefighter.

When a slow trainload of cardboard and junk car bales rolled through the Kelso freight yard, The Keeper surmised that it was heading for a scrap shipping facility on the Columbia River in Vancouver. We jumped aboard, climbed into a low-sided wagon, and made ourselves comfortable amidst the cardboard bundles. My duffel made a lovely mattress, padded as it was with $200,000 in twenty-dollar bills. Reclining on this costly skybox seat, and shielded from the damp wind by a flattened refrigerator box, we enjoyed a rolling view of the Columbia to one side and the madness of Interstate 5 to the other, where police cars from half a dozen jurisdictions raced back and forth, presumably searching for Dan Cooper, the person I had been last night.

And this of course was where the months of training in Murmansk paid off. Cooper no longer existed. He had been a temporary shell, a mask I assumed would never be used again. As the train's wheels rumbled on beneath me, and The Keeper rambled on beside me, I had time to wonder who I was beneath all the masks I had been taught to wear. Certainly I no longer was the idealist the Russians had found ripe for recruitment a year before. Oh, I still believed in the causes that had made me say yes. My own government, the United States of America, was napalming innocent Vietnamese villagers, poisoning entire jungles, and shooting protesters at home. People of conscience were renouncing their citizenship and fleeing to Canada. It had been easy enough for me to drop out unnoticed for a summer, simply by telling people I was going to hitchhike around Europe. Then I'd followed Swarovsky's instructions. I'd made my way to Hammersfest, a bleak Norwegian village popular only with tourists going to North Cape, Europe's northernmost point. As instructed, I had smoked a cigar on Pier 9, accepted a ride in a fishing boat with a man named Thor Ulvdahl, and wound up two days later in the Poliarny Zori Hotel in Murmansk.

That summer was the kind of hell that only a young man can withstand. I marched through tundra, fired Kalashnikov rifles, and studied cryptography. For a final test, they threw me out of a Russian cargo plane over the White Sea with nothing but a parachute and an inflatable raft.

In September, when Thor Ulvdahl brought me back to Pier 9 in Hammersfest, I looked much the same on the outside, but I was no longer sure who was living inside. Back in Portland, I rented a room in the required apartment building on Sandy Boulevard. I joined a garage band and an outdoor club. I led a normal American life. I didn't mind delivering the KGB packages because I believed everything was as Swarovsky said. I was helping the protesters change America for the better. I was ending the war. I was making it possible for people of conscience to come home. Perhaps I was even saving the goddam planet.

What an idiot.

The week before Thanksgiving I looked in one of the packages.

Opening the padded envelope unnoticed was surprisingly easy if you knew the KGB's methods. But it took me a while to understand what I was seeing. These weren't the data I had been expecting. When I finally understood, I almost threw up.

My country was not the only one capable of exploiting gullible young men. The most terrifying part was that I had dug myself in so deep. If I went to the American officials with the information in the courier packet, I'd be arrested for treason. Did they electrocute traitors these days, I wondered, or did they give them lethal injections? Meanwhile, Swarovsky had made it clear that KGB operatives who stepped out of line were liquidated.

I needed to vanish off the face of the earth. But first I absolutely had to intercept the packet that would be coming in reply. If I believed in anything—and I still did—I would have to show Professor Curt Lammergeier $200,000 and destroy the information he was selling.

At first I considered playing along with the exchange as described in the courier envelope. Apparently, Lammergeier imagined he was dealing with one of several competing U.S. companies, so he expected to meet an American. The KGB needed me for that role. They were planning to supply me with the cash. But they would also monitor the operation so carefully that nothing could go wrong. To outwit them I would have to do something spectacularly unexpected.

When our freight train neared the Vancouver Amtrak station it switched onto a siding and slowed at the entrance of a fenced compound. As The Keeper had predicted, we were headed for a scrap yard. Ahead, piles of detritus from America's materialism rose like volcanic cones. We hopped off and ducked away toward the riverbank. Under the railroad bridge we found a homeless camp set up like a hobo's Motel Six, redolent of tar, smoke, and bilge water. Red lights winked atop the bridge. Silvery gray water bars on the lapping river reflected the distant barracks of the Red Lion Inn on the Oregon shore. Our accommodations included some discarded sleeping bags and the charred remains of a wooden pallet.

"Home sweet home for the night," The Keeper said, unpacking a can of chili.

"Hold dinner for me, will you? I've got to call a tow truck about my car." Taking my duffle full of cash, I scrambled up onto a city street, took a good look back at the railroad bridge, and then sauntered, bored with life, to the Amtrak terminal. A yellow newspaper box outside the station door held up the *Oregonian's* headline: "Bomber hijacks Portland jet flight." I bent for a closer look.

> A Northwest Airlines jet, hijacked out of Portland Wednesday, landed at Reno, Nev. at 11 p.m. — but the hijacker was no longer aboard.
>
> Airport officials did not know whether he bailed out in flight or escaped from the plane after landing. He had four parachutes aboard.

I scanned down the story.

> As the plane was taxiing toward the terminal, it stopped long enough for the man to escape safely through an emergency exit, the FAA said.
>
> Sheriff's deputies with dogs began a search for him among houses surrounding the airport.

Perfect. Trust the FAA to waste time looking for me in Reno. Before long someone would realize I'd taken two of the parachutes — a pretty good clue that I'd jumped.

I glanced through the glass of the train station door. The brightly lit hall looked warm and dangerous. I went instead to a pay phone mounted on the wall outside. I put in a coin and dialed the nuclear physics lab at Reed College.

"Hello?" Lammergeier's voice was nervous and eager.

"It's me," I said.

"You're late. I was afraid you weren't going to call. Do you have the money?"

"Of course. I'm just being cautious. That's why there's a slight change of plan."

"A change?" He was easily frightened.

I explained gently, " A small change, just to be safe. We'll still meet at eleven tonight. But instead of making our transaction on the Sellwood Bridge, we'll meet on the railroad bridge over the Columbia."

"A railroad bridge! Why there?"

"I don't trust erratic drivers. Are you ready for your instructions?"

"I don't know. A railroad bridge at night sounds dangerous."

"No pain, no gain, Lammergeier. Do you want the cash or not?"

"All right," he grumbled.

"At ten o'clock you'll start driving north. At first take side streets and alleys to lose anyone who's following. Then take Interstate 5 north to the Jantzen Beach exit. Park in front of the Red Lion Inn and walk left along the river, to the west. When you get to the railroad bridge, you'll find a small railed walkway on the downstream side. I'll be waiting in the middle of the bridge."

"I'll want to inspect the money before we trade."

"Don't worry. Just make sure the documents you bring are originals. If it turns out you've kept copies to sell to another company, the information's worthless to us. And so are you."

I could hear him swallow. "I understand."

I hung up, worrying more about Swarovsky than Lammergeier. How long could I keep the Russians off balance?

Back at the railroad bridge, The Keeper had built a fire to heat the chili, and he'd opened a can of sardines. "Any luck getting a tow truck?"

"It's Thanksgiving," I said. "They can't get a truck free until eleven."

"Then you can stay for dinner after all." He uncorked a bottle of brandy happily, took a swig, and passed it to me. "To your health."

To be honest, it wasn't the worst Thanksgiving dinner I've had. The sweet warmth of the brandy ennobled our sardine appetizers, bringing back memories of the vodka and pickled herring my KGB hosts had proudly served for our graduation in Murmansk. This was an honest American feast, hot chili with a spoon from a tin can, under the freedom of a bridge. As darkness fell, the flickering campfire light on The Keeper's freckled face showed that he was at peace with his world. That easy calmness reflected on me as well, slowing the tension of the past day. I had jumped out of an airplane and made my way back to the Oregon border. My goal, against all odds, seemed near at hand. I would make the trade with Lammergeier, destroy his documents, and walk into a new life, perhaps as Dave McGill, the footloose chum of the affable Keeper.

We didn't talk much as we worked our way down the brandy bottle. A tugboat with green running lights churned slowly past, pushing a barge. The wake lapped on the riverbank boulders, a rolling whoosh from left to right, rippling the water lights. A long-necked bird landed on a piling, preened, and spread its wings. The red glow of the lights on the bridge above us blinked on and off, counting down to my rendezvous.

When the bottle was empty, The Keeper frowned for the first time. "What about your tow truck?" he asked.

I looked at my wristwatch. It was 10:30 p.m.. Reluctantly I stood up, tucked my duffel under my left arm, and held out my right hand. "Thanks for dinner."

The Keeper stood to shake my hand. "You're a good man," he said. "Not as good as you, my friend." I smiled a little sadly. Then I added, just for the hell of it, "If I change my mind about the truck, do you think I could go with you?"

He raised his bushy red eyebrows. "You're thinking of heading south?"

"Maybe."

He studied me, as if he was only now beginning to wonder who I was. He nodded.

"Then perhaps we will meet again. Take care, Keeper."

He saluted. "God speed, McGill."

I turned and climbed the embankment beside the bridge. The ferns and grass were wet from the drizzle, so I slipped several times. When I reached the tracks I cast a long look back to the lights of the Amtrak station, wishing a tow truck really were waiting for me there. When I walked the other way, on the wooden railroad ties. fear began to crowd my chest. The closer I got to the black steel girders of the bridge, the more it looked like a giant animal trap, built for monstrous prey. One tie, two ties, one tie again—the splintered, tarry beams beneath my feet were not spaced for the living. Railroad ties are called dead men, I remembered. I was the walking dead.

On the bridge itself, a row of planks to one side formed a narrow walkway, just far enough from the rails that a person might survive the passage of a speeding train. A waist-high cable served as the only handrail. Below, the Columbia River ran swift and dark. Ahead, the blinking red lights offered dim glimpses of a hellish half-mile tunnel to Oregon.

I stopped, thinking of the money I was about to trade away. It was enough to buy half a dozen houses in Portland. It was more cash than

I had ever seen in one place before. On an impulse I unzipped the duffel, took out six twenty-dollar bills, and tucked them in my wallet. No matter what happened, I would keep a memento of Cooper's treasure. Then I reclosed the duffel and walked on.

As I neared the halfway point, in the middle of a sea of water, a bright light appeared on the Oregon side. The girders around me hummed and clanked, louder and louder. I clutched my duffel and hid behind a diagonal beam. Like a great mechanical dragon, a diesel locomotive rumbled closer, staring me down with its blinding white eye. Suddenly the wheels were beside me, almost within reach. Boxcars and tankers thundered past, beating out a deafening, erratic percussion.

When the train had passed, my ears were ringing. I held up my watch and read the time by the red blink of the bridge lights. Lammergeier was already fifteen minutes late. I had chosen a poor rendezvous site. A college professor might change his mind about venturing onto a railroad bridge in the dark.

By eleven thirty the warmth of the brandy was gone. I shivered on the bridge, trying to think of alternatives.

And then I noticed a tiny, wobbling light at the end of the tunnel. The yellowish dot wove uncertainly, sometimes looking up to gleam my way. A flashlight.

It took Curt Lammergeier fifteen minutes to tap his way out to the center of the river. He stopped a hundred feet away, aimed his flashlight at me, and shouted, "Put down the money and back away!"

"Dr. Lammergeier," I said evenly, unzipping the duffel on the walkway, "Here's a sample, $6000 in twenties. Come take a look. If you like it, I have a duffel filled with bundles just like it." I held up a brick of bills. The twenties had been rubber-banded together, a dozen stacks of $500, held by a pair of thicker bands. I laid the bait on the planks, rezipped the duffel, and retreated twenty feet.

He approached warily, like a feral cat. I held up my open hands to reassure him. He was wearing a cheap plastic rain poncho over a business suit, and he held a Meier & Frank shopping bag in his left hand. His face was pale and puffy. Behind thick glasses, his eyes glanced nervously from the money to me.

"The bills are unmarked," I said. I didn't tell him that this particular bundle was missing six bills—the ones I had put in my wallet.

He set down his shopping bag and examined the cash, flipping through the notes with one hand while he held the flashlight with his other. He grunted. Then he put the bundle in his bag and took out a thick manila envelope. "Here's what you want. But first let me see the rest of the money."

"First let me see the plans." I pushed the duffel closer with my foot, but held out my hand.

We edged closer, each watching the other's eyes. He lunged for the duffel, but I pinned it with my foot. "The plans, doctor."

He held up the envelope and slid out a few papers. The blinking red lights revealed photographs, drawings, and specifications for a lunar landing module.

"How long did you work on the Apollo project?" I asked.

"Six years." He was shining his flashlight into the duffel, checking the bundles much more carefully than I ever had. "They fired me without benefits."

He was getting his benefits now, but did he know at what cost? I asked, "What do you think I'm going to do with these plans?"

He smirked. "You're not from McDonnell-Douglas. They wouldn't pay this kind of money for Apollo plans."

"Then who would?"

"The Russians, of course. They'd like to sabotage Apollo 16. The space program would look pretty stupid if the lunar module didn't work when it tried to take off from the Descartes Highlands next April."

I stared at him. "And you're OK with letting astronauts asphyxiate on the moon?"

He shrugged. "Someone has to stop them."

I was puzzling over this when I saw two new dots of light at the end of the tunnel. Two more small, yellowish flashlights were approaching from the Oregon shore. Not the police—they weren't looking for Lammergeier, and they certainly didn't know where to look for me.

Swarovsky.

My blood turned to ice. They were coming to kill me. Lammergeier was incompetent at covering his tracks, and the KGB were masters of pursuit. Perhaps they had planted a homing device in his car, or his shoe, knowing it would lead them to me. If the agents were running— and from the bobbing of the lights it seemed they were—I had no more than three minutes.

Meanwhile Lammergeier had rezipped the duffel, taken something out of his shopping bag, and aimed it at me.

"Hands up, Cooper."

The gun he held looked like a toy cowboy pistol, but it was probably a 22. Everything was going wrong.

I raised my hands, still holding the envelope. Then I nodded toward the lights behind him. "You've been followed, Lammergeier. Two people are running this way."

He laughed. "That's rich. You think you can trick me into turning around? I thought you were smarter than that, after pulling off the whole hijacking ruse."

"Hijacking ruse?"

The lights were getting much closer. Swarovsky could almost certainly see us now.

"I got suspicious when the TV news said the bandit asked for $200,000, exactly the amount I wanted. And you know what? The cash in this duffel matches the description, all in twenties. There wasn't a hijacked jetliner, was there? You never parachuted anywhere."

My heart was beating so fast it was hard to think. I nodded past his shoulder again. "Two Russian agents are running this way. They'll be in firing range in a few seconds."

He laughed even harder. "As soon as you telephoned, I knew you weren't with the Russians. The Russians wouldn't care if they had the original documents. Copies of the plans would be good enough to figure out how to sabotage the lunar module. No, I realized then that you had to be from the ones who want to shut me up. The world government people."

There was so little time. I took a step forward.

"Don't move!" Lammergeier pulled the duffel back with his foot, but because he was keeping his eyes on me he didn't notice the shopping bag. It tipped to one side and the bundle of twenties rolled out.

He gasped, clutching toward the falling cash. And suddenly the night shifted into slow motion, like an old black-and-white film flashing one frame at a time.

A bundle with $5880 in bills dropped forty feet to the steel framework of the bridge, bounced off a girder, and arced down into the Columbia River.

Before the money hit the water, I took advantage of the distraction to kick the gun out of Lammergeier's hand. Fear made me kick so hard that the weapon flew into his face and knocked him off balance. He staggered back, missed the plank, and teetered into the darkness with a terrified cry.

The cable handrail caught him under his right arm. But the wire sagged so far under his weight that he dangled precariously, just far enough from the walkway that he couldn't get back on his own. If he fell, the protruding beams below would kill him before he hit the river.

"Help me!" he whimpered, kicking toward the plank. But all he succeeded in doing was pushing the duffel loose. The big sack fell like a corpse. It thumped hard against the girders below and dropped down toward the black river.

"No!" Lammergeier cried, as if it were his own body that were falling.

I threw the envelope down with a hard spin, so that it splashed into the water at nearly the same time as the ransom money. Then I grabbed Lammergeier under the shoulders and hauled him back onto the planks.

Now the Russians were so close that I could recognize them: Swarovsky and his lieutenant Merkov. Their guns were raised, but it's hard to shoot while running.

"Are you really Cooper?" Lammergeier asked.

A shot whined past and smacked into a girder. A ribbon of fire in my shoulder suggested that the bullet had grazed me along the way.

"Yes." I took two steps, gave a mighty leap, and vaulted over the cable, praying that I had jumped far enough to clear the girders below.

36

Neil thought Murmansk seemed a little less grim the next morning, as Ludmilla drove them to the Otlichna warehouse in her little green Lada. Skinny seagulls soared in a metallic blue sky. The Lada had to wait in the middle of a boulevard while a fleet of black limousines unloaded a wedding party. Crewcut men in tuxedoes and bridesmaids in red chiffon carried armloads of flowers into an undistinguished six-story concrete building that Ludmilla said was a Russian orthodox church. Little girls in frilly white dresses waved flags striped with the white, dark blue, and burgundy of the Russian Federation.

The Otlichna headquarters, as it turned out, looked a lot like the church, palisaded by a fence of black iron spears in an industrial district between a sprawling railroad freight yard and the rusting merchant ships of the port. Ludmilla, unstoppably cheerful, marched them past loading bays, forklift trucks, and high-ceilinged offices in need of paint. She laughed when Neil asked if any of their employees had previously worked for the KGB. She seemed genuinely concerned when he suggested that contraband might have been included in some of the wine shipments from America.

Marial had arranged to meet a retired Otlichna employee at the train station cafe for lunch, and Neil was about to suggest they go straight there when Ludmilla showed them a room where dozens of women were opening boxes of Oregon Noir. They were pulling out the bottles and gluing on new labels. Neil couldn't read the bright red Cyrillic lettering, but the labels included a picture of a stylized gray face that gave him pause. He picked up one of the bottles and turned the label toward Marial. "Who does that remind you of?"

"The Gray Madonna."

"Ask her who does their artwork."

When Marial translated the question, Ludmilla responded animatedly, obviously pleased that they would show interest.

Marial said, "It's by Brother Daniel. Apparently he's famous in Russia."

Neil raised his eyebrows. Brother Daniel was not only a Cooper candidate, but he also knew how to paint well enough to fake the Rothko paintings. "Ask her if he's been to Murmansk."

Marial conferred with Ludmilla and reported, "Brother Daniel has been here several times. Otlichna is using the new labels to capitalize on the news that the Gray Madonna has been returned to the Solovetsky Island monastery. The idea is that bubbly wine works miracles, just like the icon."

"What kind of miracles?" Neil asked.

"She says she doesn't know exactly. We'll have to ask at the monastery."

Ludmilla led them to a wood-paneled tasting room and pressed them with samples. She looked hurt when Neil said no.

"Thanks for the tour, but we need to catch a train south."

"Already? I drive you to station."

Neil shook his head. "It's close enough we'll walk. We've taken up enough of your time."

"Enjoy your visit to Russia," Ludmilla said, and kissed them both farewell three times on either cheek.

It really wasn't far to the train station—the depot's yellow dome rose just a few blocks away—but to cross the freight yard they had to detour over a long iron footbridge. They dragged their wheeled suitcases up the rusty steps while old Russian women in black kerchiefs carried bags of groceries the other way. From the middle of the bridge, the dozens of shiny railroad tracks below reminded Neil of an icy river, flowing north to the Arctic. Half a dozen trains waited on sidings. The cars seemed smaller than in America, and the tracks narrower. On the horizon, the endless concrete towers of the city marched in formation, led by Mother Russia, the gigantic concrete woman on the river bluff.

"Concrete must have been the Soviets' idea of a socialist worker's paradise," Neil mused. "Half a million people live in this city, all in concrete boxes."

"Apparently, everyone also has their own garage somewhere else. Do you remember seeing all those little metal sheds packed together in the fields as we drove into town?"

"Those were private garages?"

"More than just garages. People go there on weekends to barbecue, talk, barter, work on their motorcycles, you name it."

"Where did you learn about this?"

Marial walked on, the wheels of her suitcase clunking on the bridge grating. "From a naval engineer I met last night."

"What else did this engineer tell you?"

She shrugged a shoulder, casting him a coquettish glance. "He asked if I wanted to play submarine."

"Is that like playing doctor?"

"A little. You lock yourself in an apartment with nothing but vodka and pickles. You remove all the clocks and cell phones, and you cover the windows with black plastic so you can't tell if it's day or night. Then you drink the vodka for two or three days until you run out."

"The fun never ends in Murmansk."

"I can't promise we'll learn much more from Anton Chernovich, the retired Otlichna worker."

"How much do we know about him?"

"He was a friend of my husband years ago. When I called this morning his wife said he'd be at the station cafe all day. That's all he does now — sit in the cafe, watch people, and drink."

"How will we tell him apart from all the other people who do that?"

"By his mustache. His wife said it's the only thing he does well."

A cold wind blew newspapers across the square in front of the station. Inside the cavernous hall, long lines of people waited at ticket and information windows. A giant schedule board announced that the train south wouldn't leave until 6:15 p.m. There would be time to buy tickets after lunch.

The cafe occupied a smoky wing behind a newsstand. The few travelers, sailors, and idlers at the square wooden tables seemed dazed. Chernovich, with an enormous mustache drooping below his fleshy nose, was easy to identify. The foot-tall beer glass before him was empty, but rings of foam clung to the inside, high-water marks from the passage of the morning.

Chernovich brightened when Marial introduced herself. He pressed her hands and talked so rapidly that Marial had no time to translate. Even the waitress who came to take their orders had trouble interrupting. Neil sat at the table, occasionally smiling or nodding, but otherwise ignored. Only when their food arrived—three bowls of stew with two bottles of apple juice and another foot-tall beer for Chernovich—did the giant mustache settle on the rim of his glass long enough for Marial to speak to Neil.

"Mr. Chernovich remembers my wedding in Riga. He says my husband was robbing the cradle."

"How old were you?"

"Eighteen, but I looked younger. He also said it was the government's idea that Otlichna should move its operation to Murmansk."

"Which government?"

She lowered her voice to ask the question. The old man responded with a laugh and a long stream of Russian. When he finally returned to his beer, Marial synopsized, "The KGB."

"Isn't he worried about saying that out loud in a train station?"

She opened her apple juice and poured it into a glass. "He says he's too old to care. Besides, he thinks all that spy stuff is ancient history."

"Then ask him if it's possible that things have been smuggled in with the wine shipments."

When Marial translated this, Chernovich laughed so hard that he sputtered foam into his mustache. Then he talked for five minutes before dipping back into his beer.

"At first they only smuggled messages," Marial said. "But after the collapse of the Soviet Union they started putting all kinds of things into the wine boxes—jeans, watches, cigarettes. Even now, he says, the mafia can place orders. For them it's like shopping from a catalog. Then they ship it south or set up shops in their garage sheds. Murmansk is an open city, as long as you pay off the bosses."

"Where are the bosses? In Portland?" Neil wondered how much Nancy Willis knew about the company she had bought. He needed to call Connie soon.

Chernovich didn't laugh when he heard this question. He shook his head and muttered a few words. Then he emptied his glass.

"He doesn't know," Marial said. "He thinks they're in Russia, but you don't ask. You don't want to know."

"How about Cooper?" Neil asked. "Has he ever heard that name?"

Chernovich repeated the name slowly. "Cooper. *Da*, Cooper." He took out a pencil, wrote something on his cardboard beer mat, and pushed it to Marial.

She tipped it toward Neil. "He says we should ask here. It's an address in Novgorod. We should mention his name. But he won't tell us anything more."

Neil slipped the circular mat into his suit coat pocket. "Tell him thanks. And buy him another beer."

Buying train tickets proved to be much more difficult than extracting information from the garrulous Anton Chernovich. They waited forty minutes in one line before discovering it sold only local tickets. For destinations beyond Murmansk's province you had to buy tickets in an entirely different part of the station. This room had lines of people waiting at six ticket windows, even though only three of the windows were open. It turned out that the people waiting at closed windows were betting the ticket agent at another window would go on break, and that the replacement ticket agent would open a different window. Many people hedged their bets by asking people in other lines to hold places for them.

While Marial maneuvered through this shifting labyrinth, Neil excused himself to find a restroom and make a phone call, tasks he assumed would take but a minute.

The "*Tualyet*" sign sent him outside, along the tracks, and into a basement tunnel. Here a fat woman at a counter blocked his path. She held out her hand, bored but officious. Neil offered his smallest bill, a hundred-ruble note worth about four dollars. She shook her head and pointed to a notice printed in small Cyrillic script. The only numeral he could see was a three. He surmised that restroom privileges cost three rubles (about twelve cents), and that this woman was not prepared to make change. By now his need to use a bathroom had become pressing. He hurried back to the cafe, bought a bottle of water, and returned with a handful of coins. The toilet lady picked out what she needed and nodded toward the room beyond. There Neil found seven ceramic holes in the ground, each flanked by a pair of corrugated footholds. Feces protruded from the holes. There was no toilet paper. Neil opted to use a urinal on the wall. Then he washed his hands thoroughly, as if to scrub out the memory of the room.

Once Neil was outside again he took out his cell phone to call Connie. He had bought the phone specially for the trip. That morning the hotel receptionist had helped him install a card that enabled the phone to work in Russia—and probably also allowed Russian authorities to monitor foreign calls.

The phone rang quite a while in Portland before Connie answered. "Wu here," she said groggily.

Neil looked at his watch and realized he had miscalculated the time difference. It was six a.m. in Portland, not eight. "This is Neil. Sorry to call so early, but I'm about to get on a train here in Murmansk."

"Lovely. Have you tracked down Cooper yet?"

"No, but I did find out the Otlichna warehouse has been receiving a lot more than just wine from Oregon. I wonder if Nancy Willis knows Murmansk is such an active trade center."

"Was," Connie said.

"What do you mean, 'was'?"

"When Martin Blodgett was shipping manager at McMinnville, he checked all the containers by himself. He could have loaded them with whatever he wanted. After Blodgett died in the Underground murders, Otlichna started a policy of double checking. Two different supervisors now make sure there's nothing in those containers but Oregon Noir."

"Sounds like someone didn't want Blodgett talking about his work," Neil said. "After Blodgett shipped out the Rothko paintings, he was eliminated. Compared with multi-million-dollar artwork, smuggling blue jeans and cigarettes was small potatoes."

"I agree, but there's no sign Nancy Willis was involved."

"How about Brother Daniel?"

"The icon painter? Funny you'd mention him."

A row of dark green sleeper wagons backed into the station, creaking and clanging. Neil cupped the phone to his ear. "I found out Brother Daniel has been to Murmansk. He painted a version of the Gray Madonna that Otlichna is using on a wine label."

"Interesting. Remember how you asked me find out what people were doing on Thanksgiving of 1971?"

"Yes."

"Well, it turns out Brother Daniel was under some stress back then. He'd spent the years from '69 to '71 as a conscientious objector, working in a Salem mental hospital. He called himself Crenshaw back then. The summer of '71 he took off for Europe, but no one knows exactly where. The next time he shows up is a week after Thanksgiving. That's when he went to his parents house in Washougal. and found them both dead. Officially, it was a double suicide."

Neil whistled. "Maybe his parents had just found out their son had spent Thanksgiving hijacking a plane."

"It's possible."

"Any other news?"

"Well, the television newspeople are still trying to figure out what happened to The Keeper. They seem to think because he had the parachute case that he can lead them to D.B. Cooper. But he's sitting tight in Susan's apartment."

"And Susan?"

"She doesn't talk much, so she's fine."

Neil had been looking at the label mounted on the side of the railroad car: САНКТ-ПЕТЕРБУРГ. Now he realized it spelled Saint Petersburg.

"Connie? My train just pulled into the station. I'll try to call tomorrow, but we're going to a pretty remote area, checking out the Gray Madonna on the Solevetsky Islands, so my cell phone might not work."

"Roger that, Lieutenant."

Marial had spent a little over a hundred dollars apiece for two first-class tickets. At the door of their car, two uniformed attendants examined their tickets, passports, and visas. Then the attendants made themselves tea from a samovar boiler in the hallway and retired to a glass-doored cubicle to play cards. The compartment reserved for Neil and Marial had two benches, a music system that played Russian classics in minor keys, and a fold-up table with a small white tablecloth.

Marial had come prepared for the twelve-hour trip to Kem, the nearest station to the Solovetsky Islands. From her large handbag she produced yoghurt, buns, and apples pilfered from the hotel's breakfast bar. Then she gave Neil an English copy of the *International Herald Tribune* and sat down with a Russian magazine for herself. When Neil asked, she explained that it was titled ДОБРЫЕ СОВЕТЫ, "Good Advice". The lead article, "Are You a Slave to Fashion?" suggested that Russian women might dare to skip the standard tight jeans, black tops, and pointy-toed high heels in favor of ХИППИ (hippie) fashion—blouses consisting of strategically draped Indian prints.

When the train pulled out of the station, Murmansk's factories slowly rolled by. The wheels soon found their rhythm—a clanking that seemed to chant, "You're out of luck, you're out of luck." After that Neil saw little outside but an endless taiga of struggling pines, white-barked birches, and blackwater swamps. Occasionally, across thawing lakes, he glimpsed low, snow-capped hills. The sweet tarry scent of Russian diesel mixed with stale cigarette smoke. Fainter were the scents of sea tang, urine, and wood.

At ten in the evening one of the two attendants came to convert the benches to beds. Neil and Marial were both tired. They kissed each other good night, crawled into their separate berths, and soon were rocking to sleep.

At six the next morning an attendant turned on the lights, announcing that Kem was half an hour away. Neil squinted unwillingly against the glare. Marial raised herself to one elbow, her red hair poofed out randomly. They looked at each other, laughed, and turned aside to prepare for the day.

It was still dark outside when they arrived. Kem's ancient wooden station had only one information window. The woman there knew nothing about traveling to the Solovetsky Islands.

"Isn't the monastery a big tourist attraction?" Neil asked Marial. She forwarded this question to the woman at the window. A moment later she translated the reply. "Yes, but the ferries aren't operated by the railroad, so she doesn't know their schedule. She says we might ask a taxi driver."

Neil and Marial rolled their suitcases to a crossroads where two long-haired men dozed in cabs beneath a streetlight. The first man yawned at them and began putting their luggage into the trunk.

"Solovetsky?" Neil asked.

The man nodded. He turned on a meter and drove along a dark, potholed road. The headlights revealed a slum of rusty garages on the left and an occasional unpainted wooden farmhouse on the right. Fifteen minutes later, as dawn began to coax grays from the overcast sky, they reached a waterfront with concrete ruins, derelict ships, and the rotten remains of wharves. They stopped at a trailer where a bare bulb lit a patio where the only furniture was a flimsy picnic table made of pine boards.

Neil missed much of the conversation that followed, but he surmised that the official ferry was out of service due to some kind of mechanical failure. The woman in the trailer sold them paper cups of soup and pointed them toward an old fishing trawler. Half a dozen people were already waiting beside the boat while a shifty-looking captain rearranged boxes and nets on deck to make room for passengers. Two young Russian men with touring bags on bicycles joked with each other. Three nuns in black habits prayed. A bearded man sat on a cat carrier, frowning. Nearly an hour passed before the captain loaded everyone on board, started the motor, and steered out of the harbor. When they reached open water—the faintly salty spray of the White Sea misting across the bow with each wave—the captain tied the wheel in place with an elastic cord and came to collect fares. The nuns, the bicyclists, and the man with the cat paid three hundred rubles apiece. Marial argued with the captain in Russian for a while before counting out two thousand rubles.

"Why so much?" Neil asked.

She shrugged. "We don't have Russian passports. The captain charges foreigners more because he says we can afford it."

The fishing boat steamed east for an hour and a half, mostly out of sight of land. A tern with black-and-white scissor wings swept above the gray waves, dipped its beak in the water, and came up with a minnow. The bird flew beside the boat, let the little fish go for half a second, caught it in the air, and swallowed it.

The diesel fumes and churning waves were starting to make Neil queasy. But then a pinpoint of gold appeared ahead, something at last that wasn't moving. Slowly the dot grew to a dozen gold onion domes, the towers of an improbable Arctic Oz.

The fishing boat steamed past skerries of bare pink granite to the bay of a long, low island. The churches of the monastery were part of a Kremlin-like fortress ringed with fifty-foot walls.

After tying up at the dock, the captain laid a plank ashore. The bicyclists balanced across this bridge first, followed by the nuns and the man with the cat. Neil and Marial went last, carrying their suitcases. All of the passengers walked across a field to a small wooden kiosk to buy postcards, maps, or coffee. Marial bought all three. She talked several minutes with the old woman running the booth.

"The monks will be in prayer until noon," Marial told Neil. "In the meantime, there's a bed and breakfast we could check into at the monastery's old boat yard."

"Will they have lunch?"

"Apparently there's a grocery in the village behind the monastery."

They pulled their suitcases along a gravel path past the fortress. A small, freshly painted sign on a wrought iron fence led them to the bed and breakfast—actually a cluster of cottages. The one they rented had brightly painted walls, a ceiling papered with flour sacks, and wavy glass windows. A giant feather comforter puffed atop the double bed like a balloon.

They washed up, changed, and went out in search of food. The village, according to the map Marial had bought, occupied the barracks of Russia's first gulag, built in 1921 for political prisoners who opposed Lenin's October Revolution. The main street reminded Neil of a Wild West ghost town, but with Soviet Army trucks instead of stagecoaches and stray dogs instead of tumbleweeds. At a store in one of the unpainted wooden barracks, they bought rolls and meat for a picnic. They ate their lunch on a bench by a cemetery overlooking the towers of the fortress walls.

Somewhere deep in the monastery a giant bell slowly tolled twelve. Neil looked to Marial. "Time to go. Let's find the Gray Madonna."

He led the way through an arched tunnel in the fortress wall to a vast inner courtyard. Ahead, domes and belfries rose above what appeared to be three connected cathedrals. To the sides, stone buildings formed a continuous ring around the central square.

A man in a gray overcoat leaned out of a doorway to their left. "*Muzei?*" he asked.

"*Nyet.*" Neil held out his police badge. He hadn't come this far to play tourist. "Marial, tell him we're from the American police. We want to talk with the Father Superior."

As Marial translated, the man stepped out to look at them more closely. Then he pointed to the far left-hand end of the courtyard. "He says the monks should be in the icon painting workshop by now," Marial said.

Neil put away his badge. He headed toward the building the man had indicated. When he knocked on the door there was no reply, so he tried the handle. It opened with a creak, revealing a long stone staircase that smelled of tar and dust. He and Marial ventured up the steps. Beyond an open door at the top they found a large studio, where sunlight slanted in from tall windows. A dozen monks in black robes looked up from their tables.

Neil decided this wasn't the right kind of place to pull out his badge. Fortunately, Marial stepped in with a long Russian speech in a friendly tone.

A long-bearded monk with a black cylindrical hat walked up to study their faces, as if he might want to paint their portraits later. Then he surprised Neil by speaking in clear, if slightly accented, English.

"I am the director of the Transfiguration Monastery. Friends from Oregon are always welcome."

"You've had other visitors from Oregon?" Neil asked.

"Oh yes. Would you like some tea?" He held his hand out to a spherical brass kettle warmed by a candle.

"Thank you, yes." Neil couldn't help but add, "What other visitors have you had?"

The monk poured hot water into Styrofoam cups and added tea bags. "Many followers of the old faith ended up in your part of America. You call them Old Believers. Originally, this was their home."

"Why pick an Arctic island as home?"

"For religious purity. We are on the thirty-sixth meridian, the same as Jerusalem, but far enough north to remove temptations and most dangers."

"But not all dangers?"

"No. Tsar Alexis drove the Old Believers out of Solovki in the sixteenth century. The official Russian Orthodox church operated the monastery for the next four hundred years. In 1921 the Communists set up a gulag here. Since 1990, when spiritual life resumed within these walls, our brothers in Oregon have offered a great deal of help." He held up his cup of tea, as if to toast.

Neil also held up his tea and took a drink. "I'm here because of a problem, father. Two months ago a painting was stolen from the

Old Believers' church in Oregon. We think it was sold at an auction in Novgorod and may have ended up here. It's a very old icon."

"The Gray Madonna?" The monk pointed to a pillar in the middle of the room, where a shelf of candles lit a small, gold-framed painting of a dark woman's face. "We are all learning from it. But why are you calling it stolen?"

Now that Neil looked about the room he could see that the monks were copying the painting, carefully recreating the flat dark face.

"The icon belongs to a church in Woodburn," Neil explained.

The monk ran his hand slowly through his long beard. "The Gray Madonna was painted in this very room more than four hundred years ago. In Russia we have a law that art should be returned to its country of origin. The madonna is home."

"Yes, but—"

"Lieutenant, perhaps you have not heard. Since the icon was returned to Solovki, the church in Woodburn has dropped its claim."

This news brought Neil up short. If the Old Believers in Oregon no longer wanted the icon, he had come to this remote island on a fool's errand. "Do you know who took the icon from the church in Woodburn?"

"No."

"Do you know how it was brought to Russia?"

"No. But I can tell you who bought it for us at the auction in Novgorod."

"Who?"

"A wealthy celebrity, and an inspiration to us all. An American named Brother Daniel."

Neil exchanged a glance with Marial. She said, "In Murmansk we learned that Brother Daniel's painting of the Gray Madonna is being used by a vodka company to sell wine."

The monk raised an eyebrow. "Why would they use a sacred image for this?"

"Because the madonna is supposed to work miracles. Although they won't say what kind."

The monk began chuckling. He had to set down his tea. "No, I don't suppose they would. Come here." He led them to the candlelit altar. "Do you have a coin? Any coin. One for each of you."

Neil fished some change from his pocket. He gave Marial a ten-ruble coin and kept another in his hand.

"Good. Then you can sample our miracle, if you like. Those who make an offering to the Gray Madonna dream of their passage to the eternal."

Neil turned his coin over in his fingers. "What does that mean?"

"It is not a miracle everyone chooses, to foresee the moment of their death. Some miracles are better suited to a pilgrimage church than to a wine bar."

A cold wind made the candles flicker. The shifting light on the icon's gold background made the face appear to move. Centuries of candlelit offerings had grayed the madonna with soot. She bent her head in sorrow. A teardrop clung to her ashen cheek.

Marial clinked her coin firmly on the sill below the icon. Then she crossed herself and backed away.

Neil still turned his coin over, thinking. He had seen a lot of death in his career. Sooner or later, every police officer did. The possibility of one's own death was part of the job. Nobody joked about it. Still, he put his coin on the altar.

That night, although they slept underneath the same, fluffy comforter on the cottage's bed, Neil and Marial did not touch. When he awoke she was fully dressed, sitting by the window, looking out as a pink dawn lit the monastery's golden domes.

"Did you dream?" she asked.

Neil ran his hands over his face. "Yeah, but nothing specific. Just snow and ice. One big winter blizzard."

Marial nodded. "Then we won't always be together, you and I."

"Why? What did you see?

"Fire," she said. "Nothing all night but flames."

37

When Neil didn't answer his cell phone for forty-eight hours — the entire weekend — Connie felt a unpleasant foreboding that he might never return from Russia.

On Monday morning, going through his mail, she found the letter, and by 11a.m. Captain Dickers and special agent Owen had called a department meeting, but with a tone of quiet desperation that Connie read as, "We're still tapping around in the dark."

And then her cell rang. "Neil?" Her heart was racing. All twenty people in the room had turned to watch.

Static sputtered from the little plastic phone, and then a tinny, rhythmic clanking. " — orry, we're — zavodsk — "

"I think it's him," Connie announced with relief. "But there's a bad connection. Neil?"

Special agent Owen took command. "OK, tell him to call back on the department line. Let's get this on the speakerphone."

A few minutes later the rattle of train wheels echoed in the conference room. "Hello? Is this better?"

"Much better, Lieutenant. This is special agent Owen. We're holding a briefing on the Cooper case. Where are you right now?"

"On a train coming into a place called Vol something. Volkhov. I paid five hundred bucks for this international phone, and this is the first time it's worked since Murmansk."

Several sergeants chuckled. Captain Dickers silenced them with an upheld hand. "Ferguson? Dickers here. Listen, a letter arrived here this morning addressed to you. It has important evidence about the case."

"What? Now you're opening my mail?"

This time almost everyone laughed. Connie said, "I opened it, Neil. You told me to check your desk."

"So what was in the letter?" The clanking in the background slowed, and brakes screeched.

Owen answered, "First, it's critical to note that this envelope was postmarked in Portland on February 28, seven days ago, when Gregory DeKuyper was still in our custody."

"Seven days ago? What took it so long?"

"It had the wrong zip code, 97001 instead of 97201. Apparently it spent the week going to Antelope and back."

"All right," Neil's voice said, "Whoever sent it was careless or in a hurry. And we know it wasn't The Keeper, because he was in jail. So who's it from?"

Connie said, "We think it's from D.B. Cooper, Neil."

For a moment there was only silence.

"The real one?"

"Yes, the skyjacker. Evidently he's alive. In Portland."

Neil paused a moment before asking, "What does he want?"

"I'll read it." Connie unfolded the sheet of paper. "Lieutenant Ferguson: I am the one you are looking for, not The Keeper. He is an innocent, good man. Enclosed is payment for a Thanksgiving dinner I have owed him for a long time. Give him one of these and keep one for your forensics department. And don't worry. I will have to tell you who I am before long, Lieutenant."

The speakerphone gave out the sigh of a man blowing out a long breath. "What else was in the envelope?" Neil asked.

"Two twenty-dollar bills."

"Are they — "

"Yes."

Luis Espada from forensics held up a plastic bag with two greenish bills. "Lieutenant? Espada here. Right now I'm looking at two banknotes, issued from the Federal Reserve in San Francisco in 1969. Not only do their serial numbers indicate that they are part of the skyjacking ransom, but do you remember the money that turned up on a Columbia River mudbank in 1980?"

"A kid on a picnic found six grand."

"Five thousand eight hundred and eighty dollars, to be exact," Espada said. "Six banknotes were missing from that bundle. Based on the sequence of the serial numbers, these are two of the missing bills."

"Could the kid have pocketed them back in 1980?"

"Nope. These notes weren't in a river for nine years. They're almost as fresh as the day they parachuted out of the plane."

A rumble issued from the phone, followed by a man speaking in Russian, apparently asking questions. When Marial's disembodied voice responded in Russian, Connie sat back and tightened her lips.

"I'm sorry," Neil's clear voice returned. "We bought third-class tickets today by mistake, so I'm in tight quarters. Espada, can you tell anything from the handwriting?"

"No handwriting, boss. The letter's done by computer in twelve-point Times Roman. It's printed on copy paper from Office Max using Hewlett-Packard ink. Anyone could have done it."

"How about DNA from the saliva?"

"Sorry. Mr. Cooper used stick-on stamps and sealed the envelope with water from a sponge. These days, even amateurs know stuff like that from television, but I'm guessing your letter came from a pro."

The FBI agent leaned forward. "Owen here. This letter was addressed to you, Lieutenant. We need progress, and so far this is our best lead. Do you have any idea who might have sent you this?"

"No, I don't. But if you're looking for progress, Owen, it's all around you."

"Where, Lieutenant?"

"You know Cooper's watching the Portland news, so you can communicate with him by going to the media."

A young sergeant in the room added, "And we've caught Cooper with a new crime."

"A new crime?" Owen looked surprised.

"Sure. It's a federal offense to send currency through the mail."

"No, it isn't." Owen grunted dismissively. "That's an urban legend. It's only illegal to send cash if it's used for chain mail letters or racketeering."

Captain Dickers tapped the table with his pen for attention. "Listen, Ferguson, tomorrow the Diplomatic Security Service shows up and everyone gets reassigned to security for the global summit. I need you back here in Portland. Now."

"That's not so easy, Captain." There was a clunk, and the clatter of iron wheels picking up speed. "There aren't many airports out here, and it's hours between train stations. Besides, there's an art auction I need to see tomorrow. I'll be back Friday."

"Cooper addressed the letter to you, Ferguson. You're our contact. What are we supposed to do without you?"

"Well, Captain, when you're dealing with a hijacker, it's always best to do what he says."

The captain frowned. He looked about the room, as if for a second opinion.

Connie said, "I know the location of the safe house where The Keeper is staying. If you want I could give him one of the twenty-dollar bills."

Espada raised his finger, "Years ago, a Seattle newspaper posted a five-thousand-dollar reward for anyone who could show them a bill from Cooper's ransom money. I think the offer is still valid."

"Do it." Neil's voice sounded as firm as if he were sitting there with his hands on the conference table. "The letter is proof that The Keeper can't be D.B. Cooper. We arrested a harmless transient by mistake. He could use five grand."

Dickers still hesitated. "We can't be seen as giving in to a terrorist."

"Cooper didn't have to send that letter," Neil said. "He says he'll give himself up soon, and you know what? I believe him. He's tired of hiding. That letter was written by a man who wants justice."

After a late-night rainstorm, Neil and Marial arrived in Novgorod — Veliky Novgorod, according to the station signs. Even in the dark, Neil could tell this was a more prosperous city than any he had yet seen in Russia. The stone buildings looked freshly scrubbed by the storm. Neon lights advertised things he couldn't read. Clusters of young men with crewcuts and black leather jackets idled along the wet cobblestone sidewalks, smoking cigarettes and dangling open beer bottles from their hands. Girls with bright red hair and wobbly heels held hands in twos and threes, orbiting the boys without seeming to notice them. A pair of girls stopped in the middle of a street crossing, kissed each other on the lips, and laughed.

Marial flagged a taxi and told the driver to take them to the Intourist Hotel. Ten minutes later the cab stopped in front of a giant rectangular building. Its pattern of lit windows reminded Neil of a computer punch card. Floodlights over the entry illuminated a three-story mosaic of a muscular woman boldly leading an army of workers, apparently unaware that she was wearing nothing but a clingy sheet, torn to reveal an unsagging pink breast.

In their room, Neil flopped onto his twin bed and put his hands over his eyes. "Cooper's not in Russia."

Marial sat beside him. She took off a blue silk scarf she had worn at her throat. "There are two Coopers, remember? I think the letter you got in Portland is from the good one."

"I know that." Neil dropped his hands and sighed. "It's just, I feel lost here."

She began unbuttoning his shirt. "That's why you brought me along. To find the evil Cooper. Not the one who writes nice letters. The one who kills people."

When she said it so simply, he realized it was true. The real D.B. Cooper hadn't harmed any of the people on the airplane he hijacked. The letter he sent Neil had been written to exonerate an innocent homeless man. A very different Cooper had shot Yosef Duvshenko and run down Connie.

"The Cooper who kills people isn't in Russia either," Neil said.

"I know. He killed my husband in Oregon eighteen years ago, and he's been killing people ever since." By now she had peeled back his shirt and had started massaging his shoulders.

"The two Coopers must be connected," he said.

"Yes, and although they're not in Russia, the connection is." She leaned herself onto his chest and looked at him through her librarian glasses, her lips parted.

Neil slowly took off the glasses, set them aside, and connected lips.

The next morning a pale, chilly sun shone through the fog along the river outside their hotel window. The art auction was scheduled to start at a downtown museum that afternoon at three. In the meantime he and Marial decided to stroll along the riverfront road, looking for the address of the possible KGB contact. Neil didn't trust Chernovsky, the retired Otlichna employee in Murmansk, but the address he had written on a cardboard beer mat was the only lead they had.

The street number matched a huge derelict concrete building on the riverbank. Circular towers, angled walls, and useless arches rose like a child's sculpture of stacked toy blocks. Weeds grew from cracks in a forecourt plaza. Plastic bottles and garbage had collected against a chain link fence. The wall with the street number still bore the shadow of removed Cyrillic letters.

"What did it say?" Neil asked.

"The People's Palace of Culture. It looks like the Soviet idea of an opera house. Not exactly where I'd expect to find a secret service agent."

"Maybe that's the idea."

Most of the windows were broken and the doors chained. But as they walked around the perimeter of the fence they found an unobtrusive door with a polished metal handle and a plastic sign.

"Novgorod Detective Agency," Marial read.

Neil pulled the door open and ventured inside. Their footsteps echoed across a windowless room that once might have been a backstage storage area. Three shaded lamps on long cords cast a pool of light over an office desk. A remarkably pretty young woman with bobbed, shiny black hair looked up, smiled, and said something in Russian while chewing gum.

Marial spoke with her for quite a while, and the girl kept smiling, but she also kept shaking her black hair. Finally Marial turned to Neil and shrugged. "She says all their agents are busy."

"Did you mention the name of the guy in Murmansk?"

"Yes. She didn't seem to know him."

Neil thought a moment. Then he reached into his pocket and held out his badge. "I'm a homicide detective from Portland. It's a city in the United States. I need to talk to whoever's in charge here."

The girl kept chewing her gum, but she no longer smiled. She examined the shiny shield and made a phone call. When she hung up she pointed to a metal staircase that seemed to vanish up into the shadows. "Our director will see you in the observation lounge."

A black door at the top of the dizzying staircase opened onto a bright white room full of curves. To the right a sweeping arc of tilted windows overlooked the river. The left wall curved with mirrored glass. In between, dozens of white leather armchairs surrounded an elliptical white table. Silver noodles with spotlights curved down from the ceiling. Neil felt as if he has stumbled onto the bridge of a spaceship about to crash into the river.

One of the chairs swiveled. A bald man with a white mustache put down the paperback book he had been reading. "Portland, is it?" His accent rolled the letter "r" and stretched the letter "i." He was a large, well-muscled man, but age had wrinkled his eyes and throat. "Are Trailblazers still winning championships?"

"Not for many years, I'm afraid."

The man pushed himself up from the chair. He extended a massive, weathered hand. "Vasiliy Swarovsky."

"Lieutenant Neil Ferguson." As they shook hands, the man's grip compressed the bones in Neil's fingers painfully. Neil nodded to his side. "This is Marial, my translator."

Swarovsky sat back down without acknowledging her. "I lived in Portland twenty years. I suppose you know that the only American citizen buried in the Kremlin came from your city?"

Neil shook his head, but Marial said, "John Reed. Not the one who founded the college. The journalist."

"Yes. *Ten Days That Shook the World.* Excellent book. Reed wrote what he saw first hand in the October Revolution. Lenin called him a hero of socialism. Even in my day, we still believed Portland could be a foothold for the workers' revolution. " He held out his huge hands. "And now look. I run a detective agency in a condemned building with free rent."

"You have a very nice office."

Swarovsky scoffed. "The only part of this 'palace' they built correctly was the observation lounge. Here party officials could watch the crowd in the auditorium below through one-way mirrors. Now the government needs someone to watch for vandals." He shook his head. "What do you want?"

Neil had not been invited to sit, so he remained standing. "I need information about a man who may have been a courier for the KGB in Portland. He hijacked an airplane in 1971 using the name Dan Cooper."

"That was long ago."

"Yes, but there's been a series of recent murders. Half a dozen in the past year. I don't think the hijacker is responsible, but he's somehow mixed up in it. He may even be in danger himself."

Swarovsky silently swiveled his chair to look out at the river.

Neil sallied on. "To stop the murders I need to know who Cooper is and how he got involved."

The big Russian man swiveled back to face him. "I cannot reveal the names of government agents, even if they are retired or dead. But I am a detective, and I might be able to locate other information for you about this man you call Cooper."

"What kind of fee would your agency charge?"

He shrugged. "Fifty thousand rubles."

Neil exchanged a glance with Marial. She took out her purse and began arranging thousand-ruble notes on the table in rows of ten.

Swarovsky laughed. "I thought you said she was your translator."

"I am," Marial said. "Money speaks its own language."

He gathered up the bills as if they were playing cards. "Money is a Russian dialect. You seem to speak it fluently."

"I learned from my late husband, Nicolai Greschyednyev."

Swarovsky suddenly stopped stacking the bills. "You were married to Greschyednyev?" He looked up at her with narrowed eyes. "Then I will tell you the same thing I told your husband. The man you call Cooper is dead. I shot him. I do not miss. I saw him fall. That is all there is."

Neil cleared his throat. "We're your clients now, Swarovsky. I think fifty thousand rubles buys us more than that."

The big man motioned them vaguely to take chairs. He picked up a hidden white telephone from the armrest of his chair and said a few words in Russian. Then he turned to Neil. "What more do you want?"

"How did you meet Cooper?"

Swarovsky sighed. "Part of my job was to recruit American couriers. People with no accent, who knew the culture as natives. During the Vietnam War this was easy, particularly if they had Russian background."

"Cooper's background was Russian?"

"Partly. His family had changed the name long ago, when they came to America."

"To what? Crenshaw? Willis? Crombaugh? Lavelle?"

"Perhaps to Ferguson?" Swarovsky smiled. "I cannot give you names. Call him Cooper."

"All right. What happened after you recruited Cooper?"

"We trained him. For this, he had to spend summer in the KGB camp at Murmansk. Recruits told people they were touring Europe.

Hitchhiking, usually, so there would be no record. In Murmansk, the training was very hard. They learned everything—how to use explosives, fly helicopters, survive in wilderness, change disguise. But most of all, they learned loyalty. We became a very close cadre. I thought, when we got back to America, I could trust him."

Marial drew in her breath. "Cooper was a double agent?"

Swarovsky slowly shook his bald head. "I think not. I think he became too curious."

"In what way?" Neil asked.

"Mostly our Portland office was helping people resist the military draft. Cooper supported this very much. Our goal was to end the war in Vietnam. But we had many goals. One day Cooper opened a courier packet and saw information he did not know how to understand."

Suddenly the lounge door opened. The black-haired receptionist backed in, wearing a short skirt and carrying a tray of teacups. She set the tray on the table, smiled, and walked back out. Swarovsky watched the hem of her skirt all the way to the door. Then he sighed, took a vodka bottle out of a hidden white cabinet below the mirrors, and held it over the teacups. "Join me?"

Neil covered his cup with his hand. Marial shook her head. Swarovsky shrugged, topped up his cup, and set the bottle aside.

"What was in the packet Cooper opened?" Neil asked.

"An offer to buy engineering specifications from a professor at Reed College."

"Curt Lammergeier?"

Swarovsky sipped his spiked tea. "Yes, I can give you this name. The man is a genius, but a snake. A traitor to all countries."

"He's dead."

"Good. He had worked many years for NASA. He wanted to sell us the plans of the lunar landing module for $200,000."

"So that's it." Neil marveled that he hadn't figured this out on his own. Rachel Lammergeier had told him her husband worked on the Apollo project, and that he loved money.

"Cooper must have thought we wanted to sabotage the Apollo 16 moon landing. Perhaps he thought we were responsible for the Apollo 13 disaster. This was not true!" Swarovsky pounded the table with his big fist, and the teacups danced. "American engineers made mistakes on Apollo 13 by themselves. We wanted the lunar landing plans only to improve our own space program."

Neil sat back, letting the story before him fall into place. "When Cooper thought you wanted to kill the astronauts, he decided to stop you by buying Lammergeier's plans first."

Swarovsky held up his palms. "No one thought this was possible. How could a courier acquire $200,000 and escape our agents?"

"You trained him to parachute, didn't you?"

"Yes, and when he jumped I knew we could not track him. So we tracked the professor instead. The next night, just before midnight, they met in the middle of the railroad bridge over the Columbia River. They must have argued. There was a struggle. By the time I arrived with my lieutenant, both the money and the plans had fallen into the river."

Marial gave him a cold look. "But you fired at Cooper anyway."

Swarovsky turned aside, closed his eyes, and took a shaky breath. When he spoke again, there was a catch in his voice. "He was my friend, but he betrayed us. My weapon was very powerful. I aimed for the heart, and must have hit his shoulder. The bullet spun him around. He fell over a cable into the river."

For a while the room was silent. Neil fingered the handle of his teacup, thinking. Lammergeier's version of this same story had turned the professor into a clever hero, a sleuth who had tracked down the skyjacker and attempted to arrest him. Swarovsky's version seemed more credible on that account. But Lammergeier had said Cooper escaped by jumping into the river. There had been no mention of Russian agents or gunplay.

"I think Cooper may have survived your shot," Neil said.

"Not possible." Swarovsky kept his face turned away, but wiped his eyes as if they were wet. "Halfway to the river there were steel beams, protruding three, maybe four meters. A falling man would hit the beams and die."

"I received a letter this week from Cooper. To prove his identity, he included two twenty-dollar bills from the original ransom."

"Someone could have found the money later, in the river."

"These bills had not been in the river, at least not for long."

"Then they are forgeries."

"They appear genuine."

Swarovsky turned and pounded the table. "He is dead! Cooper is

282

dead, I tell you. That's what you paid to find out." He took up the vodka bottle and refilled his cup. "The world is full of copycats. There was only one Cooper. Only one! These murders you talk of, they cannot be by him. It was the one thing we could never train him to do. He refused to kill. He refused to hurt anyone."

Swarovsky's eyes were now filled with tears. "And I shot him like a dog."

Neil looked down, embarrassed. "We think an impostor is responsible for the murders. Maybe it's someone who knew Cooper. Whoever it is, they're using his name for all kinds of crimes. Theft. fraud, extortion. We think this person may be connected with the Russian mafia."

Swarovsky emptied his teacup in one draft. Then he leaned back. "That I can believe. Because I lived in America, much of my detective work is about Russian emigrants. Adoptions, people wanting green cards, spouses left behind. Some of them are in Portland, and many have troubles with the mafia."

"How can we find out who runs the Russian mafia in Portland?"

Swarovsky laughed and poured himself a third shot. "Now you are asking another fifty-thousand-ruble question."

Marial took out her purse.

He held up the flat of his hand. "An incorrect translation, Mrs. Greschyednyev. I cannot answer this question, not for all the rubles in Russia. And the people who know, you do not want to ask."

"Where are the people who know?" Neil asked.

"Today I think they are in Novgorod. A very valuable artwork will be sold here today. The mafia cannot resist such a thing. You do not see the real buyers, but they are nearby."

"Where?"

Swarovsky lifted an eyebrow. "Are you fearless or foolish?"

"I don't know which."

"Then you might visit the Castle Restaurant in Pskov. But do not mention my name."

"What should I mention?"

"It is one of the most expensive restaurants in all of Russia." Swarovsky held up his teacup and smiled. "If you dare, ask for a hot dog."

Closer to downtown, the riverbank road turned into a cobblestone promenade with baby buggies, young lovers, and old men. Ahead, corralled by a pink brick wall, rose the pointy towers and silver onion domes of the city's medieval fortress.

"Considering how much we learned from Swarovsky," Neil mused aloud as they walked, "It's disappointing that he didn't tell us the two things we need most: Who is Cooper, and who is his evil twin?"

"Still, I got my money's worth," Marial replied.

"How so? Swarovsky's story doesn't rule out any of our Cooper candidates."

"True. He even added one name."

Neill looked at her skeptically. "What name was that?"

"Yours. When you listed some possible names for Cooper, he added Ferguson."

"That was a joke."

"I don't think he is a man who jokes."

Neil laughed awkwardly. "Honestly, Marial, I was twenty years old, watching Thanksgiving football games with my parents in Roseburg when D.B. Cooper jumped. You can't possibly think I—"

"Not you, no." She took his hand as they walked, and swung it mischievously. "Do you remember, after our first date at the art gala, you researched my background? I expected you would. You're a detective. But then I'm a librarian. So I researched your family, too. Did you know your aunt in California posted the entire Ferguson genealogy on a Mormon website?"

"I'm not surprised. The Fergusons are proud of being Irish."

"Mixed with English, Swiss, Danish, Austrian—and a little bit of White Russian."

"Really? I didn't know that. What are you saying?"

"I'm just asking." She looked at him from the side. "Where was your older brother Mark that Thanksgiving?"

"Mark?" Neil stopped and stared at her. "My hippie brother? You think he hijacked a plane?"

"I'm just wondering where he was."

"I don't know. He'd just finished four years at the University of Oregon—mostly smoking dope at sit-ins. He didn't actually graduate. They threw him off the track team. Finally he left to research communes or something."

"Hitchhiking in Europe?' Marial suggested.

Neil threw up his hands. "So what if he was? Mark lives in a yurt outside Eugene now, making wooden toys with his girlfriend. He's not D.B. Cooper."

"No, probably not. " Marial took his hand again to resume their walk. She didn't mention the subject again, but it left Neil pondering the expanded possibilities for Cooper. In 1971, almost any man could have slipped off the rails for the chance to go into history as a folk legend. Everyone has fantasies of breaking away to attempt the unknown. Perhaps even Swarovsky? The old KGB agent would go to his grave believing that he could not have missed, and that the crazy spark of freedom he loved had never escaped.

As they walked toward a drawbridge gate, Neil only dimly heard the travelogue Marial was reciting from a brochure. Novgorod, she read aloud, was the oldest city in Russia, with the youngest name— recently changed to Veliky Novgorod, "Novgorod the Great." It was founded in 862 by Rus, the Swedish Viking who gave Russia its name. The country's early Viking rulers exported so many locals to bondage that *Slav* became the word for "slave."

Neil snapped back to the present when a drunken man blocked their path, playing an accordion while he held a hat in his teeth for tips. They got past him only by ducking behind a woman selling balloons. The entire area near the gate was an impromptu carnival, with pony rides, beer gardens, and booths selling trinkets. Inside the gate, a forty-foot bronze monument to Russian history writhed with statues of tsars, bishops, and cossacks. Plein-air artists had covered the surrounding lawn with their canvases—oil paintings of boats, flowers, rivers, and onion domes—completed in the patchy style of Van Gogh, the neon nightmares of Chagall, or the pastel daydreams of Monet.

"This way," Marial said, following a signpost. "I've made an appointment to see the Rothkos before the auction."

"How did you manage that?"

"I told them the truth, that you're a police detective from Portland, where the real paintings are supposed to be."

"They're going to love me."

Soldiers in khaki uniforms with red stripes flanked the entrance to the Novgorod Museum of Art and History. Inside the grandly vaulted lobby, lines of tourists were waiting to buy tickets. Marial spoke to a guard who led them around the lines. He rapped on a double door to one side of the lobby.

A minute passed before a key rattled in the lock. The door opened only wide enough for a gray-haired man in a black business suit to peer out suspiciously. Marial spoke with him in Russian, but he still didn't open up. She turned to Neil. "He wants to see our credentials."

Neil held out his badge. The man studied it. Then he said, "Come in, quickly." As soon as Neil and Marial were inside, he locked the door again.

Rows of folding chairs faced a low stage where half a dozen people were sorting papers. Pink marble pillars set off galleries to either side where paintings of various sizes leaned against the walls.

"Forgive my caution," the man said, nodding his head in a sort of bow, "But we rarely have works of this value, and everyone is a little nervous. I am Sergei Semenov, director of Delos Auctions. I understand you are from the American police, Captain Ferguson?"

"Lieutenant Ferguson. Yes, we're curious to check the—" he glanced to Marial—"the provenance of the six paintings you're offering by Mark Rothko."

"Yes, of course. We too are most concerned that there be no doubt as to ownership and authenticity. The Delos Auction Company guarantees the art we sell. That is why we have engaged the services of an expert." He led them to the front of the hall, where a stern young woman in a white laboratory coat looked up from her work. She had thin brown hair and wore no make-up.

"This is Dr. Julia Barnes of the British Museum," the auction director said. "Dr. Barnes, I'd like you to meet Lieutenant Ferguson of the American police."

She shook his hand limply. "How do you do?"

"I'm fine, thanks." Neil nodded to Marial. "This is my assistant, Marial Greschyednyev, from the Portland Art Museum."

"Portland, is it?"

"Yes, we'd like to know how you think paintings from an American museum could be offered for sale in Russia."

"Evidently, Lieutenant, you haven't read my treatise in the catalogue."

"We just arrived. Perhaps you could explain things for us?"

"Certainly. The Portland museum was given certain materials from

Rothko's New York studio after his death. They claim that this donation included several valuable paintings. That is clearly untrue."

"Why?"

The British woman arched an eyebrow. "Mark Rothko committed suicide in 1970. His estate was not settled until 1975. By that time the executors had made copies of the paintings to leave in the studio for the Portland museum. They set aside the original paintings to be used for a nobler purpose. Before his death, Mr. Rothko had instructed the executors to fund a memorial to the Russian Jews of his native city, Dvinsk."

Marial cut in, "Marcus Rothkowitz was born in Daugavpils, in Latvia."

Dr. Barnes looked at her patiently. 'Of course the city has changed names now that it is no longer part of the Russian Empire. Because the memorial was intended for Russian citizens, the paintings have been brought here, to Novgorod."

"Who is the seller?" Neil asked.

The auction director held up a hand to intervene. "The Delos Auction Company protects the confidentiality of its clients."

"But the money is going to a charity?" Neil asked.

The director shrugged. "Our dealings in this matter are limited strictly to a lawyer and a bank account."

For the first time, the woman from the British Museum wrinkled her brow. "In fact, the documentation for this charity is not as satisfying as I would like. There is always a danger, with such valuable works, that the artist's intent may be difficult to fulfill. Most of the Jewish population in Russia was exterminated or forced to emigrate. The few who remain are still persecuted."

"But you believe the original paintings in his studio were replaced?" Neil asked.

"Absolutely. Here is proof." She led them behind the marble pillars to a row of six small, boldly-colored canvases, arranged on six identical easels.

Although the notebook-sized paintings seemed as simplistic as Neil remembered, spotlights made the colors float out like glowing square clouds. Seeing all six in a row was as powerful as a glimpse into an alien world.

"Only a master could have created these," Dr. Barnes said.

Neil casually walked behind the easels. One glance told him that the paintings did not match the photos he had brought. Blotches of oil paint had been smeared onto the backs like sloppy fingerprints at a crime scene. But if copies had been made before 1975, perhaps the Portland Art Museum had never owned the originals at all. In that case, the photos he had were of fakes, and nothing had been stolen at all.

"Is this where you took samples of the paint?" Neil pointed to the back of a painting, where the canvas had been lapped around a wooden stretcher and stapled.

"Yes. I conducted both electron microscopy and ultraviolet analysis. Among the usual oils and pigments I found traces of acrylic resin, phenol formaldehyde, modified alkyd, glue, egg, and several ingredients that cannot be precisely identified. In short, the paint has all the characteristics of Rothko's formula. Absolutely recognizable and utterly inimitable."

Neil took out his cell phone. "Do you mind if I take a little picture?"

The auction director stepped forward quickly. "No photographs."

"Even of the back?" Neil rolled his eyes. "Come on."

"Why would you want to photograph the back?" The director looked to the British Museum expert. She shrugged.

Neil took advantage of their hesitation to press the shutter and pocket the phone. "Thank you for your time. I think that's it until the auction." He turned to Marial. "Do you have any more questions for our hosts, Mrs. Greschyednyev?"

Marial shook her head, although her look suggested she was far from satisfied with the explanations they had heard.

The director rubbed his fingers nervously. "Then we can proceed? You don't dispute the provenance?"

Neil smiled. "I'm curious to see the sale."

On the way out of the museum Marial bought a copy of the auction catalogue, a full-color booklet in Russian. Two hours remained until the sale began, so Neil took her to lunch at a food booth on the riverbank. Seven-foot propane heaters, glowing like giant mushrooms, took the chill off a large white tent. A waitress wiped off their picnic table and said something that Neil assumed was a request for their order.

He decided to experiment, just to see if Russian waitresses even knew what a hot dog was. Swarovsky's parting words had left him curious. And one of the few phrases that had stuck from Marial's cursory instruction in survival Russian was the useful question, "Do you have?"

"*Oo vas yest* hot dog?" Neil asked.

The waitress stared at him blankly.

"*Kulbas?*" Marial suggested.

"*Da, kulbas.*"

Ten minutes later they were eating bratwurst with sauerkraut, the cafe's closest approximation to a hot dog. Marial had also ordered two glasses of *kvas*, a mildly noxious but non-alcoholic Russian root beer. She studied the catalogue as they ate.

Neil pointed to a photograph of Dr. Julia Barnes. "You don't believe her story, do you?"

"No."

"But she's from the British Museum."

Marial smiled with only the left side of her face—an expression that turned her otherwise charming dimple into a punctuation mark of disdain. "The British Museum does not collect contemporary art. If you want to see modern paintings in London you have to go to the Tate. Dr. Barnes' experience is probably limited to analyzing mummies. According to the catalogue, her doctorate is in chemical engineering."

"Then she might actually be qualified to run tests on Rothko's paint."

"Probably. But her story about the paintings' history is ridiculous. The executors of Rothko's estate were lawyers. They didn't have the skill to make copies. Within months of Rothko's death they dumped most of his paintings at garage-sale prices to a gallery in New York. It took Rothko's children years, but they finally got a judge to replace the executors. The gallery that bought the paintings had to pay millions in compensation."

Neil frowned. If the executors had not made copies, then the paintings that went to Portland with the studio furnishings must have been originals—but paint analysis suggested they had been switched with fakes. For that matter, the way paint had been smeared on the backs of the Novgorod paintings suggested they were fakes too. It was all very confusing.

"What about the memorial for displaced Russian Jews?" he asked. Marial shook her head. "That's even less likely. Rothko turned his back on his heritage. At the start of World War II he changed his name so it wouldn't sound Jewish. The whole charity sounds fictitious. You wonder how a person like Barnes can say these things with a straight face."

"It's amazing what people can believe if they're paid enough."

Marial looked at him and nodded. "The auction house must have paid her a lot. They also want to believe the paintings aren't stolen. The house usually takes a ten percent commission on sales."

"If they sell them for $20 million, that's a nice commission. Do you think they can?"

Marial shook her head. "No American gallery would pay that much." She tapped the catalogue. "Not based on a story like this. But the Russians? Who can say? The mafia here has a lot of money, and they don't mind gambling."

Neil finished his bitter *kvas* and looked at his watch. "We still have an hour."

"I know we're not bidding, but I'm nervous. There's a church by the museum. Do you mind if we wait there?"

Neil stood up and paid the bill. "Sure. I need some time to think."

The Saint Sofia Cathedral turned out to be the oldest church in Russia. Inside, tiny windows in the towers sent feeble shafts of light angling down into a fog of incense. Tourists with cameras and old women in black shawls shuffled along the walls, examining frescoes and icons.

Neil lost track of Marial in the gloom, and instead found himself confronted with a dark madonna. Much larger than the icon in the Solovetsky monastery, this Mary cradled a soot-darkened Christ in her arms. The infant gazed out with the face of a grown man, raising a hand in blessing.

Neil stood there a long time, strangely comforted by the wizened infant and his calm, dark mother. Icons of the saints were the copied images of heroes — not fakes, but variations on a theme. In his own world, he was trying to find his way through a kaleidoscope of copies. Coopers and Rothkos mirrored themselves back and forth into the darkness, alternating good and evil like the sides of a gambler's spinning coin. His head swam with the smells of beeswax and sandalwood.

An indecipherable chant echoed amid stone arches. The virgin's flat eyes gazed down on him not with sorrow, but with pity and warning. And then he knew. Suddenly the truth was terrifying and obvious. It was as if his mind had been sorting through the jungle of facts sub-consciously all this time—for the three weeks since he had heard Yosef Duvshenko's frightened voice say, "I know a crime." And only now, in a trance, he could see the truth.

"There you are!" Marial caught him by the sleeve. "Come on, the auction's about to start."

He stumbled after her. Outside, he stopped and blinked.

"Neil? Are you all right?"

"I know who Cooper is." He looked at her. "I know who he is."

"Which Cooper?"

"The real one. The skyjacker."

"Who is he?"

He shook his head. "He's doing the same thing we are. He's trying to stop the impostor. He's trying to stop the evil Cooper."

"For God's sake, Neil, if you know who he is, tell me."

"No. He's using us." Now that Neil could guess Cooper's identity, everything was starting to clear. And the picture that was forming was more complicated than ever.

"What do you mean, he's using us? Who is he?"

"It's part of his plan. We're not supposed to know. Not yet."

"Neil, you're scaring me. You've always been honest with me. You've insisted on telling me every horror from your past. Now you've figured out who Cooper is, and you won't trust me."

This accusation stung. "I'm sorry. If I'm right, Cooper needs time to work. I'll tell you after we leave Russia, I promise. Right now we have a job to do. We have to go to the auction and find out everything we can about the people who bid."

She faced him, and to his surprise, she gave him a coquettish smile, complete with dimple and smoky eyes. "All right, keep it a surprise for me until we leave Russia. But now you have to tell me something more, just one hint. Why are you suddenly so sure?"

"Because I discovered Cooper's motive."

"And what is his motive?"

"Cooper is being blackmailed."

38

For the next day and half, until they left Russia, Marial seemed to bubble with the anticipation of a child who has been promised she will meet the real Santa Claus on Christmas morning.

The auction bidding had slowed at $3 million, and as Marial predicted, no American museums seemed represented. The people in the room were all young professionals in business suits, relaying information by cell phone to the actual bidders. The whispered conversations were in Russian, Arabic, and Chinese. When the bidding reached $4 million Marial stood up as if to leave. She made her way down a narrow aisle, caught her shoe on a folding chair, and practically fell into the lap of the top Russian bidder. She apologized. He scowled, picking up his phone to redial.

Later, after the Russian man had won the bid at $4.7 million, Neil and Marial walked back to the hotel along the river. When they reached a quiet part of the promenade, Neil asked, "You stumbled at the auction on purpose, didn't you?"

"How can you say such a thing!"

"Because I think you were trying to see what number the top bidder was calling."

Marial bit her lower lip mischievously. "I did manage to catch the first four digits."

"And?"

"He was dialing the area code for Pskov."

Neil considered this. "That's where Swarovsky said the mafia might be. He warned us not to go there."

"Oh, come on. Pskov is on our way home. If we take a bus there tomorrow we'll have time for dinner before the night train leaves for Latvia." She paused for effect. "I hear they have a nice restaurant at the castle."

A day later they were looking up at the castle's ramparts. A crenelated wall traced the top of narrow cliff where two rivers joined. The fortress reminded Neil of a beached battleship. An unrailed stone stairway led to the base of a square tower with a restaurant awning.

"I feel like we're Rosencrantz and Guildenstern," Neil said.

"Who?"

"Two bumbling minor characters in Hamlet. They were sent to England with a sealed note that told the king there to kill them."

Marial thought about this. "Asking for a hot dog in a restaurant like this might be suicidal, but I don't think Swarovsky was setting us up."

Neil nodded. "He doesn't joke."

"Kiss me first, for luck."

"Good idea." He gave her a kiss. She responded with such passion, and the kiss was so delicious, that he pressed her close and held her there for a long time.

She pulled back so slowly that her lip stuck to his a moment before breaking free. She whispered, "Ready to storm the castle?"

"Now I'm ready for anything."

The door at the base of the tower opened onto a spiral staircase with worn stone steps. They climbed four stories to a foyer lit by torches. A woman in a black evening dress looked up from a podium and greeted them in Russian. Marial spoke for a while, evidently explaining that they did not have reservations. Finally the woman said, "Would you like menus in English?"

"Yes," Neil said, working up his nerve. "We just want a light dinner."

"This way." She took two menus and led them across the room. Wooden beams spanned the ceiling. Faded tapestries hung on the walls.

"Perhaps just a hot dog," Neil said behind her.

The hostess stopped. She turned to examine Neil more carefully. Her expression hardened. "Then I suggest you order from our small plate menu in the lounge."

"That—" Neil cleared his throat. "That sounds just fine."

She took them down a flight of stairs to a bar in a vaulted room decorated as a medieval armory. Racks of dangerous-looking halberds and spears flanked a wooden door at the far end. Crossed swords and muskets hung on the wall. Slit-shaped windows overlooked the river and the city.

The hostess whispered something to the bartender, a short, thick man with a black shirt and tie. "A hot dog?" he said, looking to Neil. "My uncle in Chicago likes them too. I'll tell the chef. Would you care for a drink while you wait?"

"Maybe some *kvas?*" It was all Neil could think of at the moment.

"Perfect." The bartender typed something on a computer keyboard behind the bar. Then he uncapped two bottles of root beer, poured them into glasses, and set them on the counter with cocktail napkins. "Are you just visiting Pskov, or are you here on business?"

"A little of both." Neil sat on a barstool. "We were in Novgorod yesterday for an art auction."

"Really? Did you buy anything?"

"No. At first we thought the paintings they were auctioning might be stolen."

"Stolen?"

"Yes, but it turns out they were fakes instead. The only authentic paint was smeared on the back. The rest was recent, less than a year old."

The bartender shook his head. "It's terrible, what they try to sell these days."

"I only hope whoever bought them takes them back before the auctioneer's guarantee expires. I think they have a few days."

A light blinked behind the counter. "Excuse me." The bartender stepped through a doorway hidden behind the bar's shelving.

Marial sipped her *kvas.* "Do you think we need to arm ourselves with swords?"

"I'm not sure." He toyed with his glass. He really didn't like *kvas.* They were the only ones in the lounge, and it was early enough in the evening that the restaurant was nearly empty. Five minutes passed, and then ten.

Finally the bartender returned, carrying a tray. "Compliments of the chef," he said, arranging plates of food on the bar before them. In addition to a hot dog, there was a quail and a Caesar salad with caviar.

"Wow." Neil had the feeling that his comments about the auction had just saved someone a lot of money. He decided to press the advantage. "Those paintings at the auction? We think they were brought to Russia by a man who calls himself Cooper."

The bartender frowned. "Cooper," he said quietly.

"We want to find out who he is."

The bartender shook his head. "No one knows this man. To know Cooper is to die."

The sleeper train to Riga left at 2:47 a.m., so Neil and Marial had to spend four hours in the station, waiting. Neil curled up in a plastic chair, trying to doze. His stomach hurt from the *kvas* and the rich food and everything else about Russia. At 2:30 Marial dragged him outside. She bounced on her toes to keep warm, staring into the darkness where the rails converged.

When at last the engine pulled into the station she clapped her hands. "It's a *Latvian* train!"

The sleek, modern cars were light blue with gold lettering. Neil couldn't read the words, but at least he could pronounce them, because the letters were not Cyrillic. A woman in a chic blue uniform smiled from the door. She looked at their tickets and showed them to their reserved compartment. The seats had already been converted into two neat bunks, each with an extra pillow set at an angle. Arrayed on the table below the window were two chocolate bars, a bottle of water, a magazine, and a menu. Marial picked each of these items up, one at a time, her hands trembling. "*Vesla varsa*, fresh water." She spoke the words with awe. "It's all Latvian. Everything."

"Yup." Neil shucked his coat, sat on his bunk, and began taking off his shoes.

"But Neil," she said, "Latvia never existed before, not as a real country. It was part of the Soviet Union when I left. Everything was in Russian. We had to speak Russian in school. I feel like I'm dreaming."

"Marial?" Neil dropped his shoes, sat on the bunk beside her, and put an arm around her shoulder. "I'm happy for you. I think it's half the reason you came here, to see if Latvia really exists."

"Then you understand?"

He nodded. "We're on our way there. But right now it's the middle of the night. I'm so tired I can hardly think."

She kissed him on the forehead and steered him back toward his bunk.

Neil took off his pants and crawled under the sheets wearing nothing but his shorts and the pouch with his passport. When he drifted off to the rocking of the rails, Marial was still sitting cross-legged on the other side of their compartment, reading the Latvian magazine.

Sometime later the train stopped and all the lights went on. Neil opened his eyes unwillingly. Two uniformed Russian women slid open the compartment door and demanded passports. A German shepherd on a leash sniffed their baggage, pausing with some interest to inspect Neil's socks. One of the women glanced under the bunks with a flashlight. The other stamped their passports and handed them back. "Welcome to Estonia," she said.

"I thought we were going to Latvia," Neil objected.

"Estonia first," the guard replied. "Latvia in another hour, at dawn. No border check there."

As soon as they were gone Marial said, "One more hour. But we're not in Russia anymore, so you have to tell me. Who is D.B. Cooper?"

Suddenly the lights went out. Marial clicked on a spotlight above her bunk. She had changed into a night shirt, and the light raked across it, revealing the outlines of her breasts. Her untied hair glowed golden-red on her shoulders. "Come here and tell me."

The car couplings clanked, and the train began again to roll. Neil climbed down from his bunk, his heart beating like the thump of the rails. She lifted the covers so he could crawl in beside her.

Neil sat with his back against the wall. "Do you promise not to tell until Cooper himself goes public?"

"Will he?"

Neil nodded. "I think so, soon."

"Who is he, Neil?"

"He's the only one who could have painted the fake Rothkos."

"Brother Daniel?"

"No. I should have known when he sent me the twenty-dollar bills. But it finally clicked when I remembered about my brother Mark. He really did tell us he'd spent the summer of 1971 hitchhiking through Europe."

"D.B. Cooper is your brother?"

"No, but you're very close."

"You?"

Neil laughed, "No, not me either. D.B. Cooper was my brother Mark's best friend in college. That summer they started out hitchhiking together, but then they split up. Mark went south, looking for a commune in Greece. Cooper went north on his own."

Marial just shook her head. "I have no idea who you're talking about."

"Chandler," Neil said. "The director of the Portland Art Museum, Gerry Chandler."

Later Neil would agonize over the magnitude of his error. Their trip to Russia replayed in his mind, an endlessly looping movie where everyone knows the ending except the hapless character on the screen. They had left a trail of clues a mile wide, from the retired Otlichna employee in Murmansk to Swarovsky's detective agency in Novgorod and the restaurant in Pskov. How many times had Connie told him to watch his back? They were being watched by a man so ruthless that lives meant nothing. They had just cost this killer $4.7 million by exposing the Rothko paintings as fakes. And still Lieutenant Ferguson had slept in the train station, oblivious to the passengers gathering for the trip to Riga.

And now, in a bittersweet scene that was painful to watch yet again, the detective from Portland sat on a bunk, shoulder to shoulder with the beautiful Marial Greschyednyev, spotlighted as if at a slumber party, telling her that D.B. Cooper was "Chandler. The director of the Portland Art Museum, Gerry Chandler."

Marial looked out into the dark train compartment, lost in thought. The first dim glow of dawn turned the window into a spectral square.

"I wonder," she said, as if to herself. "I had the strangest feeling."

"About Gerry?"

She nodded. "Everyone likes him, but no one seems to be able to get really close to him."

"Did you try?"

"Yes." She didn't blush. "Many of the women volunteers tried. He's attractive and unmarried. You sense he's been hurt, and if you have a heart, you want to get inside to help. But Gerry Chandler is like a Russian stacking doll. No matter how many layers you open, you're never sure who's really in there."

Neil nodded. "I'm not sure either. Even when we were on the track team together back in college, he never talked about himself. He talked about trying to end the Vietnam War. About how we were fighting on the wrong side, killing innocent people."

"The wrong side?"

"Gerry was just the kind of college kid Swarovsky was looking for."

Marial pulled her knees up to her chest. She wiggled her toes. "He's in pretty good shape for a man in his sixties. You say he used to run on a track team?"

"He didn't run." Neil recalled the trophy he'd seen in Gerry's office, and he smiled. Gerry's event was the long jump."

"The long jump!" Marial laughed. "No wonder he wasn't afraid to parachute."

"Or to jump off a bridge."

She pursed her lips and tapped them with a fingertip, thinking. "I'm still not convinced. I mean, there are so many other candidates. And what about the Rothko paintings? I don't see how that fits together. Brother Daniel is the one with the skill to paint replicas."

"Do you remember seeing Gerry's loft at the gala? There were easels and canvases all over. Gerry is a painter too. And he's the only one who had access to a supply of paint with Rothko's original formula."

Marial's eyes widened. "That's right! All the materials in Rothko's studio were donated to the Portland Art Museum. But wait. Would there have been enough of the original paint for six canvases?"

"He didn't need that much. He knew if someone tested the paintings they'd take a sample from the back, where it wouldn't show."

"So he only needed a dab on the back of each."

"Right. Except Rothko didn't slop paint on the backs of his paintings. That's why Gerry gave me photographs of the backs, so I could expose the ones at the Novgorod auction as fakes."

Marial frowned. "But why would he paint fake Rothkos in the first place?"

"Because he's being blackmailed." Neil sighed. "Somebody must have found out that he was D.B. Cooper. At first, Gerry probably had to pay money to keep the blackmailer quiet. But then, when Gerry became director of the art museum, the blackmailer wanted more. He wanted paintings worth millions."

"The evil Cooper," Marial said. "And who is that?"

Neil shook his head. "No one seems to know. Not even Gerry. But I think he's trying to find out."

A distant clanging outside grew louder and louder. Then a green light flashed in the window and the clanging suddenly dropped to a lower pitch. As the bell faded away, Marial crawled to the edge of the bunk on her knees and looked out the window. Pink clouds floated above low, rolling hills, like rosy dreams emerging from the night.

"Dawn," she whispered. "We're finally here. I'm home."

In that moment Neil felt his heart go out to her — this long suffering, alluring librarian who had spent her whole life searching.

She turned to him, still on her hands and knees. The pink light fired her hair and made her body glow through the thin nightshirt.

"Make love to me, Neil."

But then the old movie film breaks, in the same place every time, and by the time the film has been threaded back in place, the movie jerks along unwillingly. Had he really loved her? Yes, he thought, he must have been blindly in love, at least for a time. How else could he explain all the things he didn't see? The entire trip to Russia swirled in his memory with the giddiness of a honeymoon.

When the first rays of the sun flashed on the opposite wall, Marial stretched back in the pillows, naked, exhausted, still glowing white in the shadows. With her eyes closed, she smiled and said, "Coffee, love?"

Neil kissed her. "I'll get some from the dining car."

He put on his gray shirt, pants, and shoes, and walked out into the corridor, still floating in a kind of daze.

He saw, but did not see, the man in a black leather jacket quickly pushing through the door to the next car ahead of him. He heard, but did not hear, a hiss from a duffel in a pile of luggage on the floor. Trains hiss all the time. He smelled, but did not smell, a faint sour fume. Diesel trains in foreign countries are full of foreign smells.

Ordering coffee was harder than he had imagined. The diner was four cars ahead. The girl spoke no English, and only slowly understood his charade. He had no Latvian money. All he had in his sweaty passport pouch were rubles. She accepted them with disdain.

But the coffee smelled so marvelous, and he was so happy knowing how much Marial would love it, starting her first day in her homeland.

The train rocked as they rounded a long curve. Through the corridor windows he could see the sun flashing from the windows of the last cars, white bursts of light running down along the tail of a long, silver-gray snake. There! That was their window, in the next-to-last car, where she lay waiting for him, her eyes still closed.

This is where he wants the film to stop. But it does not stop.

A white-hot ball of fire blows out the windows of the next-to-last car, jerking the entire train so hard that hot coffee spills on his hands. When the boom of the blast arrives, Marial's car has hopped into the air. People scream. Metal screeches. Like a broken toy, Marial's car twists to one side, whips the car behind it sideways, and then skids along the gravel embankment, dragging one car after another off the rails to ruin.

39

Dan Cooper's Last Will & Testament, Part 9

It was the best jump of my life, fueled with adrenaline from Swarovsky's gunshot. Twirl, step, leap—headfirst over the cable railing toward the dark Columbia River. Thirty feet down, a beam from the bridge's lower support structure tore the khaki shirt I had gotten in trade from The Keeper.

When I hit the river I might as well have been cracked over the head with a block of ice. In late November, the Columbia is so cold it kicks you in the chest. I held my breath as long as I could, swimming underwater to get as far as possible from their flashlights and guns. When I finally had to come up, I discovered with some surprise that I had been swimming upstream instead of down. In my panic I had outswum the current and was underneath the bridge. The flashlights were aimed downriver, not my way at all.

Swarovsky's voice boomed, "You lost the Apollo plans?"

I couldn't hear Lammergeier's response, but then Swarovsky said, "No! And he wasn't one of ours. He was a traitor."

Lammergeier started to whine but Swarovsky cut him short. "You can go to hell."

After that the flashlights scanned the river downstream one more time. I ducked underwater, afraid they would look under the bridge. When I came up again the flashlights were bobbing through the bridge girders, heading back toward the Oregon side of the river. By this time my arms and legs were growing numb from the cold. Even my shoulder, grazed by Swarovsky's bullet, had gone dead. I floated on my back and let myself drift out from under the bridge, watching. A train of boxcars rumbled out from Vancouver, filling the ironwork with light, noise, and madly shifting shadows.

Suddenly a great weariness came over me, as if the river's chill were draining my life force. And I wondered, did I deserve to live? I was a traitor to two countries. While trying to undo the damage I had done, I had hijacked a plane and become a criminal. Why had I survived?

The flashlights on the bridge were almost out of sight, nearing the Oregon shore. I was adrift in a lost river, a river that kept secrets and money in its cold heart. Who was I in this void? Professor Lammergeier knew me as D.B. Cooper, but none of the Americans had a clue who that might be. The KGB knew, but they would never tell. Swarovsky obviously thought I was dead.

A dark hole drifted across the sky above me, a gap in the ghostly clouds. Three bright stars emerged, one after the other. I recognized them as Orion's belt, but the way they lined up I suddenly saw them as the lights of a jet plane. It was heading straight toward me. A wave filled my mouth, and I sputtered. My wet clothes were dragging me down. A part of me wanted that escape, that oblivion, that rest.

But if I died, D.B. Cooper would die with me, his debt unpaid. Suddenly I realized: This is why I had survived. Because I owed something to the world.

I spat out the water and lifted my head. Oregon and Washington were each a quarter mile away. I turned toward Oregon. Floating on my back, I commanded my numb body to move. I kicked my legs like scissors and paddled my arms like oars. Ten years ago I had used the same lazy stroke in the Boy Scouts. As a teenager I had managed to swim a mile at Camp Pioneer, circling a cold mountain lake behind my scoutmaster's rowboat. Now there was more at stake than a merit badge.

Half an hour later I dragged myself, exhausted and dripping, up a muddy beach. I collapsed on a drift log. If I rested long, I knew hypothermia would set in. I had to keep moving. I forced myself back onto my feet, climbed the steep bank at the edge of the beach, and crashed blindly into the underbrush of the rainforest beyond.

I don't know how many hours I struggled in that dark jungle before I staggered out onto a small gravel road. I followed it to the left for a mile until it crossed a set of train tracks. I realized this must be the same railroad I had taken to the Columbia River bridge. I turned right along the tracks, heading for Portland. I trudged along the tracks like a zombie.

By the time dawn lightened the clouds, the jungle on either side of the tracks had given way to streets and houses. I slid down the gravel embankment and began following sidewalks. My clothes no longer dripped and my shoes no longer squished with each step, but I must have looked terrible. People looked at me suspiciously as they got in their cars to go to work. It was Friday, the day after Thanksgiving, and although schools were closed for a long weekend, shops were opening up for the day.

At an intersection I stopped in front of a St. Vincent DePaul thrift store. A woman in the window turned over the "Closed" sign, looked up at me, and nodded. Evidently she was used to dealing with bums. Thinking to straighten my bedraggled hair I reached for my comb and discovered my wallet was still in my pocket. Somehow this struck me as odd. If you have risen from the dead, artifacts from your prior life are curiosities. Inside the soggy billfold was a forged driver's license for a man named Dan Cooper—a dangerous item I would need to destroy. The six twenty-dollar bills from Lammergeier's payoff were nearly as explosive, but only if someone thought to check their serial numbers. Fortunately the wallet contained two hundred dollars in other currency—damp but spendable. It would have to be enough to start my new life as a penitent, giving back something to the world I had wounded. Already I was beginning to develop a plan, utterly unaware of the grand forces of evil waiting for me.

My first step was to buy a new set of clothes at the thrift shop— slacks and a dress shirt suitable for a job interview. I also bought a warm raincoat and an umbrella. Next I went to a nearby cafe and filled up on coffee and pancakes. Then I took a Tri-Met bus downtown, caught a Greyhound to Eugene, and got a room across from the bus station at the Timbers Motel.

If you're in trouble, who do you turn to? I couldn't turn to my parents. I needed to lie low for a while. I decided instead to turn to my old track coach, a contact Swarovsky would never think to check.

In the morning I took a long shower at the motel, ate breakfast at a cafe named Hoots, and walked across the University of Oregon campus to Hayward Field.

I found Bill Bowerman in the big wooden grandstand. Stopwatch in his hand, he grumbled as runners in green jerseys jogged laps around the oval below. With a receding hairline and a prominent nose, Bowerman didn't look particularly athletic. But this was the man who had trained thirty-one Olympic athletes. He had led the U of O track team to twenty-three winning seasons. He was the best in the world at what he did. If anyone could get my feet pointed in the right direction, it was Bowerman.

"Coach?" I said.

He looked up and raised an eyebrow. "You? I thought you graduated."

"I did. With a degree in art."

He shook his head, as if even he couldn't imagine a use for a degree in such a field. "Are you still practicing your long jump?"

"Yes, sir." This much was true. I had just beaten my college record by miles.

"Good. As long as you've been keeping out of trouble."

I resisted the urge to tell him exactly how much trouble I had seen since we last met. Instead I said, "I spent the summer in Europe. But I've been thinking about those shoes you've been selling with Phil Knight. I understand you're starting to design your own. I wondered if you were looking to hire an art major."

He studied me silently.

I continued, "I know design, and I know track. And I'm not afraid to think outside the box."

He cleared his throat. Then he stood up and said, "There's something I want to show you."

He took me across the street to a room cluttered with gear, trophies, and books, all suffused with the faint musk of sweat and foot powder. He swept a desk clear with an arm and set a shoe in front of me. "We put this on the market this summer, while you were gone. It's a soccer shoe we call the Nike."

"The Greek goddess of victory." My study of art history had not been entirely wasted. "What's the checkmark on the side?"

"It's the new logo we're using for Blue Ribbon Sports. But about the shoe — it's not light enough, and not grippy." Bowerman opened a drawer and took out a knobby sheet of plastic. He tossed it on the table as if he were anteing up a big square poker chip. "All right, what's this look like?"

"I don't know. A plastic waffle?"

He laughed. "Exactly right. I ruined my wife's waffle iron making this thing. But look at it. All those little square bumps are light and grippy."

I made the connection. "Just what we need for a better running shoe."

He put a sheet of paper and a felt-tip pen on the table. "Draw me the shoe that goes with this sole." Then he glanced at his wrist watch. "I've got to go send my joggers to the showers. When I come back, I'll tell you if you've got a job."

The shoe I sketched that afternoon was not the design we eventually used for the famous Waffle Trainer. But it was good enough to get me started with the company that became Nike. The pay was good, and the stock shares I earned were even better. Over the next twenty years I gave away more than three million dollars to charities, schools, and museums, trying to repay my debt to the world. I volunteered at the Children's Theater under a stage name, doing makeup. Throughout it all I tried to remain invisible. To this day I have no driver's license, no home phone, and no credit card. Living without such toys is surprisingly easy, but living without lasting personal relationships can be painful indeed. I never dared to become close with anyone. Marriage was unthinkable. It was dangerous enough that I kept in touch with my parents. In fact, I even told them the truth. They laughed, of course. How many hundreds of people have said they were D.B. Cooper? And after all, I was their only child. I never dreamed they might betray me.

Swarovsky didn't find me. Perhaps he never looked. Still, I was relieved when the USSR collapsed in 1991, and the KGB was largely dismantled. The Cold War was over. Little did I suspect that my own war had just begun.

It was November 7, 1991 when I first heard the voice that would haunt my nightmares. The phone rang at my Nike office in Beaverton. I picked it up and spoke my name, foolishly thinking that this was now a safe thing to do.

A man's voice laughed—a muffled voice, disguised perhaps by a handkerchief.

"Who is this?" I demanded.

The muffled voice replied, "Your cousin. A very, very distant cousin. But I'm getting closer now."

"A cousin?" My parents had both come from large families. They had left everything behind when they fled Eastern Europe as the Iron Curtain fell in 1949. They never talked of Russia. They had changed their name from Chernovsky to Chandler before I was born. All contact with our relatives had been lost, or so I thought.

"Who are you?" I asked. "What's your name?"

"Cooper." The muffled voice laughed again. "You can call me D.B. Cooper."

"What?" Now I was terrified. Who could this be? What did he want?

"I'm the other Cooper," he said darkly. "And together we are going to help the cousins."

40

Word of the train wreck in Latvia spread through the Portland police bureau like the rumble of thunder before a storm. Sergeant Connie Wu had already Googled the news and cried her heart out by the time Dickers called her into his office.

"You'd better sit down, Sergeant." Then the captain noticed that her eyes were red, and he lowered his head. "You've already heard?"

She sank into the chair. "Just that there was an explosion on the train where—" she paused to take a tremulous breath. "Neil and Marial?"

He tightened his lips. "Some of the victims were burned beyond recognition. There was one female in the compartment they reserved. They haven't had to time to check the dental work, but from the wedding ring on her hand, it's Marial Gresham."

"What about Neil?"

"I'm afraid he's not on the list of survivors."

"But they haven't accounted for everyone yet? There's still a chance?"

The captain shook his head slowly. "If we haven't heard from him by now, we need to prepare for the worst."

Connie covered her face with her hands. "Do they know what kind of bomb it was?"

"It wasn't a bomb. Someone was stupid enough to bring a propane tank in their luggage. The valve got jostled and started leaking."

She stared at him. "That doesn't sound like an accident, captain. Someone set out to kill them."

He waved the remark aside. "You don't go halfway around the world and blow up a train just to take out a lieutenant from Portland."

"What about Lieutenant Lavelle? She's missing too."

He wrinkled his brow. "That case is troubling in other ways."

"I think the two cases are connected. Neil and I were working on it, you know."

"And you can work on it again after the energy summit," Dickers said. "Right now this department is facing a crisis. We've got a huge security job ahead of us. And, quite honestly, the loss of a lieutenant has left us short-handed. That's why I'm giving you a field promotion, Wu. I need you to step in for Ferguson."

The suddenness of the offer took Connie's breath away. She had wanted Neil's position. They had both applied for it six months ago, and he had won it unfairly as part of Dickers' scheme to cover up Neil's drunk driving. But it made her stomach churn to think of winning the promotion because Neil was dead. Being a lieutenant suddenly seemed unlucky.

"Of course, this is just provisional," Dickers added. "After the summit, when things have calmed down, we'll do an evaluation and see where you stand. But you'll be on the new salary as of this morning. Agreed?"

Connie touched her hair. It had grown back enough to cover the scar on her head, but still looked odd. "I'm not completely recovered yet, captain."

"I understand. You took quite a beating when you were thrown off that truck. Frankly, we're all impressed by how determined you've been to get back to work. As a lieutenant, you'll have some flexibility with your scheduling, but I need someone in charge. Are you in?"

She nodded almost imperceptibly.

"Good. I need you to organize security for the Russian delegation downtown at the Benson Hotel. They're taking up the whole twelfth floor. As far as I'm concerned, you can empty the other eleven. There may be protesters."

"Wait a minute," Connie interrupted. "What about Neil? Aren't you going to send someone to investigate the train explosion?"

"I can't send staff to Latvia. Certainly not now. The local police there are working on it. The whole business with the stolen paintings turned out to be a false alarm anyway. The auction house in Russia has admitted that the paintings there are fakes."

"Really?" This was news to Connie. Did that mean the paintings hadn't been smuggled out in wine cases after all?

"The originals have been in the Portland Art Museum all along," Dickers said. "Now about security for the Synergy summit. I've already pulled Sergeant Espada out of forensics to help you. He's got files of contacts for the hotel and the Russians. On Monday when they move to Timberline Lodge, you'll be reassigned to a checkpoint at the lodge entrance. Oh, and you'll need a new translator."

The swiftness of his assignments—and the ease with which he was willing to replace Neil and Marial—left her speechless.

Dickers pushed a thin dossier with a stapled photograph across his desk. "My secretary already made the arrangements."

Connie looked from the photograph to the name in disbelief. "Andrei Andropov? He's one of the car repair people that knew Yosef Duvshenko."

Dickers shrugged. "He speaks five eastern European languages and has a degree in—what the hell was it?—linguistics. If you want someone else, fine, you're in charge, hire them instead. But Andropov will be at the hotel at noon."

Her head spun. She wanted to be a lieutenant. She knew she could handle the responsibility. But right now she felt hurt and tired. She wanted Neil to be alive. She wanted him to walk in the door right now and take back his job.

"Congratulations, Lieutenant Wu," Dickers said, shaking her hand.

"Thank you, sir. I'll do my best."

"Excellent." He went to hold open the office door, but then paused. "Oh, and there's one more thing. It's a little delicate, but I don't know who else to ask."

"Yes?"

"I don't think Marial had any close relatives, but I'd appreciate it if you could check that her house is secure. The library was her primary employer, so they'll probably be organizing the memorial arrangements. As for Ferguson, of course, it's us. Didn't he have an apartment on the Park Blocks?"

The captain's voice drifted off, but Connie knew where he was leading. She said, "He also has a brother named Mark, and a daughter named Susan."

"Could you—?

She nodded, wearier than ever.

In some ways, being a lieutenant was gratifying. When Connie called Espada with instructions about the Benson Hotel he responded, "Yes, sir." When she asked the dispatcher to send a squad car to check on Marial's house, a car was sent. And she didn't have to wear a uniform. All those belts with pouches and sticks and radios that dangle awkwardly on your hips and shoulders—she left them all in her locker and changed back into her civilian clothes. The world didn't need to know she had a badge and a service semi-automatic in her purse.

But she did not enjoy calling the Midland branch of the Multnomah County Library. Connie had never cared much for Marial. The library staff, however, obviously did. The first person she spoke to broke into tears. Minutes passed before the branch director came on the line. With a quivering voice, she said they would begin the process of arranging a memorial service. Their reference department would check about the possibility of relatives in Latvia. The branch director had been a friend of Marial's since they had studied together for their librarianship degrees. She would meet the squad car to secure her house and look for a will.

Connie added, "I think Mrs. Greschyednyev also volunteered at the Portland Art Museum."

"I know." The branch director pinched off the words. "I'll call Mr. Chandler, and—" she sucked in her breath— "Oh hell, it just doesn't seem possible. Are you sure?"

"Yes. I'm so sorry."

As difficult as this call was, Connie dreaded the next one more. She circled the desk in Neil's office—her office?—as if the telephone were a coiled viper. Ever since The Keeper had gone into hiding in Susan's apartment, Connie had known Susan's cell phone number by heart. It was a Thursday morning, so Susan would probably be working at the Recyclotron, but Connie didn't know her schedule.

Finally she took a deep breath and made the call.

Susan answered after the first ring. "Hello." There was no sound in the background, no clatter of machinery. She had to be at home.

"Susan? This is Connie Wu."

Silence.

Connie soldiered on. "I need to talk with you. It's about—" she caught herself. "We just need to talk. Would you be home if I came over?"

"Yes."

"I could be there in fifteen minutes."

Another silence.

"Then I guess I'll see you soon," Connie said.

The line clicked and went dead. Connie looked at the phone in her hand, feeling lonely and a little frightened. Her own son Leighton was not particularly communicative. He rarely called and never chatted about personal things. Now she was beginning to understand that a daughter with autism could put an even greater strain on your emotions.

She took one of the department's unmarked Buicks, found a lucky parking spot in front of Susan's house, and walked up to the third-floor apartment.

Susan opened the door, averting her eyes as if Connie were a bright light. Connie stood there speechless, struck by how beautiful the young woman really was. Instead of the slightly baggy green overalls she wore for her recycling job, she had dressed in tight black jeans, a long-sleeved black shirt with an open collar, and a little suede vest that squeezed up just a bit of cleavage. Her black hair was cut short in back but hung long in front, framing her face with shiny black brackets. Inside that frame, Susan's dark eyes were a haunting gaze you could not meet. Neil's features, Connie realized, were reflected in his daughter's solemn beauty.

"May I come in?" Connie asked, reluctant to do what she had to do. "I have bad news."

Susan let Connie in and closed the door behind her. Connie looked about the room—tidy shelves of books, a framed poster of J.S. Bach—and at once she sensed an emptiness. "Isn't The Keeper living here?"

Susan shook her head. "Yesterday he rented the apartment downstairs with Dregs."

"Your boyfriend Dregs? I thought he lived under a bridge. Did you give him rent money?"

She shook her head again, waving the bracket of shiny hair. "The Keeper sold D.B. Cooper's twenty-dollar bill on eBay. And Dregs got a job."

"Really?" Connie said this with a tone of surprise, and realized at once how insulting it must sound. But the homeless drunk she had met picking up returnable bottles at the Recyclotron had not seemed employable, notwithstanding his advanced degree in engineering. To cover her surprise she asked, "Where is he working?"

"At the stage they're building for the dragon boat race. He's doing sound and video."

"Oh, I see. That's good." Connie paused and bit her lip. "Look, Susan, can we sit down? There's something important I have to tell you."

Susan sat in a straightback chair at an empty glass table. She looked down through the glass at the floor.

Connie sat opposite her and gave another deep sigh. "It's about your father. He was in Russia, researching a case with a translator, Marial Greschyednyev. They were on a train to Riga early this morning—or no, late last night, but over there it was morning, and—" Suddenly her voice caught. The words she had planned buckled up together like the train wreck itself: a fiery flash, a jolt, and a terrible explosion as glass and metal ripped through the crowd. Tears were running down her face.

"I know." Susan said, her voice cold. She shifted her dark-eyed gaze to the window. "I saw the news online. That's why I took the day off."

Connie looked up, no longer embarrassed by her own tears. Instead she was furious at this icy daughter, this heartless thing who couldn't cry. "Marial is dead, and your father—Lieutenant Ferguson—Neil—may be—oh damn, damn, damn!" She slapped the table, stood up, and turned away, her face in her hands.

For a long time Connie stood facing away, trying to control her sobs and dry her eyes.

Susan frowned as she looked out the window. Finally she said, "I was wrong about you, Sergeant Wu."

"*Lieutenant* Wu." Connie spat out the words. "They've already given me your father's goddam title. That asshole Dickers just wrote Neil off and moved on."

"I'm not often wrong," Susan said.

Connie turned to confront her. "And just how were you wrong?"

"I told my father you didn't like him enough."

Connie blinked. "What?"

"I was wrong."

"How were you wrong?"

Susan glanced up, looking Connie straight in the eyes. "I think you love him."

The gaze lasted only a second, but it pierced Connie like a pin through a butterfly. "I do not!" she protested.

Susan took out her cell phone, pushed a few buttons, and held it out.

Connie accepted the phone warily. On the screen was a six-letter text message:

"CARISA"

Connie pressed a button to check the sender, her heart beating faster. The name came up "KOSRAGS ZULNIEKI". It meant nothing to her. She handed the phone back and demanded, "What's Carisa?

"A shipwreck." Susan walked behind a counter, opened a refrigerator, and asked, "Would you like some pear nectar, Lieutenant?"

Instead of answering, Connie asked, "Are you talking about the *New Carissa?*"

Susan set two glasses on the counter. "Yes, that's the one. The tanker that wouldn't sink."

Connie remembered the incident, although it had happened at least a dozen years ago. The *New Carissa* had run aground on the Oregon Coast near Coos Bay. A salvage ship managed to pull the derelict off the beach, but it broke loose in a storm and drifted ashore near Waldport. They dragged it loose again, towed it thirty miles to sea, and tried to sink it with explosives. When even this failed to dispose of the resilient wreck, the governor had ordered it torpedoed by a submarine.

"What does this have to do with Neil?" Connie ignored the glass that Susan pushed toward her across the counter.

"When I was young I wanted a kitten." Susan sipped her drink and closed her eyes. "One day Papa brought home a little Siamese with burned whiskers. He said its first owners had left it in the woods to die. It survived by finding its way to a trailer house, but the people there were running a meth lab. A few days later the chemicals caught fire. By the time the fire department arrived, two of the people had died of smoke inhalation. Papa arrested the others. Afterwards he found the kitten hiding in a pan of water under the sink."

"And you named it Carissa," Connie said quietly.

Susan nodded. "I got the text message an hour ago. It's from a small village in Latvia. I had been so worried I could hardly move."

There was a lump in Connie's throat. She wanted to put her arms around Susan. She wanted to apologize that she had doubted this young woman's devotion to her father. Although Susan did not cry or hug, and it was difficult for her to look anyone in the eye, love obviously burned within her like a furnace. Suddenly Connie saw the jealousy that must have simmered there when Neil began dating women. And yes, the love that made Susan struggle to salvage Dregs, a homeless wreck, another Carissa.

"Why did Neil spell Carissa with one 's'?" Connie asked.

Susan set down her glass. "That scares me too. Papa shouldn't make a mistake like that. Something's wrong."

Connie thought a moment. Neil could just as easily have texted "I'M ALIVE." He used a code only Susan would understand because he wanted to hide.

"Whoever blew up the train is still out there," Connie said. "I think it's Cooper—the same Cooper who tried to kill me. He ordered people in Russia to get rid of Neil."

"Of course. But there's something else." Susan reached out, hesitated, and then set her hand on Connie's. The young woman's fingers were cold and stiff, as if she were forcing herself to touch the scales of a terrifying but potentially friendly dragon.

"Papa is not as strong as he seems," Susan said.

41

A blond flight attendant labeled "Lars" pushed his cart down the jetliner's narrow aisle. He set a foot brake and asked, "Would you like a drink before dinner, sir? It's complimentary on international flights."

"Bourbon," Neil muttered. He ran a hand over the stubble on his chin, his mind spinning as if he had been on the run for decades instead of days.

When the train had derailed and his car twisted off the tracks, the windows had popped out all along one side. He had found himself tumbling through the damp moss of a scrub birch forest. Only his shoulder and hip had been bruised. For the next hour he had helped rescue people. Little remained of the car where Marial had been waiting for him to bring coffee.

When officials in bright yellow uniforms began arriving, Neil had realized he didn't want to be on the list of survivors. His best chance of getting off Cooper's death list was to pretend to be dead. After stumbling two hours through the woods, detouring around swamps, he had found a farm. By pantomiming and finding a few words of common English, he had convinced them he was from the train wreck, but did not want to be reported. They had filled him with homemade vodka and allowed him to send a text message to his daughter. Dimly he recalled a ride to a town and a bus to an airport. Marial had insisted he keep his ID in a pouch around his neck while traveling in Russia, so he still had his passport, his police badge, a credit card, and a hundred-dollar bill. Of course the code for his e-ticket to Oregon had gone up in flames with Marial. Fortunately, the passport turned out be enough for a ticket agent to find his reservation and give him a boarding pass to Stockholm, and then Seattle, with an empty seat beside him all the way.

"I beg your pardon, sir?" Lars smiled at the disheveled, mumbling passenger.

"Bourbon on the rocks," Neil said grimly. "In memory of an old friend."

"All right, sir. If you'll just put down your seatback tray. Here you go."

"I don't suppose you serve parachutes?"

Lars shook his head. "I'm lucky if I can mix a bloody Mary."

Neil held up the plastic cup, watching the amber alcohol seep around the hollow cylindrical ice cubes. "Sorry, Marial. It should have been me."

As Connie drove to the Benson Hotel she found herself wondering why Neil had sent a reassuring text message to Susan but not to her. Connie had been targeted by the same killer. She had come out of hiding despite the threat. There's only so much research you can do when you're locked up in your home. You can do even less if you're hiding in a Latvian village.

Now that it seemed Neil might be alive, resentment began creeping in to take the place of fear. By the time she had driven the dozen blocks to the Benson, her resentment had already blossomed into anger.

The twelve-story Benson Hotel took up a block of downtown Portland. Century-old terra cotta curlicues decorated the facade. Spiraling topiary shrubs flanked the revolving brass doors. As she pulled up to the curb a white-gloved young man in a suit with tails stepped out to meet her.

"May I help you?"

She slammed the car door. "I'm checking in."

The young man looked skeptically at her black Buick and civilian clothes. Then he held out his gloved hand. "If you'll leave me the keys, I'll have someone park for you."

"Valets don't drive police cars."

"You're with the—" he faltered. "Still, you can't park in the drop-off zone."

"Watch me." She brushed past him to the revolving doors.

Connie had never been inside the Benson before, so she took a moment to size up the lobby. Chandeliers hung from the twenty-foot ceiling. To the left, four businessmen sat in plush wingback chairs at a gas fireplace beside a lacquered Chinese curio cabinet. To the right was a bar with wood-paneled pillars, a bored barmaid, two men on stools, and a stopped cuckoo clock. Straight ahead, a gray-haired man stood at a granite reception desk. Connie walked to the desk and gave her name.

"Oh yes," the man said. "Your captain asked us to clear the top floor for the Russian guests. We've taken the liberty of clearing the eleventh floor as well for security purposes. I have rooms available for you there, if you'll be staying with us."

"Thanks. I'll be here two nights." She didn't bring up the captain's idea of clearing the entire building. The hotel would want compensation, and Connie had no idea where to requisition that kind of money.

"Fine. You'll be in Room 1107." He slid a receipt and a plastic room key card across the counter. "Sign here, please. Oh, and by the way, a Sergeant Espada asked to let you know that he's meeting with a Russian security officer in the presidential suite. It's Room 1201, if you'd like to join them there."

She nodded. "In twenty minutes a translator is supposed to show up. Andrei Andropov."

"Shall I send him to the suite as well?"

"No. Keep him in the lobby and give me a call."

She had started to turn away when the man said, "You'll need this for the elevator."

She looked at the black plastic card in his hand. "I will?"

"There's no button for the twelfth floor."

"I see." This would simplify protection of the Russian delegates. But it wouldn't help if trouble came looking for her on the eleventh floor. When the elevator door opened she slipped the card into a slot marked "12". The elevator car headed up, beeping as each higher number lit. Finally the door opened onto a red-carpeted hall with a fifteen-foot ceiling. A gigantic gold-framed mirror showed a short, middle-aged woman with a bruised cheek and a hacked-up black haircut, standing in the elevator like a damaged China doll on a curio shelf. Connie frowned, marched down the hall, and rapped on the door of Suite 1201.

"Who is it?" an accented voice asked.

"Lieutenant Wu, Portland police."

The door opened a crack. The dark eye that studied her did not seem impressed, even when she held out her badge.

"It's OK," Espada's voice came from the room beyond. "She's my new boss."

The door opened wider, revealing a muscular man in a black suit. He had high cheekbones and thinning hair. "My job is caution," he said, as if this were a greeting.

Espada stepped forward. "Commander Alexi Borodin, this is Lieutenant Connie Wu." Then his face darkened. "Any word from Ferguson?"

Connie did have one word from Neil, but "Carisa" wasn't something she cared to explain. The anger surged back. "It doesn't look good," she said.

Espada told the Russian security agent, "One of our lieutenants was in a train accident in Latvia."

Borodin snorted. "I know this already."

"You do?" Connie asked.

Borodin crossed his arms. "This lieutenant was in Russia for a week. Why?"

"Because of an art auction in Novgorod," Connie said. "We thought they might be selling paintings stolen from Portland, but they were fakes."

"And that is all? He was not looking for a terrorist?"

Connie was taken aback. "No. Why do you ask?"

Borodin walked to the window and looked out across the city. "Because we have information that the people who destroyed this train may also be planning an attack at Synergy."

"Where did you hear this?" Connie asked.

"Our source is unreliable, from Pskov."

"What did he tell you?"

He shrugged. "Not much more than this." He turned to face her. "Still, I worry. The Russian energy minister has enemies. He nationalized a private oil company in Siberia. This angered many wealthy men. He signed a contract for oil pipelines through Ukraine. Nationalists in that country have sabotaged the lines and threatened his life. We know how to protect him in Russia. But here?"

Espada and Wu looked at each other. The Portland police had little experience coping with a threat of this nature. The Diplomatic Security Service should have assigned more agents to help. Obviously the feds didn't think much of an energy summit in Oregon. Connie offered, "Would it help if we sealed off the entire Benson Hotel?"

Borodin shook his head. "This hotel is not the problem. For two nights we can keep the twelfth floor safe. But then we move to Mt. Hood for the conference itself." He threw up his hands. "A remote resort on an isolated mountain, surrounded by wilderness. A snowstorm is predicted. This might be a place to vacation, perhaps, but to hold a global summit?"

"It's a little late to change the venue," Connie said. "We've worked with your government on this summit for two years. I think your energy minister even helped choose the company that organized the event."

"NovoCity Finance. Yes, we have checked them carefully. Still, I will need a list of everyone who will be there."

"That's easy," Espada said. "The staff and the delegates have already been cleared. I'll print out a roster of everyone who's authorized to be at Timberline Lodge."

"Good." Borodin slapped his hand with his fist. "This is where the terrorist will strike."

"What kind of person are we looking for?" Connie asked.

"I do not know." Borodin shook his head. "Our informant gave us only a name."

"A name?"

"Yes. Cooper. We are looking for Cooper."

With rosy clouds far below and the roar of jet engines drowning thought, Neil had wanted to keep flying forever. Three bourbons and two little bottles of Sicilian red wine had finally eased the anxiety knotting his stomach. The guilt hunching his shoulders lightened. He couldn't stop thinking of Marial. She flew beside him even now, a soft ghost. She had been so happy, radiant in that dawn, finally returning to the homeland of her dreams. Perhaps she had loved that dream more than she had loved Neil. He had always known she seduced him for a purpose. But then every love has a purpose, at least at first. And now that she was gone, he filled his empty cup with rosy clouds and a mind-numbing roar.

The Boeing descended into the twilight drizzle of the Sea-Tac airport, bumped the shiny wet tarmac, and roared even louder, like a threatened animal. D.B. Cooper had touched down here on just such a rainy evening, years ago. Could he really have been a college acquaintance? The explanation he had given Marial on the train sounded like nonsense now. His bourbon was wearing thin and his clothes were clammy. The anxious demons in his stomach were waking up. He needed the same things as Cooper: escape, cash, and anonymity.

He shuffled out of the plane in a line of sleep-deprived passengers. Alone among them Neil carried nothing. The uniformed man in the immigration booth scanned his passport and waved him through. Neil had three hours before his connecting flight to Portland, but suddenly he wanted to miss that plane. Hunted rabbits run in a zigzag. Dead men don't arrive on schedule. If Susan had gotten his text message, she must know he was alive. Did the department think he was dead? Did Connie? Above all, he couldn't let Cooper know he had survived.

He stood in front of an ATM machine, debating with himself. Finally a kid waiting behind him told him to get out of the way. Dead men don't withdraw money. He would have to make do with the hundred-dollar bill he had kept in his security pouch for emergencies. No more planes. No Amtrak trains, either. From now on, he would use nothing that checks ID.

On his way to the platform for the light rail to Seattle, a duty-free shop reached out with perfumed tentacles and reeled him in. He left with a pair of Jack Daniels hip flasks in the pockets of his rumpled suit. When he got on the commuter train he found a truckers hat and a ripped Seattle Mariners coat on an empty seat. He put them on, taking another step away from Neil Ferguson. Then he unscrewed the first Daniels and took a taste of anonymity.

The man who called himself Cooper slowly walked around the block of the Benson Hotel, glancing up at the lit windows of the upper floors. He hated loose ends, unsettled business. He had already taken care of Ferguson. Next on his to-do list was a cop named Wu. He knew he would not have to wait long.

Connie Wu rolled over and lifted her head so she could see the red numbers of her bedside clock. It was still only 10:34 p.m. She had to sleep. Her shift in the lobby would start at 4 a.m. no matter what, and the day ahead threatened to be long. But her mind was still driving through the obstacles the past day had left behind.

When Andrei Andropov showed up for the translator job, she had planned to send him home. But first she had decided to interrogate him. He had insisted absolutely that the mafia racketeer of the car repairmen was dead. There had been no more threatening phone calls. No instructions for transferring money to blind bank accounts. The Russian community was chipping in to help the widow, Nadia Duvshenko, and her daughter Sonya. Andrei himself was selling his shop and applying for an opening in the language department at Mt. Hood Community College in Troutdale.

At that point in the interview the first vanload of Russian delegates had started spinning out of the lobby's revolving doors, looking lost. None of them spoke English. There had been no time to find a different translator. She had let Andrei take them to their rooms.

Connie wished she had more security staff. Other than Sergeant Espada and half a dozen of Borodin's agents in stiff black suits, all she had were three reassigned Southeast Portland patrolmen. Tomorrow she would get six motorcycle cops and—this was the honest truth—four meter maids. She would need every last one of them. Tomorrow the Russian delegates wanted to tour the Vestas windmill headquarters on 14th and Everett. In the afternoon, they were visiting a factory for flexible solar panels in Hillsboro. Worse, they wanted to walk to dinner at Ivan's Oyster Bar. The energy minister had been to the restaurant on an earlier visit and knew Ivan Crombaugh personally.

Connie threw off the covers, walked to the bathroom, and washed down a couple of calcium tablets with a glass of water. Sometimes that helped settle her stomach, if not her thoughts. Then she went to the window and looked through a slit in the curtains to the street eleven stories below. Nothing alarming. A taxi. There were a few stragglers on the sidewalk, but they looked too bored and disorganized to be protesters. An old man looked up, as to check for rain, and walked on.

She shivered, closed the curtain, and fingered the Glock automatic she had left on the bedside table. Suddenly she felt lonely and vulnerable, on a mostly empty hotel floor shared by Andrei Andropov.

She knew it was foolish, and far too late in the evening, but she took the cell phone out of her purse and called Susan Ferguson.

The phone clicked after the second ring. Connie sensed she was connected to another silent, dark room.

"Susan? This is Connie Wu."

"I know."

"I'm sorry to bother you this late, but I just wondered if you'd heard anything else from your father. Maybe another text message?"

"No."

"Oh. OK. Thanks."

Then the line went dead with a click. Connie bit her lip.

By midnight Neil's first pint of bourbon was gone, and everything was starting to make sense. He was bad luck. The people he loved, died. He survived only because he hated himself. He was a danger to everyone. Now that people thought he was dead, he needed to stay that way.

He caught a late-night Greyhound bus to Oregon. The driver had to shake him awake in Portland. "Rise and shine. Any luggage?"

Neil shook his head, sending an arc of pain from temple to temple. On the sidewalk outside the bus station he studied his reflection in a plate glass window. With a stubble beard, a Freightliner cap, and bloodshot eyes, he could hardly recognize himself. That was good. Then he looked at a newspaper box. It was Friday, March 11. His daughter Susan would compete in the dragon boat races tomorrow afternoon. On Sunday the police would be busy covering the start of the energy conference at Mt. Hood. If he went to his apartment—or to work—he would have to explain why he was alive.

The anxious demon in his stomach asked for just a little more. He uncapped the second pint, took a drink, and started walking.

Gravity led him to the river, where workers were assembling grandstands in Waterfront Park for the boat races. As he shambled past a stage, a voice called out, "Hey, Daddy!"

The voice stirred an old fear. Neil started walking faster. But a moment later a hand caught him by the coat sleeve. Neil spun around awkwardly, staggering.

"Holy shit," Dregs whispered. "It is you."

"No." Neil yanked his sleeve free.

"Susan knew something was wrong." The scar on Dregs' face still made his left eye sag, but nothing else about him seemed the same. He wore neat black slacks and a black sweater. His hair was pulled back into a professional ponytail.

"Is she safe?" Neil asked.

"For now. She's worried about you." Dregs nodded toward the pint in Neil's pocket. "That won't help."

Neil started to walk on past.

Dregs caught him by the arm. "Once I said we're a lot alike, you and me."

Neil narrowed his eyes. "You've changed. What happened?"

"An old man knocked some sense into me. And now I've got something for you, right over there." He pointed to the empty promenade behind the stage.

Normally Neil would not have looked. Normally he would have been quick enough to dodge the blow. As it was, the fist caught him squarely on the temple, spun his head around, and left him sprawled on the grass.

"Assaulting an officer," Dregs said. "Book me, Daddy."

Neil bent forward and retched.

"There's a killer out there, Lieutenant. Your little girl needs a detective, not a coward. Now get your fucking ass out of the gutter and find him before he kills someone else."

A woman's voice called from a sound booth beyond the stage, "Dr. Egstrom? Could you help with the television uplink?"

Dregs whispered fiercely, "Susan still thinks you missed something in the Underground." Then he turned and strode toward the stage.

42

When Gerry Chandler walked home from the Portland Art Museum that evening, armed only with his umbrella, fedora, and briefcase, he had an ominous sense that Cooper himself might be waiting for him. Even if your blackmailer is a phantom, betrayal can make him appear in person, a messenger of death.

And sure enough, as Gerry waited for the crossing light by the Crystal Hotel on Burnside, he noticed a glow from the glass wall of his penthouse loft. He had not left a light on. He was sure of that. But what could he do? It was twenty years too late to call the police. All his plans for escape suddenly seemed foolish. He had never been able to hide from the man who called himself Cooper.

Surprisingly, Chandler felt relief, rather than fear, now that the long, dangerous game was finally about to end. As he crossed the courtyard he granted a sad smile to the pigeons trying to land on the splashing fountain of welded beer kegs. He waited as the chains rattled, lowering the old freight elevator. He rode it up to the top floor, took out his key, and walked the length of the hallway to the final door. But then instead of inserting the key he tried the knob. And of course it was already unlocked.

He took a deep breath and walked in, ready at last to meet the monster who had turned his world into a living hell.

Even in the entryway he noticed an unpleasant, sour smell. Gerry set down his briefcase, leaned his umbrella against the wall, and hung his hat on a peg as usual. Then he walked out into the studio — a huge room with familiar easels, a glass ceiling, and a view of city lights against a darkening sky.

The man was sitting in his office chair, tipped back lazily with his feet on the desk. That much Gerry might have predicted. But the man was also oddly shabby, with a stubble beard and a torn Seattle Mariners coat. Stranger still, the man's face seemed familiar.

'Good God," Gerry managed to say. "*You* are Cooper?"

Neil tipped his head to one side. "No, *you* are."

"But how—" Gerry paused. "I thought you were dead."

"Maybe I am. I sure feel like it."

"You look terrible, Neil."

"Thanks. It's my new disguise."

"You were in Russia. How did you get here?"

"Someone left a hide-a-key above the doorframe. Police tell you not to do that, Gerry." Neil tossed a sheaf of handwritten papers onto the desk. "I've whiled away the afternoon by reading your last will and testament. Good stuff."

Gerry groaned. Although Neil was not the tormentor he had expected, the lieutenant now knew enough to complicate things even more.

"Don't worry," Neil said. "I'd figured out most of it already. You were the only one who could have faked the Rothko paintings. And the only reason to do something stupid like that was if you were being blackmailed. But you didn't know who the blackmailer was. So you sent me on a suicide mission to Russia to find out."

Gerry shook his head. "I didn't think he was a killer, not at first. He called himself the 'other Cooper.' I thought he just wanted to help relatives in Russia. But then you told me he might be connected with the Underground murders. By then I was trying to stop you from going to Russia."

Neil looked at him steadily.

Gerry paled, remembering something else. "Marial. What about Marial?"

Neil shook his head.

Gerry turned aside, pinching his eyes closed. Neil let him suffer in silence. When Gerry could speak again, his voice broke. "Who could do this? I've tried for twenty years to find out who the other Cooper is."

"And so did Marial, and so did her husband. They're both dead. A lot of people have asked this question, and a lot of them are dead."

Gerry's shoulders sagged. "What can we do?"

"Maybe only dead men can catch him."

Gerry looked at him uncertainly.

Neil shrugged. "I'm already dead. The other Cooper thinks he blew me up. And most people think you've been dead for years."

"You mean the original D.B. Cooper?"

"That's right. Most people think you died when you jumped out of the plane."

"Except I just sent you a letter with a twenty-dollar bill from the ransom. That pretty much proves I survived."

"There are ways of changing that."

"You mean by dying? I have a feeling the other Cooper is already looking for a chance to kill me. He told me to get him the Rothko paintings. Instead I gave him copies. He's out there waiting."

"You need to disappear, Gerry."

Gerry thought about this a moment. "Disappearing is an art. It would be hard to disappear so he can't find me. I'd have to come up with something spectacularly unexpected. And then what?"

"Then two dead men might be able to set a trap even the other Cooper doesn't suspect."

Gerry frowned. "What are you thinking?"

Neil stood up and took off his ripped coat. "I'm thinking I really need a hot shower. Any chance I could do that while you find us something to eat?"

Connie was about to dress for dinner when her cell phone rang. The screen said S FERGUSON. Connie took the call at once. "Susan? Have you heard from Neil?"

There was a long silence.

"Look, Susan, I don't have much time. Have you heard from your father?"

"Yes."

Connie took a breath. "And?"

"Dregs saw him on the waterfront."

"Here? In Portland?"

"Yes. But he's—" Susan's voice trailed off into another silence.

"He's what, Susan? Talk to me!"

"He's hiding."

"Oh, great."

"I think he needs help."

"Well, how the hell am I supposed to help him if he's hiding?" Connie held the phone away and mouthed the word *Asshole!* Then she said, "As far as I'm concerned, he's AWOL. I'm not covering for him anymore."

"Don't—" Susan began.

But Connie clapped the phone shut and threw it into her purse. She didn't have time for this. She had ten minutes to dress for a dinner she wouldn't even get to eat. The Russians expected her to escort them four blocks through downtown Portland and then stand there, looking confidently secure—and presumably decorative—while they slurped down oysters.

It would have been easier if she were still a sergeant. Then she could have simply put on a uniform. As it was, she hadn't brought much of a wardrobe to the hotel. She put on a dark skirt, black nylons, and a white blouse. The gun had to be more accessible than in her purse, and shoulder holsters really aren't flattering, so she strapped on a service belt like a cowgirl. Because she had lost a couple of inches during recovery, mostly from her waist, the belt cinched down an extra notch, puckering the blouse tight across her chest. It was a little risque without a jacket, but she didn't have a jacket that matched the skirt. With five minutes left, she buried the bruises on her face with blush and eye shadow. Then she pinned a police cap on at an angle to cover her hacked hair. Time was up.

When she walked to the elevator, the big mirror in the hall no longer reflected a broken China doll. Now she looked like she was going to a Halloween party as a sexy cop. To make up for it, she took command when she reached the lobby. She ordered the motorcycle patrolmen to block the side streets. She sent the meter maids to hold back the protesters on the sidewalk. Then she used the rest of her squad to herd the nineteen Russian delegates through town, watching for suspicious silhouettes on rooftops.

The Oyster Bar seemed unchanged from her lunch there with Neil. Had that been just two weeks ago? But now the owner, Ivan Crombaugh, was everywhere. He directed the wait staff and told jokes, switching effortlessly from English to Russian. She had known he was bilingual, but it still caught her by surprise. His campaign ads for county commissioner had never mentioned his Russian heritage. She wondered if his mirrored dark glasses were really the legacy of a childhood eye disease, as he suggested, or if he just wanted the voters who looked at him to see themselves. Why else did the lenses have to be mirrors?

Because the Oyster Bar was catering one of the brunches at Mt. Hood, Crombaugh's name had turned up on the list of people with clearance for Timberline Lodge. Connie watched him, weighing the possibilities.

After dinner, when the waiters were clearing away the plates, the Russian energy minister tapped his glass with his knife. "Ivan! Come up here, please."

The white-haired commissioner crossed the restaurant. "Would you like dessert?"

"No, the food was perfect. What we need now is entertainment."

The commissioner creased his brow. "I didn't plan for musicians."

"Not music!" The energy minister waved his hand dismissively. "You know, the Portland Underground tour. The last time I was here you showed me the secrets beneath the city streets."

"That was before we knew all the secrets."

"The Underground murders only make the tour more piquant. Wasn't one of the victims a Russian? Come on, Ivan."

Commander Borodin whispered to Connie, "What is this Underground?"

"It's a history exhibit in the basement."

"How many exits does the basement have?"

"Just one, a door at the bottom of the stairs." Then Connie thought back to the tour and added, "Actually, there may be one other door, but I think it's locked."

"I don't like it," Borodin said. "I'll want to go first."

"Then I'll go last."

Crombaugh asked the delegates to line up at the head of the basement stairs. Then he led them down the steps. Connie followed them down to a dimly lit, damp brick hallway. Although Crombaugh was giving the tour in Russian, she could tell he was following the same script she had heard, warning people to watch their heads, and telling about the Shanghai men. The hallway opened up onto the dank room she remembered, where the far wall was painted as a diorama of ships in the river. One of the Russians even pointed to the actual door beside the painting and asked a question that Connie knew must be, "And where does that door lead?"

Crombaugh lowered his brow and said ominously, "Shanghai!"

Everyone laughed, and the show was over. Talking and joking, the Russian delegates walked back through the hallway to return upstairs. But Crombaugh stayed behind, and because Connie had promised to go last, she stood in a corner, waiting. Crombaugh felt his way along the wall to the door, unlocked it with a large iron key, and stepped inside. There was no light beyond the door, so whatever he was doing must have been by touch.

A minute passed before he backed out of the door, closed it, and turned around. The mirrored glasses concealed much of his expression, but in that instant Connie saw fear. She found herself flashing back to the front hood of an SUV, screaming down 122nd Avenue at sixty miles an hour, looking into the eyes of a killer—the eyes of the man who called himself Cooper.

"Who are you?" Crombaugh asked.

"Lieutenant Wu, Portland police."

He licked his lips. "What do you want?"

"Mr. Crombaugh, I'd like you to take off your glasses. I want to see if I recognize your eyes."

"Certainly my dear." He smiled and raised one hand to his glasses. Then he paused. "But only if you would first be willing to take off your shirt."

Connie stared at him. "What?"

"Your shirt, my dear. I think it wants to come off."

Obviously he was anything but blind.

"No?" He shook his head and walked past her.

43

Neil was floating in jets of hot bubbly water. He had dumped his smelly clothes on the floor of Gerry Chandler's vast bathroom — a weird backstage studio full of grease paint, wigs, and clocks. Gerry even had a life-size mannequin, dressed up to look like himself. By the time Neil had climbed into the kidney-shaped spa and turned on the jets, a great weariness had overcome him. He closed his eyes, hoping the bubbles might wash away the horrors of the past weeks.

When he opened his eyes again, it took a moment to realize he was asleep. He was still lounging in the oversized bath, and he still heard a roaring sound, but his body tingled pleasantly. How could he know for sure whether this was a dream? He checked the clock on the wall above the tub. A Jetsons-style timepiece from the 1960s, it had space-age balls on the hands. The second hand was moving backwards. Then it stopped and spun the other way, much too fast. Clocks never worked correctly in Neil's dreams.

Neil knew he could have woken up right then, simply by opening his eyes for real. But he also knew dreams like this can be a gift. He looked around, curious. The water in the bathtub was calm. The roaring sound came from outside. To his right, a small oval window beside the soap dish overlooked bright clouds and an airplane wing. To his left, the bathroom had become the aisle of an old, empty Boeing 727.

He got out of the tub, tied a bath towel around his waist, and walked down the aisle toward the back the plane, leaving wet footprints on the carpet. He wasn't surprised to find a red handle with the label, "AFT STAIR EXIT. FOR EMERGENCY USE ONLY."

When you find an emergency escape hatch in a dream you should open it, even if you're wearing nothing but a towel. Neil steadied himself, gripped the lever with both hands, and pulled.

The door popped back with a blast of cool air, and a stairway lowered into darkness. He had expected to see clouds. Instead he seemed to be on the threshold of a large, dimly lit room. There were voices. A string quartet played Mozart. Cautiously, Neil stepped down the stairs. Guests in tuxedos were holding glasses. The lights of the city sparkled from a wall of windows. Of course.

He was still in Gerry Chandler's loft apartment, but his dream had taken him back three weeks. He had walked into the evening of the art museum gala. He knew he was dressed inappropriately, but no one seemed to notice he was dripping wet, wearing only a towel. A large woman who should not have been wearing a tight black evening dress bumped his shoulder, turned, and said, "Oh! Pardon me." A young man in a white suit offered him a tray of drinks. "Would you care to try the sparkling Oregon Noir, sir?"

Neil shook his head and moved through the crowd. He knew where he was going now, and why he was here.

He found the other version of himself in the middle of the room, beneath the unopened skylight. The other Neil did not look happy. He had a black eye and was wearing the black suit he had once worn to Rebecca's funeral. Marial, on the other hand, was a vision. Her green velvet dress and emerald choker set off the highlights in her coppery hair. By trading her staid librarian glasses for contact lenses, she had transformed herself into a breathless beauty. Neil didn't have the heart to tell her that she was dead.

"Hey, Marial, you look good enough to eat." Captain John Dickers' face was flushed. He held up a champagne flute. "Let me introduce you all. These are two of my staffers, Neil Ferguson and Marial Gresham. I'm sure you know our county commissioner, Ivan Crombaugh."

Neil watched the black-suited version of himself smile awkwardly, unsure whether to say something or attempt to shake hands.

"And this is Nancy Willis, the CEO of NovoCity Finance."

The young executive with piercings and brightly colored hair ignored both versions of Neil Ferguson. Instead she said to Marial, "It's good to see you again, Mrs. Greschyednev."

Stop. He would remember this later, wouldn't he?

Neil opened his eyes.

At once the dream began slipping away. Instead he found himself worrying that he might be in a different dream. How could tell if he was truly awake?

The bathwater around him had cooled. The spa's jets were not working, which seemed wrong, but the clock's second hand moved the right way, and the wall with the airplane window had healed. Neil got out of the tub unsteadily. Fading alcohol left him nervous and hungry. Where the pile of old clothes on the floor had been, he found a fresh, folded stack with a suspicious note on top. It read, "Don't shave."

He dried himself and put on the clothes—tan slacks, a black turtleneck, and a tan sport coat. Then he looked in the bathroom mirror. Surrounded by dressing room light bulbs, an ageing hipster with grizzled stubble and unkempt hair looked back. Worse, the mannequin of Gerry Chandler seemed to be smiling at him from the shadows. It leaned against a closet, looking smug with its mustache and fedora.

"Neil?" There was a rap on the door. The other Gerry Chandler looked in—presumably, the real one. "Did you drown in here?"

"Sorry. I must have fallen asleep in the tub." Neil rubbed his aching forehead. Had he wanted to remember something?

"We're supposed to be working on a plan, remember? Come on, I've cooked quesadillas."

Neil followed him out into the dark studio, still a little dazed. The lights of the city cast shadows across the loft. A single candle, covered by a lampshade, glowed on a dining table set for two. A few silver balloons, apparently left over from the gala, floated by at head-height like ghosts.

"Good idea," Neil said.

"You told me to make dinner."

"No, not that."

"You mean the clothes? I'm sending your old suit out for cleaning."

"No, I meant turning out the lights."

Gerry sat down and unfolded a cloth napkin. "It didn't take a detective to figure out Cooper might be out there, watching this window. No point in being an easy target."

"We both need to stay out of sight."

"So what's our plan?"

Neil cut a big piece of tortilla. "Start by telling me everything you know about your blackmailer, the man who calls himself Cooper."

Gerry ate for a while in silence. Then he put down his fork. "It wasn't blackmail. Not at first. I thought of it as charity, helping politically persecuted families from Eastern Europe find a better life here in Portland."

Neil spoke with his mouth full. "Strange charity. A muffled voice on the phone tells you to transfer money to anonymous bank accounts."

"I thought he might really be related to me."

"When did you realize he was with the Russian mafia?"

"Why would I think that? He was helping people immigrate, using my money to get them jobs and apartments. I had no idea he was pressuring them."

"So you didn't care if he told police you were a hijacker?"

Gerry's head sank. "I don't know how he found out. Maybe he really had been in touch with my parents before they passed away. Maybe he had connections at the KGB. Anyway, you're right. I didn't want him to make it public."

"He first threatened you—when?—about nineteen years after the hijacking? At that point the feds could still have put you in prison. But the statute of limitations ran out after twenty-five years. Why didn't you stand up to him then?"

"Not everyone knows about the statute of limitations. "

"Seriously? You didn't realize you were in the clear?"

"I'll never be in the clear, Neil. Russia's Foreign Intelligence Service took over for the KGB. If they knew I was alive, they'd still want revenge. Besides, I committed treason against the United States. I was a courier for the KGB when they were stealing Apollo plans. How could I face that in public?"

"If no one knew about the Apollo plans, would you be willing to admit you're D.B. Cooper?"

Gerry stood up, walked to a sink by the wall, and refilled his glass with water. "D.B. Cooper was a disguise I invented. I made him disappear once. I think he needs to disappear again."

"That's what I'm thinking too. Then the other Cooper would stop trying to track us down, and we could track him down instead." Neil wiped the whiskers on his chin with a napkin. "Now let's talk about your evil twin. The Cooper with blood on his hands."

Gerry returned with his water glass. "I swear, I didn't know how dangerous he was."

"Well, I'm pretty sure he shot Yosef Duvshenko, the car repairman. And he probably strangled all five of the Underground murder victims. Three of them had been witnesses in the car repair scam. One had smuggled contraband in wine cases. The other was a Russian immigrant studying to be a flight technician. I have no idea why Cooper killed him. Anyway, that brings the body count to six."

"What happened to the man who led the Underground tours?"

"Thomas Daugherty, the mortician? Cooper must have strangled him too, when he didn't need him anymore. And he probably drowned Lieutenant Lavelle, the homicide detective who was writing a book about the case. That makes eight."

"Marial." Gerry looked down as he said the name.

"She—" Neil's voice caught. He turned aside, unable to speak. She had been so beautiful, so happy the morning they had arrived in Latvia. It was hard to believe Cooper could hire someone to blow up an entire train. "How many—how many others died on the train?"

"They're saying seven, but two are unidentified, and three are missing. He must have thought you were getting close."

Neil nodded. "He's tried to kill Connie too."

"Connie?"

"My colleague, Sergeant Wu." Neil steadied himself with a breath. "The night Cooper killed the car repairman, she got a close look at him. He was wearing a balaclava, but she thinks she might be able to identify him by his eyes. I don't know. Maybe she can."

Gerry looked across the room at the lights of Portland. "He's out there now, a man who has murdered at least sixteen people. Are you sure Sergeant Wu is safe?"

Connie had just locked down the top two floors of the Benson Hotel, taken a shower, and collapsed into her bed when her cell phone beeped.

To hell with them all, she thought. She was too tired to deal with Susan's enigmatic silences, Captain Dickers' peremptory commands, or her son Leighton's self-centered ramblings. She needed sleep.

Eventually the phone gave up. A few seconds later, however, it started beeping again.

Wearily, she reached to the bedside table and tilted the phone just enough to see the lit screen on its cover: UNKNOWN CALLER. Damn. She opened the phone at arm's length, as if it might explode.

A tiny, tinny voice called, "Connie? Is that you? Are you all right?"

She sank back onto her bed and closed her eyes, flush with anger and relief. Still holding the phone at arm's length, she bit out the words, "You asshole."

"Connie! Oh, I'm glad to hear your voice. I should have called sooner. I—"

"Don't tell me," she interrupted. "You've been hiding."

"Hiding?" The little voice in the phone paused. "I suppose I have. The truth is, Connie, I've been drunk."

"Oh, God." She wanted to be even angrier at him, but this kind of honesty always caught her off guard. She held the phone closer. Now she could hear something else, something strange and frightening. She heard the staccato sobs of a man crying.

"Neil?"

A minute passed before his voice came back, this time quietly. "I drank for two years after Rebecca died. Marial deserved more than two days. It's all the time I had."

"You're in Portland?"

He sighed. "Yeah. I found out you were right. There really are two Coopers. One of them is a killer. I think I've got a better chance of tracking him down if we can convince people I'm dead."

"That's easy," Connie said.

"What do you mean?"

"Dickers has already written you off. He left the train wreck investigation to the Latvian police. He closed the whole Cooper case and reassigned everyone to security for the energy summit."

"Including you?"

She gave a wry laugh. "I'm at the Benson Hotel, running security for the Russian delegation."

"Dickers put a sergeant in charge of the entire Russian delegation?"

Now it was Connie's turn to make an awkward confession. "I'm not a sergeant, Neil. When Dickers thought you were dead, he gave me a field promotion to take your place."

"I see."

"It's just provisional. Anyway, now that you're back, there's work to do."

"I'm dead, Connie. Remember?"

"I know. But the Russian security chief says he has a tip that Cooper may try to disrupt the summit at Timberline Lodge. I don't know what to do. We're running out of time."

"Where did they get a tip like that?"

"He admitted the source might be unreliable. From someplace in Russia. It sounded like Piss-Off."

"Pskov?"

"Yeah, I think so."

Neil whistled. "That's the hub of a rival mafia network. They really might know what Cooper's planning."

"What can we do?"

"I've got an idea, but I'm going to need a few things."

"Like what?"

"A list of everyone who will be at the summit."

"No problem," Connie said. "Although you're not going to like it. Half the suspects we've been dealing with are guests at the summit."

"For example?"

"Dickers had me hire Andrei Andropov, one of the car repairmen, as a translator."

"You're working with Andropov?" Neil's voice rose.

"I'm more worried about Ivan Crombaugh, the county commissioner who owns the Oyster Bar. He speaks Russian and hides behind mirrored glasses. He's catering a dinner at Timberline."

"Next you'll tell me Brother Daniel will be there too."

"That's right," Connie said. "He's leading an evening art walk around the lodge. Todd Lammergeier, the engineer, is showing up at the opening ceremony to accept a conservation award for his father's work in designing the Recyclotron. And of course there's the NovoCity Finance people who organized the event, including Nancy Willis herself."

"Wait." Neil stopped her. "Nancy Willis? I'm remembering something about her now."

"She's the goth girl who's a CEO."

"I know, but I think she speaks Russian."

Connie cocked her head. "Are you sure? She gave me access to her files. I didn't see anything about that."

"When I was at the art museum gala with Marial, Captain Dickers introduced us to Nancy Willis. She knew that Marial's last name was Greschyednyev, and she pronounced it right. Could her finance company be mixed up with the mafia?"

"Not as far as I can tell. I went through their books pretty carefully. The company's done well, but there's nothing irregular."

Neil sighed. "Maybe I just dreamed it up."

"Do you want me to email you the list of summit guests?"

"No. Print it out. I'll also need the key to the Underground. Is it still in my desk?"

"I kept it in my purse. You want to come pick it up?"

"Just leave everything on the seat of an unmarked police car. Leave the car keys on the seat too."

Connie sank back into her pillow, suddenly feeling the tiredness of the day. "Neil? It's too late for jokes."

"No joke, Connie. I need a car. I'll walk past the front of the Benson Hotel tomorrow morning at eight. Do you think you could have a car for me by then?"

"Neil! If I give a dead man a police car without telling Dickers, he won't just demote me, he'll kick me off the force."

Neil didn't answer. Finally Connie said, "Look, I need some kind of security. At least tell me you've got a plan that's going to work."

"It's not much of a plan, and it might not work," Neil admitted. "But I can offer you job security."

Connie heard a fumbling sound, as if the cell phone were being shifted from one hand to another. Then a voice she did not recognize said, "Sergeant Wu?"

"Lieutentant Wu," she corrected. "Who is this?"

The man cleared his throat. "I think you might know me by a name I once used."

"That's a lousy pickup line. What's the name?"

"Dan Cooper."

Connie sat up in bed, suddenly wide awake. "You're Cooper? The original D.B. Cooper?"

"I'm afraid so."

"But how —?"

"When I came home from work today, I found Neil Ferguson here in my apartment. We had a little talk, and I've decided to give myself up."

Connie's head was reeling. Was this another hoax? How could Neil have tracked Cooper down? And which Cooper was this — the hijacker or the mafia boss?

"Who are you?" she asked.

The man on the phone clicked his tongue. "Tomorrow morning, Lieutenant. When Ferguson picks up the car at eight, he'll be wearing a disguise. He'll have a manila envelope with him. That packet will include my confession, proof of my identity, and details of exactly how I'll give myself up."

"You're serious."

"Absolutely. Are my terms acceptable?"

"Can I talk to Neil again?"

There was another fumbling sound, and then Neil's voice. "Connie?"

"Are you drunk?"

"Not very," Neil said. "Why?"

"Because if the man I just talked to is really D.B. Cooper, special agent Owen is going to go ballistic. The FBI may have trouble prosecuting a crime that old, but they'll find some excuse to lock him up anyway. The media's going to be all over this."

"That's the plan, Connie. And because I'm dead, I'm not involved. Tomorrow, the one person too famous for Dickers to fire will be a cop named Wu."

44

Neil's head throbbed as he walked down Burnside Street the next morning. The hangover and jet lag had been bad enough, but then Gerry had shaken him awake at 4 a.m. to start work on a disguise. Neil's scalp itched and his nose was numb. He passed Powell's Books without daring to look at his reflection in the plate glass windows.

When he got to the Benson Hotel none of the cars in front looked right, so he walked on by. Around the corner on Stark Street, a black Buick was just pulling into a delivery zone. Connie got out, glanced up and down the street, and bit her lip.

Neil stopped, suddenly overcome by a fluttery confusion. She had lost weight, and it left her looking both more attractive and more fragile than before. Her black hair shone from beneath a tilted police cap. The flush on her face seemed almost girlish. She sighed, closed the car door, and walked past him on the sidewalk as if he were cast in bronze.

"Connie?"

She turned, startled. Then her mouth opened. "Good God."

Neil looked aside, a little embarrassed, and saw himself reflected in the car's window. His hair had been dyed black and parted in the middle. Blue wraparound glasses perched on a hawk nose. His gray stubble had become a black five o'clock shadow. The sport coat and turtleneck belonged on a Porsche billboard.

"You look terrific," Connie said. "I never would have recognized you."

Neil managed half a smile at this double-edged compliment. Had he looked so dull before?

"Our friend D.B. Cooper has a knack for make-up," Neil said. "This morning we switched noses."

"Switched noses?"

"He made casts, poured some kind of latex, and attached it with glue."

She shook her head, laughing. "I'm just glad you're alive."

"I've been worried about you too, Connie." This was the moment when he might have sought comfort by taking her in his arms. But he didn't. The ghost of a librarian was standing between them, her arms crossed.

Neil held out the manila envelope.

Connie tucked it under her arm. "Are you sure D.B. Cooper will give himself up?"

"He'll come out of his apartment, unarmed, at exactly six o'clock this evening."

"That's when the dragon boat races are supposed to end. Half the city is going to be watching the finals."

"I know. By then we've got to have the attention of the police and the media. Can you do that?"

"It depends on how good the evidence in this packet is." She lowered her eyes. "Tomorrow morning I've got to drive up to Timberline Lodge. I'll be staffing the guard booth on the entry road to the conference. What about you?"

"I've got a date with my daughter, collecting clues. I called her last night after talking with you. She still thinks something's wrong at the Recyclotron."

Connie met his eyes. "Do you have a gun?"

He shook his head.

"Then take mine."

He hesitated. "You need it more than I do. Besides, I'm already dead, remember?"

She hugged him then, an all-too-brief embrace. Then she hurried down the sidewalk without looking back.

Neil got into the Buick, pocketed the Underground key, and flipped through the four-page list Connie had left on the seat. Seventy-three delegates from twelve countries were attending the energy summit's opening banquet on Sunday afternoon. Another ninety names had been separated into categories: honorees, Diplomatic Service agents, local police, chefs, waiters, and hotel staff.

Was Gerry's blackmailer on the list? And why would he care about an energy summit? The evil Cooper had always seemed more interested in profit than in politics.

Suddenly a honk jolted Neil back to streets of Portland. The headlights of a laundry van were blinking at him in the rearview mirror. Neil muttered, started the motor, and pulled out of the delivery zone.

The lawn at Waterfront Park was a green sea full of brightly painted dragon boats. Neil pulled to the curb of the Naito Parkway and honked three times.

Susan walked across the grass, unhurried, with her head down.

Neil winced when he saw Dregs beside her. Neil wasn't keen to meet her boyfriend again. Dr. Egstrom's fist was one reason Neil's head still hurt.

"What the hell?" Dregs peered in the car window, squinting so hard the scar below his eye stretched into a red J.

"It's Papa," Susan said, opening the front passenger door. "Sit in back."

Dregs swung himself into the back seat, laughing. "Man, you had me going there. Nice disguise. You look more like an ad for Rolex than for rotgut."

Neil ignored him. He asked Susan, "Are you sure you're all right? You haven't noticed people or cars following you? Maybe outside your apartment?"

She shook her head, wagging black strands of hair past her white neck.

"Your little girl's got a sixth sense, Daddy," Dregs bellowed from the back seat.

"Will you shut up?" Neil slowed for the Saturday Market tourists straggling across the street. Then he drove under the Burnside Bridge and turned the Buick sharply left onto Couch Street.

"Well, if you don't think Suzie's psychic, why are you taking us back to the Recyclotron?"

"Because this is the one piece that doesn't fit." Neil parked the car and got out. He took off his wraparound glasses and slid them into the pocket of his sports coat.

"Isn't that what you've been saying?" Dregs asked Susan. "You've been talking about a piece that doesn't fit."

Susan took a ring of keys from the pocket of her green overalls, unlocked the door of the One More Time Women's Cooperative, and turned on a bank of fluorescent lights. As the tubes blinked on, shadows jerked across the thrift shop's tables. Salvaged frying pans, golf clubs, and rakes glared like an array of weapons.

Susan led the way through a second door marked "Employees Only." The dark workroom beyond was silent, but the sour smell of the Recyclotron loomed large. Dim shadows suggested the pipes, tanks, and conveyor belts of the huge machine.

Dregs felt his way to a circuit breaker box and flipped a switch. Suddenly a crack of yellow light outlined a small door on the far wall.

Neil approached the door. His Underground key rattled in the bright keyhole. The hinge creaked and the door swung open.

"What are we looking for?" Dregs asked behind him.

"I'm not sure." Surrounded by light, Neil ventured down the metal steps to a dank basement corridor. Susan followed, her dark eyes glancing to either side.

Dregs said, "I bet the piece that doesn't fit is really my old professor, Curt Lammergeier." Dregs' footsteps clanged on the metal stairs as he followed Neil and Susan down into the Underground.

Neil stopped in the first of the basement rooms—the old tour's gift shop. Dusty mannequins dressed as prostitutes lounged in the musty chairs of a bordello parlor.

Dreg's voice echoed behind him, "I actually thought Lammergeier might be D.B. Cooper. He wasn't, was he?"

"No," Neil said, checking the edges of the room. "He met Cooper on a railroad bridge in 1971."

"OK, so they knew each other. Years later, Lammergeier needed money. He invented a recycling machine that's too good to be true. It's profitable because the toxics disappear. Then he turns up dead, floating in a poisoned pond. Have I got it right so far, Lieutenant?"

Neil moved on to the second room, the saloon where the victims of the Underground murders had been displayed as embalmed corpses.

"Have I got it right?" Dregs demanded. "You've figured out all the other murders, but you don't have a clue about Lammergeier. He's in the middle of everything, and you don't know who, or why, or how."

"Enough!" Susan had closed her eyes. She held her hands over her ears. "Can't you smell it?"

"What?" All Neil could smell was the stench of the recycling machine and the musk of damp brick walls.

"Something sweet."

Dregs shrugged. He and Neil began searching the room. The empty whiskey bottles on the saloon's bar smelled only of dust. The shadows behind the broken chairs and tables hid no surprises.

Susan opened her eyes and frowned.

"There's nothing here, babe," Dregs said.

Neil looked at his watch. He should have been tracking down Ivan Crombaugh, Nancy Willis, or Brother Daniel—suspects who were actually going to be at the energy summit.

"You know, I need to get back to the dragon boat stage," Dregs said.

Susan closed her eyes again and shook her head. "B vitamins."

"Babe?"

"B vitamins," she repeated.

Dregs rubbed the scar on his cheek. "That's what we called—" Suddenly he looked toward the wall at the back of the room.

"What is it?" Neil asked.

"The Blitz. Last time there were cases of beer in here—the old Blitz Weinhard stuff they haven't made for years."

Now Neil remembered the stacks of stubby brown bottles. He felt a chill of fear.

Susan said what he was thinking, "That's where they put the toxic waste."

"Three cases of bottles?" Dregs asked. "That's a lot of poison. Who'd want it? And where is it now?"

A memory and an idea were starting to merge in Neil's mind. "I think I know where to check."

"Where?"

"The forensic warehouse in Northwest Portland." Neil strode across the basement toward the metal staircase. "I'll drop you off at the dragon boats on the way."

But Dregs was right behind him. "Sorry, Dad. Forensics? We're coming along."

"No you're not." Neil took the stairs two steps at a time, but then he had to wait for Dregs and Susan in order to lock the Underground door. They ended up at the car at the same time.

Susan plunked herself down in the passenger seat, her arms crossed.

One glance told Neil she wasn't going to leave the car unless he took her to the warehouse. "Look, Susan, all I've got is a hunch. I don't even know if I can get in. It's a weekend, and they might have changed the codes."

She didn't move.

Neil banged the steering wheel with his fist. He knew he could waste all day waiting for his stubborn daughter to change her mind, and she never would. He shifted the Buick into drive, hit the gas, and swerved down Second Street.

Five minutes later they pulled up to what looked like an abandoned factory on Northwest Vaughn. The windows had been bricked up. A keypad glowed red beside a blank metal door.

"Wait by the car," Neil told them. He went to the keypad, shielded the buttons with one hand, and typed in the number of his police badge. After a moment the light turned yellow. Neil hadn't used the forensics code in months. He tried the room number of Captain Dicker's office. The light went green.

He opened the door and motioned for Susan and Dregs to follow.

Inside was an unpainted concrete foyer. An elderly man in a blue work shirt looked up from behind a counter. He took off his wireframe glasses, polished them slowly, and put them back on, studying Neil's slicked back hair and sport coat. "Are you new with the bureau?"

"It's Saturday." Neil showed his badge. "I was off duty when something came up. These are—" he indicated Susan and Dregs, trying to think of something true— "possible witnesses."

"Well, Lieutenant, they'll have to sign in."

After Susan and Dregs had signed a clipboard, the caretaker gave them all latex gloves and white paper slippers. Neil checked a chart, wrote down a seven-digit number, and then led the way down a hall lined with shelves and boxes. At length he stopped before a bank of drawers.

"Here we are." Neil pulled out a drawer. It was filled with trash.

Dregs and Susan looked at each other uncertainly. Dregs asked, "What the hell is this?"

"Garbage," Neil said.

"Yeah, I know. I've seen garbage before."

"It's from the lake where Curt Lammergeier died. It turns out your old Reed College professor wasn't all bad. He volunteered at the Crystal Springs Rhododendron Garden. In the evenings he'd bring a sandwich to eat by the lake after the park closed. I told the forensic team to save whatever they found near the body."

With his gloved hand, Neil lifted aside a juice carton, a Styrofoam container, and half a dozen plastic bags. Underneath was the brown glass that had been waiting all along, caught in his memory. An old-fashioned stubby bottle—a style the Blitz Weinhard brewery had not used for years.

"Then it's true," Dregs said. "Someone poisoned Lammergeier with waste from his own invention." Dregs glanced up at Neil sharply. "You won't try to pin this on The Keeper, will you?"

Neil shook his head. A witness claimed to have seen a man lurking about the rhododendron garden that night, but it couldn't have been Dregs' roommate. The Keeper had been in a Salem freightyard that night, looking for an empty boxcar.

"Then who?" Dregs asked.

"The bad Cooper," Susan said. "You've got to find him, Papa."

Neil nodded. "But how? Even the good Cooper doesn't know where to look."

45

Connie clutched the manila envelope under her arm, as if she were smuggling contraband into the Benson Hotel. She rode the elevator up to her room, opened the envelope. and carefully shook it over a table. Two plastic bags fell out—a thin one with a twenty-dollar bill and a thicker one with a wad of blue cloth. A folded piece of paper remained caught in the envelope. Using two hotel pens as chopsticks, she extracted the note and unfolded it on the table.

> Lieutenant Wu:
> I am the person known to the public as D.B. Cooper. The items in this packet will establish my identity and my address. I understand that I am wanted for questioning by authorities. I am prepared to give myself up, and will come out of my apartment unarmed at precisely 6 p.m. this evening.
> Sincerely,

Connie examined the signature for a long time, puzzled. She took out her cell phone, but then decided not to call Captain Dickers yet. First she would need to make sure this wasn't a prank. Even Neil could have been tricked.

Sergeant Espada answered on the first ring. "What can I do for you, Lieutenant?"

"I've got a forensics question here in Room 1107. Can you get away for a few minutes?"

"On my way, sir."

By the time he rapped on the door Connie was already researching names on her laptop computer. "Come in!"

Luis Espada opened the door half way. "Sir?" His small dark eyes glanced quickly about the room.

"Sit down and take a look at this envelope. A few minutes ago a man outside the hotel handed it to me."

"A courier?"

"I think so. I didn't recognize him. What do you think?"

Espada sat in a chair opposite her. "Both of these plastic bags were in the package?"

"And the note."

He read the note and whistled. Then he took a metal rod from his pocket and turned the plastic bags over.

"What do you think?" Connie asked.

"I think D.B. Cooper is finally tired of hiding." He tapped the bag with the twenty-dollar bill. "This is a 1969 series Federal Reserve note. The serial number is consecutive with the two we received in the mail last week. It's definitely from the Cooper ransom."

"I haven't opened the other bag."

"Good." Espada said. "When in doubt, call a forensics sergeant." He took a pair of rubber gloves from the pocket of his coat and put them on. He slid open the bag's plastic zipper. Slowly, he pulled out a wrinkled, blue silk necktie. He held it up, revealing a dark stain above the embroidered letters "PAM".

Espada shook his head in wonder. "This is so Cooper."

"In what way?"

"Cooper left his tie on the plane in 1971. The only DNA evidence we have is a saliva stain, right in the middle of the tie, just like this." Espada pointed to the dark spot.

"How long would it take to compare the DNA and prove this is Cooper's tie?"

"A few hours. But I bet it matches. Only Cooper would know to pull a stunt like this." Then Espada paused. "What I don't understand is the name. Who's Pam?"

Connie turned her laptop to show him a photograph of a man with a fedora and a mustache. "If Cooper is really Gerald Chandler, he's the director of PAM."

"He's a director? So Pam is an actress?"

"PAM is the Portland Art Museum."

Espada's eyes widened. "You're telling me Cooper runs the museum?"

"That's what he's telling us."

"Then Cooper might be more dangerous than he seems. Wasn't Lieutenant Ferguson working on a case about the museum when he died?"

Connie sidestepped the question. "I think it's time to call Captain Dickers." She took out her phone and punched in his number.

Espada stood to leave, but Connie waved him back to his chair. She switched the phone to speaker mode and turned up the volume.

After a minute the captain's secretary answered. "Lieutenant Wu? Can you hold?"

"No."

"Just for—

"Don't put me on hold!"

The secretary's voice rose a note. "I have three other lines open, Lieutenant."

"Hang up on them. I've found D.B. Cooper."

"You what?"

"Found D.B. Cooper."

The line clicked. Silence followed.

Espada pointed to Connie's laptop computer. "May I? She nodded. He swiveled the screen and began tapping keys.

Finally the captain's voice came out of the plastic phone. "Wu? I'm in a meeting with the Energy Secretary. You've been a lieutenant for just two days. Tell me this is important."

"I've identified D.B. Cooper, sir."

"Oh, for God's sake, not again."

"This time it's really him, sir. He's signed a confession and agreed to give himself up."

"Just a minute."

Connie looked at the ceiling. Espada kept working on the computer. Several minutes passed.

"All right, Wu." The captain's voice was louder now, and more commanding. "You'd better have proof."

"Sir? I'll let Sergeant Espada describe the evidence." She held out her hand.

Espada mouthed a silent, sarcastic, *Thanks a lot.*

"Espada? Are you there?"

"Yes sir." He leaned closer to the phone. "I'm looking at a handwritten note, signed with a fountain pen. There's also a men's necktie with what appears to be a saliva stain similar to the one found on Cooper's plane in 1971, and another twenty-dollar bill."

"The bill's authentic?"

"I'll have to check, but the serial number is consecutive with the bills Cooper sent us last week. And the lab could run a DNA—"

"Wait," the captain interrupted. "Are you telling me Cooper just walked up and gave all this stuff to a lieutenant?"

Connie flushed. "Sir, I was given an unmarked packet by a courier."

"So you don't know yet who Cooper is?"

"But we do, sir. It's in the confession."

"And?"

Connie took a breath. "He's Gerald Chandler, sir. The director of the Portland—"

"I know who Gerry Chandler is," the captain snapped. "Someone's pulling your leg. Chandler just invited half the town to a gala at his apartment."

Espada was scrolling down a computer screen. "Actually, sir, Chandler fits the Cooper profile."

Connie stood to look over his shoulder. "Does he?"

"Take a look at Chandler's college photo. It's a lot like the police sketch of Cooper. His bio doesn't rule anything out, either. Chandler graduated from the University of Oregon in June, 1971. He started work at Nike that December, two weeks after the hijacking."

The captain's voice was quieter now. "Wasn't Chandler on the U of O track team with Lieutenant Ferguson?"

"I don't know about Ferguson," Espada said, "But Chandler sure was. He placed third in the NCAA championship in the long jump."

"The long jump," the captain repeated.

A silence settled over the table. At length the captain asked, "What else do we know about Chandler?"

Espada clicked on a tab to a different search screen. "Well, he doesn't have a police record. Not even a traffic ticket. In fact, he's not in the DMV database at all."

Connie asked, "Are you sure?"

"Yup. No driver's license. No photo ID." Espada searched some more. "No telephone either."

"Probably unlisted," the captain said.

"I don't think so, sir. It doesn't look like he's ever had a residential land line. If he has a cell phone, it's under a different name."

There was another silence. This time Connie spoke first. "Captain? Chandler wants to give himself up at six o'clock tonight. He has an address in the Pearl District."

"I know where he lives," Dickers said. "But we need to be absolutely sure before we move in. Wu, how soon can you and Espada bring the evidence to the forensic lab at headquarters?"

"Ten minutes." Without the black Buick, she would have to take a taxi, but there was always one waiting in front of the Benson.

"Have you got enough security people to keep an eye on the hotel?"

"I think so, yes. The Russians are staying in their rooms today, preparing for the conference."

"Good. I want results from the forensics lab by noon. I'll call a meeting with Steve Owen and the FBI. By two, we should be ready to move."

"Sir?" Connie asked. "We might have trouble getting into Chandler's apartment before six. Unless we can point to some more recent crime than the hijacking, a judge isn't likely to give us a search warrant."

The captain gave a tolerant sigh. "I know the playbook, Wu. This Cooper thing is getting on people's nerves. One way or another, we need this case closed before the summit."

"Papa?" Susan was looking straight ahead, staring out the windshield as Neil drove back across the city from the forensic warehouse. "What will he do with the poison?"

Her voice sounded so small that Neil glanced at her from the side. In that moment he saw his daughter as she had been when she was thirteen instead of thirty. When she had trusted her father to protect her from a world of bullies and doubt.

"I wish I knew." Neil didn't want to tell her everything. By now the poison was probably in the hands of Chandler's blackmailer—the "other" Cooper—a man willing to kill anyone in his way. He had used the Underground murders to cover up a car repair scam.

Lieutenant Lavelle's death had covered up the Underground murders. Lammergeier's poisoning fit the pattern. The blackmailer had needed to get rid of the man who invented the Recyclotron, the man who could expose him. The actual blackmail would come later. The lake at Crystal Springs had been only a small display. Three cases of bottles would be enough to poison the water supply of an entire city.

"The real Cooper isn't like that, is he?" Susan asked. As always, she seemed to have overheard his thoughts.

"No, he's not." Neil gripped the wheel and turned the corner to Waterfront Park. "The real D.B. Cooper made a mistake years ago, but he never hurt anyone, and that crime's too old to prosecute. Since then I don't think he's done anything wrong. I think he's paid for his mistake many times over."

Neil wanted to tell her more. He wanted to say that by six o'clock that evening, everyone would know the identity of the real D.B. Cooper.

Still staring out the windshield, Susan gave an almost imperceptible nod.

As soon as Neil stopped the car, Dregs opened the backseat door and laughed. He jumped out onto the lawn, pulled up his black sweater, and took out a rumpled gray backpack.

"Hey!" Neil recognized the bag. "How did you get that?"

Dregs waved the parachute case tauntingly. "It was just lying there on a shelf, Daddy."

"Give it back! It's evidence."

"Not anymore." Dregs wagged his finger. "You said yourself the crime's too old. This baby belongs to my roommate, The Keeper."

Dregs loped across the lawn toward the stage. Cars began honking behind Neil's car. Susan got out, but before closing the door, she leaned down and looked him in the eye. "Thanks, Papa."

It was such a busy day at KPDV—covering the dragon boat races, the upcoming summit, and a bomb scare in the Pearl District—that the producer of the evening show had to answer the newsroom phone himself that afternoon.

"KPDV News, this is Rick Abolt." Rick never appeared on camera himself, so it didn't matter that he wore spiked hair and a Grateful

Dead T-shirt to work.

"This is Gerald Chandler, the director of the Portland Art Museum."

"Good afternoon, Mr. Chandler. Everything OK at the museum?"

"Yes, but not at my home."

"I'm sorry to hear that." Rick swiveled impatiently in his chair, scanning a bank of screens on the wall. The tech guy at the dragon boat races might uplink the quarter final results at any moment.

"The truth is," the voice on the phone continued, "The police have surrounded my apartment. I've told them they can't come in without a search warrant, but they're insistent. I'm wondering if you might help."

Rick swiveled back, suddenly focused. "Do you live in the Pearl District?"

"Yes. I'm calling you because I noticed a news van down on the street with your number printed on the side."

"We've heard there might be a bomb in that area. Do you know anything about it?"

"There is no bomb." Chandler sighed. "There never was a bomb, not even the first time."

"Do you know what the police want?"

"Yes. I'm afraid they want me. I've told them I'll give myself up at six o'clock."

A live feed began streaming in on one of the TV screens, with a flashing note from someone calling himself Dregs. Rick ignored it, concentrating instead on the telephone. "Mr. Chandler? Have you committed a crime?"

"Not for more than forty years. That's the problem, you see. They can't prosecute a crime that old. But they'll think of some excuse to jail me anyway. Once I leave this apartment, I'm afraid the public might never hear from me again. That's why I need until six o'clock. I want a chance to tell you what I've done."

"OK, Chandler, what have you done?" Rick suspected he was talking with a nut case, but even that could make a good story if the police were involved.

"I hijacked an airplane in 1971 under the name Dan Cooper."

Rick snorted. He was definitely dealing with a kook.

"You don't have to take my word for it." The voice on the phone sounded a little offended. "I'll wait while you call the police. But use another line. I think we should keep this connection open until at least six."

"Sure, sure."

"The police officer you need to contact is Lieutenant Wu. She's one of the people outside my door, and she has evidence to corroborate my identity." Chandler gave him Connie's cell phone number. "Have you got that?"

"Yeah. Hang on." Rick idly took a phone from the desk beside his own. He punched in the number, expecting a dead end.

The phone suddenly cut into the midst of an argument, with half a dozen voices talking at once. "Stop it!" a woman shouted. "Everyone wait a minute. I've got a call." Then she said in a calmer tone, "This is Lieutenant Wu."

Rick leaned back in his swivel chair. "This is Rick Abolt in the KPDV newsroom. I've got a caller on the other line by the name of Chandler. He says he's D.B. Cooper. Does that sound even remotely possible?"

"Yes. He really is Cooper."

"The authentic, original D.B. Cooper?"

"Yes."

"You have proof?"

"We have proof." Then Connie added, "If you've got Gerald Chandler on the other line, perhaps you could connect us? I have a special agent from the FBI here who wants to talk with him."

Rick ran a hand over his face. He had to think fast. A story like this could either make his career or end it. He took the plunge. "I'm afraid Mr. Chandler has given KPDV exclusive rights to his story until six o'clock. If you want to hear him talk, you can tune in like anyone else."

"But—"

"No buts, Lieutenant. I'm going live with this. And if you try to interrupt by breaking into his apartment without a search warrant, I'll sue your goddam ass."

Dregs worried that KPDV had not yet responded to his uplink of the dragon boat quarter finals. The One More Time team had lost, but they had put up a good fight and deserved fifteen seconds of fame, even if it was only on local TV. He switched to the KPDV website to see what they were running. And for the next two hours, like everyone else who ventured near KPDV, he was hooked.

"This is Angela Flint, live from downtown Portland, where police are finally closing in on the hijacker known as D.B. Cooper." The young woman spoke earnestly into a microphone beside a white news van. She wore shoulder-length blond hair, a blue blazer, and heavy makeup. A banner across the bottom of the screen read, "BREAKING NEWS."

"The suspect, 63-year-old Gerald Chandler, began work last year as director of the Portland Art Museum. He contacted KPDV by telephone from his apartment here in the Pearl District." Angela pointed to a brick building across the street. The camera zoomed up to a row of large, whitish windows on the top floor. "I'm told we'll be linking live to Mr. Chandler in a few moments. Apparently he has agreed to give himself up to the police at six o'clock this evening. In the meantime, police have surrounded the building."

When the camera returned to Angela she was walking down the sidewalk to a yellow plastic tape marked, "Police Line, Do Not Cross." On the far side, officers clustered around patrol cars with flashing blue and red lights. She turned to the camera. "Among the officials here today, one name in particular may be familiar to viewers — special agent Steve Owen of the FBI. Hello? Agent Owen?"

Obviously she had not had time to arrange an interview in advance. But by waving and standing on her tiptoes, she eventually attracted the attention of the big crewcut officer. He walked over slowly. "Yes?"

Angela gave him a winning smile. "Officer Owen, two weeks ago the nation watched as you handcuffed a homeless man named Gregor DeKuyper. I think we've seen that clip often enough to memorize the words, 'Mr. D. Cooper, in the name of the FBI, I hereby arrest you on charges of hijacking and murder.' But a week later he was released. What makes you so certain you've got the right man now?"

Owen straightened the broad shoulders of his gray suit coat. "With DeKuyper all we had was a parachute case. It was an honest mistake. But with Chandler we've got a signed confession, a DNA match, and a twenty-dollar bill from the ransom money. He's Cooper, all right."

"Were you surprised that Cooper was hiding in plain sight as a museum director?"

He scowled and turned to walk away.

Angela threw a question after him, "Why did he agree to give himself up? And why at six o'clock?"

Owen looked back at her, his jaw set. "We have a lot of questions for D.B. Cooper. He was on the Top Ten Wanted list for years. His police sketch was in every post office in the country. It's the only unsolved hijacking in the history of the FBI."

"Yes, but you can't arrest him for that crime. After forty years, it's too late to prosecute."

Owen nearly growled in reply, "I said we want him for questioning. We'll detain him as long as it takes."

"Oh! Just a moment." Angela put her hand to her ear. "It looks like we've got that live telephone link with Gerald Chandler now.

"You do? Give me the phone."

"Actually, we've got him on a speaker at the van. Mr. Chandler, are you there?"

A technician opened the back door of the van, positioned a speaker on a box, and gave a thumbs-up.

"Hello?" Chandler's voice boomed from the van. The technician adjusted the volume, but it was still unnervingly loud. "This is Gerald Chandler, formerly known as Dan Cooper. With whom am I speaking?"

"This is Angela Flint with KPDV. Mr. Chandler, I'm here with special agent Steve Owen. He says the FBI plans to detain you for questioning."

"If the special agent has questions," Gerry's oversized voice rolled out from the van and echoed down the street, "Why doesn't he ask them now?"

By this time a crowd of perhaps a hundred had gathered behind the police tape to watch. Back in the KPDV studio on Salmon Street, Rick Abolt had just finished negotiations with CNN. With the flick of a switch, millions were listening.

"Special agent Owen?" Angela said. "This is your chance to interrogate D.B. Cooper." She tilted the microphone toward him.

Owen glanced from the camera to the van uncertainly. "All right, Cooper—or Chandler, or whatever you want to be called. How did you escape the manhunt in 1971? After you jumped out of that plane, law enforcements officers searched hundreds of miles of terrain. They never even found your parachute."

Chandler laughed, a throaty sound that shook windows. "I landed in a clearcut near Mt. St. Helens. I stuffed the parachute under a slash pile of branches, knowing the loggers would burn it in the spring. Then I walked twenty miles to the freightyard at Kelso."

"You're lying. You must have had accomplices waiting for you on the ground."

"Accomplices? No, but the world is full of good people, Owen. I met one of them in Kelso, a selfless drifter who called himself The Keeper. He knew nothing of D.B. Cooper. He gave me the coat off his back and helped me catch a freight train to Vancouver. The brandy he shared with me that night was part of the best Thanksgiving dinner of my life."

"What about the $200,000 you stole?" Owen demanded. "Where did you hide it?"

"In the river." Chandler sighed, a sound like a great rush of wind. "I was walking across the railroad bridge to Portland. It was midnight. The tracks were wet. The duffel bag of cash fell in the water."

"All of it?"

"I kept six of the bills in my wallet," the voice from the van admitted. "I've already sent three of them to you, proving who I am."

Finally the special agent smiled. "And in so doing, you proved you are guilty of a federal crime. A crime that can still be prosecuted."

With a look of surprise, Angela tilted the microphone back to herself. "Is it really illegal to send currency in the mail?"

"No, but tax evasion is. We've checked Gerald Chandler's tax forms from 1971. There is no mention of the money he stole."

"He lost most of it," Angela objected. "Are you going to arrest a man for failing to declare a hundred and twenty dollars?"

"The law is the law," Owen said grimly. "If Chandler doesn't come out, we're prepared to storm the building."

The voice from the van thundered, "You may enter my apartment at six o'clock! And not, sir, a second sooner."

46

Neil parked the black Buick on Carlton Street near Reed College. A woman in a pale blue sweat suit was standing in front of a brick Tudor home, stringing a zigzag trellis above a small bed with a row of tiny seedlings. Rachel Lammergeier was obviously determined to be the first gardener in Portland that spring to grow peas.

As he got out of the car and walked up the curving brick path to the house, Neil remembered how worried he had been the last time he met Mrs. Lammergeier, when he had had to tell her she was a widow. Her husband had been found poisoned, floating in a lake. She had surprised him then by saying, "Thank God." This time enough poison was missing to kill thousands.

"Mrs. Lammergeier?" He held out his police badge.

She used the back of her hand to push aside a shock of dark hair from her forehead. "It's about time they sent someone. I called this morning as soon as Roger left for work."

"Oh? Who did you call?"

"I wanted to talk with Neil Ferguson, the detective who left me his card. But they told me he's dead."

Neil took off his wraparound glasses. "That's not entirely true."

She sized up his sport coat, stylish stubble, and Roman nose.

He held his hand toward the front door. "Could you spare another cup of rooibos tea?"

"Why are you in disguise?" she asked.

"Probably for the same reason you called the police."

She nodded slowly. Then she put away the trellis string, brushed off her hands, and led the way inside. Instead of making tea, she sat in a wing chair in the front room. Behind her, a Bose radio on the bookshelf mumbled about classical composers.

"Someone broke into the house yesterday evening." She rubbed her fingers nervously. "Roger and I were out for dinner at the time."

Neil sat in the chair opposite her. "And Roger is?"

Rachel reddened. "He's also on the faculty at Reed. We started seeing each other a few years ago, after Curt and I separated."

Neil recalled hearing that Mrs. Lammergeier had been romantically involved with a chemistry professor. FBI agent Owen had suggested the liaison gave her both the motive and the opportunity to poison her husband. That seemed less likely now that Neil had traced the poison to the Recyclotron.

He asked, "You discovered the burglary last night, but didn't report it until this morning?"

"We argued about whether to report it at all. Roger doesn't want more trouble. But you'd told me to report anything that came up. And I have to admit, I'm frightened."

Neil leaned forward. "It wasn't an ordinary burglary, was it?"

"No. They mostly went through Curt's things, in his old office upstairs." She looked to one side. "I think it might have been Curt's son, Todd. He's always been unpleasant, but since Curt died he's been impossible."

"In what way?" Neil didn't tell her that he had just spent several hours trying to track down Todd Lammergeier. His neighbors and landlady hadn't seen him for several days. The young engineer was one of the few people with a key to the Recyclotron basement where the bottles of poison had been stored.

"Oh, he's been calling me, going on about his conspiracy theories. I guess I got used to it with his father. Whenever Curt started ranting about socialists and government plots, I'd just tune out. If you have to live with a man like that, you learn to let them think you're listening."

"Why would Todd break into your home? Couldn't he just ask to come over?"

Rachel gave him a lopsided smile. "Roger doesn't approve. He wants a clean break with the past. The instructions in Curt's will were clear. The patents went to Todd. The house and everything in it went to me. We didn't have to let Todd in."

"Do you know what Todd might have been looking for in your

husband's office?"

"I'm not sure. Todd seemed obsessed with his father's death. Once, when he called me, he blamed everything on D.B. Cooper." She bit her lip. "That proves he's crazy, doesn't it?"

"No." Neil stood up. "He might be right. Could I take a look at your late husband's office?"

"Of course." She led him to a stairway but then paused, her hand on the wooden post at the bottom of the banister. "The room is upstairs to the left, the first door in the hall."

"You're not coming?"

She shook her head. "When you've taught medieval studies as long as I have, you start to believe in ghosts."

Neil went up the stairs, took out his handkerchief to cover the doorknob, and opened the office door.

At first he thought he must have opened the wrong door. Burglars usually dump out drawers, searching in a hurry. But the floor of this office was clean and the drawers closed. Tidy rows of file folders covered a table. Three neat stacks of envelopes stood on a desk beside a computer keyboard. He wondered how Rachel had known there had been a break-in. Was the room less messy than before?

For the next twenty minutes Neil sorted through files and envelopes without learning anything that seemed important. He turned on the computer, but it demanded a password. He was still typing in guesses when he heard Rachel calling from the stairs.

"Lieutenant Ferguson? I think you might want to see this."

He glanced around the room one more time in frustration. What had Todd found here? Perhaps a ghost named Cooper?

"Lieutenant?" Rachel called again, her voice louder.

Neil opened the door and walked to the head of the stairs.

Rachel pointed to the other room. "They've interrupted the radio program, and now it's on TV too."

"Don't tell me." Neil glanced at his watch. According to the plan, he needed to be downtown soon. "They've found D.B. Cooper."

Rick Abolt had never organized a talk show so quickly. He had managed to locate a staffer at the art museum who could walk to the KPDV studio in five minutes. He had gotten a call through to a Nike executive in a BMW who was willing to swing by Salmon Street. He had begged the traffic helicopter team to fly the KPDV news anchor, Marcus Hampton, directly from the dragon boat races to the studio rooftop.

As the studio's sweep second hand touched five o'clock, Rick hit the ON AIR button, pointed to the anchorman, and gave him an encouraging grin. How many millions were watching? He had no idea.

Marcus nervously shuffled some blue sheets of paper, all of which he now saw were blank. The teleprompter read simply, "Smile!

"Good evening," Marcus said, smiling. "And welcome to a special hour of live coverage of the quest for D.B. Cooper. For more than four decades, the world has wondered what happened to the hijacker who parachuted with $200,000 into the forests of the Pacific Northwest in 1971. Tonight we intend to find out. We'll discuss the case with important guests." He held out his hand to the people on the sofa beside him, although he didn't have a clue who they might be. "We'll also have live reports from the police surrounding an apartment in downtown Portland, and we hope to talk directly by telephone to the man who claims to be D.B. Cooper."

At this point Marcus realized words were appearing on the Teleprompter screen: FIRST A RECAP OF THE CASE SO FAR. Rick was at the keyboard, typing as fast as he could.

"First, let's do a brief recap of the case so far." Marcus spoke slowly, waiting for more words to appear. "This afternoon police announced that Cooper is Gerald Chandler, the 63-year-old director of the Portland Art Museum. Chandler has agreed to give himself up at six o'clock. Until then — "

The Teleprompter ran out of words. Marcus saw that Rick was no longer typing. He was rolling his hand in the air.

"Until then," Marcus repeated slowly, and then realized what should come next. "Let's talk with the first of our guests here in the studio."

He turned to the woman on the sofa. "Welcome."

"Thank you." She was a thin, nervous woman with silvering hair. A bookkeeper? Someone's grandmother? She fingered a necklace of gaudy ceramic beads.

Marcus smiled. "Perhaps you could start by telling us, in your own words, just how you are acquainted with the hijacker, D.B. Cooper."

"Oh! I had no idea he was a hijacker. None of us did."

Marcus leaned forward earnestly. "None of you suspected?"

"Heavens, no!"

Finally he looked past her to the live screen on the studio wall. The camera had focused on her fidgeting fingers, but there was also a caption: STELLA McCRAE, ART MUSEUM SECRETARY.

"Mrs. McCrae," Marcus said, "Gerald Chandler is director of the museum where you serve as secretary. You didn't think he was criminal. What did you think?"

She looked past him into space, her nervousness suddenly gone. "Mr. Chandler is the greatest man I've ever known."

"Seriously?"

She clutched her necklace. "Gerry revived the Portland Art Museum—the whole Portland art scene—just as he'd done in Los Angeles at the Getty. He brought in new exhibits, new ideas, and new donors. He's an artist himself, you know. You should see his studio! But that's not what's important, not really."

"What is important?"

"It's him. Who he is. When he leads school groups through the museum, they follow him like the Pied Piper. He volunteers at the Children's Theater too. Without him, that company would have folded long ago."

Marcus spread his hands. "You know, I'd always imagined that D.B. Cooper might really be Matt Groening."

"The creator of The Simpsons?" The other studio guest, a well-dressed man with an olive complexion and a clipped accent, broke the studio rules by interrupting. "You're loony."

Marcus forgot the millions who were watching. "Look at Bart Simpson. That kid has Cooper written all over him. He's an anti-establishment hero. When Cooper hijacked the plane, Matt Groening and I were seniors in a drama class together at Lincoln High School. After Thanksgiving vacation, Matt seemed different."

The male guest crossed his arms. "By those criteria, almost any Portland male over the age of fifty might be the hijacker."

Marcus looked to the live screen for help. Below the man's face was the caption: PRABAL SINGH, NIKE EXECUTIVE.

"Mr. Singh," Marcus said, "You work for one of the world's largest shoe companies. What do you know about Gerald Chandler, the man police claim is D.B. Cooper?"

"I don't know what Gerry was doing in 1971. I met him five years later. I was a new hire from India, part of Nike's expansion into Asia. Gerry and I shared a cubicle. He designed shoes. I translated his work into factory specifications."

"So Chandler wasn't fighting the establishment? He sounds like a company man."

"At work, he was." Singh frowned. "But we shared the same computer system, and I helped him with his taxes, so I learned some unusual things about his behavior."

Marcus leaned forward. "Mr. Singh, can you share that with us now?"

"I'm not sure. Perhaps."

The art museum secretary broke in. "No! If Gerry has secrets, he deserves to keep them."

Singh held up one hand. 'I know. You want to protect him. But the time has come for truth."

"What is the truth about D.B. Cooper?" Marcus asked.

Prabal Singh lowered his head. "When I worked in that office, I sent my paychecks to my family in India. During that time Gerry earned three million dollars from Nike stock. Almost all of it went to charity. I don't know if he has family. Somehow I think he must not. He transferred his money to schools, homeless shelters, and art projects. All of the gifts were anonymous. No one could have known, except me. Why would he do this?"

Marcus shrugged.

"I know why." It was Mrs. McCrae, the art museum secretary. "Gerald Chandler is a saint. He's suffered in silence all these years — for our sins, I suspect, as much as for his own."

"Slow down," Marcus said. "You're talking about a man who stole $200,000 from an airline company. Apparently it's too late to charge him with that crime, but he may still be guilty of tax evasion."

Singh held up his hand again. "This I also find puzzling."

"You say you helped him with his taxes, Mr. Singh. Perhaps you can tell us if he failed to report the income from his hijacking, as police claim?"

"I don't know about his tax return for 1971. As I said, I came to know him only later. I can tell you that he was incompetent at both mathematics and accounting. Without help, he would have made many mistakes on his tax returns. This is not uncommon."

"Then what do you find puzzling?"

"Every year, after I had calculated his tax bill, Gerry would tell me to add fifteen percent."

Marcus furrowed his brow. "He wanted to pay extra?"

"Yes. He told me to calculate a tip, as if we were dealing with a restaurant bill instead of his tax return."

"That could be a sign of guilt," Marcus suggested.

Mrs. McRae lifted her chin. "Or a mark of honor."

Singh nodded. "It is a donation few would understand. But I can tell you this: If the IRS were to audit Gerald Chandler today, they would find he is not in debt to his country, but rather that his country is in debt to him."

Marcus cupped his hand to his ear. "Excuse me, I'm getting a report that Angela Flint is ready with a report from the Pearl District. Angela, are you there?"

An awkward silence followed. Off stage, Rick was desperately clicking his computer screen, trying to open the connection.

Finally a little box whirled in from the side. When the spinning stopped, a blonde woman with heavy make-up had landed above Marcus' left shoulder.

"Marcus?"

"Go ahead, Angela. What's the situation outside Gerald Chandler's apartment building?"

"Chaotic, Marcus." Jostled by a huge, noisy crowd, the newswoman clutched a microphone and held one hand to her ear. "More than a thousand people have turned out to witness what some are already calling the arrest of the century, although we're still not sure that an actual arrest can be made. At six o'clock, just thirty-nine minutes from now, the hijacker known as D.B. Cooper has promised to come out of his apartment for interrogation by the FBI. Portland's mayor has called out the fire department to help with crowd control. Apparently the police are short handed because they're preparing for Synergy, the global energy summit that opens tomorrow at Mt. Hood, just sixty miles away."

"How are the firemen coping with the situation?"

"Pretty well, considering." Angela pointed to the street, where a line of men in yellow slickers were holding back the crowd. The camera panned to a large red ladder truck, and then followed the ladder up to the glass wall of a fourth-floor studio. "They've sent an observer up a ladder to Gerald Chandler's penthouse apartment, but the windows seem to have been frosted with some kind of spray or soap on the inside, so there's not much to see."

Marcus said. "Our studio guests have mostly had positive things to say about the suspect, Gerald Chandler. What's the reaction of the crowd to the news that an art museum director may be D.B. Cooper?"

"I'm getting mixed reactions from people in the street, Marcus." The camera zoomed out to show that Angela was standing next to a stocky, sandy-haired man in a camouflage parka. "With me here is Richard Ballantyne, a tree surgeon who came downtown for the dragon boat races. When he got a Tweet about Cooper, he joined the crowd outside Chandler's apartment. Mr. Ballantyne, what's your opinion of D.B. Cooper?"

"It's not an opinion, it's a fact," Ballantyne said. "Cooper's a terrorist. He threatened to blow up a plane full of people. Because of him, extremists all over the world now use passenger planes as weapons. If there had never been a D.B. Cooper, we wouldn't all be waiting in line for body scans at airports. I say, lock him up."

Angela took back the microphone. "I also have with me Martha Browning, a cellist for the Oregon Symphony." The camera shifted, revealing a tall, smartly dressed woman to Angela's left. "Ms. Browning, do you agree that Gerald Chandler should be prosecuted as a terrorist?"

"Absolutely not." The woman lifted her chin. "Chandler never hurt anyone. So what if he took money from an airline company? Everyone hated Northwest Orient. They went out of business years ago. Since then Chandler has helped make Portland what it is—a city alive with art, creativity, and freedom. D.B. Cooper has become one of the world's great folk heroes. If they lock him up, they might as well lock up Santa Claus."

"Terrorist or folk hero?" Angela asked, looking into the camera. "One way or the other, we'll meet D.B. Cooper in just a few minutes. Agent Steve Owen of the FBI has said that the police are prepared to break into the building to remove Gerald Chandler by force if he fails to meet his own six o'clock deadline for surrender. Back to you, Marcus."

The inset photo of Angela Flint whirled off the screen, leaving

Marcus Hampton alone, shuffling blank sheets of blue paper. "We're still hoping to hold an exclusive conversation with Gerald Chandler. He's keeping a telephone connection open with KPDV, but says he is only willing to speak on air during the final five minutes before six o'clock. Until then—" Marcus smiled to his studio guests on the sofa beside him, "Let's find out more about Gerald Chandler from the people who know him. What kind of personal life did the hijacker lead? Mrs. McCrae, let's start with you."

The art museum secretary blushed bright red. "I'm sure I couldn't say."

"Is Chandler married?"

"No, he never married," she replied, straightening her skirt. "In fact, I'm not aware that he's been involved in any close personal relationships, although I suspect he's had plenty of opportunities."

"Why is that?" This was just the sort of dirt Marcus loved on his talk shows. The more his guests squirmed, the better.

"Well, it's rare enough to find a single man in his sixties who is financially secure, attractive, and physically fit. He works out at the Multnomah Athletic Club almost every day." She lowered her eyes. "Club memberships are expensive, but several of our single women volunteers have joined."

"In the hopes of meeting Mr. Chandler in a less formal setting?"

Mrs. McRae did not look up. "I'm told he wears blue tights with suspenders during workouts."

Marcus was not completely ruthless. He turned from the blushing secretary to his other guest. "Mr. Singh, most of Nike's shoes are designed for sports. Did Gerald Chandler have an interest in athletics?"

"Definitively." The Indian executive enunciated the syllables with precision. "Before joining Nike, Gerry had won a trophy on Bill Bowerman's famous University of Oregon track team. At Nike he ran around the lake every lunch hour. But I think his passion has always been skiing."

"Skiing?"

"Even at the age of fifty he was still placing in twenty-kilometer Nordic races. Before that, he preferred downhill skiing. Once I went with him." Singh frowned at the memory.

Marcus recognized the frown as a sign that an emotional story lay just below the surface. All he had to do was dig. "What happened when you went skiing with Chandler?"

"Gerry never had a driver's license, so he mostly rode the bus to Mt. Hood or Mt. Bachelor. But he kept talking about other resorts farther away. One time when we had a long weekend off, I offered to drive him to Sun Valley in Idaho. "

"Do you ski?"

"Not well. Where I grew up in Mumbai, there was no snow. Gerry gave me lessons the first day at Sun Valley. I improved enough that I agreed to go up the high chairlift the second day. I was terrified, but I made it down several times. On the last run before we were to drive back to Portland, a strange thing happened."

"To Gerry?"

"Yes. He swerved off the slope toward the tallest of the ski jump ramps, the one built for the Olympics. I think there were ropes and rules to keep ordinary skiers out, but he cut right through them, skied down in a tuck, and sailed off the ramp into the sky." Singh shook his head. "This should not have been possible with standard downhill skis. They are not designed for such a jump. But he just held his arms out like wings and flew. He landed at the bottom of the slope without falling. Then he disappeared into the crowd."

"How could he jump like that without training?"

"That's what everyone was asking in the lodge. They wanted to know who he was, and where he'd come from. I found him later, hiding in my car. On the drive back to Portland, I asked him the same questions. All he would say is that he once hitchhiked to Norway and trained in the far north."

"A man of mystery," Marcus said. "So tell us, Mr. Singh. Gerry's colleagues at the art museum say he has no close relationships with women. Is D.B. Cooper gay?"

The Nike executive neither blushed nor blinked. "I do not know about his sexual preferences. He is a private man."

"So you never really understood him?"

"From the first, I understood that Gerry is a deeply troubled man. I knew he would leave Nike eventually. He never belonged in a cubicle."

Singh turned to Marcus with a frighteningly steady gaze. "If they incarcerate Gerald Chandler, he will wither. A spark of inspiration will die. And all of us will be a little poorer."

47

The low clouds of an approaching storm brought an early twilight to the Willamette River in downtown Portland. Cold wind swept through the crowd lining the seawall at Waterfront Park. The six dragon boats in the final race were thrashing their way upstream from the Burnside Bridge to the Morrison Street Bridge, but the cries and splashes of the crews seemed a distant struggle. The fading light dimmed the colorful dragon scales to gray shadows. When Columbia Sportswear's boat edged ahead beneath the bridge to victory, nearly as many people were watching the giant monitor on the stage as were peering into the murk at the race itself.

Laura Hildebrand, organizer of the races, leaned her head into the control booth beside the stage. "Dregs? I've just been told KPDV isn't airing the finals. What happened?"

"Sorry. We got preempted. They're covering the arrest of D.B. Cooper instead."

"Damn."

"The fireworks crew on the Esplanade is ready to launch." Dregs held out a set of headphones. "You want to talk to them?"

She shook her head. "Tell them we can't start the awards ceremony for at least fifteen minutes. We've still got to haul the boats out of the river and get the crews to the stage."

"So what am I supposed to put on screen until then? The crowd's getting restless."

"Music videos?" The festival director was already turning to go, taking out a flashing pager. "Whatever you want."

Alone again with the bank of computer screens, Dregs typed in the words, AWARDS IN 15 MINS. Beside him on the stage, the text appeared on screen in giant ten-foot letters. He could hear the crowd groan. The air felt like rain. Floodlights with generators lit a field of tired faces.

Dregs smiled to himself, briefly typed in the words, LIVE FROM KPDV, and switched screens. Suddenly the ten-foot-tall head of Angela Flint was talking to a thousand puzzled dragon boat racers and their fans.

"With just thirteen minutes before D.B. Cooper's surrender, the crowd here in the Pearl District has started a countdown." The camera wobbled, panning from the blond reporter to a street packed with people chanting, "Thirteen! Thirteen!"

Angela had to raise her voice to be heard. "A helicopter is approaching the apartment building where Gerald Chandler is waiting to come out. Yes, now I can see it's our own Traffic Eye chopper. Do we have a report from the air?"

The giant screen on the Waterfront Park stage suddenly switched to an aerial view of a brick building surrounded by crowded streets.

"We do, Angela," a man's voice rumbled from the stage's speakers. "For our Traffic Eye update, the slowing we noticed earlier on the Terwilliger Curves has cleared up, but there's a big bottleneck downtown. Crowds are blocking streets from Ankeny to Everett between the Park Blocks and Fourteenth. If you're out driving tonight, steer clear of the Pearl. Even the streetcar isn't getting through."

"Can you see the penthouse apartment on the old Blitz Weinhard brewery building?" Angela asked.

"The one with the big glass roof?"

"That's it. Can you look inside?" Behind her the crowds were chanting, "Twelve! Twelve!"

The view descended dizzily toward a lattice of glass panels. "Not really, Angela. There aren't any lights inside, and the glass is frosted. But I am seeing policemen in the courtyard and on the fire escape."

"Hold that position if you can. Marcus, do we have the connection open to Gerald Chandler yet?"

The aerial view shrank to a square in the corner of the screen. Beneath a red overlaid banner, D.B. COOPER: THE CAPTURE, Marcus

Hamilton was tapping together a stack of blue papers on a studio desk. "In just a minute we'll be talking live with the man police claim to have positively identified as the 1971 hijacker, D.B. Cooper. While we wait for that interview, let's take a quick look at some of the people who have been suspects in the past."

The screen switched to a drawing of a man with a high forehead, a narrow black tie, and dark glasses. "The composite sketch created by police artists in 1971 showed a generic face obscured by large sunglasses. The FBI had so few clues that they suggested Cooper might be almost anyone's wayward uncle. The public took the suggestion to heart. Over the years, more than one thousand people have either claimed to be D.B. Cooper, or claimed that they know who he is."

A black-and-white photo of a balding man in an airline uniform filled the screen. "In 2007, suspicion fell on the late Kenneth Christensen, an army paratrooper who had worked as a baggage handler for Northwest Orient airlines. But his height, weight, and eye color were wrong."

The front page of a newspaper slid in from the side, with a headline highlighted in yellow. "In 2011, Marla Cooper of Oklahoma told the London Telegraph that her uncle Lynn was the hijacker. Marla had been eight years old at the time, living in Sisters, Oregon. After Thanksgiving that year, her uncle came back from an elk hunting trip with bloody clothes, no elk, and a confused story. We may never know what misadventures befell the late Lynn Doyle Cooper that weekend, but DNA tests proved he was not hijacking an airplane."

"Just two weeks ago," Marcus said, voicing over a video of The Keeper's arrest, "The FBI arrested Gregor DeKuyper, a homeless man under the Burnside bridge, on charges of hijacking and murder. Although DeKuyper did have the actual parachute case used in the hijacking, no other evidence could be found to connect him to a crime. He was released a week ago Wednesday."

The view returned to the police sketch from 1971. "And now police claim to have positive proof that D.B. Cooper is in fact Gerald Chandler, the 63-year-old director of the Portland Art Museum." The screen split in half, making room for a side-by-side comparison with a photo of Chandler. Although Chandler was much older, wearing a fedora and a mustache, the resemblance was remarkable.

"I'm told Gerald Chandler is now prepared to speak with us by telephone," Marcus said. "Mr. Chandler, are you there?"

At Waterfront Park, the crews carrying their dragon boats to the stage stopped to listen. On the streets of the Pearl District, the crowds chanting "Five! Five!" gradually grew quiet. Everywhere people leaned closer to speakers, waiting.

"I am here."

The voice sounded hollow and haunted, more distant than when Chandler had spoken to a news crew earlier that afternoon.

Marcus looked into the camera earnestly. "Mr. Chandler, D.B. Cooper has been a legendary fugitive for more than forty years. How can we believe that you have been living in plain sight all this time—that you really are D.B. Cooper?"

"Because I am. I have given the police samples of the ransom money and my DNA."

"Hundreds of people have claimed to be Cooper, perhaps because the hijacking and parachute escape seemed like the perfect crime. Is that how you feel about what you did?

The hollow voice sighed. "What I did was wrong. I think we all commit errors of judgment when we are young. If we are honest, we live the rest of our lives to atone for them."

"Is that why you have chosen to give yourself up now, in such a public way?"

In the KPDV studio, producer Rick Abolt had finally managed to make a digital clock appear at the bottom of the screen, blinking a countdown to the six o'clock deadline—3:15, 3:14, 3:13.

"We all dream of a chance to clear the slate," Chandler said, "But that reckoning comes with a price. When I leave this apartment, I do not expect to return."

"At this point it's unclear whether the FBI have grounds to hold you."

"I understand," the hollow voice said. On the screen the numbers blinked 2:47, 2:46, 2:45. "Nonetheless, I am leaving documents on my desk that will transfer ownership of my apartment to the Portland Children's Theater. They have been unable to find a downtown studio they can afford. Now they will have one."

At Waterfront Park, a ripple of applause spread through the crowd of dragon boat racers. On the giant screen, Marcus Hampton said. "That's quite a gift, Mr. Chandler. Are you sure you won't need your apartment for yourself?"

"Yes. I have also written a letter of resignation as director of the Portland Art Museum. Because I will not be able to help with the search for my replacement, I have transferred my remaining Nike stock to the museum, increasing their endowment fund by 1.2 million dollars. I wish them well."

Marcus knit his brow. "Mr. Chandler, we've heard of your generosity from the guests here in the studio today. But with donations on this scale, it almost sounds as if you are saying good bye."

"I am." He paused, and then said, "Good bye."

The on-screen clock blinked 1:54, 1:53, 1:52.

"Mr. Chandler?" Marcus held his hand to his ear.

The clock blinked 1:43, 1:42, 1:41.

Marcus frowned. "The line still seems to be open, but he's not responding. Let's go now to Angela Flint, in the street outside Chandler's apartment. Angela? What's happening where you are?"

Angela whirled up beside him, a well-lit face against a darkening street scene. "I'm sensing a lot of tension here, Marcus. Some of the people in the crowd have been shouting at the police to 'back off' and 'let him go'. We can't actually see the police up on the fourth floor, but I imagine they're outside Chandler's door, watching the clock and counting down toward the deadline."

"Thanks, Angela." Marcus was still holding his hand beside his ear. "I'm getting something from Traffic Eye. Can we go to the helicopter?"

The screen suddenly cut to an aerial view of the brick building. In the twilight, the disused water tanks and smokestacks of the old brewery loomed like cannons. The *whacka-whacka* of helicopter blades was so loud that the traffic reporter had to shout. "Something's happening down there on the roof. I've opened the helicopter door to get a better view."

"Is that safe?"

"Hold on a sec." The camera zoomed down to the glass roof. The frosted window panels were slowly opening upward, as if they were the petals of a gigantic white tulip. On screen, the digital clock blinked 0:35, 0:34, 0:33.

"The skylight's opening," the voice in the helicopter shouted over the din of the whirling blades. "I can see silver shapes inside. Dozens of round, silver shapes."

Marcus asked, "Could they be balloons? A month ago, Gerald Chandler released hundreds of silver balloons from his studio. He was promoting a new art exhibit."

"If they're balloons, they're huge," the traffic reporter shouted. As the helicopter turned, the silver curves slowly came into view. The digital clock kept counting down, 0:21, 0:20, 0:19.

"They're starting to rise. We're moving the chopper to the side so we can use our headlights."

Slowly, with the grace of a satellite emerging from a space shuttle bay, two dozen weather balloons rose from the skylight. Suspended beneath them, the glare of helicopter's lights illuminated a man wearing a thick coat and a fedora, sitting in a lawn chair.

"As promised," a hollow voice said, "I am coming out of my apartment."

"Good God!" Marcus exclaimed. "He's flying out of the roof! We are watching D.B. Cooper attempt yet another escape!"

As the lawn chair slowly turned, it was just possible to see that the man in the lawn chair was holding a cell phone to his ear.

"Mr. Chandler?" Marcus asked. "I thought you had agreed to surrender."

"I have never used the word 'surrender'," the voice on the cell phone intoned. "I said I would give myself up, and I am. Behold the final flight of D.B. Cooper."

The crowds outside the building began to cheer. The roar echoed up from the streets of the Pearl District.

"Do you have a parachute?" Marcus asked.

"Of course." The balloons eddied past a smokestack.

"Where are you going?"

The hollow voice laughed. "Wherever the wind takes me. East, I suspect. For all I know, to Kansas. Oh, and a word to the policemen outside my front door. Tell them they can come on in. I unlocked the door ten minutes ago."

Firemen with axes stood waiting in the hall outside Chandler's apartment, ready to splinter open the door at the command of special agent Steve Owen.

Connie reached out, turned the knob, and opened the door a crack.

"Wait," Owen cautioned. "Have your weapons ready." He drew his semi-automatic and held it before him in both hands. Then he kicked the door open wide. A dozen officers followed him into the dark studio, crouching through the shadows, guns drawn.

Owen stood in the middle of the room, looking up through the skylight at the bright cluster of silver balloons a hundred yards up in the night sky.

"Damn him!" Owen raised his semi-automatic overhead.

"No!" Connie clutched his arm.

The FBI agent shook her loose. "I'm just going to shoot out a few balloons to force him down. He won't get away this time." He aimed again at the sky.

Now Captain Dickers caught him by the wrist. "Sorry, Owen. The risk of hitting Chandler is too great. You'll have to catch him another way."

Reluctantly, Owen lowered his arm. "All right, we'll get him when he comes down. I want cars following him on the ground. And get people tracking his cell phone so we know exactly where he is, even if he goes up into the clouds."

Meanwhile, one of the plainclothes detectives had unlocked the fire escape. The four sergeants outside on the landing had been looking up at the lawn chair. When they turned, they stared in disbelief at the tall, blue-eyed detective in the doorway.

"Lieutenant Ferguson!" one of the men managed to say. "We thought you were dead."

"Idiots." Ferguson closed the door behind him. "Can't you see that Cooper is getting away? Dickers wants everyone to regroup down in the street. Move!"

"Mr. Chandler? Are you still on the line?" Marcus leaned forward at his studio desk, beside a live shot of a lawn chair floating toward the skyscrapers of Portland. "I'm afraid he's not responding right now, although the phone connection seems to be open. Let's go to our reporter in the street, Angela Flint. Angela, what's your situation?"

A shaky, hand-held camera showed the blond reporter in the thick of a crowd surging down the middle of Burnside Street. "It's like Mardi Gras down here," she said. "Since Cooper flew out the roof of his apartment, people have been pointing and cheering. The crowd is following him down Burnside toward the river. Right now he's going past the twentieth floor of a bank tower."

The camera swiveled and zoomed to a cluster of silver balloons sailing past the pink glass wall of the skyscraper.

"Everyone wants to know where he's going to come down," Angela said. "They want to know if D.B. Cooper really has a chance at another escape."

"Good question, Angela." The screen cut back to Marcus. "To help us with the answer, let's turn to Jim Fletcher, KPDV's meteorologist. Jim, what's the weather look like tonight if you're flying a balloon over Portland?"

The camera cut to a square-jawed man in a light blue suit, standing in front a wall-sized weather map. "Well, Marcus, Mr. Chandler is in for some rough sailing. A low pressure system began moving in from the coast this afternoon, bringing cold, wet marine air. We've already got a thick cloud layer over the city at about a thousand feet. Winds should increase to fifteen miles an hour from the west tonight, with cold rain in the foothills and heavy snow in the mountains."

"So where is Chandler headed?" Marcus asked.

"He's right about going east, although his balloons aren't likely to get as far as Kansas. We learned that in 2008, when a gas station owner set out from Bend in a lawn chair suspended from a bunch of helium party balloons. That flight only made it to Idaho."

"Is it possible to steer a balloon?"

"Only up and down. I'm not sure about Chandler's system, but the Bend man used a BB gun to shoot balloons when he wanted to go down. To go up, he let cherry Kool-Aid drain from a tank he'd brought along as ballast."

Marcus chuckled, but the weatherman did not. He looked at his map and shook his head. "I hope Chandler is wearing long underwear beneath that suit. With a wind pattern like this, he'll be in a snowstorm over the Bull Run Watershed tonight."

"That's Portland's water supply," Marcus said.

"By tomorrow afternoon he'd be over Walla Walla, but I can't imagine him surviving that long in an air layer this cold. His best hope would be to parachute before he gets to Mt. Hood. That won't be easy in a snowstorm at night."

"Maybe not," Marcus said, "but he's done it before."

At Waterfront Park, the throng pouring down Burnside Street began to merge with the crowd on the riverfront. Fifty dragon boats stood on the lawn before the stage, flanked by their twenty-man crews. All eyes were watching the silver dot in the sky above the Burnside bridge, spotlit by a whirring traffic helicopter.

"Portlanders!" A hollow voice emanated from the speakers on the stage. People turned to the live video on the screen. "To all of you gathered below me, to everyone watching, I thank you for your faith. I owe you more than I can ever repay."

The Keeper climbed to the front of the recycling team's dragon boat and stood in the bow for a better view. Although the old man had kept himself hidden from the media for more than a week, the temptation to participate in the dragon boat race had been too great. Now a blue stage light caught him from the side—a wild, white-bearded celebrity, wearing a gray parachute case that had become famous in its own right.

The Keeper stood at attention and saluted the lawn chair in the sky. "God speed, McGill," he said, his eyes damp.

Susan held up her oar, as if it were the banner pole of an honor guard. One by one, the rest of the One More Time Women's Cooperative raised their oars. Dregs, watching from his booth beside the stage, typed the words "OARS UP!!" in ten-foot letters on the screen. Across the field, a thousand oars rose.

A chant began spreading through the crowd, "Cooper! Cooper!"

Caught by a breeze over the river, the balloons eddied north, followed by the helicopter.

"Cooper! Cooper!" Oars stamped in unison as the chant rolled out, growing louder.

On the Eastbank Esplanade, the fireworks crew mistook the commotion for a starting signal. Rockets began arcing over the river upstream, lighting the low storm clouds with sparkling bursts of blue and red. Meanwhile the lawn chair sailed east between the twin spires of the Oregon Convention Center — as if they were goalposts, and the balloons were a silver football.

"Farewell," the hollow voice intoned from the speakers on stage.

And while the helicopter paused, unwilling to follow the balloons into the clouds, D.B. Cooper vanished, ascending into the darkness of the storm.

48

Neil had torn off his latex nose. The disguise had become so itchy and his death had been accepted with such disturbing speed that he was ready to risk coming back to life a little.

He drove the black Buick into the basement garage of his apartment building on the Park Blocks, got out to move his bicycle to one side, and parked the car. Then he took the stairs up to the lobby and checked his post box for mail.

"Lieutenant?" Mrs. Grady, a widow from the sixth floor, wobbled slightly as she peered at Neil from the side. She often lurked in the lobby with the excuse of airing her miniature dachshund.

"Good evening, Mrs. Grady." Neil collected his magazines without making eye contact. The widow organized vodka happy hours for a rooftop barbecue every Friday at five, making a special point of inviting unmarried men. Every other day of the week she started her happy hour earlier, alone.

"We've been worried. Are you all right?" she asked, slurring the words a little. Then she smiled. "You've colored your hair black, you devil."

Just then there was a ding from the elevator. The door opened and Neil retreated toward it with a nod.

Mrs. Grady sighed, picked up her dog, and wobbled out to the sidewalk, leaving a *Willamette Week* newspaper in the door so it wouldn't lock behind her. She had just set the dachshund down in a planter to do its business when another Neil Ferguson appeared, walking briskly toward the building entrance.

"Oh, my," she said. "Lieutenant?" This version of Neil Ferguson looked even more credible than the first, with familiar graying hair and the black suit he often wore to work.

"Good evening," Ferguson said. He held up a plastic bag. "I've just been down to the food carts for some take-out. You know how I hate to cook."

Mrs. Grady opened her mouth, about to agree, but then said instead, "Do you know, a minute ago I saw a man who looks just like you. He came up the basement stairs, took the mail out of your box, and rode the elevator up."

"Really? Well, there's no need for alarm. This is the sort of thing detectives deal with all the time." He smiled and pushed open the glass door. The newspaper fell out, but he picked it up and replaced it so the door was still ajar. Then he gave Mrs. Grady a little salute through the glass, crossed the lobby, and pressed the elevator button.

Mrs. Grady put her hand over her mouth. Behind her, the dachshund had begun kicking dirt.

In his apartment that evening, Neil watched the TV news with Gerry while they shared a Cuban dinner from a cardboard container — lime chicken with black beans and deep-fried plantain bananas.

"You know it's against the law to impersonate an officer." Neil took a banana chip and raised an eyebrow. He felt uneasy, eating dinner with himself. Gerry's make-up and false nose had turned the art museum director into a disturbingly realistic mirror image of Neil Ferguson. Even Gerry's voice and mannerisms had shifted to match the role.

Gerry raised an eyebrow and took a banana chip. "I never claimed to be Lieutenant Ferguson. I'm just wearing your business suit. Is it a crime to look like someone else?"

"I suppose not." Neil paused, thinking. "What I don't understand is how you could be talking on a cell phone in a lawn chair at the same time you were running down a fire escape."

Gerry looked at his watch. "It's about time for a final demonstration anyway." He muted the television news. Then he asked Neil, "Can you make a whooshing, whistling sound?"

Neil blinked.

"Oh, come on. Whoosh a little so it sounds like wind."

Neil shrugged. "Shh?"

"That's it. Now just keep it up." Gerry took a cell phone out of his suit pocket, opened it, and unmuted it. "Hello?"

Neil kept on whooshing. On the television screen, however, Marcus Hampton suddenly began mouthing words with excitement. A caption appeared below him, LIVE FROM GERALD CHANDLER.

"Yes, it's awfully cold and dark up here," Gerry said. "I'm not sure how much longer I can hold out. Are the police still tracking my cell phone?"

Marcus mouthed more silent words, nodding.

"Well, my phone battery is almost dead."

The newscaster's lips moved again.

"Tell them I wish them luck, but D.B. Cooper is signing off. And this time, I'm afraid he's never coming back." Gerry pressed the END button, closed the phone, and slowly set it on the dining table between them.

Neil stopped whooshing. After a moment he asked, "How many cell phones did you have to use?"

"Three. I bought them this morning. Two are taped together in the mannequin's hand. They relayed the call from the television studio to the phone here."

"Where is the lawn chair now?"

"Five thousand feet in the air, in a snowstorm halfway between Troutdale and Sandy." Gerry used a spoon to scrape the last of the black beans from the take-out container. "Without the cell phone connection, there's nothing the police can do. Even radar can't track a balloon in a cloud full of snow. As far as the world knows, I'm gone."

Neil picked up the cell phone. "What name did you register the phones under?"

"Daniel Blaine Cooper." Gerry smiled. "Caller ID often abbreviates first names."

"May I?" Neil opened the phone. "I've been trying all day to reach an engineer named Todd Lammergeier. He won't answer my calls, but he might pick up for Cooper."

"Be my guest."

Neil punched in Todd's number. While it rang, Gerry asked, "Is this Lammergeier related to the professor who was poisoned a few weeks ago?"

Neil nodded. "His son. I'm pretty sure the professor was involved with your blackmailer. The son's been looking for him too, and he has a head start. At this point, it's probably our best lead to the other Cooper."

A minute passed before Neil punched END in frustration. "Maybe I'll try his stepmother. Todd seems to be keeping in touch with her." He entered Rachel's number and waited.

After the seventh ring a small, frightened voice said, "Hello?"

"Mrs. Lammergeier?"

She stammered, "W-w-what do you want from me? They said on TV you've disappeared in a snowstorm."

Neil realized she must have seen the phone's caller ID. "I'm not really D.B. Cooper, Mrs. Lammergeier. This is Neil Ferguson, the detective who visited you this afternoon. I'm just using Cooper's phone."

She was silent for a moment. Then she asked, "How are you doing that? Don't tell me you're up there in the lawn chair with him."

"It's complicated. What I want to ask is, have you heard anything more from Todd?"

"Todd? Not lately." She paused. "You said Cooper might have been involved in my husband's death. Is that why you're headed toward Mt. Hood?"

Neil hesitated, trying to think of something that would be true. "More or less."

"Todd will be at Timberline Lodge tomorrow, you know. He's taking my husband's place at the Synergy conference, accepting an award for the Recyclotron."

"Yes, I know. Has Todd left Portland yet?"

"I doubt it," Rachel replied. "The conference only offered him a room at Timberline for tomorrow night."

"I'm afraid Todd may be in danger. Let me know immediately if you hear from him."

"All right. And Lieutenant? If you're really with D.B. Cooper, take care."

"I'll try." Neil closed the phone, frowning.

Gerry asked, "What's wrong?"

Neil sighed. "If your blackmailer is on the guest list at Timberline Lodge, Todd may be in more trouble than he knows. I think the blackmailer poisoned Todd's father. Todd could be next."

"Doesn't that fit in with our plan?" Gerry began clearing the table.

"We show up undercover at Timberline and get the evil Cooper to give himself away?"

Neil nodded. "I just don't like using Todd as bait."

The next morning Gerry took most of an hour to refresh his makeup. Neil had given up on his own disguise. Even the black of his hair had washed out in the shower. After breakfast they drove to the REI store in the Pearl District to buy outdoor gear for the trip to Mt. Hood.

Before getting out of the car, Gerry put on the wraparound sunglasses he had loaned to Neil the day before. "We don't want too many Fergusons in any one place. Try to shop in a different part of the store. Do you ski?"

"No," Neil said.

"Then buy snowshoes. You'll also need boots, gloves, and a parka." Gerry reached into his suit coat pocket, took out a wad of hundred-dollar bills, and peeled off a few. "Use some of these."

Neil took the money uncertainly. He held a bill up to the light to check that it was authentic. "Where did you get this much cash?"

"D.B. Cooper always has a backup plan." Gerry got out of the car and strode toward the store entrance.

Forty minutes later they met back at the car, their arms loaded with gear. Gerry carried a pair of metal-edged Nordic skis with cable bindings and spoon-shaped tips. They only fit inside the Buick sedan diagonally, so he wound up in the passenger seat with the skis angled over his left shoulder.

When Neil stopped at a light on the way out of town, he took Connie's list out of his pocket. "Let's go over the suspects again. If your blackmailer is really going to be at Timberline, we need to narrow things down farther."

Gerry unfolded the paper. Neil had circled nine names in ink:

Ivan Crombaugh, county commissioner
Brother Daniel, icon artist
Andrei Andropov, car repairman / translator
Stanley Caulfield, US energy secretary
Yuri Bolshoi, Russian energy minister
Nancy Willis, NovoCity Finance CEO

Todd Lammergeier, engineer
Steve Owen, FBI
John Dickers, Portland police

The first three names were circled twice. At the bottom of the list, one name had been added in cursive:

Lt. Credence Lavelle, deceased

"Why include a dead lieutenant?" Gerry asked. "Wasn't she the one who solved the Underground murders in the first place?"

"Yes, but she solved them wrong. And Captain Dickers thinks she may have faked her death." Neil angled onto Highway 26, following a sign for Mt. Hood.

"She still seems like a long shot. I thought we agreed the other Cooper is an older man with a Russian connection."

"Maybe," Neil said.

"Well, Brother Daniel certainly qualifies," Gerry pointed out. "I've been wondering about him. He was the most troublesome artist I dealt with at the museum, and that's saying a lot."

Neil frowned. "The problem with Brother Daniel is that he's a follower of the Old Believers. Why would he bring Russian Protestants to Portland?"

"Perhaps they really are his cousins," Gerry said. "The Russian community tends to stick together."

A sudden rain shower made Neil turn the wipers on high. "I think your blackmailer was telling the truth when he said this is about family. That's why I want to keep an eye on Andropov. He's the ringleader of the car repairmen, and most of them seem to be related."

"Why was a car repairman invited to the energy summit at all?"

Neil sighed. "Captain Dickers hired Andropov as a translator."

"An odd choice." Gerry looked back at the list. "Is that why you've circled Dickers' name?"

"Maybe."

"You don't trust your own police captain?"

Neil gripped the wheel tighter. "Dickers has been fighting my investigation from the first. He still believes Duvshenko simply shot himself in the Foreign Motors parking lot. He refused to reopen the

Underground murders case. He practically turned the department over to special agent Owen, a guy obsessed with some kind of vendetta against you."

"That doesn't make Dickers a suspect."

The rain was starting to turn into slow, heavy flakes. As Neil stared past the wipers into the whitening storm, he suddenly recalled a fragment of a dream—or was it a memory? Captain Dickers was laughing, wearing a tuxedo, with the mirrored sunglasses of commissioner Crombaugh on his left and the pretty, pierced face of Nancy Willis on his right.

"Neil?" Gerry leaned forward to look at him over the skis. "Are you OK?"

"I just had a scary thought."

"We seem to be having a lot of them these days."

"There's something I need to buy." Neil pulled off the highway into a strip mall on the outskirts of Sandy.

"Snow pants?"

"No." Neil parked in front of Bi-Mart store. "A gun."

Gerry caught his arm. The grip was so tight that Neil could not get out of the car. "No guns, Neil. That's not how I play the game."

"I'm a cop, Gerry. Cops carry guns because the guys we're going up against have them."

Gerry shook his head. "We have the advantage of surprise, and the wits of two people. If you want to shoot someone, I'm out."

Neil sat back. "That's what Swarovsky said about you."

"Swarovsky?" Gerry repeated the name cautiously.

"I ran into your old KGB boss in Novgorod last week. He said the only thing he couldn't train you to do was to kill."

Gerry nodded. "There's always another way. If you have to use a gun, you've failed. Besides, the other Cooper and I go back a long ways."

"He's been blackmailing you for more than twenty years."

"There's more to it than that."

Neil cocked his head. "You think you might be cousins after all?"

"No, I doubt we're related in that sense." Gerry looked out the windshield at the drifting snowflakes. "But we're connected, the two of us."

"Gerry, he's not like you. He kills people. You and the evil Cooper are complete opposites."

"Still, we're somehow paired. There's no such thing as pure black and white, pure good and evil. You each hold a little of the opposite inside yourself."

Frustrated, Neil started the car. He'd heard enough about such yin-yang nonsense from Dregs.

"Then you understand about not bringing a gun?" Gerry asked.

"We're both dead anyway." Neil steered the car back to the highway. The sleet wasn't yet sticking on the wet pavement. "But you're wrong about you and the evil Cooper being two sides of the same coin. That kind of coin doesn't exist."

Gerry laughed. "Look at us, two Neil Fergusons in the same car. You're arguing with yourself."

Neil did find it unsettling, talking with a man who looked more like Neil Ferguson than he did.

Gerry continued, "The split for us isn't about violence, though. It's about honesty."

This caught Neil by surprise. "What do you mean?"

"You don't know how to lie. You couldn't even wear a disguise. Me, I love deception. Stage names. Smoke and mirrors. Art exhibits. Overpriced sneakers. You're a policeman, and I'm a con artist. Two sides of the same coin."

"Then it must be a three-sided coin," Neil objected. "How can you be paired with both a mafia boss and a policeman?"

"That's the challenge," Gerry said. "Art is all about deception."

49

Neil had to pull to the side of the highway in the town of Zigzag, twenty miles before Timberline Lodge, to put chains on the front tires. After that the Buick clanked along at less than thirty miles an hour. Snowflakes seemed to fly out in all directions from the windshield. The trees beside the highway were flocked with white.

At the far end of Government Camp, two patrol cars with flashing lights blocked the start of the six-mile road up to Timberline Lodge. Neil rolled down his window and held out his badge to a policeman in a blue poncho. "Isn't Lieutenant Wu supposed to be staffing the Synergy checkpoint?"

"She's at the upper parking lot with the final check. We're just keeping out the riffraff." The policeman glanced into the car. "Hey, are you guys twins?"

Gerry grinned. "Joined at the hip."

The policeman laughed and waved them on.

As Neil drove up the road, a faint musical chord began tinkling amid the clank of the tire chains. Neil and Gerry exchanged a puzzled glance. When the tinkling music began again, Neil asked, "Do you still have D.B. Cooper's phone?"

"I thought the batteries were dead." Gerry dug the ringing phone out of his pocket. "The caller ID says 'Lammergeier'."

"Put it on speaker mode," Neil said.

Gerry pushed a button. "Hello?"

A high, worried voice said, "You're not Neil Ferguson. Is this—is this D.B. Cooper?"

"Mrs. Lammergeier?" Neil said. "Have you heard from Todd?"

"Yes, but—" she faltered. "Tell me the truth. Are you with D.B. Cooper?"

Neil looked to Gerry. Gerry shrugged, as if challenging him to lie. "Yes, he's with me," Neil said. "We're almost to Timberline Lodge."

"Good, because I'm worried about Todd. I'm afraid he may be doing something crazy."

"What did Todd say?"

"Wait, Roger's coming." Rachel Lammergeier lowered her voice. A moment passed, with the sound of footsteps and a click. "There, I'm upstairs in Curt's old office now."

Neil slowed behind an old snow plow truck. It was hard to pass because the road was narrowed by seven-foot walls of snow. The plow's curved blade made a rattling racket as it scraped up chunks of ice and dirty snow.

Neil raised his voice over the din. "Was Todd at Timberline when he called?"

"Yes. I mean, no. He'd just left the lodge on snowshoes, heading up the mountain."

"Why would he do that?"

"I told you, it's like he's gone crazy. He said he's found out who the Coopers are, and he's going to kill them."

"Coopers?" Neil exchanged a glance with Gerry. "Did he say who they were?"

"No. He said he was going to miss the toast at the opening banquet, but he was going up the mountain to toast everyone in his own way. He was calling me to say good-bye. He even gave me the password to his computer so I could find the file with his will."

The voice on the phone had been difficult enough to understand, competing with the scrape of the snow plow blade, but now static began breaking up the connection too. Either they were leaving cell phone range, or the battery was dying, or both.

"What was the password?" Neil shouted at the dying phone. Just yesterday, he had spent half an hour trying to unlock Todd's computer.

The crackling phone spat the single word, "Blitz". Then the little green power light faded out.

"Blitz?" Gerry asked.

"An old brand of beer," Neil said. "Todd Lammergeier and his father built the Recyclotron so the worst of its toxic waste was siphoned off into old beer bottles."

"Why would they do that?"

"To save money. But three cases of those bottles are missing. And one of them turned up in the lake where Curt Lammergeier was poisoned."

Gerry whistled. "It sounds like the other Cooper might have killed Todd's father. But I don't quite see why."

"We need to find out." Neil hit the gas and swerved the car to pass the snow plow.

Suddenly a much larger rotary snow plow appeared before them in the left lane, coming straight at them out of the snowstorm. Neil slammed on the brakes. The car slewed sideways, spun about, and bumped into the wall of snow beside the road. The giant snow plow growled closer, its huge, egg-beater blades chopping up the berm of ice and snow left by the smaller plow. A tall metal chute spewed the dirty mix as a geyser of powder a hundred feet back into the woods.

Just short of the Buick's bumper, the whirling blades ground to a stop. A man in a fluorescent green coat leaned out of the cab. "Hey! I almost didn't see you! Can't you read the signs? Don't pass snow plows!"

Neil lowered his window and waved weakly. "Sorry!" He put the car in reverse, his hands shaking. The Buick's wheels spun for a moment before the chains gripped. Then he backed up into the right-hand lane and followed the old snow plow the rest of the way up the mountain.

A boom blocked the road where it split at the start of the parking lot. A woman stepped out of a control booth, her face hidden by the hood of a fur-trimmed coat. She raised the boom for the snow plow and lowered it again in front of the Buick. Then she looked at the car's license plate and put her hands on her hips.

She walked to the car window and said, "Neil, you asshole. I loan you a car, and you bend the fender."

"Sorry, Connie. At least I brought help."

"Oh? Who?"

"Take a look."

Connie peered in the window at the man in the passenger seat. "Jesus Christ," she whispered.

"No," Neil said. "Two more guesses."

"I'm not sure which one is you. Is that your brother Mark?"

"You're getting warm."

"Chandler?"

Gerry gave her a thumbs up. "We spoke by telephone the other day, Lieutenant. It's a pleasure to meet you in person."

She squinted at him. "But aren't you supposed to be flying over the mountain in a lawn chair?"

"I'll explain later," Neil said. "Right now we've got to find Todd Lammergeier. He's figured out the identity of the other Cooper, the mafia boss. But Todd's planning something, and he's in danger."

"How do you know all this?" Connie asked.

"Todd called his stepmother. She says he's left the conference to go up the mountain, and she doesn't know why. I've got to find him."

Connie looked at him skeptically. But she also took a radio out of her pocket and pressed a button. "Espada? This is Wu here. I'm wondering if you've seen Todd Lammergeier. He's the engineer who's getting an award at the banquet."

The radio squawked a moment before Sergeant Espada's voice came through. "Yes, sir. Lammergeier is skipping the opening speeches because he doesn't like crowds. He went out the back door on snowshoes five minutes ago."

"What?" Connie asked. "You just let him walk out into the snow?"

"Roger that, sir. We searched him first and found out he was actually going outside for a drink."

Neil asked loudly, "Did he have a beer bottle with him? A brown, old-fashioned bottle?"

"Yes, two of them." Espada replied. Then he added, "Lieutenant Ferguson? Is that you?"

Neil shook his head and drew his finger across his throat.

Connie released the button, silencing the radio.

"Todd's headed up the mountain, but why?" Neil turned to Gerry. "You've skied here before. What's up there an engineer might want?"

Gerry shrugged. "If he went a mile he'd get to the Silcox Hut, but it's a tough climb, and the hut would be closed. Is he in good shape?"

Neil shook his head. "He can hardly walk. What's closer than that?"

"Nothing, really." Gerry thought a moment. "Well, there's a water tank. They've decorated it to look like a little castle."

"Don't tell me it's the water supply for Timberline Lodge."

"Holy hell." Gerry looked at him. "That tank's still half a mile up the mountain. If he's headed there, I can catch him."

"What's going on?" Connie reached for the boom blocking the road.

"I'm not sure." Neil really didn't know what Todd was planning. The engineer had never threatened anyone before. In fact, Todd himself was the one who was most likely in danger. Neil decided to find Todd, rather than take the risk of alarming people at the conference.

As soon as Connie lifted the bar, Neil spun the tires, clanking the Buick up around a curve into the parking lot. The snowstorm had let up for the moment. Ahead, the dormered roofline of Timberline Lodge stood stark and tall against a patch of bright clouds. Great wooden beams supported the eaves of a shake-roofed central tower. Smoke drifted from a massive stone chimney capped by an iron weathervane.

"Park here," Gerry pointed to a nearly empty overflow lot on the right.

Neil pulled up next to a snow-covered silver Prius. He caught himself wondering how the underpowered hybrid car had made it up to the lodge at all. Had he seen this particular Prius somewhere before? But then he dismissed the thought, concentrating instead on his snow gear. They quickly put on their parkas, boots, and gloves. Gerry helped Neil strap on his snowshoes. Gerry took out two long strips of fabric—furry on one side and sticky on the other.

"What are those?" Neil asked.

"Climbing skins for steep terrain." Gerry pressed the sticky side of the strips against the bottoms of his skis. Then he buckled his boots into the bindings and gripped his poles. "Let's angle across until we pick up Todd's tracks."

"Try to keep out of sight of the lodge. They'll have guards near the doors." Neil had to run to keep up with Gerry. The snowshoes were awkward and heavy, and his fingers were stiff from the cold. Gerry's skis left a trough up through the drifts behind a low row of twisted, storm-bent pines. Rime frost crusted the trunks and needles with white spikes. Neil's lungs ached from the cold, thin air.

"Snowshoe tracks!" Gerry called back.

Neil motioned with his hand to stay quiet. When he caught up with Gerry it took him a second to catch his breath. Bicycling was not the same kind of exercise as running uphill in snowshoes.

Gerry lowered his voice. "It looks like he's heading for the water tank. Why would he poison an entire energy conference?"

"Todd's into conspiracy theories." Neil looked up the slope. "Let's split up. You go left. I'll go right. Whoever sees him first tries to distract him. Then the other one comes at him from behind."

"Got it. Let's go." Gerry was already off, sliding gracefully with his knees bent.

As Neil plodded up the slope to the right, a gap in the storm parted the clouds ahead. The white crown of Mt. Hood emerged from the wisps, a tower of impossibly high, icy crags.

"Lieutenant Ferguson!" a voice called from a cluster of trees in the direction of the peak. Neil stopped, alarmed. He could see no one. The voice continued, "What an unpleasant surprise."

50

The man who called himself Cooper was not pleased. He shuffled slowly across the Timberline Lodge lobby, pushing his walker past the big stone fireplace with its crackling pine logs. No one had ever discovered his identity before. In all those years, no one! Not the police, of course. Not the car repairmen, not the rival mafia — not even his own daughter. And yet here at Timberline Lodge the conference organizers had decided to seat him next to Todd Lammergeier. Incredibly, the young engineer seemed to know a great deal about his underworld enterprises. Todd was more dangerous than his father. The boy would have to die, of course, as soon as the opportunity arose. From the first, that had been the primary rule, to leave no witnesses.

He stopped at the cloakroom and put on a long, white coat that made him look even older. He pulled on a white knit cap. Then he pushed his walker down the hallway to the disabled access door — the least watched entrance to Timberline Lodge. The guard there looked past him with the bored politeness people often show for frail old men.

"Can I help you, sir?" The guard didn't even look at his name tag.

"I just need to get my medications from the car." Cooper let his voice quiver a bit, but not too much. "I can manage by myself."

"If you're sure." The guard held the door open. The storm had let up for the moment.

Cooper lifted his walker across the threshold and set out across the packed snow of the parking lot, heading for his silver Prius. He was already thinking ahead, choosing the right way to eliminate Todd Lammergeier. The boy lacked the genius of his father. In their short conversation, Todd had swallowed half a dozen of Cooper's lies.

But then Todd had surprised him by suddenly standing up and announcing that he wasn't interested in staying to hear the conference's opening speeches. Todd had put on a coat, taken a pair of snowshoes, and convinced the guard at the back door to let him wander off toward the mountain. What had he really been up to? Cooper mistrusted people he didn't understand.

Before he opened the backseat door of the silver Prius, he studied the black Buick parked beside it. Only a trace of snow had collected on the roof of the unmarked police car. The hood was bare, suggesting that the engine was still warm. He knew this car. He had parked beside it at The Grotto a few weeks earlier. Back then he had toyed with a clumsy detective by planting a fake bomb under the hood. He had even modeled the fake after the original Cooper bomb, using a description from Gerry. To top it off, he had outfitted the bomb with a detective thumbprint from a bottle in the Underground. Eventually, of course, he had disposed of Lieutenant Ferguson appropriately, together with Marial Greschyednyev. Now the black Buick was just another police car.

He opened the back seat of the Prius, lifted the lid of the battery compartment, and took out one of the Glock semi-automatics he kept hidden there. It was time to take care of an annoying piece of unfinished business—a witness he had already tried to eliminate three times.

This was the real reason he had bothered to come to Timberline. It was time to kill Lieutenant Connie Wu.

The voice behind the snow-flocked trees said, "What a very unpleasant surprise, Lieutenant."

Neil almost replied, but then he realized the voice wasn't directed at him. He stopped in his snowshoes, breathing hard. A moment later he heard his own voice—or rather, a good imitation of it—respond from beyond the trees, "Let's talk this over, Todd."

Gerry was faster on his skis, and had obviously reached Todd first. Especially at a distance, Gerry's disguise was convincing.

Neil made his way up to the edge of the trees. In the clearing beyond, Todd Lammergeier was sitting on the snowy roof of a cylindrical, fourteen-foot tower. He wore a khaki Army surplus coat and held a brown beer bottle in his gloved hand. Judging from the broken shakes and tracks about the tank, Todd had climbed a series of iron rungs to the roof and had torn off enough of the wooden shakes to make a hole.

"If you shoot me, Lieutenant," Todd said, "my little bottle of poison will drop into this tank. You wouldn't want that, would you?"

On the far side of the tower, Gerry held up his hands. "I'm unarmed, Todd. I just want to talk."

Todd threw back his head and laughed—a strange, gasping sound that shook the white flab beneath his puffy chin.

"We want the same thing, Todd," Gerry continued. "We want to get the other Cooper, the one who killed your father."

"The one who killed my father," Todd repeated. "Now who is that, really?"

Neil crouched low, working his way to Todd's blind side, uphill of the tower.

Todd sniffed the open bottle in his hand. "So sweet. You know, Lieutenant, I'm glad you're here after all. Someone needs to know what really happened to my father."

"What did happen?" Gerry asked.

"I was there, the night he died at the rhododendron garden. The park was closed, so we were alone. My father had asked me to bring a bottle of Recyclotron juice." Todd held the bottle up with a sad smile. "He told me he wasn't really D.B. Cooper after all. He said there were two Coopers, and one of them had hired him to build the Recyclotron. Toxic juice wasn't a waste product, you know. It was the only real product of the Recyclotron."

"Why build a machine that concentrates poison?" Gerry asked.

Behind the tower, Neil was silently unstrapping his snowshoes.

"At first, my father believed Cooper shared our goals. We all wanted to stop the spread of the global socialist network. For years the socialists have been taking over the universities and the media. The nonsense about global warming was just part of their plot to scare people into letting them create a global government. My father's recycling machine was the perfect weapon to use against them." Todd frowned. "But then it turned out Cooper had different motives. He wanted money and power for himself."

"Who? Who was the man who hired your father?" Gerry skied closer.

Todd held up his gloved hand. "One more step and I drop the bottle."

Gerry stopped.

"My father never found out who Cooper was. In the end he decided everyone is Cooper. The whole world is against us, and the only way out was the escape he'd invented." Todd tilted his head. "Before I knew it, he'd taken a drink of the juice. I knocked the bottle into the lake, but he didn't seem to care. He just smiled. For the first time in his life, he actually looked happy. Everything seemed to slow down. He looked at me and said, 'Sweet. It's so sweet.'"

"I'm sorry," Gerry said, "Suicide leaves scars."

"It wasn't suicide," Todd replied. "My father was murdered. The Coopers of the world killed him in a roundabout way. And now it's my turn. A hundred of them are down there at Timberline Lodge. The elite of the secret government. After the opening speeches, they're going to toast each other with Mt. Hood spring water. All I have to do is sweeten their drink." Todd held up the bottle.

"Wait!" Gerry had glanced at Neil, and had seen that he was still creeping toward the iron rungs of the tower. They needed time, if only a minute. "Do you know the story about the Texan, the Californian, and the Oregonian?"

Todd paused. "What?"

"Three engineers went snowshoeing at Mt. Hood. You mean you've never heard about them?"

"No." Todd lowered the bottle a little.

"They climbed up from Timberline Lodge and stopped for lunch right here." Gerry pointed to the windswept pines beside him. "The Texan pulled out a bottle of Lone Star Beer and took a swig. Then he threw the bottle in the air, took out a pistol, and shot it to shards."

"Ferguson?" Todd asked. "Is something wrong with you?"

"I'm telling you a story. Don't you want to hear why the Texan shot the Lone Star Beer?"

Todd eyed him uncertainly.

Gerry continued. "The Californian asked why, and the Texan said, 'Because there's plenty more of that where I come from.'"

Neil had reached the first of the rungs. He gripped the iron bar and pulled himself up from the snow.

Gerry said, "So then the Californian takes out a bottle of Sonoma

Valley Cabernet Sauvignon. He takes a sip, sets the bottle in a snow bank, and blasts it with his Saturday Night Special. The Oregonian looks at him and asks, 'Why did you do that?' And the Californian says, 'Because there's lots more of that where I come from.'"

Todd was still holding the open bottle of poison in the air.

Gerry hurried on. "So then the Oregonian takes out a bottle of Bridgeport microbrew IPA. He drinks it dry and puts the empty bottle in his pocket. Then he takes out a revolver and shoots the Californian."

Neil was almost to the eave now, climbing silently.

"Why did he shoot the Californian?" Todd asked.

"The Texan asked the same thing," Gerry said. "And the guy from Oregon says, "Where I come from, there's lots more Californians. But a beer bottle is worth a nickel.'"

Todd sat there a moment, frowning. "You know what? My dad would have liked that story. The world may be full of Coopers, but I don't think you're one of them, Ferguson." He lifted the stubby brown bottle of poison, studying it against the sky. Then he tipped the bottle briefly toward the wispy summit of Mt. Hood. "Cheers, old man. This is for you." And he put the bottle to his lips.

By this time Neil had nearly reached the roof. Crawling out around the eave proved more difficult than he had thought. Half a minute passed before he managed to peer over the edge. Todd had just finished drinking. Neil reached out, grabbed Todd's foot, and pulled as hard as he could. The two of them slid off the roof and landed in a snowbank.

Gerry skied up and grabbed the bottle. "Empty. How long will he live?"

Neil dug himself out of the snow. "I don't know. We should get help."

"Too late," Todd said dreamily. "You know, it really is sweet."

Neil and Gerry stood over him. Neil asked, "Who is the other Cooper?"

Todd looked from one face to the other. "Two Lieutenant Fergusons!"

Neil knelt closer. "I'm Neil Ferguson. We need to find the bad Cooper."

Todd smiled. "Two Fergusons. Two Coopers. It's so perfect."

"Please, Todd," Neil said, "Tell me who the other Cooper is."

Todd's speech began to slow. "It doesn't matter. They're all dead. I poured a bottle of poison into the tank before you came."

Neil looked to Gerry in a panic. Todd really had left Timberline Lodge with two bottles.

"Gotcha," Todd said, smiling.

"You haven't poisoned the water supply yet?" Neil asked.

Todd rolled his head to one side. "When I figured out who Cooper is, he made me his partner. He was just buying time, of course. I knew he was planning to kill me. Even now, he's down there killing the only cop who can recognize him."

"Connie!" Neil felt a flush of fear. Alone at the checkpoint booth, she would be an easy target.

Todd smiled weakly. "There's a dilemma for you, Ferguson. Which will you try to save, the conference or your colleague?"

51

It had started to snow again. The old man in a long white coat was just another shadow in the storm. Connie didn't notice him until he was nearly at the checkpoint booth. But when she stepped out of the door and saw the cold look in his eyes, she knew.

By then he was already pointing his Glock at her heart. "So you do recognize me. Hands up, Lieutenant Wu, slowly."

Anger and fear burned so hot she could hardly think. The whole nightmare on 122nd Avenue raced through her mind — the horror of her fall from a car's hood, the fire of her torn scalp, and the screaming pain of her shredded palms. But most of that memory did not match what she was seeing now. The ruthless eyes she remembered belonged to a feeble, ancient man — a face she didn't know. In a moment, he would pull the trigger.

She lunged forward to knock the gun from his hand.

Incredibly, the old man sprang backwards, his reflexes sharper than seemed possible. He clicked his tongue. "Don't make me shoot you here, Lieutenant. This booth is wrong for your suicide. We need to take a walk down the road. Let's find a pleasanter spot, where you can be found when the mountain wildflowers bloom." He motioned with the gun for her to start walking.

Connie raised her hands half way. Her own semi-automatic was on the desk inside the booth — too far away — but she still had the radio on her hip belt. As she started to turn, she lowered her elbow toward the radio's TALK button.

"No, no, no." The old man unclipped her radio.

She cast him a look of rage. "Who are you?" Why hadn't he been on their list of suspects?

He smiled. "I'm Cooper, of course."

Sergeant Espada worried that Lieutenant Wu had turned off her radio. Her checkpoint was probably even more boring than his. There would be no traffic on the entrance road now that the conference had begun. And of course it was foolish to think he had heard Neil Ferguson's voice, an echo from beyond the grave.

From his position by the lodge's back door, he could hear the opening speeches of the conference droning on. Half a dozen waiters passed by, carrying trays of clinking commemorative water glasses for a ceremonial toast. Only at a conference like this, he thought, would the delegates toast each other with water.

Suddenly the Diplomatic Service agent on the other side of the door drew his long-barreled Luger. "Someone's out there!"

Espada squinted up past the icicles of the eave. Snowdrifts covered the lower half of the window. Far up the slope, a small dark shape seemed to be moving. "It's probably just Lammergeier, coming back for more beer."

"This guy ain't on snowshoes." The agent opened the door and sighted the Luger. "He's skiing like a bat out of hell."

"You can't shoot someone just because he's skiing!" Espada exclaimed, startled.

"Then call for backup, man!"

Espada fumbled with the radio. "Checkpoints! We've got an intruder, skiing down the mountain toward the back door of the lodge."

"An intruder?" Agent Owen's voice crackled back on the radio, "Don't tell me it's Cooper."

The skier flew between two trees, shot across a gully, and landed in a spray of snow on the drift outside the door. Then he kicked off his skis and threw back the hood of his parka.

Espada stared. "It's Lieutenant Ferguson!"

The Diplomatic Service agent didn't lower his Luger. "He's one of yours?"

The skier jumped down from the drift. "Quick!" he said, "You two come with me." He jogged down the hall and banged open the door to the banquet hall.

On the podium, the Russian energy minister paused at the interruption, a glass of water in his hand.

Running downhill in snowshoes proved nearly as hard as running uphill. Neil kept tripping over the flopping ends of the snowshoes, landing face first in the drifts. By the time he reached the Buick he was exhausted. Snow had begun falling so fast that he could barely see. He took off the snowshoes and ran down the road toward Connie's checkpoint, thinking only to make sure she was safe.

"Connie!" he called into the storm — and immediately realized how incautious fear had left him.

When he saw that the checkpoint booth was empty, his fear escalated toward terror. Connie's semi-automatic lay on the desk. He picked it up and clicked off the safety. Snow was already covering the footprints outside, but he could make out two sets of tracks, heading down the road. What could he do but run after them?

And then, just around the first curve, there they were — two figures beside the wall of snow at the road's edge. An old man in a white parka stood behind Connie, holding a gun to her head.

"Unbelievable," the old man said. "Lieutenant Ferguson, your determination amazes even me."

"Run, Neil!" Connie cried. "He's Cooper. He'll just kill you too."

The old man chuckled. "I suppose that's true. It seems I have to keep doing this over and over. Frankly, Ferguson, I don't know how you've survived this long. But the truth is, unless you toss your gun on the road, I am going to shoot your girlfriend."

Neil aimed his Glock at Cooper's right eye, but Neil's hand was shaking.

"Oh, honestly." The old man shifted his head behind Connie's. "Do I have to count to three? One. Two."

Neil threw the gun onto the snowy road. "Who the hell are you?"

"We've met before." The old man slipped out from behind Connie to pick up the second gun. He aimed one at each of them. "Don't you remember? Or did you think I was just another senile old man in a wheelchair?"

"At The Grotto." Now Neil recalled the drooping face and the drooling mouth. "You're Nancy Willis's father."

"And you're about to help me set up a little scene. I think it should look like you decided to shoot your girlfriend in a jealous rage." Willis motioned with the guns, indicating that Neil and Connie should walk together ahead of him. "I seem to remember a pullout down the road that will be ideal."

Connie refused to move. "Wait. I researched NovoCity's founder. You can't be Fred Willis. He had a stroke years ago. He has late-stage Alzheimer's."

"Nancy and I arranged all that. She wanted a chance to lead the company. I knew they'd never let me retire unless they thought I was half dead. She still believes I'm retired."

Neil said, "But in fact you've been running a mafia ring."

"Oh, don't call it that." Willis frowned. "It's a venture capital enterprise. A little car repair, some art sales. Look at the Recyclotron—a community service that wins international awards."

"And produces poison," Neil added.

"That's the Lammergeiers' side of things. They're psychopathic." -

Connie said, "But you think it was OK to hit me with your car and shoot Duvshenko at his shop?"

"Every business has its expenses, Lieutenant Wu." He waved the guns again. "This way, please. There is an art to doing these things correctly."

Neil took Connie's arm and whispered, "Stall."

Connie asked aloud, "So, Mr. Willis, are you really Gerry Chandler's cousin?"

Willis sighed. "Don't die here, Lieutenant. Walk, and I'll answer your question."

Connie and Neil started walking.

Behind them, Willis spoke as if he were perfectly relaxed. "My parents knew Chandler's parents in Russia before the war. Gerry told his mother he was D.B. Cooper, and she told anyone who would listen. Of course no one believed her. I didn't either, at first. When I got to Portland I had nothing. I needed a chance. I changed my name from Fyodor Vilnitz to Fred Willis. Then I gave Gerry a call, just to see, and suddenly I had the cash to start NovoCity, my own little empire."

"Which you named after your home town, Novgorod," Neil suggested.

"Very good." He stopped. "Here, this looks fine. Just step up to the side, both of you."

A snow plow must once have turned around here, creating a small gap in the walls lining the road. Attempting to climb this ramp, Neil and Connie sank in to their hips. After a few struggling steps, they stopped. The snow was falling thick and fast. Running away had never been likely. Now it seemed impossible.

Neil turned to Connie, thinking that this would be the time to kiss her, to say good-bye, to tell her that he loved her.

But she was still following his instruction to stall. "Mr. Willis?" she asked. "Don't you ever feel bad about blackmailing Gerry Chandler for money?"

"You know, I do. I think everything we do is for our children. Gerry didn't have any children, so I let him help dozens of young Russian families get started here in America. I always made sure the kids knew nothing about our dealings. Especially my own daughter, Nancy." He waved a gun toward Connie. "Could you turn a bit to face Lieutenant Ferguson?"

Connie turned. "Like this?"

"Excellent. When the snow melts, I'd like you to be looking at him."

Willis stepped up onto a berm of dirty snow where he would have a better shot. "Still, you're right. I do regret missing a chance to tell Gerry good-bye. His little ruse about D.B. Cooper made me what I am. Last night I was so disappointed. When Gerry flew out of his apartment, I felt as if a part of myself had disappeared with him."

Willis sighed. Then he raised the guns. "Let's take care of two good-byes at once."

But instead of a gunshot, there was a *whoomf!* as a shadow sailed off the cliff beside the road. Neil and Connie ducked. A pair of skis flew out of the snowstorm and rammed Willis on the shoulder. With a crunch of ice, the skier hit the road, skidded hard, and pulled upright.

Gerry Chandler took off his blue wraparound sunglasses. "Are you two all right?"

"Gerry! Thank God." Neil jumped down into the road. He picked the guns up out of the snow. Connie had to struggle to get loose from the bank. Then she knelt by the fallen man in the road. "He's breathing, but he hit his head pretty hard."

Gerry skied up to look. "Who is he?"

"The other Cooper," Neil said.

"I know that," Gerry said, "But who the devil is he?"

"He's Nancy Willis's father. The founder of NovoCity Finance."

"How strange." Gerry bent down to study the figure lying in the snow. "I've been trying to track down the other Cooper for years. And now, here he finally is. My greatest enemy and my worst nightmare."

In the distance, the faint growl of a snow plow began to cut through the storm.

Neil asked, "You've never seen him before?"

Gerry tilted his head. "I suppose he did come to art museum events along with Nancy, but I never paid much attention to him. He was just an old man in a wheelchair."

"I think you'll be free of him now," Neil said.

Gerry put his arm around Neil. "Thank you, my friend."

Connie asked, "Will you press charges against Mr. Willis?"

Gerry shook his head. "Even if I could, that's not my way."

"It might not be easy to nail him in court," Neil said. "He didn't leave a lot of evidence when he committed crimes."

"Well, I'll leave that to you," Gerry said. "This is where I have to disappear for keeps." He skied to the ramp of snow and began side-stepping up from the road.

"Where are you going?" Neil asked. "You can't just leave."

"Yes, I can." Gerry climbed to the top of the wall of snow beside the road. He stood there against the sky, already little more than a gray shadow amid the thickly falling snow.

Neil and Connie were watching Gerry so intently that they did not notice what was happening behind them.

Lying in the road, Fred Willis had opened his eyes. He lay still, trying to piece together what had happened. His head was spinning and his shoulder hurt. Somehow there were two Fergusons now. The one in the road had a gun in each hand. Another Ferguson was standing atop the wall of snow. The clatter of a snow plow was growing louder.

"I can't go back to Portland," Gerry said. "You must have realized that already, Neil. My life as Gerry Chandler is over, and my time as Cooper has passed. I'll have to become someone else now, somewhere else."

"You're leaving? Out here in the snow?" Connie asked. "Where will you go?"

"I have places I can stay under other names. Don't try to look for me. If I want to be found, you'll know. Good bye and good luck."

Then Gerry pushed with his poles and skied off, disappearing into the forest beyond the road.

At the same time Fred Willis had quietly stood up behind Neil and Connie. Willis was still confused about what had happened, but adrenaline was pumping strength into him. For a moment he considered tackling Neil from behind. If Neil had been alone, he might have managed to wrestle away one of the guns. With two cops, the plan seemed too risky. Then he remembered the backup gun he had left in his Prius. Yes, that was the safer move—to run back to the car.

At first Willis backed away quietly. The noise of an approaching snow plow covered the sound of his footsteps. Then he turned and broke into a run, his feet crunching in the snow.

Neil swiveled and raised his gun. He couldn't shoot a fleeing man in the back. Besides, it was snowing so hard that Willis was already difficult to see.

"Come on!" Connie started running after Willis, and Neil followed close behind. The road was so slippery that they couldn't run fast.

Suddenly a big rotary snow plow scraped its way around a curve ahead, shooting a white plume of snow back into the woods. Willis turned to look, lost his footing, and landed hard on a berm of dirty ice. When his head hit the ground, he stopped moving.

"Wait!" Neil shouted into the storm. "Stop the plow!" He and Connie waved their arms at the driver. The whirling blades of the giant plow growled closer, chopping up the berm. In his long white coat and white cap, Willis was all but indistinguishable from the snow.

Before Neil and Connie could reach the plow, the growl of the blades dipped half a note, and the plume of snow spewing into the woods turned pink.

The driver's door opened. A man in a bright green coat leaned out. "Hey, what's the matter with you two?"

Neil felt sick. Connie's face had gone white.

"Why all the waving?" the driver asked. "Something wrong?"

Neil tightened his lips and looked to Connie. What was the point of burdening the driver with the truth? The machinery had spread the remains of Fred Willis into the forest. Within minutes, falling snow would cover up the pink stain. Even when the snow melted, the traces would be small and scattered, hidden beneath the plow's detritus of sanding gravel and pine needles.

The man who called himself Cooper—the mafia boss who had tried to kill them both—was gone.

"No," Connie said, hanging her head. "Nothing's wrong. We just wanted to make sure you saw us."

52

That evening Captain Dickers asked Connie to break the news to Nancy Willis. The young CEO had spent the afternoon upstairs at Timberline Lodge, drinking Ice Axe Ale in the Rams Head Pub. Who could blame her, with her father missing? The old man had last been seen tottering out the disabled access door to get medications from his car. Search parties had combed the lodge, the parking lot, and the surrounding slopes where a confused Alzheimer's patient might stray. The snowstorm had hampered the search.

Neil followed Connie up to the pub, partly because he hadn't been given an assignment of his own.

Nancy was wearing black, as always, but for the conference she had removed many of her piercings and had dyed her hair a fairly ordinary red. Her eye shadow made it difficult to tell whether the rings around her eyes were unusually dark.

"Have you found him?" Nancy asked. She sat on a stool at the end of the bar. Behind her, a string of tiny lights gave the bottles on a mirrored shelf a ghostly glow. Twilight had dimmed the windows on either side to dark squares fringed with the gray fingers of icicles.

Connie shook her head. "Not yet. Now that it's getting dark, we've decided to call off the search."

"Call off the search? But he's still out there!"

"After this long, Ms. Willis, I'm afraid it wouldn't matter. You need to prepare yourself for the worst."

Nancy gave a despairing cry. She turned her head aside, as if to hide her suffering in the darkest corner of the room.

Neil was the only one who could see her reflection in the small mirrored shelf behind the bar. There, caught between the glowing bottles, Nancy Willis was smiling.

53

Captain John Dickers clicked the lead of his mechanical pencil back and forth, as if he were having trouble adjusting its length. Neil stood in front of the captain's desk, waiting for an invitation to sit down.

"I suppose you know why I've called you in." The captain didn't look up.

"You're debriefing people about the Synergy conference." Neil was among the last to be interviewed. He had a suspicion of what that might mean.

"Oh yes. That's part of it." The captain frowned. "The truth is, I wanted this to work out as much as you did. Maybe more."

"Sir?"

Finally Dickers got the pencil lead right. He set it down and looked up at Neil. "You've been a lieutenant detective for almost exactly seven months. We've had our differences, but I thought things went pretty well for the first half year."

"Thank you, sir."

"No." Dickers moved his hand back and forth, as if he were trying to erase a little invisible blackboard. "Since then it's just been one thing after another. First you botched a stakeout at the Midland library. Then you angered the Russian community by barging in on a funeral, practically accusing people of murder. You flew halfway around the world chasing stolen artworks that weren't stolen. You went AWOL for a week. Finally you frightened the delegates at the Synergy conference by telling them the water they were drinking was poisoned."

"Sir?" Neil reddened. He already knew he was being fired, but he wanted to go out with dignity. "Todd Lammergeier did in fact bring poison to the conference."

"The only thing he poisoned was himself."

"Didn't he have two bottles?"

"We found the second bottle unopened in his coat pocket. And the old wooden tank where he committed suicide hasn't been used for years. The water supply for Timberline Lodge is in a covered concrete tank farther up the hill."

"I didn't know that, sir."

The captain tapped his pencil on the desk. "The bigger problem here, Ferguson, is that you have repeatedly violated protocol. While the rest of us were trying to arrest Gerry Chandler, you climbed up the fire escape and told four sergeants that I had given them an order to meet down in the street. What were you thinking?"

"I couldn't say, sir." How could Neil tell him what he didn't know? Chandler had been the one on the fire escape, not him.

Dickers pointed the pencil at him. "Another violation is even more troubling. I've learned that you may in fact be the officer responsible for losing the case of D.B. Cooper's parachute."

This accusation left Neil perplexed. "I lost the case, sir?"

"Did you or did you not sign in at the forensics warehouse, with two unauthorized visitors, on the morning Cooper's backpack disappeared?"

Neil lowered his head. "One of the visitors took the parachute case without my knowledge, sir. I should have supervised him more carefully."

Dickers sighed. "You've been off the payroll for a week, Ferguson. The good news is that I'm willing to reinstate you. At your age, you're not likely to find other work."

Neil could hardly believe what he was hearing. In a few months, he really would turn sixty. If he lost his job now, his pension would be too small to cover his rent. "What's the bad news?"

"I'm afraid there's a reduction in pay. You'll be back as a sergeant." Dickers stood up. "Don't make me regret giving you yet another chance, Ferguson. You'll have to straighten out, follow protocol, and stay off the booze. Do we understand each other?" He held out his hand.

Neil shook his hand. "I don't suppose I'll still be assigned to the detective division."

"Actually, you will. It seems you have a defender in the ranks— someone willing to keep an eye on you." Dickers smiled as he showed Neil to the door. "You'll be working under a rising star. Our newest lieutenant, Connie Wu."

By the time Neil made his way up to his old office, the custodian had already replaced the laminated nameplate on the door. He closed his eyes and took a few breaths before he had the courage to knock.

"Come in."

He opened the door far enough to see a new coffee machine perking on the counter. Connie was stacking boxes of files on his desk. Instead of the familiar blue uniform, she wore a smart purple skirt with a matching jacket and nylons. Her hair was blacker than ever, and although it was still quite short, she had cut it at a chic angle. Everything would have been easier, he thought, if Connie didn't keep managing to make herself attractive.

"Neil!" She motioned him inside, walked to the door, and closed it behind him. "This wasn't my idea."

"I deserved the demotion, sir."

She raised her hand, as if she might actually slap him. "Don't ever call me 'sir' when we're alone."

He didn't flinch. "Sorry. Dickers just reminded me what a lousy detective I've been."

"Neil, if anyone earned a promotion, it was you."

"Really? You'd promote a drunk driver?"

"Stop it. You solved a whole series of murders, and we both know it."

"Just a series of accidents." Neil walked to the coffee machine and took a paper cup. "How do we know Yosef Duvshenko didn't shoot himself with his left hand on a whim?"

She snorted. "Sure, and trains blow up all the time in Latvia."

Neil poured his cup half full. "You know, if I ran an Underground tour, I probably would strangle people who ride buses."

She laughed. "Yeah, and I bet Credence Lavelle was so stressed about her book that she jumped off her own boat."

Now even Neil couldn't resist a grim chuckle. It felt good, even if they were only sharing the dark humor of frustration. But then a dangerous silence began to fill the room.

"What happened to Gerry?" Neil asked.

She shook her head. "I keep checking the police blotter, but nothing turns up. It's not like we can post him on the missing persons list."

"I guess his lawn chair never made it to Eastern Oregon. The TV weatherman thinks it went down in the woods between Bull Run and Lost Lake." Neil took a sip of his coffee. "They'll never find it there."

Connie was still standing awkwardly in front of the desk, as if this weren't really her office. "There's a poll on the Internet. Half the people think Cooper died, and the other half believe he got away."

"Then that's about the same as before all this started." Neil stared at his coffee. "So what are you going to do, Connie? When I became lieutenant I asked for cold cases. Look at the trouble I got."

"I know." She bit her lip.

"I went after a phantom named Cooper and found two of them. When they finally met, it was like matter and antimatter. Poof! They both disappeared. All we had to do was lie."

"Neil!" She stood before him. "Do you think I'm happy about it? Fred Willis deserved to die, but not like that. What happened was horrible. No one wanted to hear the truth."

"The day he hit you in that SUV I remember swearing that we'd make him pay." Neil took another drink of coffee. It tasted bitter.

"Cops aren't supposed to do revenge," Connie said. "I knew from the first that the mafia Cooper couldn't have shot himself. You were the only one who believed me."

"The mafia won't vanish because one old man is gone." Neil finished the coffee. He threw his paper cup in the wastebasket. "I think Nancy Willis is running the show now. Maybe she's been running it for years. But then what do I know? I'm just a sergeant."

"No, you're more than that. That's why I need you." She lowered her eyes. "Dickers didn't have much choice. You were right about making me the only cop in Portland he couldn't fire."

Neil looked at her from the side. "What did you tell him?"

"I said if he fired you, I'd quit." Her eyes were damp, darkening a purple line of mascara. "I couldn't lose you, Neil."

He mused aloud, "Is this the same Connie Wu who told me a month ago to stop asking her out?"

She shook her head. "I've changed. We've both changed, Neil." She began straightening the lapels of his tan sports coat. "I think we make a good team."

Neil knew his lapels didn't need straightening. He had bought the coat yesterday, thinking of Gerry. And still he wavered.

"Maybe we could talk about it over dinner?" Connie suggested. "I owe you one."

"Don't tell me you're hungry for oysters again."

She shook her head. "I've seen enough of Ivan's Oyster Bar for a long time. But I could try fixing spaghetti with eggplant. What do you say?"

"What do I say?" Neil smiled. "Sure."

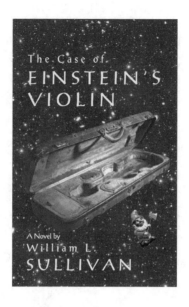

THE CASE OF
EINSTEIN'S VIOLIN

by William L. Sullivan

When Ana Smyth inherits Albert Einstein's violin case and sells it on eBay, she suddenly finds herself dodging international spies. A tip that her long-dead father may be alive sends her racing through Europe to discover her family's past—and a lost formula for quantum gravity.

THE SHIP IN THE HILL

by William L. Sullivan

Based on the actual excavation of a Viking burial ship, this carefully researched historical novel tells the story of two women struggling with power and love — an American archeologist unearthing the ship in southern Norway in 1904 and Asa of Agthir, the queen who sailed it a thousand years earlier in a quest to unify Norway against the Vikings.

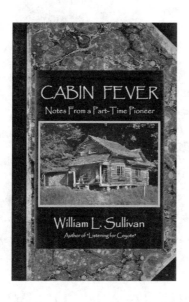

CABIN FEVER

by William L. Sullivan

Who hasn't dreamed of a summer getaway? In this poignant and dramatic adventure memoir, William L. Sullivan and his wife Janell spend 25 summers building a log cabin by hand in the roadless wilds of Oregon's Coast Range. Along the way they raise a family and puzzle out a murder mystery that had haunted their homestead for decades.

WILLIAM L. SULLIVAN

The author of four novels and a dozen nonfiction books, Sullivan grew up in Salem, Oregon. He completed his B.A. degree in English at Cornell University under Alison Lurie, studied linguistics at Germany's Heidelberg University, and earned an M.A. in German at the University of Oregon.

Sullivan is known in the American West as the author who backpacked more than a thousand miles across Oregon's wilderness in 1985. His journal of that adventure, *Listening for Coyote*, has been chosen one of Oregon's "100 Books," the most significant books in Oregon history. In summer he writes at the log cabin that he and his wife Janell Sorensen built by hand in the wilds of Oregon's Coast Range, more than a mile from roads, electricity, and telephones. The rest of the year they live in Eugene, Oregon, where he volunteers to promote libraries and literature.

Details about Sullivan's books, speaking engagements, and favorite adventures is at *www.oregonhiking.com*.